The NOVA System

Jon Scott Lee

Chapter 1

:/Initiation

Gavin sat at his desk, staring blankly at the monitor screen. The rest of his desk was empty. He had plenty to bring, but he hadn't seen the point. He worked alone on the night shift, so there wasn't anyone to even notice. He couldn't wait to finish his shift so that he would get a couple of days off for his birthday. *Not like it will matter much, but I will get some time with Kaleb. We can have a gaming and bad Kung fu movie marathon.* He thought with a laugh.

Looking back at the clock, only a minute had passed. He huffed in disgust at the absolute snail's pace that the clock had seemed to decide to move at.

With a sigh, he opened his backpack and pulled out his personal laptop. If nothing else, he could get in a couple extra hours on his secret hobby. Hacking. Well, more specifically looking for his parents. He glanced over in his backpack at the picture of his family before his mom left. The smile on his sister's face was the happiest it would be for years after that picture. The picture next to it is him and his best friend in the world, Kaleb. They had endured too many wedgies and beatings from their classmates not to be best friends. No one else got their nerdy references or their sense of humor. They were outcasted for their interests. And the fact that Kaleb got beat up by a girl two years younger than him as a freshman in high school. *That didn't help matters either.* Gavin thought as he reminisced about their relationship.

Megan, Gavin's sister, hated Kaleb, in a way, any older sister hates the friend of the younger brother who has been infatuated with them for over a decade. Gavin met Kaleb in the 4th grade at Sarah Smith Elementary School in Atlanta Georgia.

RING RING RING

Gavin forgot for a moment that he was at work. Hitting the button on his computer, he spoke into his headset. "Snollygoster Inc., this is Gavin. How may I help you?" He tried to sound cheery, but it couldn't reach his tone entirely.

"Gavin. Happy birthday. I'm sorry," and the line was dead.

What is happening? That sounded like Brett, but why would he be calling? Why would he remember that my birthday is tomorrow? How did he even get this number? Or know where I work? Gavin pondered as he pulled up the callback number, but when he tried it, it was just a burner number. Even tracking it didn't explain anything besides it was outside Washington, DC. He felt himself slipping into a self-deprecating spiral brought on by the encounter with his ex-friend.

After a lonely freshman year at Georgia Institute of Technology in Atlanta, Gavin thought he had found his people. He had joined a fraternity and roomed with Brett. He never would have taken Brett for a nerd. He was a lady's man on the track team. And yet, Brett and Gavin had programmed their own fantasy game while there. Like RuneScape but very dumbed down.

It was while programming the game that things started to turn. Brett asked him if he had done any hacking before. Not sure where it was going, Gavin answered with a half-truth. He admitted to doing some, but not to the extent he had done it. Gavin had been hacking since

6

around the time he was eight. And actively hacking and looking for his parents since he was ten after his mom had left. Then it increased five years later when his dad left, leaving Megan and him to fend for themselves.

If he was honest with himself, though, his dad left mentally the day his mom did. When she didn't return, it left Megan in charge to run everything. And his dad just fell in line with it. Like he wasn't the adult in the house. So, it shouldn't have been much of a surprise when he left, but it still hurt.

Around that time was when it all clicked for Gavin. Hacking became easy. He loved doing it, but he never wanted to hurt anyone. So, instead of taking things, he started hacking into different security systems and leaving tips on improving them. And he got pretty good at it.

The lack of malice is what made the betrayal by Brett so hard to take. When Gavin was finishing his sophomore year and getting ready to graduate with a bachelor's in computer programming and computer engineering, is when everything went south quickly.

During one of their game programming sessions after class, Brett asked if he would like to join him with a group of other 'creative programmers.' Gavin joined him and quickly learned that it was a hacking group. They had a silly-sounding name until he understood why. They were called the Giant River Otters, or GRO, because they only ever hacked as a pack. Initially, they seemed to align with what he felt was right morally. They didn't do anything for self-gain or malicious intent. Instead, they tried to help people and businesses.

Then, a few months into being a part of the group, there was an incident at the Georgia Institute of Technology. Gavin was turned in for altering grades by none other than Brett. The administration had followed the trail back to the GRO, and everyone in the group said Gavin was the one most capable of pulling off a hack like that. Hurt and feeling utterly betrayed, Gavin packed up his things and moved back in with his sister. Everything he had hoped for and dreamed was lost. He found this job working for Snollygoster Inc., a small privately owned call center, as their IT. It was nowhere near enough pay to live on his own, but it was a job. And he was good at it. Plus, they were flexible with him on when he could work. And he preferred to work the night shift, so that he could take down a system without having everyone standing over his shoulder.

As he came out of his daydream, reminiscing about the not-so-happy past, there was a ding on his personal cell phone. Looking down, it was an email from Brett. A few clicks and it opened. Across the screen flashed an algorithm. Brett always liked playing games with people. He would be the type to heavily encrypt a birthday email for no reason. Grabbing a notepad and pen, Gavin quickly wrote it down. Cycling through all the algorithms he knew already; this one didn't match.

Of course, Brett sends me an entirely new algorithm to open a freaking birthday email. Gavin thought with a slight smirk. It had been a while since he was able to use these skills. He started jotting down numbers and working through the math. Seeing a call from Kaleb, he ignored it. Kaleb likely wanted him to jump on Call of Duty with him, even though he knew he was at work. Getting close to finishing the algorithm got Gavin excited. He always felt a sense of accomplishment when he was able to complete a problem like this one. Bringing the email up on his laptop, Gavin entered in the final missing parts of the algorithm. "Ha, Brett. A bit rusty, but I still got it." He said under his breath, as no one was there.

As he hit enter to show the completed line of math, the screen came to life with coding. Gavin's eyes started to flutter. So much coding flew across the screen. He felt his head starting to get hot. His eyes burned, but he couldn't look away. Then, images mixed with coding. He felt his legs go to jelly. His arms were mush. His entire body felt like it was on autopilot and on fire. Then black.

***

Alex's phone buzzed. Looking down, she saw the text said 5. Five seconds. She looked around quickly to find a place to get away from the frat boys at the bar who wouldn't leave her alone. Seeing no way to get out, she realized she would just have to be vague in her replies. She waited for the call. The ringing started.

"Hunter secure," CIA Director Richard Hunter said.

"Hey, boss! What do you need?" Alex responded.

"Agent Johnson, we have confirmation of completion of the NOVA system. Your old partner has gone rogue and sent it to a civilian, as far as we can see. Your plane leaves in an hour. The dossier will be on the plane." Director Hunter commanded.

"Yes, Sir, I will get that paperwork to you right away." She said. She was thankful to be able to get away from the weak attempts to hit on her. "Sorry boys, duty calls." She said as she paid her tab and made her exit. That wasn't her scene, anyway.

Getting to the plane, she boards and sits down. Picking up the file, she immediately sees the picture of a man with scruffy, thick, brown hair that looks clean but could use a comb, glasses, and a friendly, goofy smile.

NAME: GAVIN MICHAEL WOODFORD
HEIGHT: 6'4"
WEIGHT: 195 LBS
HAIR: BROWN
EYES: GREEN
    OCCUPATION: CALL CENTER IT FOR SNOLLYGOSTER INC.
    LIVES WITH SISTER MEGAN
THREAT LEVEL: 0
    MISSION: INFILTRATE AND REACQUIRE ANY DEVICE WITH THE NOVA SYSTEM ON IT. DOWNLOAD CONFIRMED.

Looking at the naive and nerdy-looking man, *this will be cake.* Alex thought as she smirked. Finally, an easy mission.

***

Gavin woke up on the floor to Kaleb standing over him. "Hey man, we gotta go! How could you fall asleep at work? And on the floor? Are you an animal? Let's get you up and home. We have a big day ahead of us, Birthday Boy!" Kaleb kept jabbering as he helped his friend off the floor. He grabbed his laptop, shoved it in his backpack, and pushed him out the door. "If we don't get a move on, Megan is going to kill us!" he said, sounding scared.

"Kaleb, I don't think I can drive, man," Gavin said, slowly tossing Kaleb his keys. "You can get us to my house, right?"

Kaleb looked floored. "You know I can, buddy! You just rest your pretty little head and let Daddy Kaleb do all the work." Gavin had a splitting headache and didn't even bother correcting Kaleb on how creepy that sounded. "Just get us to my sister's," Gavin mumbled as he closed his eyes, trying to clear his mind of the coding that kept running through his mind, but it seemed to almost be worse when he closed his eyes.

Looking over and seeing his friend in pain, Kaleb offered, "How about some music?" He turns on the radio, and it was on the news channel since Gavin always streams his own music.

"And today at the CDC, the Ambassador from Kenya is speaking on the Ebola outbreak. His plane will be landing in just a few short hours." The news anchor stated.

A pink orchid, coding, a DNA strand, coding, an airplane.

"No, he didn't. He got here yesterday morning and is staying at the hotel across the street from the event center." Gavin blurted out. Surprised by the fact that it came out of him.

"Ok, Google. You don't need to tell me how you spent your time last night instead of gaming with me. You're lucky I took today off. Speaking of, do you think we could stop by the store? The boss had been after me to get the computer system working, and you taking care of it would get me some serious brownie points!" Kaleb asked in a rush, already turning the car around.

"Yeah, shouldn't take long. It's usually just a quick reboot. Let's get it out of the way." He said with a chuckle. *It is starting to feel like I should be getting paid there, too.* "But if we are too late getting to the house, then Megan will rip us apart." Gavin finished as they pulled into the store's parking lot.

They finished the reboot of the store quickly and were on their way out as the store started to open. Gavin made eye contact with a guy as they walked out the door. His brain started whirling again.

Coding, syringe, bodies, coding.

Gavin froze slightly. *That man is an assassin. Why would someone like that be here?* He shook his head and was glad that they were leaving. He wanted to get as far away as he could from him. Getting back out to the car, he took out his laptop. "Well crap, my laptop is fried." He muttered.

Kaleb looked at it, "Oh no, man! That thing is your life!" Gavin just looked at it and checked the power button a few more times. Nothing. He would have to tear it apart when he had time. Maybe if he drove himself, he would be able to sneak it into the club where his sister was hosting his birthday party. Even though he would likely know all of three people at said party.

He knew Kaleb had stayed up all night like he was supposed to. He still didn't understand what had happened to him last night. He never fell asleep at work. Even when he didn't get to sleep during the day. And other than his splitting headache, he felt completely fine. Unfortunately, being sick would've been the perfect excuse to miss the party tonight.

Getting home, he showered and found Kaleb already passed out on the couch. So, he went to his room, picked out his outfit for tonight from the preapproved options that Megan had set out for him, and collapsed in a heap face-first on his bed. Sleep came easy to his exhausted brain.

Alex watched as Gavin and Kaleb got into the car. She had made the short flight in just a few hours, and the CIA had her car waiting for her on the tarmac.

"I have eyes on the target. I will follow and wait for an opening to approach," Alex said.

"This is not a red mission yet. I will notify you if and when that changes, Agent Johnson." Director Hunter said in an impatient tone. "Make sure we don't mess this up. NSA is already in route. So, don't just sit on your hands." And the phone call ended.

I can't believe that he would say that to me! Don't mess this up? Who does he think I am? I'm not some amateur! Alex thought as she followed them. Watching them turn around and head back got her intrigued. Following them back to the store. This wasn't on her list of places. She watched and made note of the backpack that didn't seem to leave him. *That will be the first place to check.* Making an internal checklist of places to look without returning to his room.

She followed them into the store and kept her hood up. It wasn't cold, but it was an easy impromptu disguise. She watched them go in the back. They came back out fast enough that she didn't think it would be worth checking right now. *Back of this store.* Next location to review later on their list. She saw them leaving and delayed her exit so they wouldn't get suspicious. However, she was beginning to believe that they were completely incompetent at spotting a tail.

She waited a few minutes and then followed out. Seeing them in their car just getting ready to leave, she quickly got into her car and made to follow them about thirty yards back. She watched as they made it to a nice townhouse in a nicer area of town. If she didn't know he lived with his sister, then it would make sense that he was getting paid on the side from somewhere. But the townhouse made sense for a cardio surgeon and a neurologist.

She put on her thermo glasses and watched him enter the shower and then his room. She saw the other guy lying on the couch. And Gavin fell onto his bed. By his body temperature, she could tell it wasn't long before he fell asleep. So, she waited until something else happened. She couldn't take much longer, but she couldn't just knock on his door, either. *I hate seduction missions. Red missions are always so much easier.* She thought with a slight sneer.

Gavin woke up to his alarm going off. He checked, and it had been going off for 15 minutes. He bolted out of bed and got his clothes on for the party as fast as he could. "Kaleb! We gotta go, man! We are late!" He yelled from his room.

"Five more minutes, Mom," Kaleb yelled back, trying hard to stay asleep. Then, there was a thump on his head. "Hey!" He said, opening his eyes to see Gavin standing over him. "Crap! The party! Let's go." He said, jumping off the couch and grabbing the keys.

"No, no, buddy, I am driving now. I am feeling a lot better." Gavin said with a slight laugh. He shook his head at his friend's antics. "That was a one-time thing, buddy. You know I'm not supposed to let other people drive the company car."

"I know, man, but you can't blame a brother for trying. Right?" Kaleb said with a smirk. They jumped in the car and were off.

Across the street, Alex sat up in her car. She had placed a tracker on their car, so she wasn't worried about being able to follow where they went. She snuck into the townhouse and up to the room he had slept in. A War Games poster was hanging on the wall, the room was fairly tight, and there was a large TV with several gaming consoles hooked up. She looked around and checked the desktop for activity. Hooking up her drive to it, she ran her program. The machine told her the computer hadn't been turned on in several days.

She huffed in frustration after searching the room. It looked like she would have to make contact. Looking at the tracker monitor, it showed that they were at a club. She rolled her eyes. *Of course, they are at a club.* She quickly drove to her room, changed, and headed toward the club.

***

Having just endured the singing of Happy Birthday, Gavin was sitting to the side with Kaleb, discussing their next gaming night. Megan saw them and rolled her eyes. Making her way to them, she plopped down next to Gavin. "I hope you don't plan on sitting here the entire time we are here and talking video games. I have invited women who aren't on a screen here for you to meet. And have been talking you up to more of them. There are several who think you're cute. Get out there and talk to them," she urged while pushing him up off the couch.

"Megan, I hate to tell you this, but I would bet money I don't have that they were just being nice because it was you that they were talking to. I don't stand a chance with these women," Gavin said as he tried to sit back down.

"You will never know if you don't at least try. So, get your butt out there and mingle. Kaleb, you stay here. Or you are more than welcome to go home," Megan retorted. Standing and guiding Gavin out into the crowd, as he turned and mouthed to Kaleb, 'HELP ME.' But Kaleb just smiled and pulled out his phone to play a mobile game.

***

Alex pulled up to the club and, with a little flirting, could get in relatively easily. She made her way to the bar and got a drink as she scanned the club for Gavin. She spotted him talking to some woman in the VIP area. *Of course, he is. Typical guy. Too bad I didn't get the VIP access, though I am sure it won't be too hard to get an invite.* So, she waited.

After a while, and several weak attempts from guys to flirt with her, she saw him starting to come out to get a drink. He had his friend with him, who had driven him home. Turning her back to him as he made his way to the bar, she waited for him to order. She opened a second button on her blouse and waited to make her move. She couldn't help but smile slightly at how long it took them to get the bartender's attention. As they got their beers, she waited for them to get them picked up and ready to head back. *Show time.* As Gavin turned, she turned as well. Purposefully causing him to spill half a beer on her.

"Hey, watch it!" She yelped, acting startled and slightly upset.

"Oh, CRAP! I am SO sorry, Miss. Please let me help, er, get, I'll get some towels or something. Bartender! Please! Can I get a towel or something!" Gavin stuttered awkwardly, not even looking at who he had spilled the beer on. But Kaleb had. He was momentarily stunned and at a loss for words. He started pulling on Gavin's shirt sleeve. "Please! Can I get… What Kaleb?!" Gavin finally turned to his friend and then turned to see what he was looking at.

Looking up, he sees the most piercing and deep blue eyes he has ever seen in his life. Everything stopped. Nothing else matters but those eyes. Followed by chocolate brown hair and a stunning figure. But Gavin couldn't get past her eyes. *What? I. Huh? Work! That's where I'm at. Why is everything blue? Customer! Crap! Speak idiot!* Gavin thought.

"It's okay, really. I just didn't expect to get a beer shower this early. Hi, I am Alex." She started trying to smooth things over. *Okay, so maybe he isn't just like any other guy. He almost seems scared to even be near me now that he saw me. Is he breathing? Yes. Okay, that's good, at least. He is kind of cute. This may not be so bad after all. No! Be completely professional! Nice guys don't get sent government secrets, Alex!*

"I'm Kaleb, and my mute friend here is Gavin," Kaleb interjected, trying to smooth over his friend's mishap.

"Gavin." He finally blurted out, putting his hand out the short distance between their bodies.

Taking his hand, she grinned, and he smiled back. It was quite cute he was being so innocent and sweet. His smile was so full, even if he was red with embarrassment. Different than every other guy who had approached her. *Confirm where he has the item, Johnson. Come on. Get your head together. He has barely spoken, and your knees are weak? Snap out of it.* "Really, I don't mind," she stated in a slow tone.

Gavin finally found his footing, "Please, let me at least get you a drink you can throw in my face or something." He offered to be genuine and try to defuse his uncomfortable nature with humor, as usual.

"I don't think that is needed, but I wouldn't say no to a date," she said, taking a pen from her handbag and pulling his hand toward her.

"You don't have to write it on there; you are welcome to join us in our booth. I have some paper in there." Gavin inferred, not wanting to tell her he had a slight aversion to having people write on him after getting a particular part of the male anatomy drawn on him many times in high school.

"You sure you don't mind? I don't want to intrude," Alex asked politely. She couldn't help but feel a genuine blush creep over her neck and cheeks. It had been so long since she felt someone look at her the way Gavin was, not with lust or intent, but with real admiration.

"You wouldn't be. Really. Besides, it is my birthday party, and all the people there are my sister's friends. At least you would be someone I invited. Know that you don't have to stay or anything if you don't want to." Gavin rambled out. He was clearly nervous, but it still hadn't registered that she had asked him on a date.

"Okay, but only if you insist," Alex said, as Gavin gave a huge nose-scrunching smile. She started to follow him to the VIP area. *This is the goal. This was what I had intended when I made him bump me. But why am I getting a little giddy? It hasn't been THAT long. Has it? Well, I guess that was different. That was just post-mission adrenaline-fueled lust. Does that even really count?*

They got to the roped-off part, and she saw him lean over and tell the bouncer she was with him. Going through, they made their way to his backpack. She sat down next to it and started watching him rifling through everything in it. She saw a laptop, a phone, a set of small tools, a headset, two flash drives, and papers. Lots of papers.

Pulling one out, Gavin handed it to her. She smiled kindly and, trying not to sound too condescending, asked, "At this point, wouldn't it just be easier if I put my number in your phone?"

Gavin blushed and smacked himself in the forehead. "Yes. Yes, it would be. Sorry, I'll get that." He reached in and pulled out his personal phone, since he leaves his work phone at work, and handed it to her after unlocking it.

He is way too trusting. Just in general for someone living in the public. Let alone someone trying to hide the government's secrets. Unless he just believes that he can't be caught. Maybe that is it. But he doesn't give off that kind of confidence. He is bashful. Bashful. Like he hasn't spoken to a woman in years, if ever. As she quickly implanted a cloning app that instantly vanished, she put in her number and called herself. Allowing the app to pair with her phone. "There, now we have each other's numbers. I am new to the area and just would like to have someone kind to show me around a bit. If you don't mind?" she asked.

"Not at all! Just let me know. I do have some stuff planned later," Gavin said, looking at Kaleb.

Kaleb looked at him like he had grown a third head. "Like hell you do! You're free. You have nothing but time!" He nearly shouted.

"And apparently, my schedule has freed up," Gavin said, slightly embarrassed.

Alex felt her phone buzz once in her hand. She knew that meant her boss wanted a check-in ASAP. "I need to use the restroom. Will you let me back in when I come back?" She asked with a heavy flirting tone.

"Oh. Uh. Of course. Of course, I will." Gavin said, pushing his hand through his thick hair. A new blush crept across his cheeks. Making something happen in Alex's stomach.

She got into the bathroom and into a stall. "Johnson secure."

"Agent Johnson. NSA is boots on the ground. You are to stand down, according to their director," Director Hunter said in his perpetually irritated tone.

"Give me twelve hours. I'll find the device. I have already made contact and can have one-on-one time with him in the guise of a date. I can do

17

this. I can find the device by morning," Alex almost pleaded with her boss. After everything recently, she needed to prove herself.

"You have six hours. Get it done. And Johnson, this mission is now considered Red. If he runs, kill him," Director Hunter said, sounding slightly less irritated. And the line was dead.

Alex huffed. She hated being rushed. Especially for a seduction mission. Not that she ever really did them. She hated them, but had to find a way to complete this mission. And this guy, at least, wasn't all over her and trying to just get her to bed. Making her way back to the VIP lounge, she spotted four NSA agents entering the club.

Rushing over to Gavin, she asked, "So, since it is your birthday, I owe you a present. How about we go on that date right now? My treat!" She asked.

Kaleb nudged him towards her. "I would have to tell my sister that I'm," Gavin started.

"You go! I'll talk to her and let her know where you went. I have no doubt she will be MORE than happy you're on a date," Kaleb interrupted.

"Great! Let's go!" Alex grabbed his hand and headed out of the club. Getting out the door, he started towards his car. She waited for him to open her door. Watching out for the NSA agents. Thankfully, the club was so crowded. Once they were on their way, she kept an eye out for them.

***

He took her to a nicer Mexican restaurant. And as they say, she noticed he had opened every door for her. And waited for her to sit first at the restaurant. She chose to sit facing the door. *Gotta keep him safe until he can tell me where the NOVA system is.*

Once they sat and the conversation started, it startled her that he was asking about her with genuine interest. He wasn't trying to interrupt

18

her. He wasn't talking over her. Or trying to one-up her. He just wanted to hear about her. *Who is this guy? There is no way that he could possibly have whatever the NOVA system is. But I have to keep trying.*

He was making her really laugh for what felt like the first time since she was a little girl. He had an ease that seemed to make everyone, and everything relax and try to enjoy themselves. She couldn't help but admire how he handled himself. Once he got past the nerves of a first date, he was easy to talk to and highly personable in a way she hadn't experienced before. *Get yourself together. Who cares what he does. He is your assignment. Your suspect.*

As she paid and they made their way out of the restaurant, she made eye contact with NSA agent Robert Charles. She pulled on his arm. "Gavin, give me your keys! NOW!" *Come on, we don't have time.*

"What? Why? What's going on?" Gavin asked, waiting for an answer. *Is this because of my hacking? I have never told anyone that I am Vidar.*

Pulling out a skeleton key, she pushed the button, which fit the lock, and unlocked the door. Gavin stood there stunned. Alex reached across and opened the door. "GET IN!" Gavin got in, feeling himself starting to freak out. Alex turned the car on and slammed it in gear. Quickly driving down random roads, trying to lose them. Knowing she doesn't have much time.

"Alex, what is going on?!" Gavin almost screamed, gripping the car as if it was his last hope for life.

"Do you have the NOVA system? Did you get anything from Brett Martin?" Alex asked in a rush.

"NOVA? I don't know anything. Wait, Brett? What does any of this have to do with my old college roommate? I hadn't heard from him in ages until the other night," Gavin rattled off.

"That is the NSA. They don't follow the same rules as I do. To them, if the system is dead, then it is safe. And I am collateral damage. Now answer my questions. Did he send you anything? Did he give you anything?" Alex demanded.

"No. He didn't… wait. Yes. He sent me an email with an algorithm to solve for my birthday. That was very on-brand for him," Gavin responded. "ALEX LOOK OUT!"

He wasn't in time. A black SUV slammed into the side of his car. They were spinning, and Gavin couldn't understand what was going on. *Why his date went south so fast. Why did a random SUV just seem to purposefully hit them?* He saw Alex crawl out of the car. Thankfully, they were both okay. He got out himself as he saw the SUV turning toward them. "Alex! MOVE!" Gavin yelled.

Alex looked and saw Agent Charles' SUV had turned around and was starting to drive towards her. *Now, this is the adrenaline I need. Now, it is a mission. This is what I live for. This is how I feel alive. Government SUV, puncture-proof tires, that's out. They have an auto lock, two feet back from the bottom of the grill, in the break line being severed. Gotta time it right. Wait, Wait.* She reached down, grabbed a knife from her ankle sheath, and threw it at the ground right in front of the SUV.

The knife ricocheted off the pavement and up into the engine. It severed the front brakes of the SUV as Alex rolled out of the way. The front tires locked on the SUV, causing the axle to seize up and get ripped off its mounts. The front-end dived into the ground, and the forward momentum caused the SUV to flip. With her out of the way, she got up, ran, and grabbed Gavin. Seeing an empty parking lot, she ran toward it, getting out her phone to call in an air evac.

"You have to tell me exactly what was in that email, and I mean now!" Alex demanded.

"Was I not supposed to open that email? The one that Brett sent? I just solved the algorithm, and then there was coding and some pictures.

Was I not supposed to solve that? What did he get me into?" Gavin started talking faster as he was freaking out.

"I hope you had some good insurance on that car. I would hate for your family to have to pay for the damages after you're gone. Because you are coming with me now." Agent Charles came walking up with his gun out.

"He isn't yours yet. He solved it. He saw everything. And he is still alive. He IS the NOVA system," Alex said. Pulling out her gun as well.

Agent Charles raised his gun to point it at Gavin's head. "So, all I have to do is put a bullet in his head, shoot you, and I can get my long-needed vacation? I could be on a beach by sunrise?"

Alex turns her gun on him. "We have to check in with the directors to see what they want. This is unprecedented. No one has been able to do what he has done. They will want him alive."

Gavin wanted to go back and punch himself in the face. He wished he had never opened that email. He turned to run and heard a click. And froze. Looking across the street, he saw an ad for the CDC.

Some coding, a syringe, coding, an iris, coding.

"They are going to assassinate the Ambassador from Kenya at the conference in the next two hours. He takes the stage," Gavin blurted out, turning towards them.

Both agents looked at him. "Talk to me, Gavin. What is going on?" Alex said.

"I don't know. There are images and coding that pop up in my head, and I suddenly know what is happening. And some that will be happening soon. I don't understand it, and I don't want it. I want my meaningless life back," Gavin said with a slight whine.

"Loser," grunted Charles.

Looking at Agent Charles with a scowl, Alex said, "Gavin, is there time to save the ambassador?"

"I think so. But we must hurry." He took off running through the park. He knew he was only about a 30-minute run away from the event center, even as his lungs started burning.

***

Getting to the event center, Charles grabbed him. "If this is real and you're the Nova system, then you are staying out here. You're too important. So, which way?"

"The fastest or the least conspicuous?" Gavin asked. His nerves are taking over.

"Fastest. We need to get to him," Alex said.

"Fastest. Got it." Gavin jumped up and ran off. The 2 agents huff in frustration as they run after him. He barged into the conference room, looking around for him. Popping his head out the door, he saw the assassin closing a door down the hall. "That's the assassin!" Gavin said to Alex.

Charles took off after the assassin, making Gavin almost feel bad for the fool. Coming up to the door, Gavin saw that the door was electro-locked with a computer login. "He is draining the air in the Ambassador's room. Let me see the system." He pulled the computer out and did a simple DOS override to get in. Then he saw that the lock was intentionally broken. As he set in the coding, he fried the motherboard and caused the electrical wiring to fry into the door, making it open. "Got it!" Gavin said, letting the security into the room.

When Alex got outside to see Charles putting the assassin into the back of an unmarked car, she walked up to him to discuss the ownership of the asset.

Gavin walked out of the building and heard them arguing. He couldn't take it anymore. They acted like he didn't matter beyond what was in his head. So, he walked off. Catching a cab to a park by his house. He used to come here to clear his mind all the time.

As the sun rose, he heard Alex approaching him from behind. "I guess there is no way to get away from any of you. Huh?" He asked.

"Not really, but you aren't going anywhere until we get orders. Our bosses have heard what is going on and are making a decision by later today. Gavin, I have to ask you something." Alex said, feeling almost bashful.

"Yeah?" he asked, hoping it wasn't related to this. He couldn't help but like her. Beyond her obvious, attractive physical appearance, he felt a connection. He couldn't explain it, but she was everything he had ever wanted.

"Trust me. I won't always tell you the truth, but I will tell you what you need. Please, for your safety, trust me. Now, let's get some sleep. We don't know what tomorrow will bring." Alex asked. There was almost a pleading tone.

He stood to leave and said, "I will try," as he headed home to crash.

Chapter 2

:/History

It had been a few days since Alex had talked to Gavin in the park. Life had seemed fairly normal, apart from Charles now working at the Snollygoster Inc. as security with Gavin, Alex got a job at the Sub Express across the parking lot ,and the daily reports Gavin had to look over before work each day. Other than that, and Alex's cover being his girlfriend, it had been back to the daily grind, no one knowing he had saved the lives of some important people. *Oh well, could be worse. Could've NOT been able to save those lives.* Gavin thought with a shrug. Normally, something like that would bother him more, but he wondered if they were making any progress to get the NOVA system thing out of his head.

Working the day shift had thrown him off his schedule. But thankfully, the company didn't seem to care when he worked, as long as things ran smoothly.

Gavin stood to get out of his car to start another regular day, and a flash of brown hair caught his attention. Alex was standing outside the Sub Express, which he had been informed was really just the start of a CIA base with the most basic setup. He couldn't help but stare. *She's perfect...* Gavin thought, and before he could stop himself, he was walking towards her as she waved and headed inside.

He jogged up to the door and headed in. *I need to know more about what is going on with this thing in my head* as he heard her cussing about the slicing job of the meat. "I could have done better in my sleep. Did they ask some analyst to cut this?" She huffed as she turned around to see Gavin standing at the counter. She wasn't surprised. She knew he was likely to head in to see her. "Hey, Gavin," she said with a smile. To her surprise, it was genuine.

Gavin smiled back. "Hey, umm, I just wanted to see, is there a plan? You know, to get this out of my head? I can't imagine that the nation is super secure with all its secrets inside the head of a guy who makes less than $20 an hour." Gavin said self-deprecatingly with a chuckle.

He doesn't have any clue how significant this is. How special he is. How adorable... stop it, Johnson. Focus. Mission first. "Yeah, we have a plan. There is a top scientist coming to see you. We are confident he can help get the data out if that's still what you want?" She said with a slight smirk. *Why am I wishing he didn't want that anymore? I don't get attached to people. Make him feel he's special but keep him at arm's length. You've worked a mark a million times. Focus on my orders.* Alex reprimanded herself.

"Umm. Yeah... yeah! That's what I want. Just to get my life back." Gavin said.

"Okay. Date tonight. I'll pick you up at eight." Alex said, fighting the smile on her face and the urge to feel excited about more time with Gavin.

"See you then!" Gavin said with a smile, not bothering to hide his excitement.

***

After work, Gavin stood in his room; Megan was again helping him pick out his outfit for the date. "A second date with Alex, huh? Getting pretty serious?" Megan teased with genuine interest.

"It's really not that big of a deal," Gavin mumbled, knowing that Alex wasn't what they all thought she was.

"I'd say it's a big deal! She is SO hot!" Kaleb said as he continued to play Gears of War on Gavin's bed.

"Looks aren't always everything Kaleb. And why does he get to meet her first, mister?!" Megan says with indignation.

"Gavin and I keep secrets, Megers. He tells me things. Things he'd never dream of divulging to you." Kaleb said, "We could have secrets too, you know." Kaleb said flirtingly.

"Here's a secret: I loathe you," Megan said with a roll of her eyes.

"That's not really a secret, Meg," Gavin said with a chuckle at the both of them. "And it's not a big deal. We are just getting together. She wants me to show her around town more." Gavin lied without even realizing it.

Alex pulled up to Gavin's sister's townhouse. Her BMW R8 idled as she waved to Gavin. *I need to be more careful tonight. Maybe it was my last mission still messing with me. I can't afford any slip-ups.* Alex thought as Gavin made his way to the car.

Opening the door and plopping down, Gavin quipped, "Sub Express, huh? You'll need a different cover to explain driving a Beemer."

Alex couldn't help but smirk; all the tension she had built up was gone in a moment with Gavin. "I could always say that you're my sugar daddy." She said with a slight flirt. Gavin gulped great big and turned red.

"So, what are we doing? A movie and dinner? Or some drinks? Mini golf?" Gavin asked as he put his seatbelt on.

"No, not really anything like that," Alex said. Suddenly, she was stoic as she zoomed off into traffic. The ride remained fairly quiet, with mixed small talk about their day. Alex felt it would be best to minimize contact with him, given how easy it has been for them to slip into calm and easy banter.

***

Soon, they pulled up to what looked like an abandoned building, and Gavin looked somewhat confused. Alex had him let them in as he said, "Is this the stranger danger that Megan always tried to tell me was out there?" With a smirk.

Alex took a breath, "We are here to meet the scientist who will help you. He will test you to see if everything is good and to make sure that you can have them removed or not." *Ending this assignment already.* She thought surprisingly begrudgingly.

They made their way into the building, which seemed nicer inside. Clearly, it was a black-site government building.

"Great!" He said as he sat down in front of a computer screen as Alex indicated. "When do I get to meet him?"

"Oh, that won't be happening. It's best if he doesn't know who you are for your safety. You're too important." *As an asset. Yeah.* Alex said as she set to head out the door.

"So, what do I do?" Gavin said, confused.

"Just sit there and look at the images and tell us what you see," Alex replied chipperly.

"Sounds easy enough," Gavin answered.

"I'm sure you'll find a way to screw it up," Charles grunted, appearing out of nowhere. Alex closed the blinds and shut the door as the scientist walked up. After initial introductions, the test began. Gavin did perfectly, as she expected, and things started to feel off. Her senses heightened, and she felt on edge even though she wasn't sure what had changed.

Charles and the scientist Dr. Zodiac were discussing Gavin ambiguously. Something seemed off with it. She couldn't tell if it was Charles or Zodiac. But the situation was unsettling for her. She wanted this done as soon as possible. "Do you think you can get it out?" She said, getting to the point.

"Yes, I believe I can," Zodiac said slowly.

They showed him out, and she got Gavin and headed to take him home. Once again, they traveled quietly. Both are clearly in thought. *Why didn't I feel right?* Alex thought as she replayed the scene in her head. *Charles was his grumpy self. Gavin is safe. That's what matters. And it looks like he will get those out of his head soon. Both good things.* Alex started to slow down and calm down as they approached the apartment again.

"I gotta say. This is the best, only second date that I have been on in a long time!" Gavin quipped with a chuckle. He had a soft, slightly embarrassed smile.

Why does he do that? Does he know how disarming it is? Is he really playing me? Alex found she couldn't respond.

"So," Gavin coughed out, "I guess once I get this out of my head, we are all done, right?" Gavin said sadly.

"Umm, yeah," Alex said, nodding her head. And Gavin paused for a moment. *Great. I'm sure she is ready to be not babysitting me anymore. She's feeling awkward now.*

"Ok, well, goodnight, Alex." Gavin didn't wait for a reply. He vaguely heard her say goodnight.

***

Gavin got to work the next day, not sure what to feel. He liked that he wouldn't be in danger, like having to disarm a bomb again, but it also meant no more Alex. *I think I'll miss her. No, I KNOW I'll miss her. I barely know her. So, why?* Gavin thought as he started working on a computer. *I didn't see Charles on the way in. And Alex's car wasn't in the usual spot. I wonder if everything is okay.* Just then, Charles came storming in, clearly upset. *When isn't he upset?* Gavin thought with a roll of his eyes.

Charles got clocked in and then made a beeline for him. The way he walked made him feel uncomfortable. Things weren't okay. "You can't trust her," Charles whispered with a blunt and aggressive tone, "You can't trust your girlfriend. She is CIA. How much do you really know about her? Huh?"

Gavin suddenly became painfully aware of how little Alex had said about herself. Even on the first date, she avoided talking about herself much. He started to focus on her. He was thinking about the details of her. And suddenly, images flashed; he saw clips of a few of her missions, some pictures. People dead. Bodies surround Alex. Then, another of her shooting out a surveillance camera. Gavin's breath caught. He felt dizzy. And out of the corner of his eye, he saw a message pop up on his laptop.

Come see me. We need to talk. ASAP. AJ

Gavin didn't know what to think. He felt his pulse increase. *She hadn't seemed like that. She'd been so sweet. She even cared enough not to treat him like a nuisance.* Gavin thought. Charles had started running through situations with Kaleb. He seemed distracted enough for Gavin to be able to sneak out. As he crossed the parking lot, he could see a bunch of teenage boys in the eating area of the Sub Express.

Rolling his eyes, he entered as the group started to leave. "I don't want you to be having any private meetings with Charles," Alex warned as the restaurant emptied other than Gavin.

"What is with you guys? Did something happen?!" Gavin said, feeling exhausted.

"What can you tell me about this?" Alex said as she tossed a bag with a severely burnt-up cell phone on the counter.

29

"It's a mangled… No. Wait, that's a bomb! Hang on." He focused on it closer. "That's a CIA explosive?! Alex, what is going on?" Gavin almost whimpered.

"We believe that Zodiac is dead. His car was found a few miles out of town. And that was among the debris. I didn't put it there. But who was the only other person who knew what was happening last night?" Alex replied.

"No, why would Charles want to kill him? He wants out of here." Gavin whined.

"Look. All I know is that it is my job to protect you from anyone, including fellow operatives, as needed. So, right now, I need you to go back to work while I investigate. Okay, Gavin? You can do that." Alex ordered matter of factly.

"Okay. Act like I know nothing. Okay," Gavin said absentmindedly. She grabbed Gavin's hand and made eye contact with him.

"Trust me, Gavin. Please. This is real now. It's not one of your games." He simply nodded as he left the restaurant.

Gavin was walking across the parking lot, and he focused on Charles. As with Alex, soon images were flashing through his mind and then death. Bodies. Military record, redacted. And Gavin realized just how dangerous these handlers of his are. And a chill went down his spine. He walked in, and Charles grabbed him. "What did you talk to your girlfriend about?" Charles growled at him. And Gavin just gaped at him. Charles huffed in anger and left. Gavin tried to refocus on work. He was zoning out in the parts and soldering of the computers. He was in his happy place.

***

The day had ended when he noticed he hadn't seen Charles again and wasn't sure what was happening. He didn't like being in the dark in his life. He wanted to know more about what was going on. And who he was having to deal with. Especially with this Zodiac gone, there was no way to get the NOVA system out of his head. *Focus on the work, Gavin. Don't think about that right now.* Gavin headed to the car to go home, and as he pulled out his keys, Alex came running up, looking frazzled. "Alex, what is going on?" He asked with concern.

"I was wrong, Gavin. Charles is gone. We were supposed to check in an hour ago, but he never did. I reviewed the tape and saw him get taken. I got a plate number and am tracking them. But a rescue team is too far out. I'm going after him. You go home and STAY HOME!" she said intently.

"Alex. I want to help! Let me help find him!" Gavin pleaded with her.

"Just go home, Gavin. Trust me. Remember?" she replied as she took off running towards her car.

Gavin huffed. *I can help, though.* He thought as he got in the car. He got out his fixed laptop and hacked into her phone. Pulling up the mimic of it and watching her GPS following the car Charles was in, he guessed where they might be going and took off that way.

      ***

Arriving at the building, he saw the car with the plates that Alex was following. He hadn't seen her yet, so he figured he had known a shorter route. He pulled his laptop back out and got to work. He found the building's schematics and power grid access. He also hacked into the security and looked for Charles.

As he went through the security footage, he saw a man come out of the building and head toward the car he had followed.

Stars, coding, North Korean flag, coding.

Zodiac?! What is he doing here? I thought he was supposed to be dead! He's selling secrets to North Korea? That just makes sense. He is sleazy looking. Great. This thing is never and never was going to be coming out of my head. He thought as he continued through the footage.

He found Charles right as Alex pulled up. He didn't get out since she had been adamant that he should go home. So, he waited. She went to the back of her car and pulled out a bag. She glanced at his car but quickly continued towards the wrong building and went inside.

Of course. Couldn't have just had the right guess, could you? He thought as he typed away on his laptop. He quickly set a few timers for different systems and entered the building.

He headed straight for where Charles was being held, snuck into the room, and hid. He watched as Zodiac approached and woke Charles. He wasn't close enough to hear, but not long after they spoke, it was clear that Charles was not having anything to do with what the Zodiac was saying.

Soon, Zodiac went out of sight and came back with pliers. *He is going to torture him!* Gavin gasped. The shock caused him to fall backward slightly and bump into the shelf behind him. This caused a wrench to fall to the floor with a loud clang. It caused both Charles and Zodiac to look in his direction.

But right when they did, the lights all went out, and the fire alarm kicked on. There were flashing lights and loud noises in the room, causing Zodiac to be disoriented enough for Charles to kick him.

The one kick was enough to knock him out. And Gavin came running up and freed Charles. "Where is Johnson? Why are you here and not her, if she cut the power? Know what? Never mind. I'll ask when we are out of here." He reached down and punched Zodiac in the face. Then, he picked him up and slung him over his shoulder.

"How did you even get taken by a scientist in the first place?" Gavin asked in a sarcastic, teasing tone.

"Ever heard of sedatives, numbnuts? They work on us. Agents aren't immune. We just have a faster recovery time. Now, let's get out of here before his friends come." Charles said as he started out the door.

They were about to reach the door when it opened, and Alex tried to sneak in. "Welcome, Johnson. Glad you could join us," Charles quipped at her.

"What is he doing here?" she asked, "I thought I told you to go home! And how did you even find us? And before me? If you EVER pull anything like this again, I will end this! You go with Charles to a hole in the ground, and I go back to missions all over the world. You are too important to have running into danger, especially on your own, trying to play the hero! You are not a spy! You are an asset, so stop trying to act like you're more!" she finally finished with a huff.

"Congrats! While you all were sorting out your lady feelings, the rest of Doctor Kevorkian's team showed up," Charles growled in a very irritated tone.

Gavin looked up. Guns, coding, North Korean flag, coding.

"Those aren't his men. Those are his buyers," he said quietly. Charles growled in what almost sounded like excitement. Alex huffed and pulled her gun out. She crouched in the dark of the hallway and returned to the room they were in. She made her way around to the back of the buyers and waited. Nobody noticed Gavin hit a button on his watch, and the lights came back on.

The buyers saw Charles in their way and grabbed their guns. While distracted, Alex goes through with a stun gun and dropped them all. "I guess we need to call in a detainment team. I will stay. You make sure he gets home," Alex said, still sounding irritated.

"No can do. You don't have clearance to operate on US soil with the locals yet. So, YOU get to babysit him while I babysit these fools. Have fun."

Alex grabbed Gavin by the arm and pulled him out of the building in silence.

How could he not trust me and listen to me? Just like Brett always did. I thought he was different. I guess I was wrong. And now I am stuck with him for the foreseeable future. Can I handle it? Alex thought. She couldn't be there anymore. She couldn't be near him. Brett would have been trying to smooth-talk her by now. He would have found a way to try to work her pants off before they even got to the car, yet here was Gavin just quietly walking next to her, respecting the fact she was mad, and allowing her to work through those emotions herself without trying to either explain it away or guilt her into forgiveness.

But she did feel guilty. She never should've talked to Gavin like that. He was trying to help and actually had helped. If she hadn't shown up, he would have had Charles out of the building before the other guys showed. And even then, he could tell them who they were when they did show. So, instead of killing them, like they would have to without him, they were captured without bloodshed. That means they have foreign operatives to interrogate and bargain with.

Plus, he is new and doesn't understand the stakes of being a part of this world. Maybe now he would. She needed him to. *I need to have more patience with him. This isn't a seduction mission anymore, thankfully. I've never been on one and don't intend to. But I do need him to be compliant.* She thought as she got to his car. She went to start talking to him, and he just got in the car immediately without a word. *I guess that was easier, but I would have liked to talk some before he left.*

He waited for her to get back to her car and get going. As she followed him, the phone rang. "Johnson secure." She said in a dull tone. "Agent Johnson, Zodiac never made it to our facilities. He died in transit. We aren't sure what's at play here, but it feels like there is more than just him. Keep an eye on the asset, and if he seems lost to the enemy, kill him." Hunter hung up before she could reply. *Kill him? He's done nothing wrong. He didn't want this. Still doesn't want this. I know I'm an assassin. It's what I'm best at. But isn't my job to protect him? No. It's to protect the country. It's secrets. Not Gavin. The NOVA system. And it's better to be gone than with the enemy. He's right. I must prepare for it.*

***

Gavin got home and felt more tired than he had in a long time. The physical and emotional toll of the day had crested.

"Hey, you. Feels like we haven't seen you since you started dating this girl. Not that there is anything wrong with that, I just would like a slight heads up as to where my brother is," Megan said from her seat on the couch. She was still in her scrubs from the hospital. She looked tired but happy to see him. *I could talk to her about it. I just have to be vague.*

"Meg, I messed up. I made Alex mad. Like, really mad. I kinda directly ignored what she told me to do. And I am not sure how to fix it,." Gavin said as he flopped down onto the couch next to her.

Megan put her head on his shoulder, "Have you tried to apologize yet?" she asked. "You would be amazed at how much can be forgiven with a simple and real apology. If she cares about you, it won't be an issue as soon as you show her you care too and that her input is important to you." Megan sighed in contentment at the fact that her brother was finally having girl trouble that she could help with.

"Thanks, Meg. I will try, and do you think you would want to meet her?" he asked with a curious tone.

"Only if she feels up to it. Don't push her too far, too fast. But, at any point, if she is ready to meet me, then I am more than excited to meet her," Megan replied with a soft smile.

***

Later that evening, Gavin made his way to the Sub Express. *Megan said to just try to apologize, right? That's all I need to do. Easy.* Gavin thought with a huff. It definitely was easier said than done. But hopefully, maybe, she had had some time.

Walking in, he saw her and immediately started, "Alex. I just wanted to say I'm sorry. I was a real jackass. I was scared, and all of this is new. I didn't know who to trust because I didn't know anything about you. My life has been turned upside down, and it's left me facing my mortality at a rate I couldn't have imagined less than a month ago. I'm sorry I didn't listen to you. I should have. And this won't happen again. And I do trust you. I just also feel like I can help you guys more than you feel I can. I am not entirely incompetent, despite what my background might say," he said while maintaining eye contact.

He's serious. He set his ego aside and was genuinely sorry. He acknowledged he messed up. So, I guess he isn't completely like Brett. And the one part that he argued with, he isn't wrong either. I can't just treat him like a mark or a child. This is a completely different situation than any mission. He isn't a fugitive or someone dangerous. He just wants to help. "I understand, Gavin. But that's even more reason to trust and listen to me. And I guess Charles. We have lived in this world for a long time. That alone should tell you that you need to listen to us." Alex softly reprimanded.

"I know. And you're right. I will do better in the future. But I can't just not help when someone needs me. But I'll listen better. And since you have seemed to have forgiven me," he paused, and in walked Kaleb, Megan, and Chad, "I was hoping we could have dinner together with everyone in my life who has been begging to meet you. Here?" Gavin asked.

"Here? You do realize that that means you will all be subjected to my cooking, right?" Alex said with a smile. He surprised her, and it was once again genuine. Gavin smiled back.

***

That night, Gavin sat in his room after he got home from the makeup dinner with Alex and his makeshift family. He was stuck. And worse, he felt helpless. Alex had already snapped at him once. He barely trusted Charles; his world was falling apart, and he couldn't even talk to his sister about it. Not really. What was he supposed to do?

Megan had told him to apologize to Alex, but she didn't even know what the real issue was. This was entirely about trust or lack thereof. He had found he could force himself to access the NOVA system, so there was some semblance of control over his life. But it wasn't easy, and he felt weird when he did it.

There is one thing I can do to gain some control. Some kind of order. I will have to be careful, but it's time to stop sitting on the sidelines. They don't need to know. I want to help. There is no point in sitting idly and hoping someone else can fix the situation. Even if they could, I need to make the most of it. And that starts with research. Time for an old friend to come out to play. They weren't here because they knew I was Vidar. So that means I can use that to my advantage. Time to start digging.

Gavin thought as he sat down at his computer. It was like riding a bike. He got into his old coding and started reworking it. Making it fit the modern designs for sites, and after a bit, he was in. He was surfing silently through the government's data servers. He had goals in mind that he hadn't had before.

First off, who was in charge? NSA and CIA. So, the directors for those. He would need as much information on them as possible. And Alex and Charles. He trusted them for the most part. But both had made a strong point that he knew nothing about either of them. And yet he had to trust them with his life. What was it his dad used to say? *Trust but verify...*? Yeah. Verify. He was going to make sure he wasn't flying blind anymore.

The more he pulled up, the more he felt sick to his stomach. The things that they had to do to make sure that he was safe, even before he had the NOVA system. It was sad and terrifying. And some of these didn't make sense. Alex's missions didn't always seem to work in favor of the American government. Definitely not for the American people.

Charles's was fairly straightforward once you unredacted his file. 6ft 3in 275lbs. Black hair, black eyes. He knew he was big. American Indian. Military operations mostly. His real name is Mato Acothley. Likely some things he didn't even know. But all seemed to be on the up and up.

Alex's read different. 5ft 8in 175 lbs. Brunette, Blue eyes. But even when unredacted, there were chunks missing that shouldn't be. There are gaps in her training that didn't make sense. And the age she was recruited. There wasn't much on her early life. Not like Charles. Fragments. Names. Not one. Many. It didn't make sense. He would need to take a much deeper dive into her training and recruitment. Those didn't sit right with him.

Gavin noticed a difference in himself as he read. It felt similar to when he was younger. Easy to read things and recall them. He didn't feel a need to write anything down because he knew it would never leave his mind.

General Catherine Richmond, Director of the NSA, is an imposing yet diminutive woman, at 5ft even, and mostly gray with some red hair and piercing steel blue eyes. Her record more than spoke for itself. An old soldier, turned Cold War spy, turned general. She was tough as nails. Her file was full of mission after mission, success after success. Rarely ever was there a failure. And the few that were there, stood out as beyond her control. For a while, a couple of names, Hel and Coeus, popped up a lot. But then, they stopped showing up in the late 80s and early 90s.

Same with Director Richard Ethan Hunter. 5ft 11in. Salt and Pepper, black hair, and grey eyes. But his file had far less successful missions. In fact, he seemed to be mediocre before those same names as in Richmond's file showed up in his file. He had made his way to the CIA and was an apprentice to the then Director. Little more than an errand boy. And then, these names showed in his file, and suddenly, he started his rise in power. Quickly to Assistant Director, and then froze until his predecessor retired. *Maybe it was out of respect,* Gavin thought, though in the same thought, disregarded it. The freeze in the rise to power started as those names stopped appearing in his file. First one. Then, several years later, the other. Just gone.

Chapter 3

:/Facts

Gavin woke up still at his computer. He had spent most of the night looking into his "new friends" and their bosses. And he wasn't even remotely close to done yet. *I'll need to think of a faster way to unredact their files. I saw plenty to make me sick, but there is definitely more I need to know.* Gavin thought as he stretched, sure to close out of his program and bring up the computer game that would've been showing had anyone been looking before he shut his computer. It unplugged the external hard drive that he was storing all the encrypted files he had accessed, not that it was needed since his mind remembered everything easier than it had. *That's something I will need to analyze when I get the chance to relax a bit. Things that seemed hard to learn are starting to feel easier to remember. Blessing and a curse, for sure.* Gavin laughed as he put the hard drive inside his computer, lodging it between the graphics card and the internal hard drive. It is not easy to detect without knowing what you're looking at. And then he got up to get ready for work.

***

A week later, it felt like he hadn't gotten a minute alone to think about everything and see what more he could find. Either Kaleb wanted time with him, or Megan needed to talk, or the rare but wonderful date with

Alex. *Cover date. It's not real.* Gavin admonished himself. He was starting to have some trouble differentiating between what was real and what wasn't. A lot of the time he spent with Alex just felt so real. But she was always quick to remind him that it wasn't. That everything she did was for the cover. He mattered only for what was in his head and nothing more.

Kaleb had resorted to coming over early in the mornings to play video games before they both had to work since Gavin was on day shifts now. While playing Call of Duty, they were talking smack to some kids who were skipping school to play, when a new person joined the lobby. OrisTheTerrible. Gavin read it and instantly felt the NOVA system kick in.

"Earth to Gavin, you okay man? You zoned out pretty hard there," Kaleb teased him, "Thinking about Alex again, weren't you? I can't even blame you. I do from time to time myself."

"Kaleb, that is my girlfriend you are perving on. Please stop," Gavin said with a slight hint of disgust, even though he knew his friend was teasing. But the disgust wasn't for Kaleb. It was for what he saw in his head. He had to get to Charles ASAP. "Hey, I think we need to call it a day. You want to take my car to work? I have to talk to Charles about security issues at the call center. Can't be too careful with other people's credit card information," He explained with an awkward laugh. He hated having to lie to the people who loved him. But he had to keep them safe.

"Yeah, you're good. I understand. I will see you later," Kaleb said, not even sounding excited that he gets to drive. Gavin didn't notice, though. He was in a hurry.

***

Knocking on the door, Alex let him in. Gavin was slightly confused about why Alex was there. Still, as he wandered into the apartment, which was bare except for a picture of an American Indian. Focusing, he forced himself to access the NOVA system. Quanah Parker. Famous Comanche Chief. *Interesting, I wonder if that's Charles' tribe?* Gavin

40

thought as he heard voices talking to Charles and Alex. Rounding the table he saw it was Director Hunter and General Richmond. "Wow. These monitors really show the age,huh?" Gavin said with a smirk.

"This is a live feed conference, numbnuts. We are being debriefed. They can hear you," Charles grunted angrily. Gavin gulped with big eyes. knowing there was no saving the situation.

With a roll of her eyes, Alex hid a smirk. *Of course, he walks in and says that to the bosses. He either has a death wish or is just that open of a person.*

"And I understand you're being debriefed, but I figured you all would be interested in a massive arms dealer and some weapons-grade plutonium that is set to be in Atlanta tomorrow at an estate sale. Does the name Oris the Terrible mean anything?" Gavin said, trying to act like he didn't know who it was on the monitors.

There was a bit of chaos at what he said. Richmond immediately started trying to give orders, and Hunter did as well. Alex stood staring at the scene Gavin had just inadvertently caused, and Charles was busy trying to listen to the General. He had no respect for Hunter, but his face was unreadable like Alex's. They had their agent masks on and wouldn't let a distraction affect it. Having calmed down, the General ordered Charles to investigate the validity of this, and Hunter directed Alex to find out what she could about the estate sale.

They were dismissed quickly, with a flat look from Richmond and a glare from Hunter. "They seem nice," Gavin chirped with a chuckle.

Charles grabbed him, "Don't interrupt another briefing like that again, or you'll have my foot up your ass," Charles growled and then let go and grabbed his coat, walking toward the door. "Let's go moron," he said as he closed the door.

"He really is a sweet guy once you get past the hard candy shell," Gavin quipped on his way past Alex, who failed at maintaining her spy mask, and cracked a small smile.

***

On the way to the estate sale, Alex kept looking at Gavin. She knew what she looked like. The CIA made sure she was alluring. It's easier to get people to talk when they feel attracted to the person they are talking to. But she hadn't been prepared for what that Armani suit would look like on Gavin. *He looks really good. He doesn't dress right for his body type. He is way more handsome than he thinks, and I'm going to need to be careful.* Alex gave herself a pep talk. Gavin was excited. He hadn't been told to stay in the car or to go home yet. It had been a good morning. And the fact that Alex was in that low-cut blue dress with a hip-high slit, well, it didn't help his blood pressure either.

Gavin was wandering the items and watching Alex getting friendly with some of the big shots at the sale, getting more and more jealous as he watched her. "Eyes on the prize, moron. We need you to be on the lookout for Oris the Terrible. Remember. Not staring down Johnson." Gavin coughed and diverted his eyes as Alex had heard Charles over the coms. *Really, Charles. You couldn't have been more subtle?*

Gavin started roaming around and found the painting. He wondered if it had already happened. As he was standing there looking at it, a nicely dressed man came up and looked at the picture. "Beautiful painting. Isn't it?" he said.

"What? Oh, yeah. I mean, it's not really something I'd pay for. It wouldn't fit in my apartment," Gavin joked, feeling uncomfortable.

"Well, it isn't for everyone," the man said as he glanced at his watch. His movement caught Gavin's attention, and instantly, his eyes fluttered as he caught sight of distinct markings on his watch. He remembered the pictures from that morning and what the NOVA system showed him. *I messed up. Where is Charles? Alex? I'm standing next to him. Next to Oris the Terrible.* Gavin started to back away. Faking a yawn, he tried tapping on his com. Hoping to get their attention.

Just then, the front desk clerk asked if he was Gavin Woodford. "What? No. You have me confused," Gavin tried to lie.

"THAT'S HIM! I know his voice anywhere!" He heard Kaleb yell from on the phone. Oris the Terrible was eyeing him suspiciously.

He begrudgingly took the phone, "What, Kaleb?"

"Gavin, I'm trapped in the cage of emotion, man. I'm here alone. Trapped. With nothing but my games to keep me company. I'm not okay!" Kaleb spewed out in a frantic stream of words.

Gavin hung up and handed the phone back to the waiter. "Thank you," he said to them. Turning to Oris the Terrible he said, "It's been a pleasure talking to you, but I must find my date and be going. Apparently, a friend is in trouble. Excuse me." He slipped away in the direction that Alex had disappeared. Getting far enough away, he felt a little safe. He didn't notice one of the big guys that had been with Oris the Terrible was following him. "Guys, where are you? You have the wrong guy! Where are you!?" Gavin said frantically, turning a corner to what he saw were 2 doorways. A door outside and a door to the stairs.

He took off upstairs. Quickly running to the other end of the hallway and back down the stairs. Finding Alex, he told her what happened. She and Charles went to look for Oris, but he was gone. They had missed the sale.

***

Once everything had settled, the knowledge that Oris the Terrible had gotten away, and they had parted ways, Gavin was mentally scolding himself for the mess up, as he made his way to his room. As he started to mindlessly tear into the first computer, something he could fix in his sleep at 16, he began to think.

This thing in my head seems to be changing slightly. The sensation of flashing doesn't seem to carry the same weight as it first did. It seems to be picking up information and facts as it goes. Is it some kind of AI? Is it similar to the program that I messed with in my dad's office that had him so worked up about my mental health for those two weeks he actually seemed to be present? It feels similar, just it started heavier. Like a weight inside my head at all times. But the longer it is in there, the lighter it gets. And the lighter it gets; it seems to get more…. agile? Is that the right word? It's learning easier. But it's my brain. I'm learning easier. No. If it were me, then it would've been like this forever. I'll need to do some exercises with it, if I can figure something out. Maybe talk to Megan very vaguely about it, since the brain is her field. Well, no matter what, I can't just stay stagnant. Today showed just how ill-prepared I am to handle this life. And who knows how long it will be in my head.

As Gavin worked, he was thinking and spaced out. He didn't notice that in the shadows, outside his window, was a figure watching him. Alex sat and relaxed slightly at the fact he was somewhere safe. She saw him deep in thought and wasn't sure if his concentration was on what he was doing or something else. His hands seemed to be moving on their own. She knew what it was like to zone out and have muscle memory take over. It took a lot of skill and practice, and he seemed to be troubleshooting computer issues off muscle memory. He had fixed and cleared his laptop that had burnt up the first time she saw him without it seeming like he knew what he was doing.

Have we severely underestimated him? I know our bosses have. I see him go out of his way to save the day twice now, even if he shouldn't. And he doesn't question it. Simply because it's the right thing to do. But is he much more skilled than his dossier says? He did go to Georgia Institute of Technology. On scholarship. That's not easy to do. He got kicked out for cheating, so maybe he faked it? But from what I've seen, that isn't like him. He's too straight cut. He isn't like my dad.

That thought stopped her. Was she really comparing him to her father? She had never done that with anyone. Sure, maybe Hunter had taken that role slightly. But it makes sense. Why was she thinking about her father while watching Gavin? Before long, she realized he was finishing up; the entire night had gone by already, and they had to work in a few minutes. She slipped out and got ready for work in her car. *I'll keep a better eye on him. I don't think he is as inept as everyone believes,* she thought as she clocked in.

***

Gavin had finished getting ready for work and made iced coffee. As he got to work, a pretty woman crossed in front of him and caused his iced coffee to spill on her. *That's funny, that happened with Alex, too.* As his eyes met hers, he felt that familiar sensation. Dossier, her picture from the police academy, a list of missions, relation to Alex, CATS, a picture of Charles in his underwear, and Slovakia. Miranda Miller. This DIA agent is likely to improvise and leave you holding the bag.

What, do they just print out beautiful women to be agents for the government and send them into the field? And is this drink thing just a play in a book? Gavin mused as he finally had a leg up in this world that he had been uninitiated into. "I am so sorry," he said, trying to act like he didn't know she did it on purpose.

As he did, he noticed two large men getting out of a car. He knew them. They were Oris the Terrible's muscle. "No, please excuse me," Gavin said as he turned and quickly made his way into the call center. He made eye contact with Charles and hurried into his office. Charles noticed and saw the men as they came through the door. He approached them and saw a flash of red hair exit the store. Shaking his head with a grunt, he went up to one of the thugs and discretely took them out. And then followed the other to the restroom.

On her way out of the store, Miranda saw a hulking delivery driver carrying a box and heading to the Sub Express. Just where she was headed. It didn't make sense that the driver didn't go inside but instead headed straight for the roof. Following him off instinct, which is just how she had lived her entire life, she climbed up. She saw the man getting out a sniper rifle, facing toward the Snollygoster Inc. entrance. Miranda quickly snuck up on him, tased him, and then choked him out. Dragging him back down and into the store, she saw Alex at the register. "Hey. I found some trash on your roof. Thought you might want it cleaned up," Miranda quipped. Alex's head shot up at her pseudo-friend's voice.

She immediately got her phone out and called Charles. "Hey, it's Johnson. We got Oris the Terrible. Yeah. Miranda. I'll take care of him. Call Richmond," She hung up and asked Miranda, "Why are you here anyway?" Alex inquired with a bit of force in her tone. She may have considered Miranda as much of a friend as you could have in this line of work, but that doesn't mean she trusted her.

"Is that any way to treat your only friend?" Miranda said with a smirk. "I was just over at that store meeting the rest of your team, and I have to say, I'm not impressed. The lanky one is kind of cute, but he sure couldn't hold his own in a fight, and Charles is a washout. More assassin than spy," she added dismissively.

Alex was getting upset. She knew what Miranda was trying to do. She wanted information that she knew wasn't hers to have. "Well, we do good work here." Alex almost spat back at her.

"It doesn't matter anyway. Your team has become my team. I'm here to get some plutonium, and you're going to help me," Miranda said with a grin. She enjoyed the power struggle any time she was with Alex.

"I hadn't heard anything. But we were finishing up this mission," Alex started.

"You're welcome," Miranda cut her off.

Alex rolled her eyes and continued, "I'm sure we will be briefed about it in the morning," Alex said. She was used to little sleep but had a cover date tonight with Gavin. She didn't have time to deal with Miranda today.

At least she finished this mission for us, even though she blindly just attacked someone without any confirmation of who they were. But that sounds like her. I'll have to watch her closely. I don't trust her with Gavin. She thought as she saw Miranda make her way out of the store. She was sure she would be back. She wasn't through with her mind games yet.

46

Gavin got the afternoon off, for which he was thankful. He returned home and planned on crashing in his room before the cover date tonight. When he entered the room, he noticed his computer wasn't exactly where he left it. Slightly panicked, he crouched down and slid it open. Seeing the external hard drive, he relaxed a little. Booting up the computer, he ran a diagnostic and saw someone had been on it, but only saw computer games and a few scripts that were for nothing. Feeling better, he figured Charles had just snooped to make sure, and he crashed in his bed for a few hours.

***

Waking up to the sound of Alex's voice in the kitchen talking to Megan, Gavin quickly got up and changed into a t-shirt and jeans. He opened his door and heard the two women chatting. "He can be really absentminded at times," Megan said as she set the table.

"I hadn't seen that. He has always shown me that he is reliable and trustworthy. I'd trust him with my life," Alex said, looking down the hallway and seeing the door had moved. She smirked slightly, knowing Gavin was up and likely heard them.

"That's good. Maybe you're just bringing out the best in him in a way I never could," Megan said almost despondently.

"I'm always going to need you, sis," Gavin said, entering the dining room and making his presence known.

"Don't take this wrong, Gavin, but I really hope not," she said as she gave him a hug. They all laughed slightly as they finished getting the table ready.

The rest of the night went well. Kaleb came over, which was expected even though he hadn't been invited. And they played games. She saw Gavin looking at her whenever he thought she wasn't looking, to which she smirked to herself softly. But there was something else. She still felt she was being watched. Looking around the room, she saw everyone focused on the game board. She looked out the window.

Miranda. You couldn't just stay away and chill for the night. You had to butt in, didn't you?

Alex saw the shadowed form of Miranda make her way to the front door. "I hope you guys don't mind. I had a friend stop by the restaurant today, and she wanted to spend some time with me. So, I invited her to stop by tonight, even though she can't stay long." Alex said, saying the last part toward the door loud enough for Miranda to hear. Alex opened the door and hugged Miranda, "You aren't supposed to be here, now, make a damn good excuse and a quick exit, or I'll make sure you do," Alex whispered with an icy tone.

Miranda smiled and entered the rooms, introducing herself to everyone. She quickly inserted herself as Kaleb's partner. To everyone else but Gavin and Alex, she seemed to be flirting with and into him. Megan seemed the happiest about it. Gavin leaned over and whispered to Alex, "Why is she here? She's supposed to be in Argentina, and I don't like that she is getting into Kaleb. Kaleb will think she's actually into him. It will devastate him when she leaves." Gavin wasn't happy, but Alex seemed to think Miranda being distracted by Kaleb was a great thing. She hinted at Kaleb that maybe they would like to find somewhere where just the two of them could talk. Kaleb got really excited at the idea, but that seemed to be enough for Miranda to make an excuse and leave for the night.

***

Not long after she left, everyone called it a night and went home. Gavin walked Alex to her car, and with the last game they played, Brett had come up as Gavin's enemy. And his mind was focused on that. He had seen in her file what they were. but he wanted to hear from her. "Alex, what exactly were you and Brett?" he asked, with a slight twinge of jealousy present in his tone.

"Well, we were partners. We watched each other's backs. And made sure the mission got done," she said matter of factly.

"Oh, so it was more a working relationship than romantic. Well, that makes sense," Gavin said, trying to make it ok in his mind. Even though

48

he knew that she wasn't being truthful. She just nodded and headed toward her car. She was difficult to read at that moment, and he watched her leave and then headed inside to sleep. *She lied to me. Of course, she did. She's a spy, it's literally what she does for a living. This is her job. Remember? You are a job to her. The moment you forget that, is the moment she will crush you,* Gavin thought as he crawled into bed.

Alex sat in the quiet as she drove to her hotel room. *Why did he ask that? Obviously, because he had feelings for you. Feelings you can't reciprocate, no matter how easy it would feel. But why lie about Brett? Because you know it would hurt him even more if he knew. Ugh. What a mess. And it's all Brett's fault. And Gavin never asked for this. Yet he is thriving in it. He doesn't understand how perfect he is for this, and yet not at the same time, just like Bailey. He will always be more than a job.* She shook her head. She couldn't believe she went there. She needed sleep. And with that, she hurried to her room.

***

Gavin was woken in the night by his phone ringing. It was Kaleb. Again. Asking, again, if Miranda had called. Why she would call him, he had no clue. But here Kaleb was again. "She did not call, Kaleb! Oh, yes ma'am, I am the on call IT. Oh, ok, and your room number? Ok, I will be there in just a bit." Gavin felt himself flush with embarrassment. He would get back at Kaleb somehow for this. But right now he had to get to the hotel for the on-call manager.

He knocked on the door, and when it opened, he just about dropped his case. There was Miranda in a black silk robe and clearly very little on underneath it. "Wow, you take your cover job seriously, Gavin. Feet, use them," she said as she moved away from the door. She turned back to him, now holding two flutes of champagne.

"He… hello. Where is the computer?" Gavin asked, clearly uncomfortable and not looking in Miranda's direction at all.

"I don't have one," she said in a flirting manner.

49

"Then why did you call?" Gavin droned, his voice cracking from his throat getting dry.

"Because I wanted to get you alone. To get to know you better. In a less professional way. See, if I'm going to trust you with my life and, more importantly, my plutonium, then I wanted to know who I was working with,." Miranda seemingly purred.

Gavin gulped, "I should call Alex; she should be here," Gavin said as he started to get out his phone.

Miranda grabbed his phone and tossed it onto the chair by the bed. "Now, if you do that, then I wouldn't be able to seduce you." Miranda's voice almost dripped with lust as she spoke in his ear.

"And why would you do that?" Gavin said in an almost dead voice.

"Because I like having what Alex hasn't. Unless she has already. Gavin, have you already had Alex?" Miranda inquired.

"A gentleman, um, never kisses and, um, tells." Gavin stuttered as Miranda knelt behind him. He could feel her breasts on his back and her hands rubbing his chest and shoulders.

"Well, I know how she likes to mix business with pleasure, but considering her and Brett, I'm sure she isn't over her last lover yet." Gavin's brain froze. He knew but hearing it out loud was another thing.

Of course, they were PARTNERS. She didn't lie. She omitted the truth, but she didn't lie. He always got the best girls, so it just makes sense. It's not like she had given any indication that she and I are anything more than a job to her. Doesn't mean I'm not still mad at her. She could've just been honest with me. And I didn't care for how she flippantly threw Kaleb under the Miranda train, either. After this, we are going to have a talk. I know absolutely nothing about her that's real. Nothing. And she knows almost everything about me and still is flippant with my friends, Gavin thought. And he was suddenly back in his bed. He vaguely remembered leaving Miranda on the bed. Not saying a word to her as he gathered his things and left.

50

***

The next morning, he went to Charles's after breakfast and entered during their briefing again. This time, he sat quietly. Stewing slightly toward Alex. Once they were told that they would be party crashing, it got his attention. He looked up and saw the man they were to steal this Plutonium from. "Mr. Gremlin here? That's who has this Plutonium?" Gavin said with a slight chuckle. Even Charles cracked a smile at it.

"Hamaad is about to strike it big with this sale and is celebrating it with a party this afternoon. Alex and Miranda will blend in well with his usual guests. Charles, you will be their driver. Gavin, we will need you to go along to see what kind of security he has on the Plutonium that we may have missed." It was the first time General Richmond had used his name, and it didn't go unnoticed by Gavin. He saw Hunter looking at the General as well. Apparently, he wasn't the only one who noticed. He smiled a little at not being referred to as "the asset" or "the NOVA system." Seeing that she might understand that he is human after all was nice.

***

At the party, Gavin was wandering around. There was an apparent power struggle between Miranda and Alex, and he would rather not get in the middle of it. Alex had also been seeming to try to talk to Gavin since they left the briefing, but Gavin just wasn't feeling like talking to her at the moment. So, he stuck close to Charles before they got to the party. Gavin saw the security cameras, and despite his feelings, he didn't want Alex or Miranda hurt or caught. And he knew if Miranda had a chance to ditch them and blame them for the theft, she would take it. Walking up to Alex, he quietly said, "There are cameras on the north, south, and east walls overlooking the entrances. Easy enough to get by, if you know the system," Gavin murmured.

"Did the NOVA system tell you that?" Alex asked quietly.

"What? No. No, I didn't need to. We sell them at the spy section on Amazon," he said as he pulled out his phone and sent the command to loop the cameras.

"Ok, they are blind for thirty minutes," Gavin said.

"Time to move. Miranda, where are you?" Alex commanded.

"Already in the house. I got a tour from one of the guards who is sleeping now," Miranda bragged with an audible smirk.

"That wasn't the plan. Stick to the plan, Miranda," Alex said angrily as she and Gavin made their way to the east entrance, which was closest to the Plutonium. They made their way to the Plutonium, passing several pieces of art. When they arrived, Miranda was in the room already, having set off the silent alarm. Immediately upon entering the room, Gavin used the NOVA system for information on the security system. The pressure-sensitive stand was surrounded by several thousand volts of electricity. Once the Plutonium was off the stand, the room would close and fill with a toxic gas. All in under thirty seconds.

"Miranda, you didn't happen to turn off the silent alarm, did you...?" Gavin asked quietly, and as he finished talking, Hamaad and two large goons stepped into the room.

On seeing the women, Hamaad waved off the men and started flirting with them. They say that Gavin was just their brother, and he played into it completely. Miranda looked at Gavin, indicating for him to get the Plutonium while Hamaad was distracted. So, Gavin took off his jacket and threw the arm around the case, holding the plutonium, taking it out of the case and putting it in a pouch; he made a dash for the door, doing a perfect slide under it as it closed.

Seeing that the girls had knocked out the guards and Hamaad, they made a break for the beach. As they reach the stairs to the beach, Gavin notices that the guard Miranda had knocked out first after them. His gun was drawn. And not far behind him were the other two.

Soon, the rest caught on and started moving towards them quickly as they descended the stairs and onto the beach. Gavin dove behind a rock, waiting for Charles to come to get them. "Gavin, give me the plutonium. I'll take the heat, and they will leave you alone!" Miranda implored. Gavin looked at her and wondered just how stupid she thought he was. He reached into his pocket and dumped the plutonium into the second sack he had Charles make him, then pulled the first sack out that it had been in. In the sand, he felt a rock about that size and slid it into the sack before tossing it to Miranda.

She turned and ran, hitting a button on her watch that caused a jet ski to pop up out of the water. She jumped on it and took off. "WHY DID YOU DO THAT?! NOW WE ARE DEFINITELY DEAD!" Alex screamed at him. Her lack of faith in him was never more apparent than in that moment. He kept his mouth shut, not wanting to fight while getting shot at.

Just then, the black Hummer popped out from the other side of the beach, hitting two guys and blocking the rest from firing. "Did someone order an Uber?" Charles quipped as he pushed the door open. Alex jumped in the back, and Gavin up front.

They were soon out of immediate danger, and Alex rounded on Gavin. "Why did you give her the plutonium! You KNEW she was going to leave us there!" Her phone rang, and she answered it with just as much anger. "Mir, and where are you?"

"I'm gone, Alex. I knew you would make it out of there alive. You always do," Miranda said flippantly. "It was a pleasure working with. Wait. Where is my plutonium!" Miranda yelled into the phone. Alex's eyes shot up to see Gavin holding the second sack with the plutonium in it.

"I don't get the fuss about these rocks. Do you, Charles?" Gavin said calmly. Charles grunted, amused at Gavin's antics for the first time, as he glanced back at Alex. Making eye contact and giving a slight head nod and shoulder shrug. Alex hung up the phone and sat quietly in the back on the way back to Atlanta.

53

The next evening, as work finished, Alex went to Snollygoster Inc. to see Gavin. He looked up and smiled as she entered the door, but it didn't reach his eyes like it normally did. *Something was wrong more than me getting onto him during the mission, s*he thought as she greeted him. "Want to come over tonight?" she said, trying to sound like a girlfriend. *It was always easier with Gavin than it had been with anyone else, s*he noticed. It sent a shiver down her spine.

She had already been on this assignment of protecting Gavin longer than most of her other missions had taken. The post-mission briefing had been quick and easy since they had the plutonium. Charles would handle the rest that was needed, which freed her up for some cover maintenance.

"Sure. I'm off in a half hour, and then I'll run home and change and pick up pizza?" Gavin offered, clearly trying to sound more excited than he seemed.

"Sounds great. See you around seven," Alex said as she turned to leave.

***

Gavin appeared at her hotel room; he'd never been there before and felt a little out of place. It was a really nice extended-stay hotel. He sat down, and Alex started talking to him. "Clearly, Miranda got to you. You have been off since she got here. Talk to me, Gavin." Alex asked of him.

"A little. She told me the truth about you and Brett. I don't understand why you lied about it to me," Gavin sadly stated.

"Because it didn't feel relevant," Alex said with another half-truth. *Relevant. Sure. Just pile on him. Tell him how little his feelings mean to you.* Alex berated herself. Gavin kinda scoffed,

"Yeah, I guess not. Is there anything about you that is real? Can you tell me anything? A name? Favorite band? Anything?" Gavin pleaded. He was desperate to make a connection of some kind. *Why won't he stop? Do I really want him to stop? Do I want him to give up on me? It would be easier for both of us. This is complicated; it wouldn't be, if he stopped caring about me. Like everyone else has. It's easier that way.*

Alex looked at her hands in her lap. She didn't like these feelings he brought up in her. But she knew she couldn't speak. "I'm going to get the napkins and pizza," Gavin said as he stood, dejected at her lack of willingness to let him in. Misunderstanding why.

Just say something. You're losing the one person who saw you. Sees you. The one person who cares about more than your body. Your skill set. Your record. The one person who actually wants to spend time with you outside of a mission or a bed. Say. Something. "It's Katelyn. My middle name is Katelyn. That is something real about me," she croaked out in barely a whisper. She was sure he hadn't heard her because she got no response. No reaction. But Gavin did hear her. She finally told him something real. He knew. He schooled his grin slightly as he picked everything up. And walked back to her.

Chapter 4

:/Trust

Gavin sat down in his room. It had been a quiet several days of working at Snollygoster Inc. and nothing more. He was thankful for it but was still waiting for his program to decrypt and unredacted the files he had pulled. Which meant there wasn't much more he could do. Checking the status, he figured a few more days, and he'd have what he needed. In the meantime, he focused on figuring out more about the NOVA system and how it worked. Everything he had found told him that maybe three people knew how it worked, and one was a traitor to the United States. Zodiac. The other two he didn't have a name for.

They must have only put their code names in the NOVA system, or he hadn't figured out how to access it yet. He'd noticed that the NOVA system seemed almost like a muscle, as though it was an extension of himself. The more he worked it, the easier it was on his brain. It no longer caused headaches when he accessed the NOVA system a lot. And he felt like he did when he was young. Things were easy to learn and easy to remember. *That had always made therapy more difficult.* He mused, thinking about how it would've been easier just to forget the trauma of their parents leaving.

Feeling the guilt, the loneliness, that empty feeling that a kid left alone got. He always felt for Megan. She never showed that it bothered her for a long time, and even now, she only talked about how much stronger they were together. But right now, his brain felt new. Fresh. As he focused on the information he had, it would trigger him to access the Nova system. He could spiderweb through an entire network and not even realize it had been an hour or two. But he didn't have control yet. He'd spiral into a hole without being able to guide his mind to what tunnel he wanted to dive into next. *Always something more to work on. And who said I'm not an athlete?* Gavin smirked at his thoughts. He'd already found that Alex wasn't her real name. Neither was one of the multitudes of other aliases that were in her file. The only thing not listed was her real name, along with several months of gaps during her training. She had quite the record, and this had been the longest she had ever been on a single mission.

While Major Robert Charles has an exemplary military background. As Mato Acothley. Engaged before deployment. Several medals of valor. He died in service and was brought back as Robert Charles to live the undercover life of an NSA agent. Gavin had also been looking into many other cases dealing with assets. He noticed a major difference in all of those. They were all getting something. Protection from people wanting them dead. Money for their expertise. Some even had desk jobs and cushy lifestyles provided by the taxpayers.

And yet here he was. *Literally being taken advantage of. Not getting paid, I'm in danger all the time, and treated like I'm hostile. Not to mention not able to live his life in any way. Okay, so my life hadn't been great before the Nova system came to me, but at least it was mine to make that decision.* It was then he realized he would have to change the things he wanted if he was going to accept this life for the time being. He just had to wait until he had leverage on the people it mattered about: General Richmond and Director Hunter.

Once he has that, he may be able to push for a few changes. Yes, there were laws against what was happening, but it didn't honestly seem like they abided by the same rules as citizens had to. He had a few options, but one was far better than the rest. It was just a matter of time before he could implement it. Refocusing his mind, he felt how differently the NOVA system made him feel.

He wandered into the living room and saw several of Megan's books on the shelves. Many of them were on the human brain. He grabbed a few. *Couldn't hurt to know more about my hardware. I know computers, but brains are the exact same. Let's see if I can find a way they integrate and take care of this thing myself, h*e thought as he started flipping through the book, scanning it, and reading things he felt may be relevant.

***

That night, he had a date with Alex that Kaleb was tagging along. It was good for the cover for him to approve of Alex in his life. It would help him not question every time he spent time with her, instead of getting jealous as he had been. He kept calling it "An Essence of Kaleb." Which always made Gavin laugh. Alex was likely not going to have a good time, but he would, and it wasn't like they were really dating.

The evening consisted of all of Kaleb's favorites—starting with teriyaki crab from the Golden Dragon, Kaleb's favorite meal. As they reach the restaurant, the door was locked for a private party, so Kaleb got them in the back with a key that one of the cooks gave him. While picking up the crab, Gavin was looking around and accessing the NOVA system on one of the waitresses there. Lin-Chen Cho, China's top spy, was serving at table nine. Gavin tried not to make it obvious that he was watching her. He pointed her out to Alex, and then they proceeded with the evening as planned with bad kung fu movies, Gavin and Kaleb even more poorly acting out the scenes, and then Alex reported it.

They were all in Charles' apartment the next morning for a briefing. "Team, we appreciate you reporting the enemy spy, but there are more pressing matters. One of ours has gone missing for a week, and we believe he may be in your area."

A picture of the target came, causing Gavin to access the NOVA system: Edward Mahnovski, computer genius and inventor. He was recruited at twelve, graduated college at fourteen, and has been unheard of since. He invented most of the tech they have used, or upgraded it.

"He killed his handlers and escaped and has been on the run. We can't lose him with the knowledge he has. He is to be brought in at any cost," Hunter said.

Gavin saw Alex stiffen. "I'm sorry, sir. Does that mean you would have him killed?" Gavin asked hesitantly.

"He has already killed two agents and could easily incite a war with his knowledge of our systems. So yes, there is a green light to eliminate him, if needed," Hunter responded as though it was the only option he was considering.

Is this how he views me? I know too much, and if I were to go free, then it would be easier to kill me than to try to bring me in? Gavin thought as the meeting came to a close. Alex was watching Gavin's reaction to what the order was. She could tell he was starting to identify with Edward and wasn't sure how to handle that. *If that order comes through for Gavin, then I'll do everything I can to prevent it. I can't lose him,* she thought as she proceeded to head to work.

***

Kaleb wasn't at the store that morning, which wasn't too odd, but Mike, his manager was asking for him. "If he doesn't show again today, then he is fired," Mike bellowed as he stormed off into the office. Gavin called him, but Kaleb didn't answer. After checking with his mom, Gavin knew where Kaleb had to be if he was no longer at home asleep. And Gavin headed out.

Walking into the arcade at the pier, he spotted Kaleb playing Guitar Hero and headed towards him. As he approached, he froze. There was Edward, playing against Kaleb. Sending a text to Alex, Gavin went over and started chastising Kaleb for not showing up to work. Saying it was time to grow up and act more like an adult. As he did this, Edward seemed startled and went to leave. Not wanting to lose him, Gavin quickly took off his watch and slipped it into the pocket of Edward's coat. As Edward ran, Kaleb looked dejected and hurt as he slumped out of the arcade and returned to work. Gavin was leaving the arcade when Alex showed up.

"Where is he?" Alex asked.

"Kaleb? He headed back to work, thankfully. Or I hope. I should check," Gavin rambled slightly.

"No numbnuts, where is Edward? You know, the geek who could kill everyone here?" Charles growled as he came up behind Gavin.

"Oh, he left," Gavin said as Charles groaned, and Alex looked upset at him.

"What? Don't worry. I slipped my watch in his jacket." Gavin showed his empty wrist. And then Charles pulled up the tracking app on his phone and clapped Gavin on the shoulder with a grunt.

Grunt #5: "Good job." Huh. I seem to be getting that one more often. Gavin mused as they made their way toward the cars.

"You two head back to work. I'll track the target," Charles said as he climbed into his car. It was his day off at the Snollygoster Inc.

"Oh, Gavin here. I wanted you to have this," Alex said as she handed him a picture of him and her. She was in the Princess Leia metal bikini.

Gulping audibly, Gavin choked out, "Umm, we never dressed up like this..."

"I know. But it's good for the cover if we have pictures together to explain our disappearances to everyone. The CIA is pretty good with Photoshop," she replied with a smirk. *Why do I always feel better when I know he likes how I look? And why do I feel guilty about the bug? It's only for his protection.* Alex thought as Gavin was visibly enamored by the fake photo, feeling slightly sick to her stomach.

Later that evening, as Charles tracked Edward, he called Alex and Gavin to come on the stakeout, in case he could access the Nova system on anything while they were there in the van. As they sat there and watched, several people went in and out of the restaurant, and Gavin ordered some delivery, which got him an angry grunt from Charles and an eye roll from Alex. But as he ate, he looked at the takeout menu and accessed the NOVA system on the symbol on the front. Chinese flag. Shrimp. Triads. Jun Hong. "Guys. I think I know why Lin-Chen is here," Gavin stammered.

"That isn't our mission, Gavin. We have to stay focused," Alex reprimanded.

Gavin focused more and felt the NOVA system, making more connections. "That's what I'm trying to say. I think we could do more than just our mission."

As Gavin finished talking, they heard gunshots inside the restaurant. Alex and Charles jumped out of the van, yelling over their shoulders, "STAY IN THE VAN!" Gavin slumped and nodded his head slightly. He was worried and busied himself, looking around the van more. Spotting a tranq gun, he grabbed one and slid it into his jacket. *Never hurts to be prepared. Or something like that. I wasn't a Boy Scout*, he thought, as he resumed watching.

He saw a limo pull up out front, and Jun Hong got in the car. He got out to try and stop them, but as he did, Lin-Chen came bursting out the door, running directly into Gavin, who had his tranq gun in hand. It accidentally fired off two rounds into Lin-Chen, and she fell forward, tackling Gavin as she did. As he lay there on the ground under Lin-Chen, two burly men came out carrying a man in a trench coat. He was tied up and tossed into a car, and they took off as Gavin was yelling for someone to help.

Alex came out the door and saw Lin-Chen on top of him, "What did you do, Gavin?!" she said, starting to panic. Then, she noticed the Chinese woman still breathing.

"I'm sorry. I saw this tranq gun in the van, and then she and Jun Hong were leaving, but I had to stop them. He got away, though," Gavin rambled as he tried to explain himself. "I think they had Edward…" Gavin started as Charles came out, pushing Edward as he went.

"Good work Woodford. We got both. Looks like you might have some competition, Johnson," Charles grunted in a tease as he chuckled to himself, pushed Edward into the back of the van, and zip-tied his arms and legs.

Back at Charles's apartment, they had Edward and Lin-Chen tied up. While Charles and Alex reported everything to the General, as Hunter seemed unavailable, Gavin watched the prisoners. He was alternating between rooms.

Edward was the first to talk, "You aren't a spy, are you? You're like me. Trapped in a life you never wanted. Forced to work for the government while they give you nothing and take every freedom and decision you had away from you. Watching your every move."

"I'm nothing like you. I wouldn't betray my country," Gavin said defensively.

"Betray? Is that what they told you? I did what I had to do to get freedom. I work a bit for the triads, and then I get Chinese citizenship and a place to live without being under constant surveillance and pressure to build the next toy or bomb for the government. All I ever wanted to do was live my life," Edward said, sounding dejected. Gavin was hurt. He did relate to him, even if he didn't want to admit it. He couldn't let him go, though. The triads hurt people, too. So, anything he would do for them would cause innocent people to ruin their lives or end them.

"You watch, Gavin. When you start to trust these people, they will make sure you don't have a choice. You won't have privacy. You aren't part of the team. You are expendable to them. You are a means to information and skills. That's it," Edward warned. "I made most of these toys. I know their setup. There are surveillance monitors in every room here. And I bet it isn't for his house." Gavin tried to ignore him. But he knew he was right. And he knew if he wanted to have any part of his life for himself, he had to take that warning seriously. Getting up to leave the room, he thought about what was said but couldn't take any more of it. *At least in the other room, it would be quieter.* Gavin thought as he moved next door.

He was wrong. Lin-Chen had woken up and was none too happy to see him. "You idiot. You let them take my brother! If anything happens to him, I will make sure it happens to you too!"

Gavin felt it punch him in the stomach. Suddenly, what he heard from Edward wasn't as important. His mind flooded with images of losing Megan to these people, how he'd feel, and what he would do to get her back. He rushed into the living room right as the briefing ended. "Guys, I made a huge mistake," Gavin uttered as he entered.

After he explained everything to Charles and Alex, Charles laughed at him. "Alex, please. What if it was Megan? I can't let her brother just die," Gavin pleaded.

"Find something to go off of, and maybe," Alex said, feeling herself start to feel for him in this. *Am I really going this soft? No other asset I've ever handled have I given so much leeway. But Gavin also always comes through. He isn't a normal asset, even if the brass wants us to treat him like he is.* Alex thought as she went off to check on the prisoners. Gavin sat down at the computer, and after a few minutes of discrete hacking, he had a base of a plan.

He asked Charles, "What if I got Lin-Chen to convert to USA?" he asked.

"You mean defect...?" Charles said thoughtfully.

"YES! Defect. That's what I mean. That's a thing, right? Like. That's something spies do?" Gavin asked quickly.

"Not the good ones. And she is a good one. What makes you think she'd be willing to?" Charles said with a slight hint of disbelieving hope in his voice.

"She isn't on a mission here. This is a personal trip. Meaning her government didn't see it as important to save her brother. Someone who works for the ambassador to the USA for China. Someone who would have the ambassador's ear and influence over future decisions with China. And the triads would have that if they turn him," Gavin said. "Or if they kill him and replace him. And Edward was working for them. He knows where they keep people and where they would be." Gavin pushed, hoping to sway Charles or Alex, who had come back into the room during his explanation.

"That might actually work," Charles said hesitantly. "One of us will have to get her to agree and to sign the papers. And since this is your grand plan, you get to do the honors," Charles taunted Gavin as he left the room. Turning to Alex, who shrugged at him, Gavin walked past her to try to talk to Lin-Chen.

Gavin walked into the room, again getting a barrage of what he assumed were curses and insults in Chinese. "I'm sorry. Please listen. Please," Gavin said, thankfully it worked, and Lin-Chen seemed to calm down and be quiet. "Look. I want to help you. But I'm going to need something from you. You may not like it, but it may be the only way." Gavin started his explanation.

"I'm listening. But I doubt you could help me any," Lin-Chen said with slight disgust in her voice.

"I want to help you save your brother. I do. I want to make it right. But I need you to agree to defect," Gavin said with a wince.

"WHAT?! I could never and would never betray my country," Lin-Chen replied in disgust.

"Why? Why would you stay loyal to a country that didn't see it necessary to save your brother? I saw the requests they denied. You've known this could be an issue for months, and they ignored you. I'm offering you a way out. You go back, and how do they treat disobeying a direct order? You were told to stand down, and yet here you are. How would they treat you after all you had done for them? And it's not that bad here, really. I mean, we have pretty good Chinese food." Gavin tried to soothe the Chinese operative.

"And if I betray them, then they come after me. They don't want what I know getting out," Lin-Chen replied, clearly considering the offer.

"We don't leave our informants and defected agents out to dry without protection. Unlike some other communist countries, we all know," Charles said with pride as he stepped into the room.

"We would provide protection and a new identity," Alex reiterated. Gavin looked at them both with a thankful expression.

"And how do I know I can trust you all?" Lin-Chen asked.

"What other choice do you have?" Gavin responded, "Any other option, and you likely end up dead."

Lin-Chen's face was unchanging. She knew her options. She knew that she had no choice but to trust that they would hold their end of the bargain, and if they didn't, then at least they had laws against cruel ways of killing her. "Ok. I agree. Bring me the papers and save my brother," she said, sounding defeated.

As she started signing the papers, Charles entered the next room to interrogate Edward on the triad compound. Gavin found whatever research he could on the triads and their territory. As he finished, he turned to see Charles coming out of the room, wiping his hands. "Took a bit, but he talked. I know where they would be keeping the brother," Charles said as he pulled up a compound map and started laying out the plan with Alex.

Gavin was careful to ensure that his handlers didn't see his hacking and could only see him pulling up things that looked like he could pull off Google. *Edward is right, unfortunately. I have to worry about whether I can trust them or not. And as much as I would like to think I can trust Alex, there are a lot of reasons to wonder.* Gavin thought as he heard them start to get packed. He was to run support from the van and stay out of harm's way. He grabbed a tranq gun with two extra clips, just in case. As they went out the door, Charles activated the detention system for his apartment, locking in Lin-Chen and Edward.

Arriving at the compound, Gavin quickly got into their system. Watching the cameras, he called out the men and their placement to Charles and Alex on the coms. He watched them infiltrate, take out the guards, and make their way into the room where her brother was being held. Right as they entered the room, he lost visual. "Guys. I'm blind. I can't see you. What's going on?!" Gavin was getting worried.

"Gavin! Get out of here!" he heard Alex say before the coms became static. Gavin's blood went cold.

He grabbed the keyboard and unleashed Vidar in full. He was quickly back into their system. Whether they saw him as such or not, these were his friends. People he cared about. He wasn't walking away.

He got access to the cameras again and saw that they were surrounded. He killed the lights, locked all but one door in and out of the complex, and watched his handlers take out half the men before grabbing Lin-Chen's brother and diving behind the couch. They were trapped. Gavin brought the lights back on full power and set off alarms. It disoriented everyone but Alex and Charles, who made a break for the door.

Gavin pulled the van around to the exit, leaned back, and hit the button to open the gates. Charles opened the driver's door, so Gavin jumped in back with the others, and as Charles sped away, Gavin hit another button. He locked down the compound while sending a video of Lin-Chen's brother being held captive to the Chinese ambassador and several Chinese and American news outlets. As they finally got to safety, the alarm was set off on Charles's phone. "Crap, Edward got free and grabbed a company car. Now we have to track him down," he said as they sped off.

***

Arriving at the apartment, they rushed in. Lin-Chen and her brother were reunited and had no intention of going anywhere. Gavin quickly got on the computer and started tracking down the stolen car. Finding it, he accessed the NOVA system. It was near where Edward was recruited on the pier.

Alex and Gavin went to the pier and searched for Edward. Gavin raced to the arcade, not seeing him. Gavin put his head in his hands, and down through the slots, Gavin spotted the red and white of the car. Quickly running down under the pier, followed closely by Alex, Gavin saw Edward had started the self-destruct on the car. "What are you doing, Edward?!" Gavin said with an intense indignation.

"Isn't it obvious, Gavin? I'm making sure that they can't get any more guys like us. Use us. Treat us like we don't matter. We aren't just tools for them to use and throw away like they think we are. I joined a literal gang to avoid having to go back to being locked up in a bunker for years. That's where you will end up eventually, Gavin. And when you have lost your usefulness, they will kill you. That's how they play the game," Edward ranted as Gavin kept trying to access the NOVA system on the car, the adrenaline pumping through him, causing him not to think.

"Edward, they aren't the terrible people you experienced. They wouldn't do those things to me," Gavin said, his mind trying to solve too many problems at once.

Stealing a glance at Alex, his heart broke. Her face was the agent mask. *She doesn't want me to read her at all. That isn't good.* Gavin felt betrayed.

I have to remove the bug from that picture before he finds it, Alex lamented. *If he does, I will lose all credibility with him. Then again, maybe I deserve to.* Alex steeled her nerves. "Gavin. The bomb!" she reminded him as he looked at her.

Gavin's mind cleared, and he remembered the manual he had read several days before. Gavin didn't hesitate and cut the green wire as the bomb deactivated, and Alex took Edward into custody again. "You'll regret trusting them, Gavin. You shouldn't trust anyone who doesn't trust you," Edward said, his eyes looking crazed and his voice almost sounding distorted.

Alex put him in her car, "Are you okay, Gavin?" She asked.

"Huh? Yeah, yeah, I'm good. I'll umm, I'll get a ride. I have to get back to work anyway. I'll, uh, I'll talk to you later," he responded with as much of a smile as he could muster. Alex got Edward in her car and pulled away. Gavin watched them leave as he got a cab back to his apartment.

Alex met up with Charles to drop off the prisoners, and Lin-Chen stopped in front of her. "That Gavin, he isn't an agent, is he?" she said somewhat knowingly.

"No. He isn't," Alex answered, trying to keep from divulging more than she should. *He is so much more than that. And he doesn't even know it.* Alex thought to herself.

"I could tell. He was real. He meant every word he said. And genuinely wanted to help. Word of advice from someone who's been doing this a long time." Lin-Chen leaned in, continuing, "Don't let them take more than you owe them. Because once you start, they won't stop," she said as she was pulled away. "And don't let them ruin someone so pure," she spoke louder as she was shoved into a transport truck. *I don't intend to let them do to him what they did to me. He deserves so much more.*

***

As Gavin walked into his room, he started looking around. He found several bugs in his room, the living room, the kitchen, and even Megan's room. *Edward was right. They don't trust me.* Then Gavin got a sinking feeling in his stomach as he returned to his room and grabbed the picture Alex had given him. Opening it, he saw the bug that was placed on the inside of it. He tossed it into the trash as he fell onto his bed, feeling defeated.

Alex stepped through the bedroom window. "Gavin, what's wrong?" She started but stopped as she spotted the picture in the trash can. "Gavin, I'm sorry," she started but then didn't know what else to say.

"No. It's ok. I get it," Gavin stated, sounding dejected. "I'm like him. Like Edward. I may not be dangerous myself. But what is in my head is."

"It's for your protection. Only for protection," Alex pleaded. *Please understand. I'm begging you to understand.* She started to get a headache.

"Until I say or do something they don't want or like. Right? Until I no longer give results? It's ok. I get it. You don't keep your old computer around that holds all your info. You wipe the hard drive and get rid of it," Gavin said in a monotone voice. "I'm pretty tired," he said, as an invitation to leave.

"Ok, I am sorry, though, Gavin. I should have told you," Alex apologized. *Please understand, Gavin.* She thought as her headache got worse. She climbed out of the window and headed toward her car, rubbing the side of her head.

Once she was gone, Gavin hopped up and was on his computer. *I do understand that they have to watch me. But that doesn't mean they need to see and hear everything.* Gavin thought as he typed away on the keyboard. Soon, he had access to Charles's cameras and audio bugs. He started scrubbing some of the footage, creating several loops of him in bed in different outfits or playing video games. *There. Now, when I want some privacy, I can have it.* Gavin thought as he started to dive into the decrypted and unredacted files.

***

Alex's phone rang as she got into her car. "Johnson secure." She said in her agent's voice.

"Hello, Agent Johnson," Hunter started. "How did the mission fair?"

69

"Both targets have been apprehended and are on their way to a secure location. Do you have orders, Sir?" Alex asked as she struggled not to let the headache affect her speech.

"As of now, continue to play nicely. When I need my Enforcer, I will call her. Until then, we will always have Miami," Hunter said in a chipper tone for him.

"Thank you, Sir. I will be on standby," Alex said in a pure-agent tone. Her headache was gone.

***

Gavin's deep dive into Richmond reveals nothing about who Agent Hel and Analyst Coeus were. But he did learn several points of hers that were significant to many of her missions, and she worked closely with them. She seemed to take a lot of the training methods that she implemented after she took over them. She appeared very results-driven, and if you could scratch her back, she would make yours comfortable. He could work with that.

The dive into Hunter's file was shorter. Even unredacted, he still had a lot of pieces missing from his files—entire years. But the pieces he did gather, he didn't like.

Hunter was a dangerous man to everyone. He was a man who knew what he was doing and seemed always to have a plan. The rise to power that paused when Agent Hel and Coeus went missing seemed to cause him turmoil. But again, he based a lot of training methods on their success. He almost seemed professionally enamored with Hel. But Gavin couldn't see why. He would have to keep digging.

Then, a file popped up. He knew it hadn't been there before, and as he scanned it for any malware, tracers, or spyware, he checked the program. It was still running, so theoretically, it could've grabbed this one, but he isn't sure why. He reread the file name as he got ready to close out the computer screen and hide what he was doing. *Project Oghma.*

Chapter 5

:/The Process

A figure watched Gavin through the webcam on the computer. Noting all the files he was accessing, all the names he scrolled over, every click of his mouse. "Oh, Gavin, what have you gotten into?" they say as they close their laptop and walk out of the burning building, stepping over bodies on their way out.

***

Gavin woke up to his alarm, the controller still in hand and in his work clothes from the day before. He stretched, feeling his sore neck from how he had fallen asleep. He got up and got ready for work. He had those few quiet moments in the shower. It had become his island of peace. He needed it every day, just to have time away from everything. But today, he couldn't keep his mind from thinking about some of what he had read. He still couldn't get into the Project Oghma files. His worm was still working its way through the encryption, which would take time.

What he found on Hunter was concerning. The man had little digital footprint, even within the CIA database—no military service. There is no science background to speak of. He just randomly started working for the CIA out of college. After being a mediocre analyst for a few years, he became an agent. Within a month, he was already working his way up the ladder.

How could he do that? How would he be a better fit for these positions than some other candidates with a better resume? Gavin was baffled by it. He knew he'd never be able to know without knowing the rest of his file. There wasn't any way for him to get that without breaking into the hard copies of the files. And he couldn't get away for that long to do it. So, his curiosity would go unsatisfied for now. Instead, he focused on the snippets of coding for the NOVA system he had found. They weren't like anything he had learned in school or during his hacking days, but somehow, they felt familiar. He had just started analyzing it, when he realized he would be late for work. He rushed through the rest of his morning routine and then out the door.

"Hey. Idiot, get in here!" Charles barked at him and returned to his apartment, leaving the door ajar. *And a good morning to you, too, Charles. Yes, it is beautiful out,* Gavin snarked to himself as he followed the larger man's orders.

Walking in, the Director and General half-heartedly greet him. "We need the NOVA system to listen to this," Hunter said, not even looking at Gavin.

"I mean since you asked so nicely," Gavin quipped. Charles smacked him on the back of the head with a grunt while Alex's face hardened. *Dang. Tough crowd today.* Gavin had thought it was amusing. "I'll take a listen," he said with a more serious tone. "Shroud, this is Looking Glass." Gavin used the NOVA system on both code names. Shroud, aka Richard Hunter. Some of his files popped up. His recruitment of college professors, off-the-books black sites he created, and interrogation techniques he invented. More was there, but Gavin cut it off. He didn't know he could do that, but the images were dark, and he felt he had more to listen to.

Then, Looking Glass. Aka, Professor Louis Williams. GIT professor directed the recruitment of candidates for several CIA projects, including fieldwork, Project Tyr, Project Ara, Project Oghma, and Project Spartan. "I made a mistake. I made a copy of the intel. It's hidden. Someone's after me. It's what they want. I'm initiating protocol 10-56. I'm sorry," Williams finished.

72

"No. No. I'm sorry, but no. I can't help. In case you forgot, Williams was the professor who thought I hacked in and changed grades on his computer. He is one of the reasons I couldn't graduate college. I don't exactly have a great relationship with him. So, no. I can't and won't help you. Good luck." Gavin fumed as he refused.

"You won't be seeing him. He is no longer with us," Richmond stated. "We need you to find the intel. He would have hidden it in a dead drop on campus. You will go with Agents Johnson and Charles to GIT and look for it."

"We know that your sister and her boyfriend have invited you to the football game this weekend. Accept the offer and go with them. Agent Johnson will accompany you, and Agent Charles will meet you there." And the video feed ended.

"Glad I get a say," Gavin mumbled.

"Look at it this way: you will get the closure you didn't get before." Alex tried to placate the situation. "Yeah, and you get to dig into the professor's life that kicked you out. That's going to be fun."

Charles grunted as he left to pack. Gavin huffed as he flopped down at the table. Alex placed a file in front of him. "Could you glance through this and get any leads our analysts may have missed? We have already checked his home and his office." Alex asked. Her tone is soft and friendly. *Gavin, we need this. Just cooperate and get it over with.* Alex felt like every time she saw pain in his eyes, it made it harder to push him. *I have a job to do. I can't be soft like this. Where's the Queen of Death, Johnson?* Alex chastised herself as she walked over to her suitcase to ensure she had everything. She shook her head.

Gavin dove into the file. Flipping through the pages, he would feel the NOVA system activate on a few things every few pages. If he felt the NOVA system's information wasn't leading to anything, he used it as a practice to end it before it was completed. He wasn't making any progress until he saw it. Williams had worked closely with Brett over the years, including while they were still in school. "Hang on, guys, I may have something," Gavin said. *Could it really be? He was using it for our dumb games,* Gavin pondered.

"Did you use the NOVA on something?" Alex said with some eagerness in her voice.

"No, I didn't have to," Gavin answered, sliding the file over to her. "You see, he worked a lot with Brett. Even while we were still in school. And when he and I were roommates, we would take study breaks."

"How touching. Relevance, moron?" Charles scowled at him impatiently.

"I'm getting there. So, as I was saying, during those breaks, we would play games in the library. Acting like we were spies. And he'd always seem to have more ammo than I expected. So, he'd always win," Gavin explained, slightly embarrassed to admit he wasn't even as good of a spy as Brett Martin back then. Charles just looked at him with a slightly condescending smile. "I think he had a spot, a book he would hide things in."

"Great! Where is it?" Alex replied, ignoring Charles as he tried to tease Gavin. "It's on the third floor of the library. You go up the stairs and take a." He paused. *Take a... Which way is it?! Crap.* "I can picture it, but I can't remember exactly."

"Looks like you have even less of a choice now. Go pack, wheels up in thirty," Charles barked as he turned to finish packing.

***

Arriving at GIT, Gavin froze. Everything looked the same as when he left under duress just five years earlier. *Some things never change, I guess. Only thing that has, is me and some of the people here.* Gavin thought as he looked around campus. Captain's frat buddies were all starting to pregame and having a great time. "Hey, Meg, I'm going to show Alex around the place. See if it helps get some closure," Gavin said,

74

"That's a great idea, Gavin! Hopefully, you can find what you need to move on," Megan said, sounding like she was hoping for some relief from his self-punishment.

I can't keep disappointing her. Gavin thought as he turned to walk away. "The library is this way, across the Quad," Gavin said as he took off in a determined walk.

He seems confident in this moment. Determined. Driven. Sexy. What?! Johnson, get your crap together. He is your asset. If you want to keep him in your life, you have to keep your mind in the right place. Keep him in the right place, Alex thought as she took off after him.

***

Arriving at the library, Gavin realized that he needed an ID to scan to get in. As he started to worry, Charles walked up and handed him his old ID. "We got it reactivated. Sorry, I couldn't do anything about that stupid picture, though," Charles teased with a smirk.

"It's okay, Charles. I know you think I'm pretty," Gavin said, patting the big guy on the shoulder. Charles grunted in response. *I swear these two are like brothers sometimes,* Alex thinks with a smile and a shake of her head.

Gavin, smirking at irritating Charles, went in and immediately headed up to the third-floor study area, missing the front desk clerk picking up the phone and calling out. He started walking down the aisle and turned. He remembered exactly where it was at. Turning down an aisle, he stopped and started pulling out books. *It has to be here somewhere. This is the spot.* He looked it over and realized that it's not the same book. "They have reorganized the books. It could be anywhere now," he lamented as he felt defeated.

"Gavin, why would they have a dead drop in a book that could get checked out at any time?" Alex asked, "Check the shelving." She told him, as she started to do the same. Gavin's face lit up. *Of course!* He turned and ran his finger under the bottom of the shelf. Just like he saw

Brett do dozens of times. Feeling a nub, he hit it and down dropped a small drawer.

He pulled out the flash drive in it and said, "Got it!" Immediately, there was gunfire hitting the books around them. They all ducked down and took off towards the back exit with the enemy on their tails. The rain of bullets coming down around them seemed to be zeroing in as they dove into a classroom and locked the door behind them.

Gavin went to the computer and put the flash drive in. "Hey, you shouldn't be looking at that." Charles reprimanded.

"I need to know what they are after, so that we can have an actual plan. Things rarely work out well when you fly blind," Gavin said. *Oghma. Is that what I'm decrypting at home?* Gavin thought as he opened the file.

He's not wrong. But we don't have orders to look at that. Alex thought. "Charles is right, Gavin," che started but was interrupted by Gavin's gasp.

"I'm on here," he said almost dreamily. "Why would I be on here? What is this?" He started freaking out. Just then, the doors at the back of the classroom opened, and bad guys poured into the room, firing down on them. Alex and Charles returned fire as Gavin hid. *There was contact info on this thing,* Gavin remembered as he formed a plan. "Guys, get me out of here. This computer is shot, literally, and I have a plan," Gavin said urgently.

"Okay. When we shoot, make a run for it. Ready?" Charles commanded as he reloaded. "Go!" He said as he and Alex stood and shot at the guys shooting at them. Taking out two in the process. Gavin ran and dived out the door. In the back of the room, a shorter man with a stocky stature saw Gavin bolt and decided to follow him.

Gavin found a computer lab and put the flash drive into one already on. Opening it, he saw the Oghma file again and then saw the Tyr and Ara also. Click on the first file, Tyr, he started pulling up people. The list was long, and as he called a few, he notified them of the situation. Off to the side, the stocky man watched Gavin. Realizing he will soon be outnumbered, he sneaked in, placed a tracer on Gavin, and got out quickly. Leaving the rest of the men to die or be captured.

Gavin finished up and pulled the flash drive from the computer. Heading back to check on Charles and Alex, he saw several people with guns rush into the back of the classroom. He ran to the door and looked in. Charles and Alex slouched down, looking relaxed, as the bad guys were surrounded by the people Gavin had called.

***

After everything was wrapped up and the game was over, Gavin and Alex returned to the townhouse. They had fun at the game. Both enjoyed being "boyfriend and girlfriend" more than they cared to let on. Being away from surveillance, Alex had let her hair down more. *I have to reign it in now. I can't let him think it's okay to act like that while we are in Atlanta.* "Hey Gavin. I... I wanted to talk to you about today." Alex started. Feeling awkward about it all.

"I enjoyed it. You know, after all the shooting was done," Gavin said with a big grin, causing his nose to crinkle.

Why does he do that? Does he have any idea what that smile does to me? Why is this so difficult? And why does my stomach twist in knots when he smiles at me like that? "I had a good time, too, Gavin, but we must get back to being more professional once we are back. You can't be picking me up like you were. Okay?" Alex explained.

Gavin looked like someone had punched him in the gut and taken his War Games poster simultaneously. "I understand. It was just good for the cover. That's all," Gavin said as you could see him shutting down and closing off emotionally.

Gavin, understand. Please. I could get sent away if they see me acting like that. Alex tried to reason without saying a word. Gavin's smile was gone, though. He reached back into his bag and pulled out his laptop. Inserting the drive. "You can't continue to look at that, Gavin," Alex said, but you could hear her heart wasn't behind it. She had already hurt him.

"I have to see why I'm in here," Gavin said, almost ignoring her. Clicking on his name, his profile popped up. Quickly looking over it, he saw several designation prospects under his name. Including all the projects that Williams recruited for, as well as analyst and fieldwork designations. *No mention of Vidar, thankfully. Not that I'm too surprised. Their computer people are looked down on and likely aren't hackers or are hackers I shut down for them,* Gavin mused as he gave it a glance. Then he noticed an MP4 link that he clicked on. Up on the screen popped Williams. Gavin noticed Alex watching the video as well. Williams went through the typical recruiting video intro, and then Brett walked in and convinced him to not recruit Gavin. That he was too weak and couldn't handle the mental aspects. It would be better for Gavin in the long run, and he would ensure that Gavin never came up on their radar again.

After the video, Gavin had a mixture of emotions. *So, he was trying to protect me. That makes me feel slightly better about everything. But he also just about called me inept and naive. I'm glad I never told him about Vidar, either. Mr. BrLA247. Weak hacker, if you could even call him that. I'm sure he was basically the male version of Miranda. Though Miranda likely does it better. He took the option away from me, and then what? Changed his mind?* Gavin thought. His ire built towards Brett as he sat there. "At least you know now that I didn't break the law," Gavin said sarcastically. Sensing Alex tearing up next to him. *She's in love with him. Still.* Gavin fumed to himself as he fought with his jealousy.

"I never questioned if you did or not, Gavin. But now we know Brett had always been looking out for you. And that he sent the NOVA system to you because he knew you could handle it," Alex said while thinking, *even if he was a selfish and arrogant ass. At least he did that right. Cared enough about you to disobey orders. Gavin just has a way of getting under your skin, apparently even with the most hardened agents.* She hadn't noticed Gavin making a discrete copy of the files, putting a tracking code on the drive, and then pulling it out. He handed it to her.

78

"I guess I don't need this anymore since I have my answers," he said and then turned toward the window. The rest of the trip was spent in silence.

***

Arriving at the house, they had let Charles know to meet in Gavin's room. Alex was waiting with him as Charles climbed through the window. Charles took the drive from Alex, and they both started to leave as Gavin felt he should apologize to Alex for his actions. As he turned to say something, they were gone. The shorter, stocky man had been watching them and saw that Charles had the drive.

Gavin locked his window and shut his door. Leaning over, he hit a few keys and started a loop of him playing video games. Opening the Oghma project files from Williams, he recognized some of the names of his classmates on the list. Connecting to his desktop, he transferred the files and cleared his laptop. He checked the decryption process, and it was about done. He was getting antsy to see what the file held. Sitting there, he realized that the NOVA system was a computer program. The issue that had happened with him at times, it was written like it was for a computer and not a mind. The books he had read from Megan's library from her classes. From what he had deduced, the NOVA system already required a certain amount of electrical activity in the brain to not overload and fry it. He couldn't quite tell how it interacted with the brain, but he knew his head felt hot if he allowed too many accesses to NOVA. And that's when the headaches would happen. *I have to find a way to minimize the heat or counteract it,* Gavin mused.

Then he thought about and did something he hadn't thought about doing before. He used the NOVA system to start a dive into Brett's file. Looking through what was in the NOVA system, he saw his training was missing a few months, like Alex's. It wasn't exact, but it was close enough to make it noticeable. He also noticed that almost none of Brett's personal information was in his file. And he used his actual name. Call sign Smirking Raven. *I assume they don't get to pick their call sign.* Gavin laughed to himself. Brett's file was exemplary. His missions were all completed, no matter the body count needed to complete them. But he had a habit of not bringing partners back with him.

Until Alex. Alex seemed to make him less reckless or was good enough that it didn't matter. A life only seemed to matter if it was ordered for it to matter. Gavin couldn't understand that. That didn't seem like the Brett he knew in college, but maybe the Brett he knew never was real. He'd been recruited their freshman year. Training started before sophomore year. But it seemed like the only life Brett ever cared about was his own and Gavin's. Looking at the clock, he realized he'd been going for an hour already. Hitting a couple keys, he set the timer to turn off the loop and get in bed.

***

As the sun rose the next morning, the short man continued to watch Gavin's window. Waiting for his opportunity. He watched Gavin get up and meet the big agent in the courtyard. He watched them enter the car and follow them to the Snollygoster Inc. He went in to browse the store while he stayed close within hearing distance of Gavin.

Gavin thought it would be another one of those slow, post-mission, regular work-only days. He was mindlessly going through his tasks and fixing whatever menial computer issue was brought in. It was getting close to lunchtime, when Charles came up. "The drop is happening soon. Want you to be over getting a sandwich when it happens." Charles said as he started out of the office. Gavin was close behind him. Seeing them leave together, the short man followed.

Getting over there, there were no other customers. Before anyone could react, the man opened the door, fired a tranq dart into Alex and Charles, and threw a vile of something into the room before he quickly shut the door and stared at his watch. Once Gavin turned and saw him, he felt the NOVA system activate. Morgan Henson, ex-gymnast turned international thief, steals and sells hard-to-get high-end information. He waited several minutes before he reopened the door and came in.

"Hello, I believe you have something that I'm looking for. A flash drive with some very sensitive information on it. Information that my friends will pay very handsomely for. Before you think of doing anything crazy, know that the toxin I gave you soon will compel you to give me the truth. You see, it slowly kills you, and just a little before you die, you tell the truth without meaning to. I didn't give a very potent dose, so you and your friends have some time. But if you refuse, I have another vial. Now. Tell me where the drive is, and I may give you the information you need to save your friends," Morgan said nonchalantly. Gavin immediately grabbed the drive from Charles's pocket and tossed it to Morgan.

"Okay, now how do I save my friends!?" Gavin pleaded.

"Oh, I said I may. Not that I would. Besides, I don't know if this is the real thing or not. I'll just have to take it and find out. Best of luck to you, and don't worry. Your friends should wake up before you all die," Morgan taunted. And then he was gone.

Gavin was worried but knew he could track the drive once it was plugged into any computer. He just hoped Morgan did as he said he would and went to check it immediately. He returned to Snollygoster Inc., grabbed his laptop, and returned to the Sub Express.

Coming through the door, he saw Alex and Charles start to wake up. "Good morning, status report. We've all been poisoned. The guy came for the drive and has it. I'm tracking if he has plugged it into a computer yet, and we will all start compulsively saying the truth and whatever comes to mind, right before we die. Just another day in my life. Did you all sleep well?" Gavin rambled, everything falling out of his mouth before he could stop it.

"What? How did you know to track it? Can all flash drives do that?" Charles said groggily.

"No, they can't all do that. I installed a tracking program on this one to track where it goes, thinking it would be fun to see where the best computer engineers for the government are stored. But it came in handy," Gavin explained.

"Where did you learn to do that?" Alex asked as she got up off the floor.

"I'm a hacker. It's what we do," Gavin said before he realized he had just given them his secret. Looking at them, neither of them seemed phased by it.

"And I shoot guns. It's all but your job title, numbnuts," Charles growled as he walked towards Gavin.

Breathing slightly easier, Gavin noticed the tracker came on. "Got a location! That has to be where he is living. He must have an antidote there. Let's go." They hurried out the door.

Arriving at the place, they scoped it out quickly. And headed inside. "My god, you're so pretty," Gavin blurted out as they waited for the elevator. "And Charles, your jawline was chiseled by the gods, I swear."

"Uh, thanks," Charles said, clearly uncomfortable.

They got to the door and knocked. And Morgan called out, asking who it was. "The CIA, NSA, and me, who is a little harder to explain!" Gavin yelled out.

"Ugh, you know you don't HAVE to talk, you moron," Charles growled as he shot the lock on the door and kicked it in. Guns drawn; they enter the main room of the apartment.

"Hello, I assume you're here for some antidote. But you won't mind if..." And he took off toward the exit. He got two steps, and Alex kneecapped him, sending him to the ground writhing in pain.

"Not very good gamesmanship, Johnson," Charles said with a smirk.

Pulling Morgan into a chair to torture. "Wait. Before you do anything. Find some toxin and give it to him," Gavin said.

"Gavin, that's a great idea." Charles took off to find some, which wasn't hard to do. The case of it was sitting on the table by the stairs.

82

"Veritaol. Alex, doesn't the CIA handle this stuff?" Charles called to her.

"Yes," she said, clearly keeping her answer short. Going over to the case, she pulled out a vial and a needle. Pulling it in front of Morgan, she knew he would know how much she gave him. When it was just enough to kill him in five minutes, she pulled it out and stuck the needle in his arm. "Tell us where the antidote is," Alex said as she injected the toxin into him.

"What are you doing?! That will skip the truth part. That will just kill me," Morgan said, freaking out. They let him up, and he immediately took off for the antidote. Following him, after he drank some, they grabbed a vial each.

"Wait, Alex. Wait. I must ask," Gavin pleaded as they stood close to each other. "While I have the chance, I have to ask. Do you see this thing of ours, this under-the-cover thing, going anywhere?"

Oh, Gavin. Why did you ask that? You're asking the wrong thing. I can skirt around that one. Of course, I don't see a future for us. Hunter and the CIA would never allow it. You're my asset. And of course, now I have to hurt you. You sweet man. Why couldn't you ask if I had feelings for you? "No. I don't," Alex said finally. Her heart felt heavier than she could ever remember.

"Thank you for your honesty. Though I suppose that isn't really your choice," Gavin said with a half-smile and pain in his eyes. He downed the antidote.

"Not bad." Alex drank the antidote as well. Though she didn't feel as though she deserved it. She fought off tears threatening to escape as they all returned to their prospective jobs.

***

Heading back to Snollygoster Inc., Gavin felt his world drained of color. Alex had outright rejected him. *This is a job for her. How many times does she have to make that clear? Even if she is really, REALLY good at her job. This entire situation just has my heart so confused. I have such deep feelings for her, but it's clear that everything from her side is just really good acting. It's time to try to move on, even if I can't actually move on. I can't love someone who doesn't love me back. I can't keep doing this to myself.* Gavin thought as he heard someone starting to talk to him in a fast-paced, high-energy tone.

Looking up, he sees a very cute and peppy girl. Brunette with curls, shorts, and a cute face. "I can't lose this. I can't go back to who I was before this phone. It's my entire life. It has everything in it."

"Hey hey hey, calm down. My name is Gavin. Tell me what's wrong." Gavin tried to placate her.

"Hi, my name is Erin."

"Erin? Really? Anyways, Erin, this is kinda of my world. You know? Phones, electronics, computers, all these things. It's what I do. What I'm good at. So, I know I am a stranger, but if you let me take a look, I will take good care of it for you," Gavin said with a brighter smile than he had since leaving the GIT football game.

"I can't. What if something happens and you lose everything?" Erin started again.

"Woah woah woah, don't go back there. Deep breaths. It will be ok. Trust me. Think about something that gives you peace and makes you happy. Go to your happy place," Gavin said quickly.

"Cake, chocolate, pudding, candies, bacon, maple syrup," Erin said with her eyes closed. Visibly calming down as she said it.

"I'm sorry, what?" Gavin asked with a slight chuckle.

"I think about desserts a lot to calm me down," Erin said as if it was the most natural explanation in the world.

"Who doesn't?" Gavin said with a bright smile.

84

"I own the bakery down the street," Erin continued, "Please fix my phone for me," she added, slightly embarrassed.

"Let me take a look, Erin," Gavin said, reaching out. He took the phone, quickly did a battery swap, hard reset, and reinstall. Which fixed it. "There you go. Good as new," he said, holding the phone out to Erin.

"Really?! That fast? No way!" Erin said excitedly. She started going through everything quickly, a happy smile on her face. Every now and then, she would glance at Gavin through her eyelashes. "Gavin, you are my hero," she said, stepping closer.

Just then, behind Gavin, a tall, beautiful blonde appeared. "Hi, I'm Alex. Gavin's girlfriend." And at that, Erin's face fell. And surprisingly to Alex, so did Gavin's a little bit. With a cringing, forced smile, Erin said goodbye and left quickly. "Gavin, we need to talk," Alex said as she pulled him toward Gavin's office.

Pulling Gavin into the room and closing the curtains and door, Alex turned to him and said, "First off, what was that? You were clearly flirting with that girl. What would your coworkers think?" Alex felt more jealousy than she had expected.

"I was just being nice. You know? Good customer service," Gavin said, trying to avoid the awkwardness, realizing this was the perfect time to get into the situation and how messed up it was for him.

"And so, what if I was? She's a nice and pretty girl. Who seemed to actually like me for me. And I want something real. Not something that all it does is confuse me and hurt me. The longer we do this, I feel like I'm just fooling myself more than anyone else. It's not like I could actually get someone." Gavin tapered off, running out of steam. And then he mumbled, "I think we should break up. Well, fake break up."

Alex was shocked. She didn't know that this was how Gavin had been feeling. *Why can't you see it? You can always see the real me in everything else. Even if I don't tell you. Why is this different?* "I'm sorry, Gavin. But we can't. There isn't a way to explain my being close to you other than if we are dating. I'm sorry if you feel trapped. I'll try to make it easier for you," Alex said. Alex's head started to hurt. She needed to leave. "We will talk more later," she said as she quickly walked away, wiping the corners of her eyes.

She drove fast to her hotel room. She felt the tears starting to fall. Her head hurt so bad. *Why couldn't he understand? Because you make sure he can't ever see how you really feel. But I do let him in. More than I have anyone. Which is super dangerous. You have known him for a few months, and he is making you question orders. He is dangerous to you. But the orders he makes me question, I SHOULD question. No. There are no orders you should question. That isn't what you do. You follow orders. Not question them. What am I thinking? Even if you did defy orders and tried to have something real with him, he wouldn't want you. Not if he knew what you did before you came here. Not if he knew the real you. Even before the CIA. You haven't been a good person in a LONG time.*

You haven't been innocent in what feels like forever. Even this life is better than what you deserve. What you've earned. No one would want you. No one does want you once they know the truth. You are rotten fruit wrapped in a healthy-looking peel. You're dead and rotten inside. And there is nothing you can do to change that. Following orders is all you have. It's all you deserve to have. You don't belong here with him. You will only ruin him. Corrupt him. Until he is just as dead as you. It's already started. You can see it in his eyes every time you remind him of why you're here. Even if you care about him. Do you care about him? Do you remember what it's like to care about something other than the mission? He deserves better than you. More than what you must give him. All you will do is ruin him. All you're good at is death.

The tears were flowing. She had reached her hotel and made her way into her room. She screamed into her pillow. Her head throbbing. *I deserve this pain. This is what I get for not following orders. For trying to be more than what I am. For reaching for the sun. For something real. This is what I am. Pain, hurt, and death. It follows me everywhere. It defines me. It defines my life. But the way Gavin looks at me. It's like he sees more. But there isn't more there. There isn't more to me than death. Destruction. I'm tainted. Defiled. Dirty. And there isn't any kind of water that can clean me. That could get the blood off my hands.*

You can't erase the past, and so you have to accept that that is who you are. Your past is all you have. Your past and orders. Orders are my only future. Orders mean that it's not me acting. No, you make the decision to follow them. Gavin has proven that. He has shown you there are other ways, better ways, to complete the mission. That it isn't a detriment to value life as a spy. That you aren't weak just because you don't embrace death. He completes the mission with minimal damage. With only self-defense. Yes, Charles and I kill, but we do it to protect him. Not to assassinate. Everyone underestimates Gavin. They don't understand how much he brings to every mission. To every day. How much he makes things okay. How his innocence is paramount to all. Somehow, he is innocent but not naive. And that confuses everyone. Just because he doesn't have darkness, doesn't mean he hasn't been through darkness. Somehow, he doesn't let it claim him.

She screamed into the pillow again, her head feeling like it was splitting open. *No, I have to be hard. It's how I deal. It's who I always have been. I don't talk about my feelings. That's for Gavin. And people like Gavin. Like Megan. They accept me as part of them, but I'd never be part of them. I'm not the same. I am darkness. I am death. And I'm nothing else. Death and orders. That's who I am. That's what I deserve. I can't allow that to consume Gavin like it has everyone else I've been around. Everyone else I've cared about. Everyone else I loved.*

Alex sobbed into her pillow, tears streaming from her eyes. Her entire body hurt. It felt like she had been tortured for days. She had never felt pain like this before, and it was only dimmed slightly by the pain she felt in her head. *Why would anyone like them want me? I have nothing to give them because there is nothing left of me to give. All I am, all that is left, are my body and the skills I have. And I can't give him my body. That would just confuse someone like him. Gavin feels too deeply for meaningless sex. His heart is in everything he does. He can't detach. Nothing is meaningless to him. Especially something like sex. I can't allow him to be consumed by my darkness. I can't allow him to see the real me, either. Arm's length. So that I have him in my life, but don't allow my darkness to consume his light. He still deserves better and will get it once the NOVA system is out of his head. He will forget all about me and the darkness I brought into his life. I'll be but a shadow in his life. Like I have been in so many. In all, I didn't kill. And in the families of those I did kill. Death. It's what I am, what I deserve.*

Chapter 6

:/Bombs

Gavin trudged into his room, tossing his bag on his bed, flopping down in his computer chair, and running his hands through his hair. He felt lost.

I get why we couldn't break up, but she has to know how hard this is for me. She has to know how I feel about her. Everyone says it is written on my face every time I see her.

And then his head sank into his hands as though it had just become too heavy for his neck. *But they say the same thing about her. And that is clearly wrong.*

After a few minutes, Gavin finally collected enough and booted up his computer. He was thankful for the distraction from his thoughts and feelings about Alex. He was entering the password and turning on the loop he made. He scrolled down, and it was finished.

Project Oghma.

The file had been decrypted. And Gavin was surprisingly nervous to open it. He's never been a confident guy unless he was hacking. But this. This had ties to his past heavily. This got him kicked out of Georgia Institute of Technology. This caused him to spiral into inaction and complacency for five years emotionally. It derailed his life. It made him lose a friend. And now he might be able to figure out why.

He clicked on the file and scrolled through the sub-files and document titles. He could tell from the listed names this project was the NOVA system. In this folder was all the information on it he needed. He saw how it works, what it was meant to do, what it could do. Digging into it deeper, he found the history of it. And there again.

Coeus.

He was the creator of the NOVA system. So that explained, at least in part, why he was so tied to Hunter and Richmond. Testing started in 1989 for humans, but the first successful test was listed in 1990. Gavin felt something about that was familiar. Though he couldn't quite say what it was.

He started pulling up the diagnostic charts and data. Comparing them with what he had thought, learned in Fleming's class, and what he had begun learning from Megan's neuroscience books, he has started understanding more of how it worked in his mind. And even more, he was understanding how to alter it. While he wasn't sure if he could remove the program from his head, he did know that he would be able to add or remove aspects of it. Alter its programming. And adjust it to fit his mind and body better.

He was getting excited. He knew he would have to keep this hidden. But being able to change what was in his head allowed him some semblance of control again.

And then he remembered the other files—the other projects. Pulling out a flash drive, he brought up the other project files. Again, it was lists of recruits, with their interviews and information. There were hundreds of names. The Oghma project recruits file was small and only a handful of names. But this one had their schools listed as well. They didn't all go to Georgia Institute of Technology. This was the complete recruitment list. He started scrolling through the names.

Gavin froze. He could barely breathe. He reread the name again. And again. There, listed among the other recruits: Agent Alex Johnson.

Gavin clicked on her file, which had everything he expected—no list of her birth name. But the name was Stacy Moore, and her alias in High School. He had seen all this from what the NOVA system had on her and what he had dug up. It wasn't anything new. So, he hopped over to the other lists, and she was in everyone. In fact, the only list she wasn't in was Project Oghma. *What ARE these projects if Oghma is for the NOVA system download?*

Vidar started salivating. He closed out the files and brought up a browser—time to dig.

Within minutes, he was into the secure government servers. He started searching for anything he could find on Project Tyr, Project Ara, and Project Spartan, copying them to his external hard drive. Of course, he would have to run his decryption software over it before he could look into it more. But he was ecstatic at what he had found.

Another idea came to him, and he started reviewing the files and looking into any of the agents listed. Many of them were no longer in the service. And most were dead. Everyone listed in the Oghma project didn't survive past the first two stages. And after seeing the files on its programming, he could see why. They were literally frying their brains with electricity.

After looking through the Oghma files and seeing all the data, Gavin felt confident enough to start the programming to alter the NOVA system. And to his excitement, according to his research, he might be able to add skills. He would have to be careful, which always meant it would take time. But it would be worth it to no longer be helpless. To be able to defend himself, even if just slightly.

Looking at the clock, he realized he had been working on this for several hours, and his loop would end soon. So, he saved everything off and closed it out. He was setting the loop to end with him walking to his bed. And he got up and laid down.

Through the computer, someone was watching him again. "Nicely done, Gavin. You are making far more progress than I expected. Maybe we will be able to take them all down. Just as they deserve," they murmured as they watched. Sitting in a train station and watching two agents make a handoff. As soon as the agents parted, they took off after one. They needed to catch the agent. Everything depended on it.

***

Waking up, Alex still felt conflicted. She hadn't slept well. Dreams of being ordered to shoot Gavin were mixed with dreams of running away with him. And she wasn't sure which was affecting her more. *It doesn't matter. Today is back to protecting him.*

She got out of bed and took a shower. Feeling the hot water falling over her always made her feel better. But she knew it was temporary. She always turned up the heat to make it feel like it was cleaning her, but no matter how hard she scrubbed, she still had that blood on her hands. Shaking her head clear of those thoughts, she got out and ready for the day.

When she pulled in, Charles and Gavin were already at the Snollygoster Inc., but she wasn't ready to face Gavin again just yet. So, she headed straight for the Sub Express.

***

Gavin had just finished formatting a hard drive when Kaleb came strutting up to the desk. "Hey buddy, so you don't mind that I went to try my luck with that cute deli owner, do you?"

"What Kaleb? Why would I mind that? I'm with Alex," Gavin replied without looking up.

"Because I saw your mind cheat with her yesterday. Mind cheater." Kaleb teased, "Okay, but really. I went over and talked to her. And she had this flier on her board. Dude! A new hot club! We have got to go stand in line and never get in!" he finished with an eyebrow waggle.

"Look, buddy, I don't know," Gavin started as he looked at the flier. Suddenly, he was hit with images.

A shipyard, Jorge Valentine, Pendulum, guns.

"I don't know if that's a good idea. Clubbing is always one of those things that is way more fun sounding than it ever actually is. You know?" Gavin said, trying to dissuade his friend from going.

"You're right. But it's the coolest we have ever gotten to be. To say we went to those clubs," Kaleb stated dejectedly.

"I know, Kaleb, but we never got in," Gavin said with a laugh.

"One day. One day we will." Kaleb said as he walked off.

Gavin found Charles, letting him know what he accessed the NOVA system on. "Interesting. I'll let the General know," Charles said.

"I actually have a plan on how to go about this mission," Gavin said tentatively.

"Oh really? The moron has a plan," Charles growled impatiently, "Well, let's hear this."

"So, I could verify some of their information, financial and the like. As well as get in under IT for the club to fix their system. And then I'd be able to have access to tap their cameras and place some bugs," Gavin explained.

"That's actually not half bad. I'll let the general know. Wait. Why would they need IT?" Charles asked.

Gavin smirked, "Because I just planted a virus in their system a minute ago. And they just called for service, and I intercepted the call. I will be their personal IT," Gavin stated.

Charles shook his head with a slight smile. It looked unnatural on his face. "Okay, kid. You did good. Let me call this in."

That was rare. Charles complimented me. Huh. Gavin thought as he returned to his desk, waiting for word to proceed. After getting approval, Gavin went to the service call while Alex and Charles monitored from a van outside.

"I don't like this. He is too exposed in there," Alex complained.

"This is his job. They have no reason to suspect him of anything. You just don't like being apart from your boy toy," Charles took a shot at her being compromised.

How dare he! Me? Compromised? I'm not compromised... am I? Alex pondered as she watched the feed of Gavin working on their network. Again, she wondered if they underestimated him. Just how much he was capable of. But her thoughts were cut short by Stavros Valentine, Jorge's son, and the club manager, approaching Gavin.

"Could you hurry up? We have to prepare for tonight, and I can't allow my guests to see someone wearing polyester here," he said with a sneer.

Gavin paused, embarrassed by the other man's jibe. "I should be done here in a few minutes," Gavin said as he returned to work.

"Good. And once you're done, my assistant will sign the form. Now hurry, weakling," Sierge said with a condescending chuckle as he walked away. Gavin curses under his breath.

Alex heard the exchange and badly wanted to bolster Gavin's confidence. But with Charles there listening and having already been called out for being compromised, she stayed quiet about it. "Come on, Gavin. Just get it done and get out of there. He's not worth our time," Charles said to the surprise of everyone.

"Oh, I've been done for a while. I just wanted to annoy him. We charge by the hour for service calls," Gavin said with a smile to which Charles laughed and smirked a bit.

***

94

Later that evening, Gavin was sitting in his room with the bedroom window shut and blinds closed, working on his new NOVA system files, when his computer froze.

He went to restart it when a text popped up on the screen.

/:YOU CANT TRUST THEM. THEY ONLY WANT THE NOVA SYSTEM:/

Gavin read it and reread it. Glancing up at the camera, he shifted in his seat. *How do I know I can trust it isn't them spying on me? Ha, because I know they couldn't get through my security anywhere near how I can theirs. Especially without alerting me. So, who is this?* Gavin thought as he continued to look at the monitor.

"And how do I know I can trust you? I don't even know who you are?" Gavin whispered into the mic.

/:YES. YOU DO. YOU SEARCHED FOR ME IN COLLEGE, THOUGH YOU DIDNT KNOW MY NAME AT THE TIME. YOUVE SEEN IT SEVERAL TIMES NOW:/

Gavin's eyes got big. He remembered the hacking battles he had had to reach for The Ghost—the person who had been the only one to thwart any of his hacks in college. And now, thinking about all that had changed and that he had learned. He connected the dots. "Coeus?"

/:YOU NEED TO CONTINUE TO STUDY THE FILES. FIGURE OUT HOW TO REMOVE IT. IT IS THE ONLY WAY FOR THEM TO LET YOU GO:/

"I have a plan. And I'm sorry, but I don't fully trust you. You created this thing and vanished. I've had enough people disappear from my life," Gavin said with a slightly bitter tone.

/:I UNDERSTAND. ON REVIEWING YOUR WORK, IT IS GOOD. BETTER THAN MINE. AND IF I AM CORRECT, YOU HAVE SOMETHING THAT NO ONE ELSE DOES. NOT EVEN ME. IF YOU CAN ACCESS IT. REMEMBER IT. YOU WILL BE

FARTHER AHEAD THAN ANY COULD EXPECT. THE NOVA
SYSTEM WAS DESIGNED TO UPLOAD INTELL TO AGENTS.
BUT WAS MEANT TO BE SCRAPPED AFTER A MAJORITY OF
THE AGENTS DIED WITH A MINIMAL UPLOAD, AND THE
ONES THAT DIDNT WERE NEVER THE SAME. HAD SEVERE
MENTAL BREAKDOWNS. I KNOW YOU, EVEN IF YOU DONT
THINK I DO. GOOD LUCK MR GAVIN:/

Gavin froze again. The screen went blank, and then a symbol popped
on the screen for a second, causing Gavin to access the NOVA system
on Coeus and the NOVA system. It gave validation to what he had just
told him. And then his work was back, with a few corrections. But
Gavin's mind focused on the previous message's last few words. Mr.
Gavin. Only three people had ever consistently called him Mr. Gavin.
And he seriously doubted Mrs. MacArthur from the 3rd grade was a
hacker.

In fact, he really only knew one person who fit all the blanks. One
person who knew computers better than him. One person who went
missing when he was sixteen.

"Dad?" Gavin whispered to the screen. Knowing Coeus was still
watching.

Gavin sat and thought. *What did he mean if I can access it? I remember
almost everything from my childhood. Especially since I was nine,* and
then it came to him, almost like accessing the NOVA system. Gavin
remembered wandering into his dad's office when he had left the door
open. There was a computer with a bunch of screens. The computer had
a command prompt to start the sequence. And when he had hit it. *Holy
crap! I've had a NOVA system since I was nine!?* Gavin tried to process
this, but he didn't understand. *How could I still be functioning?* He
thought as he remembered everyone who had died from the first upload
during Project Oghma.

Thinking back on everything, it made sense. He hadn't forgotten hardly
anything since then. He thought hard at that time. Those images. His
dad created the NOVA system. And he was the first successful trial. As
far as he knew, it's the only successful upload. From his study and how

96

he felt, his brain activity got a boost and kept him from being hard-wired starting at age nine. And then again, when he received the recent update. That's why he could learn things faster. He had the mental acuity of a 9-year-old, with the prior learning of a 25-year-old.

He thought about it more and focused on when he accessed the NOVA system. It was a massive NOVA system file, but it felt different. Like he suddenly picked up an arm he hadn't used in seventeen years. There were some aches and cramps, but having it flow through his mind felt amazing.

The access to the NOVA system felt like his mind rebooting. It was like he had just cleared his cache and cookies. And he looked at his War Games poster hanging next to his desk. "Don't worry dad. I have a plan," Gavin said with a smile. His heart hurt to know his father was out there, but now, knowing he created the NOVA system made it understandable as to why he left. And having it, made him feel a little closer to his dad.

He was brought out of his thoughts by his phone ringing. He quickly ended the surveillance loop he had made, cleared out the files he was looking at and the coding he had been working on, and answered. "Gavin, you need to get over to Charles's right away. We have a mission and need you," Alex said.

***

Over at Charles's, the general reviewed what they had picked up from the surveillance Gavin had put in at the Valentine's Club. According to the intel gathered, a single crate was coming in of huge value to Pendulum. They had paid Jorge to transport it to Atlanta for them. "Team, my people believe that it is a bomb. We need you to find it and for the NOVA system to figure out how to disarm it. Dismissed." And she ended the video call.

Gavin stood there and waited for them to ask him something as he watched them plan the assault. He struggled to focus on the task at hand with the emotional and mental bombs he just had to go off. *You can't trust them.* His dad had told him that. But could he even trust his dad? *I mean, I get why he left now. But he still left his kids behind.*

"Gavin! Hey, are you listening?" Alex said with a concerned look in her eye. "Charles and I will infiltrate the docks and take down the guards. Once it is clear, we will bring you in, Gavin. You will then disarm the bomb, and we will call in cleanup to take care of disassembling it and getting it out of Atlanta. Fairly simple and straightforward."

"When have our missions gone to plan?" Gavin said with a laugh.

"That's what makes them fun," Charles said with a smirk as he slammed a magazine into his M-4. He grabbed his bag and checked out the door. "Let's go," he said as they filed out.

***

Arriving at the docks, Alex and Charles got out, telling Gavin to stay in the car. Not long after, Alex leaned out the gate and waved Gavin in. "There's no one here. Can you check the manifest to see if you can find anything?" Alex said as she continued to scan the area vigilantly. *He is so confident when working with computers. You can tell he is where he is meant to be. It's kind of sexy.* Alex paused momentarily before she mentally shrugged and focused on the mission.

Pulling up the manifest, Gavin found today's expected shipment buried in a mountain of meaningless deliveries. "Here it is! Dock 7 crate 14956." Gavin said, drawing Alex's attention to the screen. As they turned to leave, Jorge and Sierge walked in.

"I don't remember calling for tech support on the docks," Sierge said with a wicked smirk. He had a gun pointed at Gavin, while Jorge pointed his at Alex. "Move, bimbo, next to your boyfriend," he said in a thick Russian accent as six more men filed into the room. All armed. "Now, you will tell me why you are here and who you work for, or I will start taking limbs," Jorge threatened.

Charles had been heading back when he saw Jorge and his men heading toward the office where Gavin and Alex were. After a quick count, he didn't feel like dying just yet, so he waited and watched what happened. He waited for them all to be in the office, then cut the power to the room.

Alex was starting to feel her blood pressure rise when suddenly the lights went out. She knew it had to be Charles. She remembered where her captures were and sent two throwing knives in that direction, hearing two screams and several shots fired into the ceiling. *Two down, six to go.* Alex thought, and she reached out for the nearest bad guy. Turning towards him, she grabbed him by the collar and yanked his head down into her knee. As she jumped, three shots hit right where she had been.

Gavin knew chaos was about to happen when the lights went out, so he immediately dropped to the floor. After hearing the screams and shots fired, he kicked out at the man closest to him. He made contact and knocked him down. *There is my opening.* Gavin crawled as quickly as he could toward the door.

Charles heard footsteps and looked behind him to see fifteen more men heading towards him and the office. He shot one as they approached. He was causing the rest to seek cover and moving between the boxes to continue a rain of fire on them. "Guys, we have more company. Find that bomb and get it taken care of. Now!" Charles bellowed into the mics.

Alex saw the door open, and Gavin slipped out of the office. *Good job, Gavin. Now, I don't have to worry about collateral damage.* Alex thinks as she grabbed the gun of another assailant. Hitting the button to eject the mag, her skilled hands quickly removed the slide from his Glock, and she threw it at another guy. Dropping down, she kicked the knees of the one in front of her sideways, hearing the crack of his joints dislocating and his bones breaking. *Another one down. Four left.*

Charles kept firing and taking down one at a time as they would pop into the open. After several close calls, he asked, "How much longer?"

Gavin replies, "I'm finding the container. Hang on and call back up. I doubt this is all of them at this point."

Alex felt her blood run cold at the thought of Gavin being at the bomb alone. She grabbed two more knives and threw one into a guy's hand, causing him to fire and shoot one of his cohorts. And the other she threw to turn on the lights. She kicks off the wall already on the floor, causing her to slide across the floor towards the door. As she got near it, she grabbed the gun that was just dropped. Four shots, and everyone in the room was either disabled beyond following her or dead. Quickly, she got up and took off after Gavin.

"I'm at the bomb and opening the crate," Gavin said into the coms as he heard more gunfire behind him. His hands shook as he grabbed the crowbar.

Alex was at a dead sprint heading towards the container she knew Gavin would be at. Her mind running faster than her legs. *I can't lose him. I can't be who I was before him. I need to be with him.* She was losing her mind. Her head throbbed as she rounded the corner into the container.

Gavin turned to see Alex. His eyes were wide. *I don't know what to do. I don't know how to stop this.* The timer on the bomb slowly ticked down. "Come on, NOVA system. We need you," Gavin said, slightly hitting the side of his head.

"Gavin. You need to get out of here!" Alex said desperately. *I can't lose you.*

"And leave you? Not happening," Gavin said firmly.

Alex huffed, drawing the gun she had grabbed on him, "I'm not asking."

"Or what? You'll shoot me? If I don't leave to avoid dying, I'll die? Great logic. And how do you run from a bomb this big?" Gavin said standing tall.

"You are so frustrating! Why can't you follow orders?" Alex said, her voice raised.

"I consider this a rare moment of bravery. Maybe you just bring out the worst in me!" Gavin retorted.

"And you in me!" Alex replied.

:07 seconds left. Gavin took a deep breath. Now toe to toe with Alex. "It's been great knowing you. Alex," Gavin said calmly. *I guess if I'm going to go, at least it's with someone I love.* Gavin thought. Not even worrying about the honesty he just had with himself. *What does it matter?*

:05 seconds left. *Why won't he run? Why does he feel I'm worth dying with? Dying for? Why won't he ever just save himself?* Alex couldn't fathom this level of selflessness. It wasn't a part of her world. Her life. Everyone had an angle. Everyone wanted something. And yet, here was a man who she had watched time and time again, just wanting to do what was right for the sake of it being right.

:03 seconds left. Gavin closed his eyes. His heart was racing. He was sweating. He wasn't ready to die, but he accepted it. Wishing he had more time. And suddenly, he felt a force crash into him. *This is it. Wait.* He felt her lips form to his. Her tongue darted across his lips—her need for him.

:03 seconds left. *I can't let him die without knowing how much he means to me. He deserves that much.* Launching herself into him. Her lips pursed, and her eyes shut. Her world might as well have exploded as soon as her lips met his. She grabbed onto his shirt, pulling him into her. She felt a heat rising inside her. She'd felt passion before. Brett was good at it. Even if it was manufactured. But this was something new. It didn't make sense. Gavin had never gone through the seduction training that she and Brett had, and she had lost herself in him. She can't contain herself in this moment.

Sure, she could play it off like it was an end-of-life kiss. But it was far more. The warmth inside her told her that. The need was there. The drive to get as much of him as she could, while she could, was there. But there was also... *why are we still here?*

Gavin eagerly returned the passion Alex was pushing into him. Grabbing her back and pulling her body flush with his own. Gripping at her jacket, she'd warn. He needed her closer even as she was so close, he could feel her heartbeat against his chest. Her soft lips latched to his like she was drawing her life from him. He felt the passion grow. This went beyond any ex girlfriend. This felt like the world made sense. His heart was finally whole. Alex's hands went to his hair, slightly pulling at his curls. And then she froze. He was still kissing for a moment before he felt she had stopped. *Why? Why did she stop? It was perfect. It was... we are still alive.*

Gavin slowly released her and lowered her back to the floor. Unsure as to when he had picked her up, to begin with. His heart is racing for a different reason now. He had a goofy grin slowly forming on his face that he couldn't stop.

I kissed him. I kiss HIM. I can't walk that back. It was a mistake. He will think that there can be something now. And now I will have to push him away even harder. Why did I do that? What happens to my control when I'm with him? Alex berated herself. "Well. This is slightly awkward," Alex said breathlessly. *Why am I still breathless? You know exactly why. That kiss might as well have taken your virginity again.* Alex fought a smirk at that thought.

"Completely comfortable on my end," Gavin said dreamily.

Just then, Charles came running around the corner. "Oh, don't worry about me. I handled the fifteen guys. Alone. With no word about the bomb," Charles growled, clearly irritated even though he was excited about the gunplay. "So, what? Was it a dud? I thought we would all be dead by now."

Yeah, me too. "We aren't sure. We will need a team to come and inspect it. But for now, let's call it in and set up a perimeter. And get Gavin back home," Alex said, snapping out of her daze.

"Roger that," Charles said, "Come on, kid. I'll call you a ride as we walk." Alex was already on the phone calling a team to clean up before calling in a bomb squad.

***

Gavin got back home and sat down at his computer. He was still wired and unsure if it was from the bomb or the kiss. *Probably the kiss. This was what? The third bomb in four months? You get numb to that kind of stress. Right? But you don't get numb to a kiss like that,* Gavin thought with a laugh. He was on cloud nine.

He decided to go back through the surveillance he had pulled to review. And he started quickly scrolling through things. Most of it was boring and not noteworthy. Every now and then, he stopped to laugh at Kaleb or Chad until he found a phone call between Richmond and Charles.

"Charles secure."

"Hello, Agent Charles. I'm just checking. Everything is in place for when the new NOVA system comes online?" the General inquired

"Are you sure this is necessary, General?" Charles replied.

"Gavin Woodford has served his purpose well. But now he will die to keep those secrets safe unless another option becomes available," the General said in a clipped tone before ending the call.

Gavin sat there and listened to it several times. He wished he couldn't believe it, but it made sense. It still hurt him. It felt like a betrayal. He had trusted these people. And while he understood that it didn't make sense to keep him alive when there was another one up and ready, he didn't see how the work they had been doing would not count for anything. Thankfully, he had done his research. Typing on his computer, he created a secure line out. He was making security on it impossible to break. Then he pulled up a video call.

As it was answered, before anyone could speak, Gavin sternly said, "Hello. I think it's time we had a talk."

Chapter 7

:/Plans

Alex had watched from behind a plexiglass wall as the bomb squad confirmed it wasn't a bomb. And then, as the CDC confirmed, it wasn't toxic or a bioweapon. After all was guaranteed to be safe, they went to work at getting it open. Alex was half paying attention as they worked on it. Instead, she worked with the cleaning crew to get the bodies gone and dealt with.

She heard the pressure release of the canister opening. "Holy crap, I thought I killed him already," she heard Charles say. *That narrows it down.* Alex thought sarcastically as she turned to see for herself. Every part of her froze as she saw who it was. All of the oxygen seemed to have left the room for Alex.

There in the canister was a sleeping Brett.

***

Gavin stared at the monitor. Vidar was out to play in total and had plans on top of plans. With fail safes at the ready in case something went wrong.

"Mr. Woodford, what is the meaning of this? And how did you get access to this line from an untraceable computer?" General Richmond asked curtly. "General, I do believe that it would be in your best interest not to talk during this conversation until I am finished," Gavin stated. And then hit play on the phone call recording he had just listened to. General Richmond's face grew tighter until her upper lip disappeared entirely.

As it finished, Gavin continued, "I'm not here to guilt you. First, trying to guilt you into a decision would never work. Even if you did use to work with my father." At that, her face paled. *Good. I'm getting through.* "Secondly, I do believe that I have a better option. As I don't fully believe that killing me was ever your idea."

Richmond seemed to relax slightly. "What can I do for you, Gavin? And what can you offer?"

"I think you know some of what I can offer," Gavin started.

"Yes. The NOVA system is of great value to us," Richmond said, sounding somewhat perturbed.

"No. Not just the NOVA system. I am going to tell you something that very few people know," Gavin retorted with an intense stare.

"I think I can handle your secrets, Gavin," The General said with a slight eye roll. He was trying to regain composure and control of the situation.

"Does the name Vidar mean anything to you?" Gavin said with a smirk.

General Richmond's eyes shot open. It did mean something. It meant something to anyone with any sort of clearance in the government from five years prior. It was the name of the only cyber-terrorist that never had a single demand and never caused any issues. It was the weirdest case she had ever had to assign.

They'd had next to nothing on the person. They were as much of a ghost as Coeus was. They only knew they were in the system if Vidar allowed them to know. And not one of their best analysts could understand what Vidar was doing or why. It was almost like the analysts had more respect for Vidar than they did each other. And no agent had been able to get close to them.

"Yes. That name means something to anyone who has heard it. Now, how do you know it?" Richmond was getting impatient.

"You really thought the son of Coeus was helpless? With a scholarship to GIT in computer programming and engineering? Your past assignment record gave an indicator that you were a better detective than that," Gavin said.

"You looked into my record?! I should have you thrown in a hole for that!" Richmond fumed.

"Yes. I did. Yours and most of Director Hunter's. Which is why I'm coming to you. Why, I believe it wasn't your idea to have me killed. And why I believe you will agree with my plan moving forward," Gavin said confidently. "And if you think tossing me into a hole in the ground is going to stop me, then you never really listened to what I was capable of as Vidar."

General Richmond paused. She knew what he was saying. He had access to more files now than she did, not only because of the NOVA system but also because of his abilities. If his statement was true, he was better than any computer expert they had on the payroll. "How can I know for sure that you are who you are claiming to be?" she asked. She was hoping that she may be able to really have Vidar on her payroll soon.

"Easy. I could tell you some of the hacks I performed. Or I could hack into something your team has deemed unhackable and get you what you want and more," Gavin said flippantly.

"You seem confident in this. Ok. Tell me Vidar's last hack," she said.

107

"Ok. 2002, I finished one of my fall midterms before getting kicked out. I hacked into the CIA and NSA servers, leaving a note pointing out your vulnerable back door accesses and where the firewalls weren't filtering out the information they should. However, that wasn't my last hack. That was just the last one I had let you know I was in. My true last hack was the same day I got kicked out of GIT. I had been searching for my parents. Seeing if there was any information on them in the FBI database," Gavin said.

He knew this was true. Richmond had no choice but to believe he was Vidar. "Okay, Gavin, you have proven what you can provide for me. Now, what is it that you are wanting?" she asked.

This is honestly going better than I expected. Gavin mused. "I'm glad you see my worth. Firstly, I want any kill order withdrawn. I feel that is a no-brainer, but it needed to be said out loud. Secondly, I would also like a designation as a field analyst. You know, as do Charles and Alex, my aversion to killing. I understand the need for it, but I couldn't bring myself to do it except for extreme situations. However, with this thing in my head, I wouldn't be able to just stay in the van all the time. It isn't who I am. So, I suggest weapons training and self-defense. I can use a tranq gun. And if any of your chemists develop a better tranq, I can use that first. It will also allow more people we can question rather than bodies to clean up. Third, I don't want anyone in the government to know this—especially no one in the CIA. While I think Alex will do her job and is a good agent, I don't trust Hunter. His past and how he has handled this situation so far make me feel he isn't being upfront. Which I suppose is the CIA way. Lastly, and this is important. I need your support. I need to be able to tell my sister, and, as much as you don't like him, Kaleb. I need him, and he is loyal to a fault. He won't tell a soul if he thinks it would endanger me. As far as my sister and her fiancé, I have an experimental computer program running in my brain. My sister is a neurologist and one of the better ones in Atlanta. Her fiancé is a cardiothoracic surgeon. I couldn't think of two better people to help watch my health and care for me than them. They will keep any secret I pose to them, and they will make sure I am healthy at all times. They can also be in-house doctors for the rest of the team. And then Agent Johnson will no longer be stuck in a fake relationship with me," Gavin finished.

The General knew that everything he had said made sense. But she wasn't sure if just giving him everything he had requested was right. It appeared desperate. And while she had become a bit desperate for control of this operation, she couldn't have him knowing that. She also had to consider that, while Gavin Woodford hadn't been a threat to her or anyone else, what Vidar was capable of was most assuredly a threat to anyone who might cross him. In this digital age, he was becoming increasingly a threat and one that would be far better suited as an NSA field analyst.

"I can agree to most of this. With a few additional parameters. You will need to convince me about Kaleb Grimes. He is not allowed to know right away. You make solid arguments for your sister and Doctor Chad Kennedy. I can make those arrangements immediately and contact them and their bosses," Richmond started.

But Gavin cut her off, "I would like to be a part of the conversation with my sister and Chad. I feel I owe it to them to tell them myself," he said. The general nodded.

"I understand that and will allow it. We can set something up for that. As far as Agent Johnson, I disagree. She is to remain as your cover girlfriend. It explains her presence in your life better than anything else could. And even if we don't need to hide it from those closest to you, your coworkers and any strangers you may meet will need to have a reason not to question her spending time with you. But I do understand the need for secrecy with this. And I will tell Agent Charles when and if it becomes relevant to," Richmond explained. A glint in her eye that was easily missed came and went quickly.

"Now as far as payment. I can assign a code name of your choosing to be a senior field analyst for the NSA, effective immediately as soon as we have signatures. As well as back pay. If you would like to move out of your sister's apartment, we can make arrangements for you. I believe an apartment in the same complex will be available soon. If they are your doctors, I would like you to remain close to them. As well as close to either Agent Charles or Agent Johnson. And as you are requesting to no longer be in a cover relationship with Agent Johnson, I'd assume moving into the same apartment as her is out of the question," the General stated.

"That all sounds reasonable. I would like to request operational financing for myself as I will likely be building my own devices for my team in the field and computers. I would like to prioritize my effectiveness in the field," Gavin said.

"Agreed. We will get a line drawn up for you and a company card to use," Richmond said. "Will there be anything else? Or should I have my administrative assistant send the paperwork to you immediately?"

"I think everything is in order. I will wait for your approval to tell Kaleb, and once I sign the paperwork and receive my back pay, we will set up a time to tell my sister and Chad. Thank you, General. I look forward to working together. And we will be keeping this private for now, correct?" Gavin said.

"That is correct. You will receive the paperwork shortly." And Richmond cut the feed.

Gavin mentally celebrated. He had done it. He has gotten almost everything he had asked for and protection from a kill order. He would no longer have to deal with feeling like a disappointment to Megan. And he could work with her on the NOVA system. Her expertise would be invaluable. Hopefully, he wouldn't have to hide his life from his best friend.

Not getting away from a cover relationship with Alex meant he didn't feel like asking her out for a real relationship would be appropriate. If she said no, they would have a lot of awkwardness between them. And that could hinder their ability to work together and communicate on missions. And he couldn't have that. Not with so much on the line. With either of them able to get hurt so easily. And something with Alex is better than nothing with her.

General Richmond leaned back in her chair after she had poured herself a scotch. She had done it. After all these years. And everything she had been through. She had gotten control of a human NOVA system. It may

110

not be the ideal way for it to happen, but you could do worse than the son of Coeus, who happens to be Vidar, as the NOVA system. Now if she could convince him to find Coeus. Then, things could start to get back on track for her.

***

Alex stared at Brett's body. He had only been breathing and hadn't come to yet. She and Charles avoided direct contact with him. They had overseen his transport to a secure CIA facility. He had lost weight. He looked slightly frail. But he looked remarkably healthy for someone who was supposed to be dead and had been shot through the chest. He was strapped to a chair in a cell as she and Charles watched him through a two-way mirror. Doctors had been in and out. One said he had been speaking in his unconscious state. He kept saying Gavin's name, but it was hard to tell. Alex only knew because she had heard it so much. Another doctor came out, saying he should be conscious soon after checking him over again. And so, they were all cleared out. They were leaving Brett alone in the room.

Brett blinked his eyes. He tried to move his arms to wipe his eyes clear, but they were strapped down. He couldn't move except for his head. As he sat there, he could feel his bonds loosening slightly. It would take a while to get loose, but he knew he could now. Pendulum may have him, but he wouldn't allow them to keep him long if he could help. He had no idea how long he had been out this time. But he knew he had to get to Gavin.

Alex watched several agents go in and question Brett. But he wasn't answering anything. She had seen him take inventory of the room. She knew he was in better shape than he was letting on. She just didn't understand how he was still there. She knew the only person he would talk to was Gavin. And maybe her. But she couldn't take those risks.

Charles walked back into the observation room. He had just gotten off the phone with updating Richmond, who had been unreachable for a few hours. "We are to bring in Gavin," Charles grunted. "The natural born interrogator," he quipped sarcastically.

111

Alex disagreed with this judgment call. But she couldn't disregard a direct order, even from the General. So, she went to find Gavin.

***

Gavin had gotten to work in a great mood. Alex had kissed him the night before. After that, he got approval from the General to bring in Megan and Chad. He would get the funding for the parts and computer he needed to create a device to update the NOVA system. And he was going to get paid. Things were looking up.

He knew he would have to stay at Snollygoster Inc. as a cover job, but he didn't mind now. He wouldn't have to deal with feeling like he constantly disappointed Megan. And that meant more than he could say. He had texted Alex that morning, but she hadn't responded.

He was busy working on a laptop virus when Alex walked in. The look on her face did not look like someone ready to continue the kiss that they had had.

"Hey, what's wrong?" Gavin asked.

"Gavin. You need to come with me. You're needed for an issue," Alex said in a pure agent voice.

"Alex, what's happening?" Gavin asked hesitantly.

Alex sighed deeply. *Things were complicated enough. Are complicated enough. Why couldn't Brett have stayed dead?* she thought as she said, "Gavin, the bomb was Brett. He's alive and asking for you."

Gavin was stunned. He silently followed Alex out of the store and to her car. *Brett is alive. Of course, he is alive. And, of course, he comes back now. Now that things had just started to look better. Like I wasn't such a failure anymore.*

Alex glanced at him periodically as they made their way to the facility where Brett was being held. She knew he was glancing at her from time to time as well. There was tension there, but not the same tension as had been there the night before. She both wanted to talk to and console
112

him, while not wanting to address it and act like everything was normal. She just isn't good with emotions.

Arriving in the observation room, Gavin looked in at Brett. He kind of jumped, startled. "It's one thing to hear it, another to see he is back from the dead with your own eyes," Gavin said quietly.

Charles looked between Gavin and Alex and then back. Shaking his head, he replied, "He has been asking for you and won't talk to anyone else. So good luck in there. And remember, he's a trained assassin. So don't get too close," Charles said, riling Gavin up.

Alex glared at Charles. "You will be fine, Gavin. We are right outside the door."

Gavin gulped heavily, took a deep breath, and opened the door. He approached Brett, saying quietly, "Hey, Brett. Buddy. It's me. Gavin."

Brett kept his head down, "I don't believe you," he said in a menacing tone.

Gavin immediately turned toward the door and tried it. It was locked. "I'd like to come out now," he squeaked.

"Did they send you in here?" Brett asked.

"Who is this 'They' Brett?" Gavin said adamantly.

"WHAT HAVE YOU DONE WITH THE REAL Gavin?!" Brett yelled.

"Well, unless we are in some weird twilight zone, and I'm some kind of clone who doesn't realize he is a clone and thinks he is the original. But it is a clone. It will eventually have to be either used for parts of the original or turn evil and want to consume the original. Then yes. I am the real Gavin," Gavin said quickly. He was nervously spouting off in nerd talk.

Brett finally looked at him. "Prove it. tlhIngan Hol Dajatlh'a'?" Brett said. Gavin looked around at the two-way mirror and, embarrassed, quietly replied,

"HIja'. bIpIvqa'law'," Gavin replied.

"Your Klingon is a bit rusty," Brett teased, visibly relaxing at the confirmation it was Gavin.

"Yeah, well, I've been a bit busy since you sent me that email," Gavin said aggressively.

"So, you opened it," Brett said.

Gavin stepped closer, getting upset with him. "Yes, I opened it! What else do you do with an email?!" Gavin said in a flabbergasted tone, "And since then, my life has been flipped upside down. Was it not enough you got me kicked out of GIT to ruin my life?" Gavin was letting loose on him and didn't realize how close he had gotten.

Brett broke his arm free from the straps. He grabbed Gavin around the throat and spun him around. "Undo the other one. Now!" Brett commanded.

Gavin undid it as Alex and Charles entered the room with guns drawn. "Alex?" Brett said as he grabbed the syringe on the table by him and held it to Gavin's neck. "Back off. Both of you. Well, hi, Charles. Care to try again?" Brett said snidely at Charles. Charles just grunted and kept his gun steady.

Brett maneuvered them into the room and down the hall without presenting a good target for Charles or Alex. Getting to the elevator, he demanded the code from Alex. Who reluctantly gave them, and then they waited for the doors to close.

As soon as the doors were shut, Brett dropped the syringe to his side and laughed. "You didn't think I'd kill you, Gavin. Did you?"

"Yes, Brett! Yes, I think you are fully capable of killing me," he said in a rushed voice, clearly on edge.

114

"Gavin, I haven't gone rogue. I was on a legitimate mission. You have to believe me," Brett pleaded.

"And why should I, Brett?! What possible reason in our history have you given me to trust a word you say?" Gavin groaned.

Brett didn't show it, but that cut deep into him. He knew it was true. He knew that Gavin had no real reason to trust him. But he was going to play it as though he should.

"Why are we stopping? That's too early," Brett said as he grabbed Gavin again, who whined. He was holding the syringe to his throat, and the doors opened. There stood one man. And as soon as Gavin saw his face, he felt the NOVA system coming on. Tim Horace, presumed dead, ex-CIA, Pendulum . The doors were closing when he felt the NOVA system ending.

"Who was that?" Gavin asked. "A bad guy. He was who brought me back. He thinks I'm the NOVA system," Brett said.

"But he's supposed to be dead. Ex-CIA. Tim Horace," Gavin said before he had meant to.

"Woah, is it always that fast? The intel?" Brett asked.

"Yeah. Pretty much," Gavin murmured.

Brett looked deep in thought, feeling the elevator start to slow down again. He turned to Gavin and said, "I didn't go rogue. Tell Alex it's always hard to say goodbye. And about operation Windstorm." And as the the NOVA system went through the information in Gavin's mind, Brett inserted the needle into Gavin's shoulder. Once the NOVA system was finished, he gave Gavin the sedative and escaped through the hatch on top.

As he came to, the information from the NOVA system was still fresh on his mind. However, he had some trouble articulating what he was trying to say. Eventually, he could inform Alex and Charles about the mission Brett had been on. How Pendulum was behind it, and how they had deep CIA information. Alex looked pained the entire time. Whereas Charles just looked more pissed off than usual.

Gavin tried to put it out of his mind as he returned to work. After a while, he felt he should try talking to Alex. So, he headed across the parking lot to see if they could smooth things over and get back to being relaxed around each other.

***

Alex had finished the paperwork and was back at the Sub Express when the door opened. She sighed. She had figured that Gavin would come to talk about everything. And as she looked up, she saw Brett standing there. She reached for her gun, "What do you want Brett? Do I need to call Charles?"

"That's not necessary." Brett kept walking toward her slowly. Reaching the counter, he started to lean. "I haven't gone rogue, Alex. Did Gavin tell you?" Brett said in a breathy voice.

"Yes. He did," Alex replied. Not noticing herself, she got comfortable.

Brett was leaning over the counter now, inches from Alex's face. "I need your help, Alex. I need you to bring me in," Brett continued in the same breathy voice. He was emphasizing when he said 'need.' Alex felt herself lean into him. And as their lips met, Brett pulled her into the kiss.

Gavin looked up when he reached the tables outside the Sub Express and saw Alex leaning over the counter kissing Brett. Like she had told him the night before, his world shattered. He had a hard time breathing. He couldn't help it. He turned around and walked back to the Snollygoster Inc. dejectedly.

Getting to his desk, Charles came up to him. "Alex called and said she had Brett and was taking him in. Don't worry. I'm sure the CIA will have a new catalog with all the fresh skirts for you to choose from," Charles said, then turned around and headed back to his desk

116

I'm sure she is, maybe after a quick stop to get reacquainted. And she didn't even bother herself to say goodbye. Gavin was lost in his pitiful world of moping when he heard the bell ring. Looking up, he saw Tim Horace there. He was hitting the button on his watch and looking over at Charles.

"Oh, don't worry about your NSA handler there, Gavin. We are taking care of him." Tim said in a menacing voice, "Where is Brett Martin?"

Gavin looked panicked. "I don't know where he is. If I did, I would tell you, but I don't," Gavin stammered.

"That's fine. I'll take you and see if that's true," Tim said as he grabbed Gavin by the shirt and made him come around the deck. Holding a gun, he started walking him out the door.

Kevin came up in a panic, "Gavin, the phones are down. What do we do?" Kevin was drunk and didn't realize what was going on.

"Say more than a few words to him, and I will kill you both right here," Tim threatened.

Gavin looked at Kevin and said, "Grapefruit." And Kevin's eyes got big as he rushed off. They had safety drills all the time, and even Kevin knew that Grapefruit meant there was a fire.

Tim continued to walk Gavin out a few more feet before Kevin came over the intercom, "Ladies and gentlemen, please evacuate the store. NOW! EVERYONE OUT NOW! GRAPEFRUIT, GRAPEFRUIT, GRAPEFRUIT!"

Suddenly, chaos broke out. People were running everywhere, bumping into them. One knocked the gun out of Tommy's hand. Gavin got knocked loose, immediately dropped to the floor, and went to his office. Charles quickly followed him.

Charles put his hand on the coffee table, and a light scanned it. He was opening up to a gun safe. Pulling out an M-4 and a tranq gun, he turned to Gavin. "This is where the fun begins." Hitting a button in the gun

117

safe, the glass was reinforced with bulletproof glass. "Stay in here. And guard the doors. Stay low." Charles made his way toward a door.

***

Alex had made it a few miles when her phone dinged. Gavin's emergency distress call was going off. Alex spun the car around. "Where are you going?" Brett asked. "Gavin is in trouble. He is my mission," Alex said in a dead tone. She hadn't talked much since they got in the car.

They pulled up around the back of the Snollygoster Inc. and made their way through the loading docks. Brett looked over at her as they looked at the main shopping area. "Ready, Mrs. Smith?" Brett asked in a jovial tone. But Alex just gave a dead smile in reply. And they started into the room.

Charles had shot a few of them, but they were starting to surround him. Gavin was crouched down and watching. Then he saw a flash of brown hair. Looking in that direction, he saw Brett and Alex making quick work of the bad guys. Feet and fists were flying everywhere. *Man, they are a great team.* He thought sadly.

Alex and Brett took out ten guys as Charles took out another seven. Brett saw Tim from the corner of his eye, gun pointed at Alex. And before he can react, a shot went off.

It seemed like time was frozen. Everyone held their breath. Everyone except Gavin, who had just shot Tim in the neck with his tranq gun by his office. Tim collapsed to the floor in a heap.

***

While Gavin and Brett talked, Alex and Charles called for clean-up and detention crews. "I never meant to ruin your life, Gavin. I always thought you'd bounce back," Brett explained.

"You took everything away from me, Brett. All my dreams were for after I had graduated from GIT. I had nothing," Gavin said.

"For what it's worth. I'm sorry. And sorry for getting you into this life now," Brett said. "Well, what's done is done, I guess."

After a few moments of silence, Gavin saw Charles was off the phone and started to head that way. Brett headed into Charles' office for a debriefing and briefing on his next assignment.

After about half an hour, Brett came strolling out in a tux. Walking up to them, he said his form of goodbye. "Charles." Charles just grunted and walked off. "Gavin. Be careful."

Gavin asked, "Where are you headed?"

"I'm sorry, Gavin," Brett replied, "Not even you can know that."

Then he turned to Alex, and Gavin tried to act like he wasn't there. "Alex," Brett said, taking her hand. He started rubbing the inside of her wrist with his thumb. "We will always have Miami," Brett said as he turned and walked out.

Alex's face was a complete agent mask now as Gavin turned to try and start talking to her. "Alex. I'm sorry. For everything that happened." He started but then stopped when she was giving no response back. He felt rejected all over again.

***

Gavin got home and was lying in bed, tossing and turning. *It's over. She is going to leave. I can feel it. Why would she stay? I've run her off because I'm not a spy.* When he thought about what Brett had said, *we will always have Miami.* And suddenly, his eyes shot open. He reached for his phone and called Alex repeatedly when she wouldn't pick up.

***

Alex was in her room. She didn't remember getting there. *What is happening to me?* She thought as she looked around. Her hand was on her phone, which was buzzing. All while the room phone was going

119

off. She looked down, and she had her suitcase in her hand. And her go bag was sitting on the bed. She had packed to leave for good.

She looked down and saw Gavin's smiling face. And she dropped her phone. Her head started throbbing. She grabbed her bag and threw it across the room. And she then kicked her suitcase. Throwing off her clothes, she climbed into the shower. *Why don't I remember getting here? And packed?* Alex thought as she collapsed against the shower wall and started to cry, not understanding where the emotions were coming from or why her head was hurting so bad.

Chapter 8

:/The Replacement

Gavin kept his distance from Alex for a while. He was busy, was his excuse. But really, he didn't know how to approach her. He hadn't seen her for almost a week after Brett left. He had assumed she went with him. And when he did finally see her, she looked ragged. Like she hadn't slept well in days. And definitely didn't seem happy to see him.

She is holding it against me that she wasn't able to leave and do what she wants with who she wants. I can't blame her for being mad. I had thought that that kiss meant something. But it was just an end-of-life kiss. And I happened to be there. Gavin was morose.

Charles noticed but didn't say anything. He had started training with Gavin in weapons. And to his surprise, the kid was a fast learner.

For the last week, it was limited to a tranq gun, which Charles detested. But he understood where Gavin was coming from and respected his stance. Though he would never tell him that in so many words. Gavin could already identify weapons, their use in situational combat, and disassemble and reassemble them faster than any cadet Charles had seen. And his aim was immaculate. It was like watching a painter, really. But if Charles had to hear one more line about Duck Hunt.

121

"Hey, Charles. I was wondering if I should start any hand-to-hand combat training," Gavin said while poorly mimicking some kung fu.

"I think that that is a good idea. But Alex would be the go-to on that. She is the expert in close quarter killing," Charles said with a smirk. He knows the tension. He also knew that letting Alex beat on the kid a bit may help matters get back to normal.

"Oh. Ok. I guess I should go try to talk to her then," Gavin stuttered out.

Charles gave a grunt. *Number 3: "I don't really care what you do, just don't let me hear about your lady feelings,"* Gavin thought with a smile. And then that smile faded when he thought again about talking to Alex. He had found it odd what Brett had said, but he couldn't find anything in the files he had pulled to help him. And he was still waiting for the other project files to decrypt. They were massive. And he knew that once he had them decrypted, it would take a while before he could get through all the information. So, he tried to focus on acting normal and made his way across the parking lot.

***

Alex had spent the last few days filing all the paperwork she had. At least, that is what she kept telling herself. She knew she was really just avoiding Gavin. She didn't know what had happened. She had kissed him. Then Brett showed up. Gavin understandably reclused and had hardly reached out in the last week.

Charles had been keeping her appraised. She may be avoiding Gavin, but she wasn't avoiding her duty. She made sure that Charles didn't need her. He said that Gavin had asked to start some training. Not a bad idea, but it still scared her. He didn't need more of a reason to get out of the car.

I still don't even understand what happened. Why I was packed to leave. Why I don't remember packing or even leaving the Snollygoster Inc. I don't remember anything after Brett said goodbye. Did he say Goodbye? He must have. He came out of the Gavin's office and then.

Fuzzy. Just like a few days before. He had come into the Sub Express and then fuzzy. Why can I not remember?

She looked up and saw Gavin heading toward her. *Can't worry about that now. Have to fix this, or I have to get reassigned. And even with everything. I can't leave Gavin.* She thought as she made herself look busy wiping down the counter.

Gavin walked into the Sub Express, and he wasn't sure what he would say. He knew there was a lot that they had to discuss. And yet, he just wasn't sure he was ready to. He isn't ready to talk about it or give her up. He had tried this last week. But it's not that easy. Every time, he thought about her. *Her smile. Her laugh. Those eyes.* He shook his head. *Focus, Gavin.* "Hey," Gavin started awkwardly with a half-smile.

"Hey," Alex said. She was surprised at how nervous she was. And at the same time, just talking to Gavin brought her calm. *Something I've never had in my life. Seeing him brings a peace I haven't known.* She shook her head. "What's up?"

"I… I wanted to talk to you… I saw you kiss Brett," Gavin blurted out. His face was as shocked as hers was.

I had kissed Brett? When did that happen? Is that what happened while I was fuzzy? "Gavin, I..." Alex started.

But Gavin interrupted her, "No, Alex it's ok. It makes sense. He always did get the best girls. I just wanted to tell you that I'm glad you're still here. And I will strive better to be more professional going forward. I don't want to be a burden on your time here. Or at least as little of one as possible," he said with a self-deprecating smile.

NO! That isn't what I want. Alex's inner voice screamed. *Why can't you see it? Why can't you understand? You are enough for me. You are more than I deserve. Why can't I just say this? Because then you will, for sure, be transferred. Straight face. Don't let anyone see. He's always been able to read past the mask. Hopefully, he can again.*

123

Gavin saw that he wasn't getting a response from her, so he continued, "I actually, umm, I've been doing some training with Charles to, uh, you know, better protect myself. So, it's not always on you guys. And he said that I should talk to you about learning hand-to-hand combat. He said you're the best." Gavin got quieter as he spoke. Until the last part was just a whisper.

"Oh, he said that did he? That was nice of him," Alex replied. *What are you playing at Charles? You could train him on what he would need to know. Simple, basic self-defense. He doesn't need a black belt in six art forms. Though I won't complain about one-on-one time with minimal clothing and his body on mine.* Alex finished that thought with a slight blush. "Yeah. Ahem. Yeah, we can do that. When did you want to start?" Alex asked.

"I mean, I'm free tonight. Unless we have a mission, I really rarely have much going on," Gavin lied. He couldn't say, 'Well, I spend most of my evenings working on either new programming for the NOVA system or building devices for the NSA. Specifically designed to help us in the field. Oh, and by the way, I'm no longer labeled an asset officially.'

"Great. So, pick you up around six?" Alex offered. "It's a date," Gavin said. Getting flush, he realized what he had said. "No. I mean, that sounds good. Not a date. I wouldn't consider it a date. I mean, unless you did. No. It's not a date. It's just training. Like friends. Or partners. Work associates. Yeah. You're like my boss. Training me. I'm going to shut up now. See you later," Gavin ducked his head and walked out the door.

He really truly doesn't understand how adorable he is. Alex thinks, her brain feeling a million times lighter than it had in over a week. She had a slight smile on her face. *A date.* She slowly shook her head and continued wiping down the counter that didn't need cleaning. It just gave her hands something to do.

***

Brett Martin stepped off the airplane in Omaha, Nebraska. Pulling out his phone, he dialed the number. "No, she didn't follow protocol. I know. I'm about to get a train to Chicago and will be out of the country by the end of the day. No, this was something else. I am going to The Westgate to see what's going on. Of course, I will report back as soon as I know more. Keep me posted on the activity here and keep your head down. I think this is just the beginning," he said as he hung up and climbed onto the train.

***

Gavin got home from work, quickly changed into his workout clothes, and remembered that it was only 4 p.m. He had three hours still before Alex was going to pick him up. So, he sat at his computer and worked on some stuff. He had several programs he was developing, as well as the programs for the NOVA system. It seemed that this shock to his life was the kick in the pants he needed to get back to doing what he loved.

He was elbows deep in his coding when the computer dinged, signaling an incoming video call. He brought up the call, and General Richmond was there. "Hello, Analyst Michaels. Your call sign will be Chaos. You can thank Agent Charles for that. No, you don't pick your call sign. Your senior Agent does. And in your case, former handler. Alex was not privy to the information that you had joined our ranks and, as such, had no input. You should be receiving your first check soon, along with your funding card and key to your new apartment. As soon as you would be able, I would like to get Drs. Kennedy and Woodford on board as well," the General started.

"Furthermore, it has come to my attention that you accessed several files you didn't have the proper paperwork for. I will let it slide this time, seeing as you have the highest clearance in the nation. Being the NOVA system has its perks. But don't make a habit of it. If you really want something, ask. If I can't get it, I'll sanction you to get it. Orders make a difference in this world.

"On a more personal note, I would like to talk to you about some of what you had hinted at from my past. After I had thought about it, I felt you should know more of the story. I can't tell everything because it is not mine to tell, and I don't know it all. But I can tell you that your parents did not want to leave you. They did it only to protect you.

"Yes, I worked closely with your parents for many years. As did Director Hunter, which you already know. Your mother's call sign was Agent Hel, and, as you know, your father's Coeus. Your mother was the top CIA agent in several generations. Many of her records still stand at the Farm, only surpassed by Agent Johnson." She paused there, noticing a slight hint of pride on his face at the mention of Agent Johnson.

"I am telling you this because I know you would dig until you found it anyway. This will save us both valuable time. If I knew more, I would tell you. I only ask your searching for them not interfere with your other work.

"I am going out on quite a limb here for you. Please don't make me regret this," Richmond concluded.

Gavin sat there for a moment, processing. The general hadn't ended the call, indicating she awaited his response. But he was struggling to accept everything she had just told him.

"Thank you for telling me all of that. I won't let it affect my work. I have several things that I believe will help revolutionize the way spies infiltrate a building. And a few other things I'm not yet ready to share. Agent Johnson will be coming to get me soon to start my hand-to-hand combat training. And I will get with you on a good time to bring my sister into the mix. Though I think for now, don't tell her everything about Mom and Dad. Please. It may be too much for her," Gavin said after a long pause.

"That sounds good. Will training with Agent Johnson be an issue?" the General asked.

"I don't believe so. We talked this afternoon, and she seemed to be her normal self. I will give a briefing after tonight's session," Gavin said.

126

"That would be good. If that is all?" And with that, General Richmond ended the conversation.

***

A few hours later, there was a knock on his window. Gavin cleared off his desk and closed out the programs. He knew no one would likely understand what it was, but better safe than sorry.

Opening the blinds, he saw Alex in an oversized shirt and leggings. He waved and then unlocked the window, and she pulled it open. "Are you ready?" Alex asked, her voice seemed hesitantly excited.

"Yeah. I was just working on a few things. Trying to get over my programming block. You know how it is," Gavin said.

Alex smiled softly with her little side smile. "Ready to go?" she said as she reached out her hand.

"Yeah, but why don't we use the front door?" Gavin joked. "The window can only be locked one way. And my sister isn't home. So, we don't have to hold hands," Gavin said, trying to keep it as professional as possible.

Alex felt like she had gotten a slight punch to the gut with that last comment. Here was Gavin reminding her that it was a cover. *And what if I feel it's worth the risk.* She surprised herself by thinking. And with that, they left.

She headed back to her apartment. "So, where are we training? I hate to say it, but you might draw some attention at a gym. And the Snollygoster Inc. doesn't offer much room," Gavin said, trying to keep the tone light.

"Actually, we are going to train at my apartment. I have a heavy-speed bag set up there and room for us to spar. Not a lot, but enough. And it would keep you away from prying eyes," Alex said.

"It's not me that would have all the eyes on them," Gavin murmured, but Alex heard him and grinned slightly.

They started with some light warm-ups once they got to her apartment. And then ran the heavy bag and speed bag. She showed Gavin what to do, and he quickly picked it up.

After a while, Gavin had worked up a sweat. He didn't have the muscle or endurance that Alex did, and it was showing. But now it was time to spar. Gavin got his headgear on and gloves. While Alex grabbed her gloves and took off her shirt.

Gavin froze. It felt like time slowed as inch after inch of Alex's skin was revealed. She was just standing there putting on her gloves, leggings, and wearing a sports bra. *Dear god, what is she doing to me?* Gavin felt like he couldn't breathe. He couldn't move. He could blink. *And I thought I could be strictly professional? HA right. Stop staring at your idiot. She's probably more than uncomfortable,* Gavin berated himself.

Alex smirked to herself. *Looks like I picked the right outfit. This will teach him not to get distracted while in a fight. Yeah. That's why I wore it. It had nothing to do with the warm feeling I get when he can't take his eyes off of me. Or the fact that a simple gasp from him turns me on more than the most eloquent dirty talk from anyone else. That has NOTHING to do with it,* Alex thought as she continued to smirk.

"Ready?" she said, turning to Gavin.

He cleared his throat a few times. "Yeah. Uh. Yeah, of course. But I can't hit a girl." Gavin said.

Alex laughed. *Of course, he can't. He's a real man. Even if the woman could kill him, he can't fathom violence against a woman. That's how his sister raised him, no doubt.*

"Tell you what. If you can land a punch on me, I'm buying dinner. And I'll also toss in a new video game for you," she said with a teasing tone.

"Oh, game on," Gavin said with a laugh.

It's nice to be comfortable with each other again. Even if I'm not EXACTLY comfortable, Gavin thought as they got into position. Alex started moving, and it was all he could do to keep up. She got on him several times with no force. He knew she was toying with him, but the speed with which she moved was mesmerizing. As she kept moving, he felt it.

She felt the NOVA system logging her movement. Slowly, he was seeing what she was doing. It definitely wasn't instantaneous like when he accessed the NOVA system, but this was almost like he had booted it up in safe mode. Like it had a learning feature. He wasn't sure which NOVA system it was that was doing it. The first one his dad wrote when he was nine, or the one he got from Brett.

He felt himself seeing the movements in ways he never had before. *Had I ever tried, though? Not really. I wasn't focused on athletics or martial arts. I focused on classwork and computers. That's what I learned. What I loved.* Gavin thought. Did one of the NOVA systems just help learn?

He felt his brain starting to get hot. His head started to hurt. Right as he began to be able to block Alex's punches, his eyesight started to darken around the edges. And suddenly, the world went black.

Alex thought it would be fun to mess with him a bit. So, she started doing some highly advanced Muay Thai and Krav Maga quickly. Only tapping him instead of hitting outright. To begin with, he just stood there, his eyes darting back and forth. *This is different. I've never seen someone do this. Obviously wouldn't work in a fight, but he is studying me, even at this pace,* she thought.

Then his arms started moving. Slowly at first, and then after a few minutes, he blocked most of her attacks. Even if she changed to Tae Kwon Do, he kept up. *I've never seen anything like this.* She was stunned. No one had kept up with her before, not like this.

And then suddenly, he collapsed.

"Gavin!" Alex screamed as she hurried over to him. Picking him up and cradling him in her arms. They had been sparring for almost fifteen minutes straight, at high speeds. *Maybe he just was dehydrated. I must have pushed him too hard this first time. Damn it, Johnson. You know better. He is a novice.* She was worried. But he had already started to wake up. His head felt extremely hot.

What is going on? Gavin thought groggily as he came out of his unconscious state. He slowly opened his eyes to find he was nuzzled into Alex's mostly naked torso. In fact, his face was almost entirely on her breasts. His eyes got huge, and he shot up. *Big mistake.* He got lightheaded again and had to sit on the chair that was right next to him.

Alex rushed over and got him some water. "Gavin, I am so sorry. I must have pushed you too hard for your first training session. I'll keep that in mind more. And maybe we can also start some workouts during the week," Alex said apologetically.

"Yeah. I must have. And sorry if I fell on you or something. I didn't mean to." *Touch your amazing body. But I can't finish that sentiment. And you don't need to know just yet about the NOVA system doing this. Not until I know I can trust you,* Gavin thought. His head was still whirling. However, he wasn't sure if it's because of the fainting spell or where he woke up.

"No. You're ok. I came over and held you after you fell. I had to check to be sure you were okay before calling Charles or your sister," Alex said, sounding worried still.

"I'll be ok. Just a bit light-headed still. But I do think I'm done for the day. And I didn't hit you, so dinner is on me," Gavin said with a laugh. *I'll talk to Megan about this once she has read everything.*

Alex laughed and lightly swatted his arm, and she stood. "Sounds good. But how about we order something in? I don't feel like changing." *Unless you want to watch. CALM DOWN, Johnson!* Alex said. She shakes her head. *Where is this coming from? I need to settle down. The way he is acting, he wants it to be professional,* she thought as she got a drink of water herself.

"Deal!" Gavin said as he got out his phone to order some pizza.

***

The next day, Gavin had dinner with Megan and Chad, intending to tell them then, so they had a heads up when they met with the General. Which also was planned for after dinner.

As they all sat down, Gavin killed the feeds for the apartment and put them on a loop. Charles could find out from the General later if she wanted him to know. "Megan, Chad. I have something I want to talk to you about. It's fairly serious," Gavin started.

"It must be if you used my first name. What's up, bro?" Chad chimed. He's always the supportive guy.

"Yeah, Gavin, you can tell us anything. You know that," Megan added, a hint of concern in her tone.

"Ok. Let me start by saying that I will be moving out soon. The apartment across the courtyard is coming available, and I plan on snagging it," Gavin said to which Megan got excited.

"Are you moving in with Alex?!" She squealed.

"Umm. No. On my own," Gavin said. A bit sheepishly.

"Oh. How can you afford it?" Megan asked earnestly.

"Well. That is the other thing I wanted to talk to you both about," Gavin started. "I have a second job. In a way."

Megan looked at him in an odd way. She knew that there was more to this. "What kind of job?" she asked.

"I know that this is going to sound crazy, but I promise I'm not losing my mind. And I will prove it to you after we finish eating," he prefaced. Megan looked at him expectantly, while Chad didn't know where to look.

"I'm working for the government," Gavin said and winced.

Megan rolled her eyes and looked at him, "Seriously, Gavin. What's going on?" Megan sounded frustrated.

"I am serious, Meg," Gavin insisted, "I started working as an analyst for the NSA, but there is more." He proceeded to tell them the story of how he got the NOVA system.

The screen behind them in the living room came alive with General Richmond. "He is not lying. Hello Dr. Woodford, Dr. Kennedy. I am General Richmond, Director of the NSA. And I have given Gavin approval to read you in. I can assure you that none of what he has just told you is a lie. And yes, I was listening. He is an incredibly valuable asset to the United States Intelligence Community.

"His analytical skills are also second to none. Which is why I hired him instead of keeping him as an asset. When he mentioned he could have you as a neurologist to keep tabs and potentially help understand and control the NOVA system in his head, I had to take that opportunity. And seeing as your fiancé is a skilled surgeon, it would be prudent to have him on the team as well," Richmond stated, "Obviously, we would pay you well, you could keep your potion and tenure at Foreman Medical, and we would upgrade you to your own lab and NSA certified assistant. They would not have authorization for your research, but they could do anything you told them to."

Megan was stunned. She didn't expect this kind of news. And Alex wasn't ever actually Gavin's girlfriend? That didn't seem right. She saw how that woman looked at her brother. She had feelings for him. Real feelings. "Ok. I'm not happy I have been kept in the dark, but as a part of it and as his doctor, I will at least have more of a say as to what he is involved in. And what kind of danger he is exposed to. I can limit that, correct?" Megan asked.

"I wish someone would," General Richmond sighed. "Yes, you will have a medical say regarding permission to go on a mission. As long as it isn't abused." She gave a stern look to Megan.

"Of course, I will do my best to keep the fact that he is my brother and my patient separate. And we can discuss pay and everything else at another time. I can only speak for myself. But I am in," Megan said with a tight smile.

I'm going to hear about this a lot. But I'm glad she didn't freak out, Gavin thought.

"Awesome. I am definitely in!" Chad said.

"Very well, I will have the paperwork drawn up and sent to you by the end of tomorrow. We will move forward from there. And we will soon have a base of operations strictly for Team Woodford. I will keep everyone updated on that. Thank you for your time." And with that, the General ended the call.

"Hey, that's far more than she normally gives for a goodbye," Gavin joked with a cringing look at Megan.

"We need to talk," Megan said sternly.

***

Coeus made his way out of an unmarked building. He hadn't been detected. Just like he planned. He pulled up his wrist computer and typed an encrypted message.

/:IT IS DONE:/

He sighed as he climbed into the cab. He hoped Gavin had been able to get his side done already.

***

After their talk, Megan felt better about the situation. She was still unconvinced that Alex didn't have feelings for Gavin, but she wouldn't pry. Much. She WAS a part of the team now and needed to ensure what could be affecting the NOVA system. But Gavin had asked her not to. And even more, Chad had told her to back off. She would respect them.

Gavin was worried his sister would push things with Alex. He always wanted it to be Alex's choice. Not for her to feel obligated to be with him. Whether through duty or Megan. He wanted it to be for sure what she wanted. *I don't feel that that is too much to desire. I want her to be happy. That's more important than being with her.*

***

Gavin was spacing out at work the next day, thinking about the last few nights. But even while spacing out, it was hard to miss the pizza girl coming in for another delivery. Kyle and Kevin, two of Gavin's coworkers, were standing too close to her, too close for anyone to be comfortable.

As he waited, he watched her interact with his sleazy coworkers. He had never seen someone being so kind to them. Even if they had to. After she left, they were busy staring at the recording they got, and they missed her stopping at the new credit card display as she left.

That's more than odd. She was nice to them, and now this. She's not normal, to say the least. Charles and Alex have taught me that if something acts suspiciously, treat it accordingly. Gavin thought as he went over to the credit card display as she walked out.

He looked it over, and it wasn't that hard to see. A bug. He accessed the NOVA system. Specifically, a GT-722 CIA bug. One that went missing during a raid several years ago. And now belonged to Pendulum. Grabbing it and disarming it, he walked over to Charles. "I think we need a lunch. Right now," he said curtly. Charles nodded with a grunt and followed him across the parking lot.

Tossing the bug on the counter, Gavin explained what he had accessed the NOVA system on. "That kind is high-quality audio but needs a receiver. Somewhere close by. Within 30 yards," Charles growled.

"The pizza delivery girl planted it. And she has been in every day this month with a delivery for Kevin and Kyle. So, I think there are more. And that she is Pendulum," Gavin said. "Let me see the bug. I may be able to build a scanner that picks up its frequency to the receiver so that we can find the receiver and make it irrelevant."

Charles didn't seem happy about it, but Alex struggled to hide her fear. *They are going to take him away from me. Take him away and put him in a bunker. I can't let them take him. I can't say goodbye. But now.* Her mind was beginning to get hysterical. She couldn't let that happen. Not when things were just beginning to make sense.

"Please do that. And we will try to hunt down this pizza delivery girl," Alex said, focusing on not letting her voice portray her emotion.

Gavin took the bug and went to the cage in the back of the store. He knew no one would bother him while he was in there. They never do, so that he doesn't put them to work. And even if they did, they wouldn't understand what he was doing.

After he found the correct frequency for the bug to the receiver, it was easy to create a scanner for that frequency to locate the receiver. He made it to be reversed as well and be able to identify the bugs, too. With her visiting that often, he figured this wasn't the only bug.

While he did that, Charles kept General Richmond up to date. She told him that Hunter would push a kill order, especially since the new NOVA system, which had been his baby, was almost operational. She told him to keep an eye on Alex as well as Gavin. She wasn't sure where the younger lady's loyalties lay just yet.

They had agreed that Gavin would return that night to hunt down the bugs and receiver. And now it was just to find the pizza girl. That was Alex's job. She got the Snollygoster Inc. security footage and an image of the girl. She was running her through the database when Gavin walked in. "Hey, I figure it is a fake name, but I asked Kevin and Kyle where they ordered the pizza from and who they asked for," Gavin said with a shrug. "Here is the number they call, the card she gave them, and her name on her badge."

"That is actually really helpful. Thank you, Gavin. I hadn't thought to talk to them," Alex said, a bit surprised that Gavin had done such great investigating.

"Yeah, well. I'm not sure you'd have been able to get everything from them as quickly as I did. You're female, and they get really weird around women," Gavin said with a laugh.

"Ha, well, thank you either way. I should be able to hunt her down a lot easier," Alex said as she started to pull up the restaurant's information. Gavin had gone back to work, and so she called Charles. "Hey, I'm thinking we get what we can tonight and have Kevin and Kyle call in another order tomorrow. I can come by while she is there, and it will be easier to take her by surprise than to try to go hunting."

"That's a good plan, Johnson. I will get things set up over here." Charles ended the call and got to work setting up for tomorrow's discreet ambush.

***

That night, Gavin entered the Snollygoster Inc. with Charles and Alex. He started searching for the receiver, entering his boss's office. He got into his safe and found the receiver, just in time to see someone drop into Snollygoster Inc. from the vent in the roof. He dove under the desk.

Alex watched the person coming down the rope, making her way over to where they would land. She wasn't taking any chances. She had a gun drawn and ready to take them out. Just then, a drunk Kevin and Kyle burst in from the hall to the break room.

Gavin heard Kevin and Kyle and made a break for the door. He saw the intruder looking in the other direction at the chaos that was his coworkers. And so, he crawled into the racks across from the entrance. Putting the tracker in his pocket and pulling out his tranq gun.

The person went into the boss's office and looked in his safe. *It's the pizza girl.* Gavin thinks as he starts trying to get out of the line of sight. He sees her turn towards Kevin and Kyle. And so, thinking quickly, he leans into the aisle and fired his tranq gun into their legs. Kyle dropped with one. But it took three for Kevin before he finally fell. *That man's body is craving a detox,* he thought with a shake of his head.

Turning, he saw feet. "I believe you have something of mine," a feminine voice asked, with a gun pointed at his head.

Just then, a foot kicked the gun up. Alex jumped in front of her and kicked her back. They started fighting. Fists flying, feet striking ribs and arms. Alex ducked to take a swipe at her legs. And then the pizza girl dropped. Out cold. She turned to see Gavin still on the ground, with his tranq gun raised.

"Sorry, I figured that was faster," he said with a slight grin. Alex rolled her eyes, trying not to smile herself. *He really does have my back.* Alex thought happily to herself. *Why does that make me feel safer than I ever have? I've had good partners before. Brett was good.* Alex was really struggling to figure out where she was within herself. Always feeling at odds.

They finished finding the bugs and the receiver, and Charles put Kevin and Kyle back in the break room. They reported in and left.

Gavin walked Alex out to her car. "Hey, thank you for having my back tonight," Alex said shyly.

"Always. It was really no big deal. You could have taken her, and you always do that for me," Gavin said dismissively.

Alex just smiled at him. *Just tell him. Tell him he means more. More than the job. More than the mission. More than anyone else has. Tell him.* Alex thought. *You can't. They will reassign you. You won't be able to stay. And then what will happen? You know Hunter. You know he will send you far away. It will take any goodness you have left away. And he'd enjoy that. Your soul is completely dead.*

Her smile faded. "It's my job to protect you. Not yours to protect me," she said as she made her way to her car. "I'll see you tomorrow for training, Gavin," she said as she opened the door and climbed in.

Gavin was left there. The mood shifted so drastically that it almost felt like a cold wind came through. He watched the taillights of her BMW for a while. And then made his way back into his room. Megan and Chad were working. He was alone. Other than the cameras, he was about to put on a loop. *Just when you think there is more. It was always just the job,* he felt as he got to work on his programs.

Chapter 9

:/The Mind

Gavin was working on the program for the NOVA system, when he had an incoming call. Answering the call from the General, he was surprised to see her looking slightly disheveled. "What's wrong, General?" Gavin said, worried.

"Analyst Woodford, the NOVA system2 was scheduled to be booted up tonight. Hunter had pushed for an execution order by Charles. He didn't believe Alex would do it, for some reason," she started. Her voice clipped, and her tone somber. "It has become irrelevant. When it was booted up, it exploded. Killing several agents along with Hunter himself."

Gavin froze. *Hunter is dead?* He was struggling to come to terms with it, but he noticed that the General had more to say. "Please continue, General," Gavin said.

"I know it's a lot to take in, but there is more. You have had several accesses to the NOVA system on the terrorist faction called Pendulum. Is that correct?"

"Yes, General," Gavin replied.

"My intelligence has led me to believe there is more than just Pendulum out there. They are, in fact, part of the largest infestation of domestic terrorist groups we have seen to date. Pendulum seems to be just a branch of them. A subsidiary of their global operations. Soon, there will be a Collective expert brought onto the team to help with their knowledge of this group. I wanted you to know, so you can get a head start on investigating this group," Richmond said.

"I will begin looking into this immediately," Gavin said. Eager to get to work.

"Report back anything that you find. Directly to me. My eyes only," Richmond said, and then she ended the call. Gavin immediately got to work.

***

Alex sat there staring at her phone. *He's gone.* He wasn't a father figure. She wasn't delusional. But he had been a constant in her life for the last ten years. Since her dad got sent away by *this same man.* She thought with a shrug. She knew her dad deserved it, but he was still her dad. *Will I be recalled now? With the reshuffle of the CIA? Am I going to get reassigned?* Alex started to worry.

She looked at her phone again. Trying to process what she should do. *I can't get reassigned.* Just then, her phone rang again. She didn't recognize the number, but that was standard. She answered it numbly.

"Johnson secure."

"Agent Johnson. You don't know me, but I have followed your career for a while. This is Director of the DOC David Lawson. I am calling to give you your new assignment and designation." Director Lawson said.

Alex panicked. *If they want me to leave, I will quit. I'm not leaving. I can't. I just...*

"You are to be labeled as an agent of the DOC, designation to CIA, on permanent loan to the NSA for a special project. You will be permanently stationed in your current assignment. And we will be setting up a base there for you all. We have purchased a good portion of the shopping complex and will be performing renovations soon and quickly. General Richmond will contact you soon to give you any new designations you need. I know your time under Hunter was unique, and you spent a lot of time with him. If you need some time off to grieve, we understand. Please let us know if there is anything more you need. And welcome to the DOC." And with that, the phone call ended.

Alex sat there stunned. *I'm not leaving. I'm here permanently with Gavin. I have triple security. This has never been done.* She didn't know how to process everything yet. And then her phone rang again.

"Johnson secure," she said with less intensity.

"Hello, Agent Johnson. I wanted to call and speak with you directly, one on one." General Richmond said. "I assume you have now been updated on recent events?" she asked as tentatively as she could.

"Yes, ma'am. I have been brought up to date on the situation as it stands," Alex said. Her training is taking over.

"Good. Then, this should be a simpler call. I am happy to have you designated to our team. You are the first agent to ever be labeled with complete coverage. You have no end to your jurisdiction as of the moment you sign the new contract. Being DOC, you have a designation of CIA and loaned to NSA. But the DOC covers all other branches as well. Of course, you, me, and the team are the only ones who will know this."

Alex nodded. Her voice seemed to falter. It was just getting to be all too much. Then, realizing that Richmond couldn't hear a nod, she choked out a "Yes, Ma'am."

"You will have the rest of the day and tomorrow to figure out whether you want this. If you decide not to, you will return to the CIA only and be reassigned elsewhere." Richmond continued.

"The extra time is not needed. I know I will accept now," Alex interrupted before she was able to realize it.

Richmond smirked at this. "Good. I was hoping you'd say that. You're allowed to take the funeral off and the days around it. As well as tomorrow. Take time to process before we get back to work. Once we do, it will not be able to stop for a while. Thank you." And Alex was alone with her thoughts once again.

***

Alex went to get Gavin, and they went on a run. Running had always been able to help clear her head. She got lost in thought a few times, thinking about Hunter being gone and what all that would mean for her as a person and her career. She was surprised that Gavin did a decent job of keeping up with her, but she was hardly winded when they finished. She took him to her apartment again for more training. Slower this time.

He looks good, sweaty. She struggled to not feel the heat rising in herself. "Okay, Gavin. So, we will go a lot slower this time. We can start with basics." She positioned herself in a stance. "Just copy me to start with." And Gavin got his body in the same position.

They progressed through several positions and then started to pick up speed. Gavin was learning quickly, and he felt okay so far. *Maybe it was just the sheer speed of the last time.* He thought as they went through more positions. Moving faster now. Then Alex turned to him. They went through the positions against each other. *This feels like it should be a montage.* Gavin thought with a laugh.

"What's so funny?" Alex asked.

"Oh, I just was thinking that we were making our 80s kung fu montage where the hero is trained by the legendary warrior who had given up violence, only to be sucked back in by the loss of their loved one," Gavin replied, trying to mimic the trailer voice at the end.

Alex was laughing. She was having trouble keeping her position. *I've never laughed so easily.* "So, does that make me the legendary warrior?" Alex said with a sassy smirk.

"Alex, most everything about you is legendary." Gavin said in an earnest tone. Causing Alex to blush slightly. "And if I can't fight, I could always make them laugh, just to throw them off guard, and then strike!" Gavin said as he reached out and poked her side, tickling her. To her surprise, it worked. She jumped. She hadn't known she was ticklish.

"Oh, you're going to regret that, Woodford," she said in her best Charles impersonation. She lunged at him. All protocols and positions were forgotten. She tackled him as she was laughing.

"Hey! This isn't fair! You're supposed to be training me!" Gavin said as he was laughing. Falling onto his back, he tried to get away. But not too hard. He was enjoying this torture. "Do your worst!" he said, followed by a shriek as she softly jabbed his ribs.

Alex landed on top of him. Straddling his torso, she tickled him a bit, causing him to squirm underneath her. *This moment is perfect.* She thought as he tickled her back. Forcing her to grab his wrists and pin them down. His squirming had had an effect on her.

Both were breathing heavily as she held his hands above his head. Slowly, they became acutely aware of the position they had ended up in. Neither made a quick escape to end it. Staring into each other's eyes, Alex felt it. She felt the love in his eyes. The same look was always there from the moment she bumped into him at the club. And it almost brought her to tears.

Getting up off of him, she coughed. "That... may be enough training for today," Alex said. Trying desperately to regain her composure.

"Yeah... Um... Yeah, I'm starting to pick it all up." Gavin said, blushing as he struggled to not stare at her exposed torso or her cleavage that showed more as she bent over to stand. *It's okay, Gavin.*

143

I want you to look. I could have gotten up a hundred other ways than my boobs in your face. I hope you see that. Alex pleaded in her mind.

"So, dinner? I was thinking sushi. Care to join me?" Gavin asked, trying desperately to sound nonchalant though his voice had a clear strain. *I just need more time with you*, he thought. Alex sighed contentedly to herself. She had hoped he would offer.

"That sounds wonderful. Just let me find my shirt," Alex said, sounding far more flirty than she had intended to. Gavin's eyes got big, and he excused himself to the restroom.

***

Alex showed up the next morning at Gavin's. Megan let her in, and she made her way to his room. His things were in boxes. "Are you... moving?" Alex asked hesitantly. She knew that Richmond wouldn't let him just take off.

"Yeah, kinda. I'm getting the apartment across the courtyard," Gavin replied cheerfully.

"Oh! Is... is Kaleb going to live with you?" Alex asked. *I'd be happy to.* Alex thought with a shake of her head.

"No, I'm getting it by myself," Gavin said with a smile.

How can he afford that? Alex thought with a jolt. But she kept it to herself. "That's exciting! A big step for sure. I just thought, as your girlfriend, I might have heard about it," Alex said, looking around. She was slightly perturbed at the fact she hadn't been told that he would be moving out of his sister's apartment.

"Yeah, it has happened fairly fast. With everything going on, I just didn't have time. I'm sorry," Gavin said as he kept packing.

"There was time last night," Alex said, sounding hurt. Just then, the NSA moving crew came in, got his things, and took them to his apartment. Alex stood there and watched as everything was taken out. She felt severely out of the loop, and it wasn't a feeling she liked.

144

She left soon after the movers arrived. As she got in her car, she pulled out her phone. "General, why was I not made aware of the fact that Gavin was moving? There are major security protocols that need to be established," Alex started as soon as Richmond picked up.

"Hello, Agent Johnson. I expected this call. The move has been vetted by me, and Agent Charles has established the security measures for the new apartment." The older woman said calmly.

"And what about our cover? If he is moving out, which I didn't know, that would not be a good look for the cover. His sister may suspect something already because of it. She did give me an odd look when she let me in." Alex huffed.

"Agent Johnson. I can tell you; you have been kept up to date on what you have needed to be. When we feel there is more you need to be informed of, we will ensure that that happens." And the General ended the call.

More? There could be MORE that I don't know about?! Gavin probably thought I'd been told. He was likely commanded to move. They forget who they are dealing with, Alex thought as she got to her apartment.

***

Gavin felt weird about Alex not knowing about him moving. Or any of the changes. But he knew it was for the best. He could tell her soon, if it became necessary. The General still didn't fully trust her, but with Hunter gone, things changed.

The NSA movers quickly got him set up, and the NSA footed the bill to refurnish his new place. It felt cold, but it was his. He walked around the apartment. He liked the lab he had. Everything was to his specifications in there. He knew that that would be where he spent most of his time. He checked his room to ensure everything was set up, then returned to his lab.

***

Brett got off the phone. He had just been notified that Hunter was dead. He felt nothing. Hunter had been his mentor, and he felt nothing. He had just met with the Westgate. He got the information he needed, and a text came in. '**It is done. Going to phase 2**.' He closed his phone and boarded a plane for Washington, DC. He had some people to meet with before his part of phase 2 could start.

***

Gavin got everything set up in his lab, and suddenly it hit him. He felt guilty. *Alex asked me to trust her. That's the only thing she has really asked of me. And I haven't. She has no idea what's going on with me. I've been mad at her for withholding information about herself. I felt hurt. And yet, here I am doing the same thing.*

As he finished the setup and powered up his computer, which he had set up beforehand, it dinged. The files were finally unencrypted. He brought it up, and there were hundreds of files. Dated and organized per agent. He also got a notification from a program he had set up to notify him of any newly loaded documents containing Hunter's name. With so much missing from his file, he needed more. Even now.

Per protocol, they cleared his office once the Director was announced dead. They uploaded private documents and journals to a secure server. But Vidar could get in. And it was more than he could have hoped for. Quickly running a formatting program over the files, he downloaded them to his computer before they could be encrypted. He started reading his journal:

<u>1996</u>

I had found her. So vulnerable and doesn't even know it. The perfect candidate for the Spartan program. My enforcer. At fourteen, it will take a lot of care and molding, but it will be worth it. Her father is the way in. He is all she has. Take him away, and she is mine. I feel it. She will be Hel's successor. Unbreakable and without any connection. Perfect. Her training will start immediately upon her acceptance.

146

I didn't take her out of school. She needs to appear as normal as possible. The ridicule will only aid my status as her savior and alienate her from the rest of the world. Unless I see fit, she will have no connection.

She will become Agent Alex Johnson. I will give it to her like a title. She will earn it upon her "graduation." Once she has completed the programming.

She is stronger-willed than I had imagined her to be. No matter. There isn't a will I can't break. It's just a matter of finding the soft spot.

It took more than expected. But she is broken and ready to rebuild. Her will is mine to mold now. There was no need to record what was needed to hurt her. She won't be telling anyone. Besides, she knows me as law enforcement. It wasn't something I enjoyed, but anything for the greater good. Just like Hel.

Her mental training is going well. She is starting to respond to basic, simple programming. Soon, she will carry out complex commands. The Westgate is good. Really good. I still have to break her every now and then. She is so strong-willed. But the Westgate tells me that it is good. This means her programming will be less likely to break.

There are a lot of rules with the programming. Hopefully, it will work as planned. She has progressed quickly in one month. Thankfully. She seems to not always remember when she follows a command. Especially once she started breaking the programming, we had to bring her back in.

"We will always have Miami." What kind of Casablanca bull crap is that? It works, though. She followed orders without question. Sure, it's a heck of a lot faster than the Farm's way. She is ready through Project Ara and on to Project Tyr.

Project Tyr is going great. She has taken to it like a fish to water. Her body is showing it, too. It is far less now that she breaks from her programming. Only needing to be reigned in one time this month now.

She made it through the strength training. Not to strategy and technique. She will be a weapon by the end.

1997

She finished her red test. No emotion. Perfect execution. I couldn't be prouder, but you don't tell a knife you are proud of it, after it's done cutting. I pulled strings, and she graduated high school right after her red test. And she is almost ready for the last phase of project Tyr.

She has been out of commission for a few weeks now. Due to the body alterations and hormone therapy. No breaks this month. She has given up to her programming entirely. The perfect recruit. I regret nothing.

1998

College proved helpful to her. But it took longer than I'd have liked. Even if she could go on missions during it, she would graduate in 1 more year. She is doing two years' worth at a time. She will have a master's by twenty. If I let her continue. For now, having a degree at eighteen will suffice for her purposes. No one else knows.

2000

She has to serve a year in the Secret Service. I guess I wasn't allowed to send an 18-year-old recruit on solo missions. Good thing the official file says she hasn't been on any. I'd be locked away for life if they knew her body count already. But she is effective.

2001

9/11 happened today. Which for me means I have a promotion to celebrate. The director was in the part of the Pentagon that got hit. Too bad. Now, no one can question me on my projects.

2003

Alex has been paired with the Assassin Squad. I will have to watch her closer. She is better alone. However, I have a few recruits to pair her with. One agent is up-and-coming, and the other is a close second. They are my protégés. I will leave all of this to them when I retire.

2004

I'm glad I didn't put her in the Oghma project. Even though that was her next training. Everyone died. The new NOVA system isn't ready. But Alex almost is. I will be pairing her with Agent Martin soon. He will be extremely useful.

My super spy pairing has been put together. And it works better than even I expected it to. It is like they are one unit. But without emotional attachment. Without entanglement.

2007

She seems to be tired. A solo mission is needed soon. Denver can watch her. He knows what would happen if he isn't loyal.

The entries ended there. Gavin was having trouble breathing. He tried to call Richmond, but she was unavailable. He wasn't sure if he should tell anyone else. Especially Alex. *Though at some point, she deserves to know.*

***

Brett got off the plane and headed to the Lincoln Monument, as were the plans. A man watched him as he approached and sat at the designated bench. The man walked over to Brett. Looking up, he spotted him and got up and followed the man. They made their way away from everyone. Down an alleyway. Into an abandoned building.

The man turned to Brett and asked, "Are we good to proceed?" The man's face was unchanging. Cold. His eyes were distant. Like he wasn't looking at anything and had nothing to live for. He seemed almost void of life.

"Yes. Everything is set," Brett said, wanting to get out of there. Something felt off. He sensed danger. Looking around, Brett asked, "Are we done here?" Sounding annoyed.

The man watched for Brett to look away again. And before Brett could react, he pulled out a pistol and fired two in the chest one in the head. Brett's body fell with a thud to the concrete floor. "We are done here," he said in a dull voice and walked off.

***

Alex sat at her computer. This wasn't her specialty, but she knew how to handle one well enough. She started going through documents and payrolls. She had clearance in most branches of government. So, she started with the basics. If the apartment was being paid for by the government, there was a money trail. Always was.

She scrolled through the payout and found the one for the apartment. A standard NSA payout for a building. No surprise there. She checked several other places and felt she was constantly reaching dead ends.

Maybe I'm overthinking this. Maybe he really is just moving out. It would make sense from Richmond's side. Security would be easier. Less of a need for the cover. Which disappointed her. *We could make a space for his training there until the base is ready. It makes sense.* She was about ready to give up when she saw something.

There is a note on a case for a raid in the Middle East. Message by NSA Analyst Michael. Before now, they had always listed his input on cases as an anonymous source. And now an analyst for the NSA, without letting her know?

After finding that, it was easy to start finding more and more. More proof that Gavin had been keeping things from her. More proof that Gavin didn't trust her. She was hurt. Deeper than she thought she would be.

I have been questioning on leaving the CIA to make sure I can be with him, and he decided to not tell me he is no longer my asset but is

150

actually my analyst support. How dumb am I? Am I really that far gone that I read someone's kindness as love? He treats everyone with that kindness, doesn't he? How desperate for kindness I must be. And then he started acting more professional to give me a hint. And what do I do? Start flaunting my body for him, like some horny teenager.

He's too nice to just tell me he isn't interested. Especially after he tried to break up with me, and then I kissed him. He seemed into the kiss at the time. But I guess my lips were just there. I won't make this mistake again. He doesn't want me. I have to respect that, even if I want him. Did want him.

Alex was extremely hurt. She wasn't sure if she'd be able to face Gavin for a while. But knew she would have to. There was a meeting scheduled for later with the General. But she wasn't sure if she should talk to him or just get the meeting over and leave.

Last night had been so great, and then this. Why last night? Why make her feel that way? I hadn't misread that. He was flirting. Maybe he is more like Brett than I thought he was capable of. She checked the time and got ready for the meeting.

***

Gavin kept calling and calling. Trying to get someone. Anyone. To get a message to Richmond. She needed to know this. Even if he got in trouble, finally, she called back.

"You have made it clear you have been trying to get in touch with me. Were all thirty-seven calls really necessary?" Richmond asked. No amusement showed in her face.

"Trust me, General. I think that you will agree it is necessary." Gavin collects his thoughts after he tells her it's for her ears only.

She nods the go-ahead after her secretary leaves the room. Gavin starts, "Okay, so I know you may be mad at me, but I got the documents from the filing of Director Hunter's effects." He winced.

"This is why I hired you. Please continue," Richmond said, unphased.

"So, I was reading through some of it and came across a journal of sorts. It caught my eye because it has Agent Johnson's name on it. Right from the start, I was appalled. I'll send everything to you for you to read through. But the lowlights of it are he recruited her basically out of middle school. Blackmailed her because of her dad's background at fourteen. Brainwashed her. Sent her on unsanctioned assignments, I'd assume, for himself. She had her red test at fifteen. And has been manipulating her since. It mentioned the Westgate in it. I've never heard of them. And it said that she can forget a chunk of time whenever her programming language is used to bring her back in," Gavin said breathlessly.

General Richmond's eyes grew wide. "I will have a talk with her after the meeting tonight. And I believe you should talk to her as well. She may have a soft spot for you. Now I need to prepare for this meeting. Please make your way to Charles's in the next hour or so." And the call ended.

Gavin was half tempted to call Alex then but knew there was too much that they had to discuss. And so, he just sat there. He fretted briefly as he watched the minutes tick off the clock.

Alex got to the apartment complex, still beating herself up mentally and feeling like a fool. *How could I be so stupid? Spies don't fall in love. This is why*, she thought. She could hear her dad saying that she was a fool for believing there was someone as good as she had seen Gavin. *Everyone has an agenda. And if they don't, then they are a fool.* Gavin was no fool. But she hadn't thought that he had a plan. And maybe he hadn't. Perhaps he was innocent. And she just misread the situation entirely. *That's not likely. But it is possible*, she thought, forcing herself to climb out of the car.

She walked in and saw Gavin. He looked pale, like he'd seen a ghost. Scared. And he kept glancing at her. *Did he know I'm mad? Could he tell that quickly?* She dismissed the thought. Something was up. Something didn't make sense. She walked up to him, making up her

152

mind. "Gavin, after this meeting, we need to talk." She saw him flinch at that statement. But he nodded his head.

"I agree. We do need to talk," he said in a somber voice.

That's weird. He's acting like he has bad news for me. Like the idea that he doesn't want me isn't bad enough. She thought as she got back across the room from him.

The screen came to life with General Richmond's face filling it. "Good evening, team. I wanted to bring us together to discuss a few things. And then, I could have a private word with Agent Johnson, please?" Seeing them all nod, she continued. "Good. Now, matters at hand, you are benched until the new base is operational. It shouldn't be but two to three weeks. Until then, I expect the NOVA system's training to continue as it has. As well as learning to work and communicate together as a team. We are facing more than we had thought. Our analysts have found indications that Pendulum isn't our only threat or even our biggest threat.

"Instead, we have found that they are just a branch of a group calling themselves 'The Collective.' We are still figuring out what resources they may have. We have had one agent working on this for several months now. He will be joining the team for the foreseeable future. Please welcome to the team special agent Christopher (Topher) Anderson."

The door opened, and in walked this super spy-looking guy. "Hello, team. Let's get to work."

Chapter 10

:/Communication

Gavin sat in his lab after he had been dismissed from the briefing. He was waiting for Alex since he needed to talk to her, and she had said she needed to speak with him. He knew she didn't seem happy with him, but that didn't matter. What he had to say to her was far more important.

I have to tell her. I have to tell her everything. She deserves to know at least about herself. Gavin thought as he pondered how to tell her. He knew it would be hard for her to accept if she didn't know.

He then heard a ding from his computer, notifying him that a video call was waiting. Answering it, he saw Richmond looking at him with a stern face. "Gavin, it is time to read Agent Johnson in on your findings. It will mean that she can seek the help she will likely need. I will offer her an NSA psychologist to help her through these issues from her past. Hopefully, it will allow her to move past this and be a better operative."

"I agree, General. She needs to know what has happened to her. And who is responsible," Gavin said with a somber tone.

"But I don't believe it is a good time for her to learn about your employment with the NSA. Not yet," Richmond continued.

"I understand, General," Gavin said as Richmond ended the call.

Gavin queued up every file he had about her and waited. The longer it took, the more he got in his own head. Worried she wouldn't take it well. *She had seemed upset that she didn't know he was moving first. But it happened so fast. Plus, I couldn't explain everything to her. Could I? Hunter had control of her. And who knows who else. Maybe Brett. Or maybe he had just heard the line. I don't know. But we don't know if she will just snap.*

He walked into his living room and peeked out the window through the shades. *Great. Now, I'm the creepy neighbor.* He thought with a shake of his head.

The door to Charles's apartment opened, and Anderson and Alex stepped out. As Gavin watched, he didn't know why, but Anderson made him nervous. Agent Anderson and Alex were saying something, and then they shook hands. Anderson leaned down and gave Alex a kiss on the cheek. *It's ok. It was just a greeting. Right? That's a thing in Europe. And maybe that's where he was stationed. Yeah, that must be it.* Gavin thought nervously.

Alex then walked towards his door, and she looked right at him. Having gotten caught spying, Gavin felt embarrassed. He walked over to the door and opened it as she knocked. Alex entered the apartment and walked past him without saying a word.

"Alex, I'm sorry I didn't..." Gavin started as he shut the door.

"Sorry for what, Gavin? Not telling me you were moving? Could you imagine what would have happened if your sister or Kaleb had come in while I was just finding out? Isn't that the kind of thing you don't keep from your girlfriend in a relationship?"

"But our relationship isn't real, Alex. You have told me that many times," Gavin said dejectedly.

Alex felt like someone had landed a solid blow to her gut. *It's more real than anything I've had, Gavin. What can't you understand about that? But you lied to me, just like everyone else. You kept something really important from me. Just like every other man I've known has. You lied.*

"Well, as your handler, you should have told me too. There are security risks to take into account. Did you at least tell Charles? You haven't told me anything about this," Alex said, fishing for information. *How much was he willing to confess? That tells me how much I can trust him moving forward.* Alex thought.

"Alex, I told Charles. You've been busy. And he lives across the court. So, I figured he could set it all up easier." Gavin told a half-truth. He felt guilty. *But how often has she lied to me? Or omitted a truth?* Gavin thought as he tried to calm her. "But that's not important. Follow me. I have something you really need to see," Gavin said quietly.

Alex's interest was peaked. *Something he feels is more important than our relationship and feelings. This can't be good.* She follows him into his lab. Looking around, she sees scattered electronics and parts. It's like he has been building something. Tools are all organized neatly against one wall. And a new computer and laptop with a 3-monitor system. *A reminder of everything he is hiding from you.* Alex felt a pang in her chest. *Stop it, Johnson. Spies don't fall in love.*

Gavin solemnly looked at her as he directed her to the computer screens. "I found these files and felt you deserved to see them." He seemed to be struggling to speak. Like he was nervous for her to look at these files.

At first, she wanted to be dismissive, but then she saw her name. The more she read, the more she couldn't look away. It was her. Almost all of her. The next screen showed pages and pages in Hunter's vernacular. The more she read, the more nervous she got.

"Where did you find these?" Alex said in a quiet but intense voice. *I didn't even think about that. Crap. She's going to want to know how I got them. Well, good job. I know Richmond said not to, but I have to come clean.* Gavin prepared himself.

"The CIA secure servers," he said with a slight wince.

"And how did you get access to those?" Alex asked coolly. She was too calm.

And it was freaking Gavin out. *Screw it.* "There is something about me that I've not been telling you," Gavin started. Alex finally turned to him, the cursor hovering over a video clip link. She had a look on her face like she already knew. "I'm Vidar," Gavin said.

Alex's jaw dropped, with a genuine look of shock. And her mind went back to the meeting they had had.

"Let's get to work," Anderson said. He looked around at the team. He knew Agents Charles and Johnson by reputation. He had been able to read their recent case logs. Turning to Gavin, he said, "You must be Gavin. The Human NOVA system." Extending a hand, which Gavin shook.

"Special Agent Anderson has been working exclusively on The Collective for months. He has uncovered most of the intel that we have on them. He has been in charge of many successful and important operations. His only blemish is his hunt for Vidar," General Richmond stated. Alex found it interesting that she mentioned that. It had been everyone's failure. No one caught Vidar.

"You're serious?" Alex said. She had even been sent to find Vidar with no luck. Gavin nodded in reply. "So that's why she accepted," Alex said to herself while turning back to the monitors.

"What? What do you mean?" Gavin asked.

"I know, Gavin. I know you're not an asset anymore. Do you think you could hide it from me? I thought you trusted me, Gavin. I thought of anyone, you would be honest with me. But I guess I was wrong."

157

"Alex, I..." was all Gavin got out before Alex clicked the video link.

On the screen was a 14-year-old Alex bound to a chair. Every time she would say no, she got electrocuted. Every time she did as she was asked, she was allowed to have some food. She didn't understand why she didn't remember this. She clicked on the following clip. 14-year-old Alex was beaten whenever she didn't do what she was told. The next clip was a 15-year-old Alex with a shock collar around her neck. Every time she missed a target with her knives, she was shocked. She moved on to another clip down the line. And there stood a 16-year-old Alex. She was covered in blood, but no marks on her. Handcuffs hanging from one wrist. Her shirt was torn. She had a completely blank look on her face, being asked what happened:

"I completed my assignment," Young Alex said.

"And what was your assignment?" Hunter asked.

"I'm not allowed to talk about assignments given to me by my superiors," Young Alex said in a cold, dead tone.

"Very good, Agent Johnson. You're dismissed," Hunter said, sounding happy.

Alex turned from the screen. Her body was shaking. She had had small reactions to the commands on the screen, but not enough for her mind to lose focus. *I was brainwashed. Is that why I have lapses in times that I can't remember anything?* Alex was unfocused.

"Alex. Alex, I'm here for you. Talk to me," Gavin said. *How can I talk to him when he didn't trust me?*

"I need to go," Alex said. And she immediately got up and walked straight out of the apartment. She made it into the courtyard and took a deep breath. She was about to go to her car when she heard him.

"Hey! Alex, are you ok?" Anderson came jogging up. "You look like you saw a ghost. Everything ok?"

158

"What? Yeah. Just, a lot on my mind," she replied, trying to ignore him.

"I saw you going over to talk to the asset. Are there any issues with him?" Anderson asked.

He doesn't know about the status change. Maybe no one does but Richmond? Gavin still should have told me. Why can't he understand? "No. No, he is fine. I'm just thinking about the last mission. Everything is okay," Alex said as she continued to her car.

Anderson grabbed her wrist to stop her. "Alex. We are a team now. You know you can tell me if something is bothering you. Right?" Anderson said. He looked at her with concern.

Letting out a breath that she didn't know she was holding. "Thank you. I really appreciate that. But I'm ok. Just need some alone time," Alex said with a soft smile. *Maybe he won't be so bad. He seems kinder than almost everyone else I have met in the CIA.*

"Well, if you change your mind, I'm just a call away. I have a flat downtown. Let me know if you need anything. Ok?" Anderson said while giving her another kiss on her cheek.

"Thanks," Alex said with a slightly bigger smile as she got into her car.

Anderson watched her drive away. Once she was out of sight, he pulled out his phone and dialed. "She's farther out than we thought. I'll start working on bringing her back in. Yes. Yes, I know. This isn't my first time. I know she is special, but I must earn her trust. She's vulnerable again. It will work. Trust me," he said in a dull tone. His eyes had gone dead.

***

The next day was Gavin's day off, and Megan had booked most of it with her. He got to the hospital and made his way to Megan's office. When he walked in, she had scans of his brain a few years ago already up. "Checking out some old homework?" Gavin asked with a laugh.

Megan looked up with a half-smile. "Something like that. I wanted to have a baseline to go off of. I figured even depressed; your mind couldn't have been TOO messed up before this thing got put in there," she said teasingly.

"There is actually something that I've been wanting to talk to you about with that. But let's get the scans done first. And then we can discuss it," Gavin said, and he got up on the hospital bed.

"No, Gavin. We are going to go to the MRI and CAT scan machines to take a look. So, come with me and bring the gown. You will have to change," Megan said as she made her way through the door.

After the scans, Gavin waited for Megan to speak, but she just kept clicking from one screen to another. And then back.

"This doesn't make sense," Megan finally said.

"What doesn't make sense?" Gavin asked. They had done so many scans before, during, and after accessing the NOVA system. Thankfully, Gavin had worked with it so that he could control the NOVA system on command.

"These scans. The only one that's different is the scan while accessing the NOVA system," Megan huffed, sounding exasperated.

"Meg, that's what I wanted to talk to you about," Gavin said placatingly. "I think I had some version of a NOVA system uploaded when I was really little."

"WHAT?! Gavin, that's absurd. I would have known. Did you forget I basically took care of you from the age of eight on up?" Megan said with a roll of her eyes.

"Meg. Dad created this thing. And I think, if I remember correctly, I uploaded one on accident when he left his office door open one time," Gavin said quietly.

"Gavin. Are you sure?" Megan started. "Then that would mean you have lived with this thing in your head for over a decade!" Megan was floored. She hadn't expected that at all.

"Yeah. But I only recently got the government upload. And even more recently, I got control to use both on command. And when I was trying to use it to learn self-defense, I blacked out," Gavin said.

"Hmm. Well, that means we need to go and access the NOVA system more while scanning. Are you up for it?" Megan asked.

"Yeah, I'll be fine. It doesn't hurt anymore, unless it's a physical action that I use the NOVA system on," Gavin replied as they made their way to the machines again.

After several hours of tests and scanning, Megan looked at the images again. "Ok. This makes more sense, although I'm not sure they actually meant to design it this way," she said.

"What? What's going on?" Gavin asked.

"Well, look at these. When you activate the NOVA system, you display hyperactivity in different parts of the brain. It's the correct spots in the brain that are supposed to be active while doing what you are thinking, but they show multiple times more than a normal person's activity," she explained.

"And it seems to have higher access to the rest of your brain while doing it. So, while most people show activity in just one area and one hemisphere when you access it, it emphasizes one spot but shows activity all over. And it makes sense that you struggled more with using it to learn physical skills. It appears that your Motor Cortex and Cerebellum are somewhat underdeveloped since you were never the active type," she said with a motherly look at him. Gavin just shrugged with a bit of a grin. "This means that how this seems to have activity in your brain causes an extra amount of strain on the rest. Creating an 'overheating' effect," Megan finished.

161

"Well, that makes sense. I know Alex wants me to put in more work to get in shape, but maybe Chad would help me as well?" Gavin asked. "And you think that this is something that could go away with working out?"

"Yes, I believe that would help. But I do believe that if you get emotional and try to access the NOVA system, similar things would happen. Your brain would be trying to process too much at one time, and you would pass out to allow it to slow down without damage," Megan explained.

"So, I came to the doctor to be told to eat right and exercise? Really?" Gavin said with a smirk.

"Gavin, this is serious. But yes," Megan said with a chuckle. "It's something we will have to work on and watch. Now, what's going on with you and Alex?"

"I honestly don't know, Megan. I found some stuff, and once she knows about you being on the team, I think she will be pissed, but I hope she will talk to you. She has been through a lot," Gavin sounded defeated.

"You need to just talk to her. I don't care what Richmond says or thinks. That woman loves you. I know it. She might be a spy, but no one can fake the look she had in her eyes," Megan encouraged him. Then, she grabbed her files and said, "Now, you have created a lot of extra work for me to map out. So, get out of here."

"Okay, Meg. Still on for dinner tonight?" Gavin asked as he stood to leave.

"Counting on it."

***

Gavin hadn't heard from Alex all day. But they had training scheduled for that night. Gavin planned on talking to her during the training. He figured it would be good for them both to clear the air.

He went home to change and work on a few things before heading to Alex's apartment. As he walks into the courtyard, he sees Kaleb. "Hey buddy, I'm so sorry I have been a bit more absent. Just been busy with Alex," Gavin said. *Please don't want to hang out. I just don't have time. I'm working on a way to let you know. But we can't yet, buddy.*

"Yeah, it's no problem. I just came by to see why you weren't at work today, but then remembered it was your day off." Kaleb said with a smack to his own forehead. "Also, I have a girlfriend! So, we should totally do a double date sometime."

"That's great man! I'm happy for you! And I'll talk to Alex about a double date possibility. Ok?" Gavin said non-committal.

"Yeah. Sure. No problem. Well, I'm off to see her. We have a 'stay-in' date planned. If you know what I mean," Kaleb said with a wink and a nudge of Gavin's elbow with his own.

"Yes. I understand perfectly, Kaleb," Gavin said with a laugh as he watched his best friend ride off on his bike. Once he was gone, Gavin made his way into his apartment to change. Kaleb peered his head back around the corner of the entrance. He watched his friend enter the apartment across the courtyard from Megan's. "What have we here?" he said, and then actually headed out for his date.

Gavin changed clothes and made his way to Alex's. As he walked down the hallway, he saw her door open. And out stepped Agent Topher Anderson. Gavin froze. "Oh, hey, Gavin. I was just on my way out. Alex said that you and she had to go over some mission stuff. Or had some training. I'll see you tomorrow. They are opening up our new base." With a smile, Anderson turned and left. Gavin didn't see the smile turn into a smirk as he entered the elevator.

Gavin couldn't keep moving. *Anderson? Really? The guy has the personality of a test dummy. Is that really what she is into? I can't believe it. Another hunky spy type. It figured. She has a type. And I'm not it. I doubt I'll ever be it. How is she any different than my ex? Here I was about to tell her everything. And she's busy with Anderson. I'm sure she doesn't have to deal with him being emotional and needy. Or having to keep up with her in the spy world. Or protecting him.*

Why do I keep forgetting that all I am is a job? Even if she seems to enjoy hanging out with me. That's all I'll ever be. Is a job. Gavin turned sadly and left. He went home and wallowed in his mind. Further spiraling into the emotional abyss. Convinced he had lost Alex yet again.

***

Alex sat in her room. Gavin never showed. She had checked his tracker and saw that he was still in his apartment. *Or at least the signal is. He is Vidar. He could have hijacked the signal at any point.* Alex thought as she sat there. *Maybe he just got caught up in work and forgot.*

She had been alone since Anderson left over an hour ago. *I don't know why he needed to come over here to let me know that the new base would be ready in the morning. A call, or even just a text, could have achieved the same goal.* Alex thought it was odd. But at the same time, it's kind of sweet. And she felt a calm in his presence. A familiarity. But she figured it was just that he was a spy.

She shook her head to clear her mind of that train of thought. Maybe if Gavin didn't have her, she would settle for Anderson. But even a dishonest Gavin was better than a good spy. *Really, who am I to call anyone dishonest. I practically defined it for most of my life.* Alex thought with a roll of her eyes.

After seeing what was in those files, he likely needs a break from being around me. I'll give him tonight. He deserves some time to himself. And I could use it to get through this myself. That was a lot to deal with. And Anderson seeming to not want to leave me alone isn't helping. At least he is nice, but I need space to think.

So, Gavin does know my past. Almost all of it. And still, at least, did like me. Is that what changed? Why doesn't he trust me? Would I trust me? Doubtful. I didn't even know that they had done that to me. Hunter. Hunter did that to me. I'm glad he's dead. Alex kept having the images of herself, dork, those videos go through her mind. That dead look in her eye. *It's no wonder Gavin had backed off. I would have, too, after seeing that.* She flopped onto her bed. Her head in her hands. She'd never felt these kinds of emotions before.

***

Gavin was lying in bed. He heard a rustle and rolled over to see Alex standing in a small nightgown. Her hair was down. Her eyes were vibrant. "Gavin. I feel trapped. I can't understand why I don't remember things. And I feel like there is something pulling me back. Keeping me from being the person I want to be. I need you. I need you to help me. Please," she pleaded with him. Crawling onto his bed towards him.

Gavin gulped. "What... what can I do to... to help?" he stammered out.

"I need you to hold me. And tell me things will be okay. That you're there for me," Alex said as she got closer. Leaning in for a kiss. Gavin blinked, and she was suddenly covered in blood. "And die!" Alex called. Her eyes were dead. Her face is the agent mask entirely. She looked like an older version of how she did in the videos.

Gavin shot up out of bed. He looked down to see his bed empty. He threw off his blankets and looked under the bed. He was alone. He grabbed his tranq gun and went through the house. Completely alone. He sighed. *What is happening to me? It was just a dream, but there was something there that felt real. Was real. I can trust Alex to not kill me. But can I trust her brainwashed self to not? She wouldn't. Would she?* Gavin didn't know the answer. He looked at the clock next to his bed. 3:13 AM.

He felt fidgety after that dream. He did a small workout. Then, he booted up his computer. Worked on a few things for what felt like a long time. He glanced at the clock. 3:47 AM. It had only been a half an hour.

Gavin huffed to himself. He knew what he needed to do to get some peace of mind, but it wasn't something he wanted to do. *Megan is right. Of course, she is.* He thought with a small laugh and a roll of his eyes. *I need to talk to Alex. Be upfront with her. Otherwise, it's going to tear me up.* He had noticed the longer he went without talking to Alex about everything, the more accessing the NOVA system would affect his head.

He tossed on some pants and a shirt, grabbed his keys, and was out the door. On the way over, he realized how crazy what he was about to do was. He would see her in the morning in a few hours. But he wasn't sure he could wait a few more hours. He pulled into the parking spot and made his way to her door.

***

Alex was lying in bed. She hadn't slept much. Even though she was emotionally exhausted, she couldn't get her mind to calm enough to let her sleep. She kept thinking about Gavin being disgusted by her. She watched as the clock flipped over to 4:00 AM. She sighed, knowing she would get a briefing on the new base in just five short hours. She was brought out of her reverie by a knock at her door. She grabbed her gun and hopped out of bed silently. Creeping to the door, she looked out the hole to see Gavin standing there, fidgeting. She quickly put her gun away, came back, and opened the door.

"Gavin?" She asked, her voice portraying an amount of grogginess that she wasn't feeling. "What are you doing here? Is everything okay?" She sounded worried.

"No. Not really. I'm safe, but we need to talk. Really talk. Can I come in, please?" Gavin asked tentatively. He was clearly nervous. Worried that she'd be mad. Or just say no. He held his breath.

Is he going to be honest with me? Alex thought as she stepped back. Gesturing for him to enter her apartment. "Talk to me, Gavin. What's going on?" Alex said as she sat down on her bed.

166

Gavin took a deep breath and let it out. He paced the room and seemed to be refusing to look at her. *I know what you're wanting to tell me, Gavin. Just say it.* Alex thought as she sat there. Finally, Gavin grabbed the chair, pulled it closer to her bed, and sat down. He looked at her with an intensity she hadn't seen from him before.

"Alex," Gavin began, "I have several things I need to talk to you about. I… I know Anderson was here, and he is much more your type. He is strong and a great spy, and well, he is everything that I'm not," he said. "And I get it. I get what you see in him. His record is flawless. He is the Clyde to your Bonnie. You with him makes sense. But I hope we can still be friends." Gavin sounded like a wounded puppy.

Gavin. That isn't what I want. Tell him. Tell him it's not what you want. Tell him you want him. Come on, Johnson. Tell him! Alex sat there. Her mind screamed at her to put him out of his misery, but she still also knew he was keeping things from her. And without honesty between them, there wasn't any point in a relationship.

Gavin coughed and continued, "Ok. Yeah, and there were some other things. I didn't want you to go into the base tomorrow blind. I'm not sure what Charles knows, but I do know that Anderson has been kept in the dark on purpose. As… as well as you. I've been worried for a while that this is just an assignment for you. That is all I am in the job. And once the job is done, no matter the ending, you're gone," Gavin expressed, emotion filling his voice.

"Gavin…" Alex started, but Gavin cut her off. "Just let me finish. Please. And then you can say whatever you like. Ok?" Alex nodded in reply. Her heart hurt from what he was telling her.

"I'm not your asset anymore, Alex. You're here, for sure. As long as you want to be. And possibly even longer, for which I'm sorry. But I'm your field analyst now. I informed Richmond of who I am, or at least my hacker persona, and she agreed to take me on to the NSA payroll. I didn't see any other way out that didn't involve a bullet between the eyes from either you or Charles," Gavin said.

"Gavin, I'd never…" Alex tried to interject.

"Please, Alex. I'm sorry. But let me finish." Gavin sighed. "After seeing the files with you in them. Seeing what Hunter did to you. Had done to you. And at such a young age. It made me sick. But it also made it harder for me to trust you with everything. I have a lot at stake here, Alex. My friends, my sister, Awesome. My life. I have so much to lose. And what had I gained in the time that I had been forced to be in the United States Government's care? Protection. Sure. I've seen what maybe could have happened. There is so much I have to tell you. But other than that, my life was still the same. I was still this college dropout loser working at Snollygoster Inc. who just had a really cool hobby. I was the most important intelligence asset in the world, and I was still nothing more than an IT guy," Gavin said dejectedly.

Alex didn't know what to say. She wanted to console him; tell him he wasn't a loser. But she understood where he was coming from. Why he said what he did. He had been Vidar. Attended Georgia Institute of Technology on a full-ride scholarship for computer programming and engineering. He wasn't some no-talent loser with no future. And then the CIA, in the form of Brett, took that from him. And now the exact same people who took that from him expected him to follow orders blindly, and for free. *How could I have just asked him to trust me that first night? Because it's what you're trained to do. Seduce the mark, however, is needed. This one's needs just happened to be what you apparently wanted in a man,* Alex thought bashfully.

Gavin continued, "I knew I was capable of more. More than any of you expected from me. Even you, though you actually tried to support me. I saw the footage of briefings where you stood up for me, or at least didn't pile on to their negative talk. Yes, I hacked my surveillance feeds a while ago. I know. Bad asset. But I didn't like being watched and having no way to know who was watching me," Gavin explained.

Alex couldn't really blame him. She wasn't given much of a choice when she was 'recruited' into the CIA. She ended up going to The Farm with the rest of them, but she was so far ahead of everyone else that it was pointless. The only thing she didn't know was seduction. And so many guys were more than willing to help her with that part. It made

168

her feel sick now, thinking back on that time, while she looked at the sweet and caring man sitting across from her.

"So, yes. I'm now officially employed by the NSA. I am getting paid and will produce equipment for us on missions. I report directly to Richmond, and she is going to be pissed that I'm sharing this all with you before she gave the ok. But I feel you deserve to know," Gavin said sadly. "Also, I have more control over the NOVA system than I have led on. You see, I am able to access the NOVA system on command. The other night, when we were training, and I collapsed? I was using the NOVA system to help me learn the moves. I have been talking to Megan about this. Part of my requirements to Richmond were that she allowed the people I am close to know. Especially since this is an experimental program in my head, and my sister is a darn good neurologist. And Chad will be the team doctor for all except Anderson. He is to remain kept in the dark until Richmond, and I feel we can trust him," Gavin finished with an exaggerated exhale.

Alex sat there stunned. That was so much to take in at once. Especially after all she had seen earlier. She thought she had uncovered everything when she figured out that he was working for the NSA. But this was so much more. *Tell him. Tell him. He deserves to know. He has come clean on more than you knew. Tell him. "Gavin. I love you." Tell him.*

"Gavin. I…"

Chapter 11

:/Pavlov

Come on. Just say it. It's just two more words. That's all. Love. You. You can say that to him. You know it's true. Just tell him. Alex encouraged herself. Building up the strength, she took a breath.

"It's ok, Alex. You don't have to say anything. I know I messed up, and I should have told you before I called Richmond. I just… I wasn't sure what was all going on. You know? They had a kill order on me for when the new NOVA system was up and running. Hunter was really pushing to off me. And you were Hunter's best. And then I saw why, and it made it even harder. But when I finally talked to Megan about it all, she made it make sense in my mind. She is just… she's wise. And has always been there for me. And knows how to handle situations that I don't." Gavin started venting now that the cork had been undone.

So, Alex just sat back. Partly thankful that he stopped her from saying what she was about to say. And partly dreading the fact that she couldn't tell him. She felt that now she was no better than him. Keeping secrets. *That's all I have ever done. No one has known the entire truth about me. No one has wanted to. And that's what makes you terrifying, Gavin.* Alex breathed.

"I just want us to go back to how we were. Friends and happy to be around each other. We may not have to go on as many dates now that my sister knows the truth. But my coworkers and Kaleb don't. So, we

170

will have to keep up appearances there. I'm sorry if that is a bit weird for you," Gavin said with a slight cringe.

I enjoy every second I can get with you. Gavin and Alex both thought at the same time.

"It's okay, Gavin. I don't mind," Alex said. *Truth is, I wish it were more. I have enjoyed every touch, every kiss, every glance into each other's eyes. Those meant more to me than I can express. And hopefully, one day, I will be able to show you and tell you just how much you truly mean to me.* Alex thought with a morose sigh. She was disappointed in herself, but she knew that it was better this way. If she said it now, it would likely sound more manipulation than anything else.

"I actually think it would be better if we still acted that way, even if they already know. At this point, it would be too much to try to remember who we can and who we can't act like, boyfriend and girlfriend, around. It's safer to keep that intact. I'll talk to Richmond about it moving forward," Alex said, sounding happier than she had since he left her apartment almost a week earlier.

Gavin noticed the shift in her attitude and felt better. *Maybe there is a chance. Just don't get too hopeful. She is still doing a job. But she isn't evil. She still cares.* Gavin thought as he started to stand. "I better get home. Since we are going to tour the new base in a few hours."

He started heading to the door.

"Gavin, wait," Alex said. Almost sounding timid. It caused Gavin to freeze mid-step. He didn't really know how to feel about it. She is the strongest person he has ever known. Never scared of anything. And she sounded like she was scared.

"You said we are friends, and you're right. But friends talk about things together, and I haven't been a good friend to you," Alex started. "I've hid behind the rules of protocol that Hunter tended to harp on. But Gavin. I don't know what's happening to me. Happened to me. I know you know everything that is in those videos and notes. And I remember

171

a lot of them. But I do have gaps. And I've been having headaches since coming here. Whenever I don't follow orders, I get a headache," Alex said with her head down. "I don't blame you for not trusting me."

"Alex, would you be willing to talk to Megan? And Richmond is wanting you to see a company psychologist," Gavin mentioned. "I think both would be a good idea. Especially with everything that you got put through. I'm so sorry that happened."

"Yeah. Yeah, I think I would be open to that. I just don't know how to process all of what you showed me," Alex said, still struggling to make eye contact. "It's ok. It was just a lot."

Gavin walked over to her and gave her a hug. He wasn't sure how she would react, but he knew it was the right thing to do. And going off of how she clung to him, she thought it was the right thing as well.

After Gavin had left, Alex lay in her bed. She wasn't sure how this was going to play out. Her head was throbbing. But now she knew why. Now she knew. Her face hardened. *It was never Gavin that I needed to push away. They did all of those horrible things to me, made me a puppet, turned me into a killer, and expected me to be obedient to them? I may not be good enough for Gavin, but I'm going to make damn sure that they don't tarnish him like they have me.* And with that thought and newfound resolve, Alex drifted off to a better sleep than she had had in a long time.

***

Gavin returned to his apartment and felt he wasn't done for the night. He went to his lab and sat down at his laptop. Vidar was curious about Anderson. He started looking, and everything was redacted. Everything was blacked out. The only thing available on anything was his name. So, Gavin got his program started to unredact and decrypt the files. Something wasn't right. Gavin didn't feel okay about this.

Coeus was watching Gavin. He saw the name Anderson get typed, and he pulled out his wrist computer.

/:NEW SUBJECT. Anderson. CIA. FULL REPORT.:/

He started typing, seeing what Gavin had been doing. He wasn't happy that he was proactive in seeking employment with the government. But he understood the need. "I hope you know what you're doing, Gavin," Coeus said to himself. His wrist computer dinged.

/:ON IT:/

Coeus smiled as he made his way out of the burned and destroyed NOVA system room.

***

Gavin woke up at his laptop. He struggled to get up. He was exhausted, but he knew he had to be on today. After getting ready, he headed to meet Charles, and they made their way to the new base together.

"I didn't get to ask you," Gavin said as they were waiting in traffic. "How do you feel about Anderson?" he asked, turning to Charles.

Charles grunted and replied, "Eh. Just another CIA skirt. Maybe you can talk to him about your lady feelings, too." He finished with a smirk and a glance towards Gavin.

Gavin just laughed. He didn't have it in him for banter this morning. He wondered how Alex was doing. As well as there was some slight excitement to see an actual CIA covert Black Site base.

Walking in, Gavin was slightly giddy. He saw massive computers and monitors. He also saw Anderson already there, but chose to ignore that. Instead, he made his way to the server room. Making sure he wasn't being watched, he quickly put his own drive into the server dock. It was loaded with a program that would direct back to his computer at home. He intended to make this as mutually beneficial as possible.

He pulled the connected screen up just as Anderson walked in. "I understand that you have a very high clearance, Gavin, but you are still only an asset. I don't think you need to be messing with that. These

173

aren't the computers you work on at Snollygoster Inc.," Anderson said with a condescending smile.

Just wait. I know you aren't entirely clean. There is something there. I can sense it. Gavin closed down the screen and made his way to the main conference room. Alex was already there, sitting at the table. She looked up and smiled at him but then went right back to the papers she had in front of her. Charles wasn't in there yet. "Why didn't you get Charles?" Gavin said, trying to not sound annoyed.

"He's in the armory. You're welcome to be the one to interrupt his alone time with his guns," Alex said with a smirk. Anderson wasn't taking his eyes off her. Gavin rolled his eyes and made his way toward the armory. "Cowards." He said under his breath. Which made Alex chuckle.

As Gavin left, Anderson made his way behind Alex. He started to rub her shoulders. "You're super tense. Do you need to talk about anything?" he said as he rubbed her shoulders.

What is he doing? Think maybe I'm tense because you're touching me? Alex thought. "Oh. No, thank you. I appreciate the offer, but I think I'm ok," Alex said tightly.

Anderson leaned down close to her ear and whispered with a smirk. "Ok. But remember, we will always have Miami."

***

Gavin entered the armory and saw Charles with his gun torn apart, cleaning it. "Hey, we have a briefing in five minutes. How do you like the new base?" Gavin asked.

"It's alright. Finally, we have a decent and full operation we are running here in Woodford. And I get a room for my girls," Charles said as he stared lovingly at his wall of weapons that were on display.

Gavin suddenly felt like he was interrupting a private moment. He hadn't seen a look of love like that from anyone other than Chad and

174

Megan. *If that's how I look at Alex, then it makes sense that people can read it on my face.* He thought with an amused laugh. "Well, I figured you wouldn't want to miss our first meeting as a team in this place," Gavin said, then turned around and left the room.

***

Alex froze. Her mind went blank for a moment. Her shoulders relaxed as they were being rubbed. *Who was rubbing them?* She glanced up. *Agent Anderson. He is handsome. It could be worse.* She felt her body start to respond to his touch. She couldn't remember how long it had been. She closed her eyes and enjoyed the feeling. A soft moan escaped from her lips.

"Oh." Gavin had just turned the corner into the conference room and saw Anderson rubbing Alex's shoulders. And Alex seemed to be enjoying it.

"Sorry to interrupt what is going on, but if I could have everyone's attention, we can get started," General Richmond stated sternly as the monitor came to life. "Where is Agent Charles?" she asked.

"Right here, Ma'am. Sorry," Charles said as he came into the room.

"Very well. I assume you were all getting acquainted and familiar with The Citadel." The General continued as she stared darkly at Agent Anderson, who hadn't moved from behind Alex. But had taken his hands off her shoulders.

Alex's mind was reeling from the moment she saw Gavin. Her head ached badly. *Why was I okay with Anderson rubbing my shoulders? Why'd it feel so good? Gavin was upset. He must still have feelings for me. If I say this was the residual effect of the brainwashing, then that's just an excuse. Right? I can't use that as an excuse. I moaned, for crying out loud.*

Suddenly, Agent Anderson's presence felt stifling, like the mere fact of him being in the room made the air thinner. She was struggling to breathe. She looked at Gavin, but he wasn't making eye contact. She focused all her energy on calming herself and schooling her features. But her head felt like it had been cracked open.

Gavin noticed her wince. *I need to get my hands on the surveillance for this place. I'm jealous, but there is something wrong with her. Is this the brainwashing taking effect?* Gavin thought.

"Mr. Woodford, am I interrupting some serious thoughts? Or may I continue?" Richmond said, though the sternness in her voice never quite reached her eyes. She kept glancing between Gavin and Alex. She also noticed Anderson standing close by Alex.

"I'm going to give you all a few more days to get accustomed to each other, as well as the base. I expect by the end of the week, you will be able to continue missions and start hunting down The Collective. We have wasted enough time. Now, I would like to speak to the asset alone. So please, everyone, see yourselves out," she finished.

After everyone had gone, she said, "Gavin. I saw some of what was happening before I started the video on your end. Yes, I know how to do that."

Gavin put his hand down. "I want you to pull the video feeds from surveillance and audio and see what you can get from their interaction."

"It is a relief to hear you say that. I don't feel Agent Anderson can be trusted. I have a feeling there is more going on with him," Gavin replied to her.

"I am well aware of your hesitation to accept him into the group. Without solid proof of there being anything more than him trying to steal the girl you're interested in, I'm afraid that there is not anything I can do about it. Now, get to work on figuring things out. I am aware of your incursions into the servers. It may or may not be easier to just give you the passwords, but I would appreciate you notifying me before you access the servers in The Citadel," General Richmond said, trying to not sound amused.

176

Gavin winced. "Actually, I may have already made an attempt there." The General's face went flat. "Continue," she said.

"Well, I put a flash drive in that was loaded with a program to allow me access from my home lab. I had planned on using it to up the safety protocols on the servers here, as well as using the computing power here, while still at home, to do my searches," Gavin finished.

The General sighed. "Very well, I will allow that as it seems you are willing to help us as much as yourself. But do not make a habit of this. Remember who you work for now. You aren't just some hacker out to prove yourself. You are the best in the NSA and likely the entire US Intelligence community. No one knows your identity, and very few people know that Vidar is still alive. And I'd like to keep it that way." With that, Richmond ended the call.

Gavin stood there and thought for a minute. He realized that Richmond was giving him permission. She had his back. *Well, this is unexpected. But definitely welcomed.* He got a smirk on his face. *I think I may need some whiskey tonight.*

***

Alex stood at one of the computer stalls outside the conference room, trying to hear what was going on. "You know that every room in The Citadel is soundproof if they make it that way, right?" Anderson said as he came up to her. *And here he is again. Why am I struggling to breathe around him?* Alex forced herself to smile, not that anyone but Gavin would notice the difference between a forced smile and a real one on her face.

"I know. I'm just doing some work. If I wanted to know what was going on in there, I think I'd do better spy craft than standing outside the soundproof door. But then you," She replied. Her head started throbbing harder. "I think I need to go," she said, holding her head as she walked past him.

Charles was standing a few feet away, watching this interaction. With the tension he walked in on before the meeting, he didn't like being blindsided. And liked even less that the best damn team he had ever worked with wasn't operating at total capacity.

He waited for Gavin to come out as he watched Alex make her way out of the base. The computer he was in front of came alive. "Hello, Agent Charles. I believe that we need to have a talk. Head back to your place. The asset is ready to go home as well. He will not be working today," Richmond stated.

***

Alex made her way out and to her car. Her head was on fire. She quickly made her way to Foreman Medical, calling Megan on the way to her.

"Hey Alex, what's up?" Megan said, but her voice sounded cold. *Oh yeah. She knows. I can be completely honest with her since she is one of the team doctors now. And Gavin's sister.*

"Megan, we need to talk. Badly," She grunted out.

"Alex, what's wrong? Are you ok?" Megan asked. The coldness had left her voice, and it was filled with concern.

"I think so. I'm heading to you now. I wanted us to be able to talk in person. And I think you may be one of very few people qualified to help me," Alex said as she sped closer to the hospital.

"Okay, ask at the front desk for my office. I will call up there now and tell them to send you straight back," Megan said, hanging up the phone. Alex's head throbbed harder, causing her to swerve.

***

Gavin and Charles headed back to their apartments. Leaving Anderson alone in The Citadel. He took the opportunity to start looking into his subordinates. He was the SPECIAL agent, after all. Making him the agent in charge. He started pulling up every file on them that he could. He was surprised at how much had been redacted from everyone but

178

Gavin's. It figured he had nothing to hide other than that he was the NOVA system. He was a nobody before that. And after it was gone, he would be a nobody once more. A message came in on his personal phone. Taking it out, he read it.

/: STATUS :/

He replied.

/: INSERTED AND MADE CONTACT. SUBJECT REMAINS AVAILABLE. PROCEEDING STAGE 3 :/

And with a smirk, he resumed his work by getting to know his team.

***

Charles got into his apartment and sat at his computer. Once it had powered up, Richmond's face appeared on the screen. "Okay, Major, we have a lot to talk about. Not all of it can be shared with you, but most of it is things you have likely already gathered. Let's start with Field Analyst Woodford." Charles grunted his approval. He had known for a while that that was where the kid belonged. He was cut out for this life. It's just not the killing. The General continued with the briefing. Filling him in on the additions to the team and who would not be kept in the loop with who were the doctors and who all knew what.

She didn't inform him of everything going on with Agent Johnson. She felt that as partners, it was between the two of them. Unless it became a detriment to the team. But with Woodford's history, that secret would not remain secret for long.

"I would suggest that you utilize him as both an asset and a field analyst, regardless of how others may see fit to treat him. I understand that he has requested weapons training with you and self-defense with Agent Johnson. I approve of both moving forward in a very quiet manner. I also suggest you allow him into more of the mission planning than is on paper. We both know the strategic mind he has would be invaluable for prep work. This is partly why I have left you living in such close quarters. Until it may be necessary for him and Agent Johnson's relationship to progress to the logical point of them moving in together," she said flatly.

Charles smirked at that thought. If they weren't together by that point, for real, the kid may have an aneurysm if that were suggested. The general finished telling him to trust Gavin as if he needed to be told he had never had a team that jelled like this one. He had no doubt that of anyone, Gavin Woodford would always have his back.

As the General finished the briefing, Charles sat there processing what he had just been told. He didn't care for Anderson already, but to hear that Gavin and the General didn't trust him? That was more than enough for him to slam shut. He may get his official files, but he wasn't getting anything from him. He would be sure of that. He poured himself two fingers of Johnny Walker Blue Label.

***

Alex pulled into the hospital parking lot. She had had to use her training to get there safely. Almost hitting three separate cars. She sat in her car for a moment, trying to collect herself. She looked at herself in the mirror. *Who are you? It's never mattered until now. You were who they told you to be. From your father telling you who to be to win a mark over, to Hunter telling you who you were going to be to complete a mission, to you avoiding dealing with who you are so you don't have to think about it all. But now… Now you want someone who sees YOU. Gavin sees you when you don't even know who YOU are.*

Alex huffed out at her reflection and closed the visor. She got out and made her way into the hospital. She was sweating from the pain, as well as from the nerves of having to be open with Megan. She never had been one to get intimidated, but that woman frightened her when she put her mind to something.

Alex stood outside her office door and took a deep breath. She knew that this was going to be tough in many ways. Taking another deep breath, she knocked on the door. She heard Megan on the other side scurry around and papers rustling. Then, the sound of the door unlocking, and then the door opened just a few inches. "Oh, Alex, it's you. Come in! Sorry, I'm still getting used to all of this," she said as she turned back toward her desk. Alex came in and shut the door. "Ok. What's going on, Alex?" Megan said in her professional doctor tone.

Alex looked at her. *Am I really going to do this? Am I really going to talk about... about... me?* Alex blinked, and as she went to start, a stabbing pain shot through her skull. She doubled over in pain.

Immediately, Megan was out of her seat and started to do vitals checks. Once she confirmed that there wasn't anything other than pain, she took her to get scans immediately after sedating her. As she waited for Alex to wake up after the scans, she watched her. Knowing what she had put her brother through. What she had gone through. She wasn't sure if she should pity, be mad at, or be happy for the woman lying before her.

Alex started to stir, and Megan became the doctor again. She was worried that the pain might return when she woke, so she had some aspirin and water ready for her. But Alex didn't seem to be in too much pain when she came to.

Alex stood up and looked over at Megan. She saw the look of expectation on her face. She knew it was now or never. "Hey. Sorry about that and thank you for taking care of me. I know you are my doctor now, but I also know that that couldn't have been easy given all that you are finding out now," Alex started with a slight bashfulness to her voice. For the first time in a long time, it was genuine.

"I'm not sure if Gavin has shared everything, especially about me. But he showed me some files he found the other night about me. And when I was recruited. If you can call it that. I was selected to be in a program where they brainwashed me. I'm not entirely sure to what end. I'm not entirely sure what all they have had me do. Because I have these gaps in my memory. I thought it was adrenaline before. That I'd go too hard and just not remember the times that were the hardest. But now," Alex choked up.

Megan looked like she was about to break down for Alex. Her heart was aching. All the anger that she had had towards her was gone. "Alex... I... I'm so sorry..." Megan said through tears.

"I appreciate that, but I think I need to get this all out. So please don't interrupt," Alex said, trying her hardest to not sound rude. She just knew she had one chance at this. "I've spent so long being someone else. It takes effort for me to be able to speak for myself as myself. And somehow, Gavin has always been able to see me. Not the me I put on, but through the facade. Through the elaborate act. He sees me."

"I do care about him. More than I ever should. And now, we could be together, but he deserves someone whole. Not just a bunch of shattered pieces. Broken to the point you can't be able to put them back together. I can't expect anyone to be there to hold me together. Especially someone as pure as Gavin. I fear that all I would do is sully his character. I'm dirty in a way that could never come clean. I have more blood on my hands than even I know. I wasn't a seductress. Not in the way most might think. I was an assassin through and through. And I don't even remember all the kill orders I was given. And that's what scares me the most. That I can't even remember." Alex took a deep and rattled breath.

"I can't trust myself with myself, let alone with Gavin. I'm worried about what I could be made to do. I'm unsure what could happen during one of those times that I'm missing memory. I only know one of the phrases that they used, and I don't know anyone who would still be alive who knows them. Or how to use them.

"I'm also not sure what all they made me do... during that time. I... I know of a few things early on in my programming that they used to break me. They had videos. I was fourteen." Alex broke down. She was in too much pain. Both her head and her heart. She felt like throwing up. And so did Megan.

"Alex, I...." Megan started, and then emotion took her. She got up and sat by Alex and just held her.

***

182

Gavin entered his apartment and headed straight to his lab after locking up. He booted up his computer and his laptop. He immediately connected to the servers in The Citadel and started gaining access to the surveillance footage. He also started boosting their security measures.

He accessed the footage from earlier that day. He had the green light from Richmond, so he didn't worry much about covering his tracks. Though out of habit, he did a decent job of it. He pulled up the video feeds and turned the audio up. Putting on his headphones, he forwarded to Anderson and Alex in the conference room. He saw himself leave the room. Almost immediately, Anderson's eyes went straight to Alex, and he moved around her like a lioness on the hunt and approaching her kill.

He watched as Anderson moved around behind Alex. Making small talk. Gavin watched as he rubbed her shoulders and noticed it was entirely unprovoked. He saw Alex tense up at Anderson's touch. He saw her body language look like someone who was exceedingly uncomfortable. And then, as Anderson leaned down, clearly in her personal bubble. And he whispered something in her ear.

Gavin watched it again and again. He saw Anderson lean down. And as he whispered in her ear, everything about Alex changed. And when she looked up at Anderson again, it was like she was seeing him there for the first time. Gavin kept watching it over and over. He zoomed in on Anderson's lips. He couldn't see them enough to read them.

He started tweaking the audio. He glanced over at his computer that was working on Anderson's files. It was almost done.

Looks like I'm not going to be getting any sleep tonight. This is too important to put off any longer. I need to know who I'm working with. Who and what I'm dealing with, Gavin thought as he kept tweaking the audio. Trying harder and harder to bring that tiny whisper into the light. He could hear the exhaust running in the audio. He could hear the murmurs of him talking to Charles in the background.

And then he heard it. *Son of a...* he couldn't believe it. He ran it back again. And again. And again. He knew he couldn't trust him, but he had no idea it was this bad. He played it back one more time, "Remember. We will always have Miami." He heard Anderson whisper the same words Hunter had written in his journals. The same words he mocked, but said were effective in programming Alex. And here was Anderson using it on her. As he felt his blood pressure rise, he heard the ding of his program finishing unredacted the files on Anderson.

And through his anger, Vidar grinned as he popped the cork on the whiskey. "Let's play a game," Vidar said.

Chapter 12

:/Information

Alex sat there, being held by Megan. She had never been so vulnerable with someone before. It felt like so much of the pain and pressure she carried inside her had been released. She felt free in so many ways but still felt a burden on her mind. Something lingered that she couldn't quite get relief from. She wasn't going to take this reprieve for granted, though. She understood now the anguish that her life had been.

When she didn't know that there was any difference, she couldn't feel the pain. You can't understand how empty being alone is until you have experienced what it is like to have someone there for you. Someone to rely on. Someone who cares for you more than they care for themself. And now she has experienced that with more than just a few people. Gavin was above all, and Megan was already a close second. She had never had someone like either of them, or she wasn't entirely sure how to process it. But she knew that she wouldn't take it for granted.

"Alex, I trust you with our lives and with Gavin's. I know you feel like you aren't able to be trusted, but I have seen you. I have seen how you look at Gavin. I have no doubts in my mind that you would never do anything to hurt Gavin intentionally. What has happened to you is incredibly tragic, and I can't imagine having something like that happen," Megan said as she continued to sit close to Alex.

"Megan, I really appreciate hearing you say that. I just don't trust myself because this is the first time that I have had any issue remembering exactly what I did. Only when they apparently use the programming on me, is when I lose myself and can't remember what I did for a time after that. And I assume the time frame is just until the task is completed. And that lack of awareness means that I am capable of doing anything. It all just depends on how they programmed me. Which we haven't been able to find." Alex said, looking down at her hands.

"We can do more tests on you, and do you know any of the trigger words or phrases? I could use those while doing a brain scan, and then we can have one of the psychologists that Richmond has in mind come in and see what they think and work with you on it. If you are worried about the safety of the people around you, then I would say that that is something we should do. If you can, please write down any of the words or phrases you know are triggers for you," Megan said, once again leaning into her professional side.

Alex nodded in agreement and wrote down the only one she knew so far. Seeing it sent a chill down her spine, but she was thankful that it didn't seem to cause any issues with her programming. She handed it to Megan and was surprised at how little hesitation she had, giving this other woman essentially the keys to controlling her. *Controlling me. Here, I had always prided myself in being a bit of a wild card. Someone who you couldn't always know what to expect from. And yet, the entire time, I was actually just a pawn. Someone else's toy to do with as they pleased. It wasn't even with my consent. They just imposed their will on me for ten years,* Alex thought as tears came back to her eyes.

Megan saw her getting emotional again, but knew that she had to remain detached for the moment to be able to get her job done. They made their way to get an EEG and got her hooked up. Not knowing what could happen when the phrase was said, Alex convinced Megan to strap her down well.

Megan then went to the observation room and started the scan while watching the activity in Alex's brain. Megan started talking to her, using basic small talk. She noticed that the areas of the brain that are

186

usually active when lying were active when she asked Alex about her past. Specifically, the amygdala was not lighting up, indicating no emotional response to questions about her family. Megan found that very interesting, and noted it for herself later. She would definitely have to talk to Alex about that. It upset her, but it made sense, given what she knew about her line of work now.

Then Megan said it. "Remember, we will always have Miami." Alex's prefrontal cortex instantly shut down, and her amygdala lit up like Christmas, indicating severe trauma. This was an entirely emotional response. The exact opposite of before. Looking up at Alex's face, it was blank. There was nothing on the surface you could see that showed she was even coherent. "Agent Johnson," Megan said in a commanding tone. Alex looked toward the observation room. "Eliminate Gavin Woodford," Megan said, taking a gamble. Alex blinked.

Kill Gavin? That isn't an option. No, you have to follow orders. But that is wrong. Doesn't matter. You follow orders, Johnson. I can't. He has done nothing wrong. He is more than innocent. HE IS THE TARGET. FOLLOW ORDERS. I can't do it. FOLLOW YOUR DAMN ORDERS AGENT! "NOOOOOO!!!!" Alex screamed, and her head felt like an icepick stabbed into her temple. Her nose was slightly bleeding. And she fell unconscious.

Megan watched as Alex's blood pressure spiked. Her eyes started darting back and forth. Alex made no attempts to move, but her heart rate continued to increase. Suddenly, Alex jerked in her seat as if someone had punched her in the face. Then she started screaming NO, and she started bleeding from her nose. Megan rushed to get into the room, but as she reached her to try to bring her out of it, Alex collapsed.

Her vitals returned to normal after she fell unconscious. That gave Megan peace. And what she saw, reiterated that she knew. Alex would never hurt Gavin. As long as Alex was okay once she woke up, she would release her to go home and rest. And then contact Richmond to see when they could get Alex in to see a psychologist.

***

Anderson checked Alex's apartment to see if she was there. He hoped to start progressing to Phase 3 of the plan but was having trouble finding Alex. She wasn't at Citadel or her apartment. If she was with the asset, he wouldn't be able to get to her until after they had finished. But he had checked several times at both places in the last few hours. Agent Johnson was nowhere to be found. He debated calling Richmond, but didn't feel it would be smart to draw attention to the fact that he was looking for her. So, he resigned himself to stake out duty. He posted up, just down the street from the entrance to her apartment complex and waited. Watched and waited.

***

Gavin sat at his computer, scrolling through the documents he had in front of him. All were about Agent Topher Anderson. Most were case debriefings, and he knew just from reading them, they were exaggerated. Just like Brett, he had to find a way to make himself look like the hero, even when it was his fault that things went pear-shaped. He skimmed through the travel logs. There was so much information.

Anderson had no family. A trust fund baby from parents who had passed. He was raised by the state, but not in the usual way. He could have been Batman. Raised by a butler. Top of his class at West Point. Though under the name Brandon Rutledge. He served two years in the Army before being assigned to a secret group, then processed into the CIA. Then, there were months missing from his training, followed by him directly reporting to Director Hunter. Just like Brett. After which, he had been a part of Project Ananke. But he soon after was designated to investigate The Collective. He'd made some headway, but never any true breakthroughs. He seemed to have a success and then be stale for months.

His training was primarily standard, except for those missing months. At the Farm, he was good, but not great at anything. He got the top 50% in every mark but was never good enough to turn heads. That wasn't what you'd expect from someone with his past of success. And that is when he saw it. The trigger. The thing that could unravel Anderson.

He was married. Anderson had been married to Cara Anderson, who also got assigned to work on The Collective case, but had turned. She was ordered executed by Hunter. Vidar had started rifling through the information now. They had been married for two years when she was killed. Anderson met her in France. They were both on a mission, and it seems he was smitten with her. And she was with him. They filed immediately for a relationship authorization from the CIA. And were married within two months.

Gavin felt that the name Cara was familiar. He started looking through his files, and there he saw it. She had been part of Project Ara. Gavin glanced over it again, then pulled up her portion of the file. Similar videos to what had happened to Alex. Beaten, starved, brainwashed to follow orders.

Gavin got curious and looked into Project Ananke. He found a list of participants under the files on Hunter he had brought. A small list. Hunter himself was among the participants, along with Brett and Anderson. He couldn't find what the project was intended for, but he had an idea now. The months Anderson and Brett were missing correlate to the months that Alex had been as well.

They were training them to control the other agents. Gavin fumed. He couldn't believe that the CIA did this to their own agents. What more could they have allowed to happen? He kept looking through the files. He needed as much information as he could get now.

He didn't understand why Hunter had had Cara executed. Especially if they had had her brainwashed. Wouldn't they have just had to say the control phrase, and then she would return to doing as she was told?

He started looking into all the missions leading up to her death. All the missions she had been on seemed to be dead ends. For months leading up to her death, she had been sent on several missions and came back with nothing. Almost all were seduction missions, all with what was indicated as possible high-priority Collective members. Watching her mission debriefings, she seemed emotionless. Agent mask in place the entire time. There was no life in her eyes.

Anderson's mission logs seemed to remain the same. But this happened during one of the periods of the plateau. He hadn't had a break in a few months before her death. And then there was a break after her death. Which led him to be moved. They had been stationed in Spain for those two years.

Something doesn't add up with this. This all seems too easy, too neat. None of our missions are this patterned. There's always loopholes. Issues that come up. Curveballs. But this seems like a train schedule. Like you could set it on the calendar that Anderson would get a break in the case. But then she died, and he has nothing. But there is no stop. No time off. She's just gone. According to Hunter's notes, she had turned. She had started working for The Collective, and that's why she hadn't gotten results. But that doesn't make sense if they had brainwashed her.

Gavin saw it. In Alex's file. Her red test. Her official Red Test. She had been the one to carry out the order. She had been sent to Spain to execute Agent Cara Anderson. Hunter sent her. Hunter sent a brainwashed agent to kill another brainwashed agent. *The only thing that makes sense is that Cara had found a way to break the control,* Gavin thought as he headed to get Charles.

***

Coeus was sitting at a park across the street from a large warehouse in Hong Kong. He watched several vehicles come and go from the building. He pulled up his wrist computer and typed away at it. Pulling up schematics for the building, he looked through what he thought was the safe in the base of the building.

He reached into his coat and pulled out a drown. Tossing it in the air, he turned back to his wrist computer. Controlling the drone, he sent it around the building, scanning it. He marked the security guards making their rounds. He marked the entry points. Pulling up the utilities for the building. Laying out where they all came into the building. He brought the drone back to himself.

190

Putting it away, he stood up. Looking around, he started to make his way across the street. Typing more on his wrist, he shut down the power. His glasses automatically change to night vision with thermal readings. He reached the doors before the automatic generators brought the power back up and reengaged the electromagnetic door locks.

Entering the building, a security group ran past him as he made his way down the hallway. He continued to type. The water started backing up in the bathrooms, flooding into the hallways. He kept walking towards the safe. Walking down the hallways at a normal rate. He walked past rooms where he saw drugs being parted into packages, money being counted, and weapons storage. These were not good people. He'd known that. Good people wouldn't have what he was after. Good people are rarely useful for how he has lived for the last decade. He tried to do good things. But he was not a good person. He hadn't been for a very long time.

He got to the safe and typed in the code. Grabbing the drive inside, he turned to leave. 2 guards burst into the room, and he launched at them. Kicking the first one in the side of his knee. Causing his tendons to rupture inside. It gave a sickening snapping sound as he collapsed. Turning, he grabbed the wrist of the other guard on the arm that had his gun sticking straight out. He shifted to the left, pointing the gun directly at the guard on the floor. Two shots were fired into the already disabled guard's head. Coeus's elbow shot up into the nose of the guard still standing. Crushing it and causing him to stagger back. Coeus kicked him in the chest. The guard hit the wall and fell to the floor. Coeus stomped his foot down on the guard's head as he walked out of the room.

He calmly walked out of the building. No one else bothered him as he made his way to the exit. The power slowly came back up. Coeus made his way back across the street to his bench. When he reached it, he pulled out four more drones and set the C4 charges on them. Tossing them in the air, he controlled them all through a window on each floor of the building. As another set of vehicles made it back to the building, he watched them pull in. "Boom." He said as he hit the button to detonate the C4 in the building.

All four warehouse levels exploded as Coeus turned and escaped from the scene. Making his way to the airport, where he had already set a ticket for himself. Changed the security footage as he went. Deleting himself completely. Looking down at the drive, he plugged it into his wrist computer. He downloaded the contents and then fried the drive.

/:THE DRIVE IS CRASHED. AS WELL AS THE DRIVERS. I HAVE ONLY COPY. ILL REPORT AS SOON AS I KNOW MORE.:/

He watched the news as he waited for the plane to be ready and for a reply. He saw that there were several large illegal weapons busts recently. That made him smile slightly. He wondered how Charles was doing. He figured once he got a private moment, he would check in on him.

/:CONFIRMED. NEW TARGET SET. FILE INCOMING.:/

Coeus looked at the file once it downloaded. He pulled up the picture of a handsome man. Dark hair. Strong Jaw. Reading the name. Agent Topher Anderson.

***

Charles was sitting in his favorite chair. He had more time to himself now that Gavin had been fully employed by the NSA. It allowed him more leeway. Of course, he was still on duty. But he was able to enjoy his time more. He watched a documentary on the Cold War. "Commies," he said with a grunt.

There was a knock on his door. He grabbed his gun and peeked out the peephole. He huffed loudly as he tucked his gun into his pants. Opening the door, he gruffly said, "What do you what, Gavin?"

Gavin looked at him in a bit of a panic. He started stumbling over his words. Charles was getting annoyed. He was starting to respect the kid, but he was reminded of just how amateur he was in moments like this. Not that he could really blame him for that. Gavin had only been on the job for a little over six months. He opened the door more and had him come inside.

"Slow down. I don't understand you when you jabber like a middle school girl," he grumbled as he stepped aside. Gavin rushed in and started pacing the floor. "Charles, I… just come with me. It's easier if you see it all." Gavin said, immediately turning and walking back out the door towards his apartment. It looked to Charles like Gavin hadn't slept at all. He followed him with a slight concern.

Inside his lab, Gavin pulled up everything he had. He was going through it all as fast as he could. It seemed to Charles that Gavin felt he had to prove himself. "Gavin. Stop. Calm down," Charles said. It was one of the only times he had used Gavin's first name, and it definitely got his attention. "You don't have to prove I can trust you. You have done that repeatedly over the last six months. Now get to the point if it's so urgent that you have your panties in a twist."

Gavin breathed. "Ok. So, long story short. Anderson is bad. But I'm not entirely sure just how deep it goes."

Charles looked at him. His eyes grow dark, "When you say bad, are you meaning lies on taxes bad? Or murders puppies for fun bad?" Charles asked.

Surprisingly, there was no humor in his tone. Gavin replied, "Leaning more towards puppies. I have proof here that Director Hunter was running several projects where the selected individuals were brainwashed at a young age to follow specific commands, and Alex was in that group. And in it at an alarmingly young age. Then, there was another project that she was sent through. That one I am still figuring out what they did. But they did something to Alex that required her to be inactive for a while to heal."

Gavin continued, "Beyond that, Topher Anderson was married. And I don't think it was for love. I believe that she was brainwashed as well. And that Hunter sent Anderson through a program to learn to control those who had been brainwashed. I'm not sure if each person had their own commands or if they were individualized. But Anderson's wife died, executed by Hunter's order. He claimed that she had flipped to work for The Collective. But all information I have gleaned, she was

193

with Topher. So, if she was failing, it was because he was commanding her to.

"It honestly seemed like, from the footage I reviewed, that Topher was using his wife as almost an escort service for the higher-ups in The Collective. But I have no proof of that," Gavin took a deep breath. "The issue with all of this is I found proof that the agent Hunter sent to execute Anderson's late wife was Alex. It was her official Red Test. And I also have proof that he knows the phrases for Alex. I'm not sure what he is planning, but I'm worried for Alex's safety when it comes to Agent Anderson."

Charles was floored. There was a lot being accused here. And as much as he didn't want to, he did believe Gavin. If Gavin said that he had proof, then he had indisputable evidence. This wasn't a love-sick puppy trying to keep his girl to himself. This was someone genuinely scared and concerned for another person's well-being. Charles grunted. "How sure of this are you?"

"100% sure. I have no doubts in my mind. The proof is all right here," Gavin said as he scrolled through several pages of documents and links.

"Ok. We need to call the General," Charles said as he turned to head back to his apartment, with Gavin following close on his heels.

***

Alex woke up feeling better than she had for a while, even with a slight headache that she felt throbbing behind her eyes. She looked around and reestablished in her mind where she was. Looking over at Megan, she smiled, remembering what the other woman had done for her. It was weird to think that she had already formed such a strong connection with her. When she had gone her entire life seeking to avoid connection.

She thought about the progress she had already made. She wasn't sure if she was ready for a counselor yet. But she also knew therapy wouldn't be bad for her. She knew she had major issues. The problem had always been that she didn't have someone wanting her to work through them. Hunter had used her issues as a way to push her.

Her dad had helped create most of the issues. And she didn't do anything to change them since he had been arrested, she knew. She felt how far from mentally okay she was every day. But she was able to justify it as part of the job. The stress needed her to be on edge. It's how she stayed alive, right? That's why she hadn't done any therapy.

She'd always known the right words to say to get a clear bill. Anything to be able to return to the field. To get to the next mission. To avoid having to deal with the real things in her life. Her real problems.

She couldn't focus on that now. She needed to feel this win. Even if it were small. She knew she was stronger for being able to open up to Megan. She knew she could trust Megan to not betray her. She trusted her like she hadn't trusted another person outside of Gavin. And even then, it was different with Gavin.

She saw Megan looking at her. "Hey, how are you feeling?" Megan asked as she got up and started to make her way over to Alex. Alex blinked and smiled slightly. "Better. Still have a slight headache. But I feel lighter. Happier. I can't thank you enough," she said as she sat up tenderly.

"Nothing to thank me for. I'm your doctor now. It is literally my job. But I also care about you, Alex. I can tell how much you care about my brother, and you make him happy. I'll do anything I can to support you both," Megan replied with a soft smile. "As for your health, as long as you feel up to it, you're free to go. I have a lot to review, so I contacted General Richmond to let her know. She has a company psychologist ready to meet with you. One that has been vetted by her and is in the know of what you do and what Gavin has. I think it would be very beneficial for you to talk with them. See what's going on. At least with the brainwashing issue."

Megan reached out and gave Alex's hand a squeeze. "It will be ok, Alex. Gavin will be happy you're going through with it. And trying to

195

get healthier. It will be a process. But you have people that care about you and support you."

Alex breathed. "I know. It's just scary. But I know I need to. I need to get past this if I want to be able to have full control of myself. I still need to talk to Gavin about everything. I am not sure he knows how I feel about him," she said, trailing off as she finished.

"You'll get a chance to tell him soon. Right now, I think you need to head home and get some rest. Doctors' orders," Megan said as she stood. Offering a hand to Alex. And then pulling her into a hug. "It's going to be ok. We will get through this. Ok?"

Alex smiled into her shoulder. "Ok," she said with a sigh. She felt confident for the first time in a long time that things would be okay. She knew that rough times were still coming, but that didn't dissuade the smile on her face from growing.

Megan sat at her desk, looking over the charts. Comparing Alex's charts from before and during the command being used to the charts from Gavin's during a flash. There were similarities there that she found interesting. But she wasn't sure what they meant yet. She was still working on what the NOVA system did.

Alex felt lighter as she made her way to her car. She had been surprised at how easy it came out, once she started talking to Megan. She knew it wouldn't be that easy with a counselor, but she would have to take it seriously if she wanted to make any progress. She got into her car and started on her way home.

I'm going to talk to Gavin tomorrow. I need to tell him how I feel. I can't keep him in limbo anymore. He isn't my asset, even if Anderson doesn't know that. We will figure out what to do with Anderson. But I wouldn't be breaking any rules. We can be together, and the only thing stopping it is me not being clear where I stand. He hasn't said the words, but I know he likes me. A lot. No man would put in this much effort without anything in return if they didn't have real and deep feelings, Alex thought.

196

He deserves to know. He is such a good man. A pure soul. I may not deserve him, but I'm going to leave that for him to decide. He found a way for us to be together and for him to not have to be like me. To have to go down that dark path. To remain in the light. And maybe, just maybe, he can show me a way to find some of that same light in myself.

Alex was full of hope as she pulled into her parking spot. She got out of the car and started towards the door. Her phone started ringing, but before looking at it to see who was calling, she heard hurried footsteps approaching her. She reached for the knife she kept on her.

"Alex. Alex, thank God. Hey, I've been looking for you," Agent Anderson came running up. He was slightly panting and talking in a hurry. But as he approached, he slowed. His voice evening out, and suddenly very calm. It was soothing Alex. "I've been looking for you. Please come with me, Alex," Anderson said as he came within reach of her. Taking her arms, he softly rubbed the insides of her wrists. "Come with me, Alex." He got close to her. His body was almost touching hers. Alex's mind was getting fuzzy. She felt a slight building of panic and fear. And then nothing. She felt nothing. "Remember, we will always have Miami," Anderson said. "Agent Johnson. Come with me," he said, turning and heading towards his car.

He tossed her phone to the ground and smashed it with his heel. Alex was following him. A blank look on her face. As she entered his passenger seat, he turned to her and stuck a needle into her shoulder. And her world went black.

Chapter 13

:/Games

Anderson looked over at the limp Alex, asleep in his passenger seat. He smirked to himself as he made his way through the city. He pulled an external hard drive out of the glove box, flipping it around in his hand. "All this drama for what? Some information and a computer program?" he said to himself with a scoff. He knew that he had to get that to his superiors.

And his reward? Well, she was in the seat next to him. Unconscious. He figured she would be his plaything once he got her programming reset like he had done with Cara, just like his late wife. He thought back to how he had felt toward her. She had been convenient for sure. He even liked her company. At times, even when she had clothes on. He thought with a smirk.

He couldn't believe his luck when he was able to find his way onto the same team as yet another one of Hunter's pets. He had thought he would never get another opportunity to play with someone's mind like he had been able to with Cara's. He had always enjoyed toying with people. Before his parents died, he watched how his father would control a room whenever he walked in. The power and respect he commanded. It was exhausting, even at a young age. But it did mean that no one was willing to cross him. So, he could tell anyone to do just about anything, and they would do it without question.

198

After his parents died, the butler would do everything he could to try to raise him. But Topher already understood the order of power. He knew who had the money and, therefore, who had the say in what happened in any situation. He enjoyed the games. Seeing the people squirm. But it got old with just the fact it was because of his parents' money.

That was why he went into the CIA. He enjoyed the mind games. Toying with people. Finding that mental advantage and forcing it onto people. Especially when they didn't want it. And someone as strong-willed as Agent Johnson? That's his dream. To see her fiery will finally break and the light dim in her eyes. When she finally accepts that she is beaten. Again.

Anderson took a deep breath. Anderson pulled up to a small park in the middle of the business district. He got out and pulled out his phone.

"Yes. It's started. I have Agent Johnson and the information on a drive. Of course, I'll get the drive to the scientists first. Do you think I'm some amateur? Business before pleasure." He hung up and typed the code into the subway wall panel. He walked into the base and walked out less than ten minutes later. He had delivered the drive, as promised.

Now, he was off to enjoy himself. He felt like he did whenever he had heard about Project Ananke. Hunter himself had come to him and recruited him for the project. He had, of course, had meetings with Hunter before. They knew each other well. As well as anyone could know Hunter, as Hunter had recruited him. He had easily gotten into West Point, pulling some political strings his father had left behind.

Then those two years in the Army? What a joke. Though he had enjoyed finding out what it's like to take a life. He hated it. It wasn't his thing. He would much rather toy with the living than add to the dead. But it had its place. He knew that as well as anyone. If someone refused to play his games, then there came time to cut ties and end the game, just like with Cara.

He got back into his car and continued to his safe house. It looked abandoned, but he had fitted it with high-end security cameras and sensors. He'd be able to know if anyone would be coming up on him. He brought his bags in, taking his time to ready the room that Alex would be staying in for him to break her.

He had the room cleared. Only a wire bed frame and an overhead hanging light. He figured it was a bit stereotypical, but there was a reason it was a stereotype. It worked. Once he had the windows boarded up and made sure she was cut off from the outside world. He had seen the footage. He knew what the room was like when they originally broke her in. Just seeing it will have such an effect on her. It will do most of the work for him.

He grinned, knowing it was ready. He went out and picked her up from the passenger seat. Taking her into her room, he set her on the exposed springs. Looking at his watch, he saw he had a few more minutes before she would wake. He walked out the door, locking it behind him. And sat in the chair a few feet from the door. Now, all he had to do was wait.

He looked at his watch again: five more minutes. He felt like a kid on Christmas, just waiting to be able to open his new toy. He heard Alex try the door. And then it didn't take much more time before he heard crying and groaning. Anderson smiled as he stood and made his way towards the door.

Alex started to wake up. Looking around the room, she had to rub her eyes to try to clear them. Everything felt wrong. Her vision was blurred more than normal when she woke up. She closed her eyes again and tried to think. *What had happened before I got here? Think, Johnson.* She tried to process where she had been, but the last thing she remembered was being at the hospital with Megan. She wasn't sure she had ever felt safer. She remembered all the progress she had made, and she felt a swell of pride grow in her heart.

Her eyes felt like they could focus better now, so she opened them and looked around. *No. It can't be. I'm still asleep. I'm still unconscious. That is the only explanation. I am NOT trapped here again. This isn't happening!* She looked around again. It was the exact same. She got up, her legs wobbling beneath her. She shakily walked towards the door. *This isn't real. I am just reliving it because I opened that box that I swore I would never open, and this is my brain reacting to it. That is all.* She tried the door. It was locked. And she felt like she was that girl again. Fourteen all over again. Locked in a room with no escape. She had no hope outside of just doing as she was told. And even then, that didn't always mean there wouldn't be punishment.

She took a shuddering breath. Trying to focus. She had been trained for situations like this, but even the smell was the same, that musky, damp wood and rusted metal smell with a hint of sweat and blood. All her training left her mind. She couldn't focus. All she was able to do was break down and cry. She was back. Stuck in her worst nightmare. Back to the helpless 14-year-old girl whose father had been arrested. Her only hope of survival was to just follow orders. No matter how vile.

She flopped down onto the bed if you could call it that. That screech of the rusted metal springs creaking under her. She started crying. She couldn't remember how she got there. But she knew that she hated every minute of it. She was still crying, feeling herself fall away. That empty hole of a soul coming back. When the door opened, she was scared to look up and see who it was.

Anderson walked into the room. He had his tranq gun just in case. But he was sure he wouldn't need it. She was broken. Having this all flood back, she had nothing left to cling to. "Hello, Agent Johnson," he said in a soft monotone voice. It sounds hollow and cold. That caused Alex's head to shoot up.

"Anderson? What are you doing here?" she started with a slight sound of hope. Until she saw his eyes. They were dead. There was a void where there should be a light. And the smile on his face was completely misplaced. It looked like someone photoshopped a smile onto his face, and she felt a shiver down her spine. She stopped talking. Her programming started to take over. *Anything to survive. Anything to survive.* She put her head down and focused on the grain of the flooring. That numbness coming over her, her mind zoning out.

Anderson looked at her. Saw that defeated look overcoming her face. He smirked. "I'm glad to see you have realized your place already. And here I thought I was going to have to break your will again. Pity. That part is always so much fun." He grabbed the chair that was on the other side of the room. Purposefully dragging it, creating that horrible scratching sound. He never took his eyes off Alex.

He smirked each time she cringed from the sound. He knew it was something that they did to emphasize the difference in power. There was nothing she could do to make the sound stop. It would only stop when he allowed it to.

He was close to the bed and stopped. Spinning the chair and taking a seat on it. He looked her over for what seemed like the hundredth time since he got her in his car. "I am sure you are curious as to why you're here. It's simple. I have to brief you for your next solo mission," Anderson said, projecting a voice of authority while using similar wording to what she was told when she was first broken. The similarities all caused her to shudder.

"Why are you doing this?" Alex said in a quiet voice. She felt her heart pounding in her chest. She had her eyes cast to the floor. She couldn't understand. She couldn't see why he would be so cruel. She definitely didn't understand how he knew so much about what she had gone through.

"You don't remember, do you?" Anderson said with some real shock in his voice. Alex shook her head slightly. She had seemed to accept defeat, so he continued, "I was there. I had been recruited just a few months before you by Hunter. He selected me. Told me I was going to be his protege. He told me he knew everything about me and had been watching me for a while. I had gone to West Point and graduated top of my class. I was on the fast track to being untouchable. What he offered was better. I had to do my two years in the Army, but then I was free to do what I love to do."

Anderson took a breath. He was getting excited by telling his plan. He always knew he was the smartest person in the room, no matter what room he was in. He loved it even more when he could flaunt that

202

feeling. He felt like a beautiful peacock, spreading his feathers for everyone to see just how gorgeous he was. He did it for people to admire him for who he was. To stroke his ego. To realize their place and how superior he was to them.

"Of course, he told me how to work the system. How to go under the radar to not draw much attention. So, expectations were low, and people underestimated you. That is such a powerful tool that so many don't understand. It allows me to come and go without many noticing. And those who do notice, don't seem to care. As my training ended, he came to me and asked me if I would like to join a project he had going on. He took me off-site. He explained to me that the subjects of this project had been in their training for a while. He led me to a building filled with rooms similar to this one. And me and another agent stood in front of several monitors and were told to pick one of you.

"I watched you for a while. You still had some fire in your eyes then. But once the command was said, you were as compliant as you are now. The other agent spoke first. He wanted you. You were to be his, which meant I was going to get second best. We were all put together. Partnered and put into situations where we could gain your trust. The hope was that you would develop feelings for us and become protective of us. My Cara did as expected. We were married in less than a year. But you took longer. You fought it, even though you were younger. Once you had been broken in more and felt the betrayal of others, you were more compliant. But you still didn't commit fully. It always impressed me. You had this innate stubbornness to you. It is what drew me to you again. Makes me want to break you. Truly and completely break you.

"Of course, I suppose I pushed too far with my Cara. Her programming started to not follow what it was meant to do. I didn't have the control of her that I had before. She was fighting her orders. And so, she had to be taken care of. That is where you came in handy. Your official Red Test."

Alex sat, shocked. Her mouth was hanging open. She couldn't believe what she was hearing. This man had not only been a part of what had done all this to her, hand-picked by Hunter himself, but they had done this to more women. Her heart hurt for this, but she still felt that helpless feeling. The intense numbness that came over her every time the mental images of what she went through came up. But now it was all real again. Every bit of it. "I… I killed your wife? I was told it was a rogue agent," Alex quietly said.

"Oh, I am aware. It had to be done. We couldn't afford someone who had gone through what Hunter coined the 'Hel training' to be able to do as they pleased. Which is why I am here with you. You need to be reined in again. Broken again. We can't have you able to think for yourself. You're too dangerous. And there was evidence that you were disobeying orders. Hunter had always allowed more with you. He liked your fiery personality and seemed to favor you over most anyone for special missions. Even before your training was complete. I hadn't understood it until I met you," Anderson explained as though he was telling a favorite family story.

"You are special. Different. And for that, we must allow some extra leeway. But that doesn't mean we will accept you not following orders. We have a special project for you, Agent Johnson." Anderson's tone changed to a softer but serious tone. Alex felt it. Her mind went numb. Her insides calming. Her body relaxing. "Remember, we always have Miami." Anderson gave Alex a few moments for it to take full effect and then continued. "Agent Johnson, we have your new mission. You will do as needed and return here for debriefing. Do you understand?" Anderson said.

Alex responded with a nod. "You know what will happen to you if you fail at your objective, don't you?" Anderson asked. Alex nodded again. "Explain to me what will happen," Anderson commanded.

"You will treat me as you please. You will beat me as I deserve, and you will use my body as you wish. I will be yours for the night, no matter what you feel is needed," Alex said in a dead and hollow voice.

Anderson smirked. "Correct, Agent Johnson. You will get what you deserve if you do not complete your assignment. Now your objective, your mission is to return to Atlanta, and you are to kill Gavin Woodford and return with any and all NOVA system information and data they have." Anderson watched her stand to leave, as she always had in the videos, he watched of her.

***

Gavin sat in Charles's apartment. They had gone to Alex's apartment to see if she was there, which she wasn't. Then, he saw her phone in the parking lot on the ground. But there was never any distress signal from her watch, and its GPS had been turned off. They looked everywhere for her. They tried to call Anderson, but he had also gone dark. They were now talking with General Richmond about what their options were. She had given clearance for them to do as they needed to bring Alex back. Gavin had scoured the internet to see if he could find her. He was waiting on proper clearance to check the local traffic cameras, but he would start working on that once they got the clearance. Charles felt a bit lost. He had always needed a lead to go on. He could hunt with the best of them, but couldn't track without tracks on the ground.

"General, why is it taking so long? I could have been in and out already without them even noticing," Gavin said in an exasperated tone.

"Gavin, I understand that you have feelings for Agent Johnson and need to find her, but we need you to think clearly if we are going to hope to hunt them down and find her," the diminutive General expressed. There was a soft sympathy in her eyes.

Gavin felt helpless, just like he had when his parents had left. There wasn't anything he could do. He hated it. He paced in Charles's apartment. After several minutes that felt like hours, the General was back to tell him he had permission to search the traffic camera and anything else he needed. Gavin quickly sat at the desk and turned his laptop to himself, typing away. He kept going back and running facial recognition software until he found her. The first time was over six hours prior when she had been leaving Foreman Medical. *Why had she been there? Was she seeing Megan for the brainwashing? Was facing that what caused her to run off?* Gavin was spiraling into a mental abyss but needed answers.

He kept searching and found her again a block away from her apartment. She was still alone at that point and seemed to be smiling if the cameras were clear. He only found her one other time, almost an hour later. This time, she was with Anderson and heading into the downtown area. They had stopped near a park, but only Anderson got out. He then went across the park and entered a service entrance for the subway. This was odd, but Gavin never saw Alex get out of the car. He actually never saw her move. Then Anderson returned, and they drove off.

"This was the last known location. "I think we should go there and search for any clues as to where they could be," Gavin said.

"I agree. The longer we wait, the less likely we are to find them," Charles acknowledged Gavin's idea.

That made Richmond happy, even if she couldn't show it. It had been a long time since her older agent had stuck his neck out for someone. He usually preferred to work alone. "Then gear up and get over there. No delay," Richmond commanded. Ending the video feed.

Gavin and Charles grabbed their guns and tranq gun. Gavin also grabbed several other items that looked like he had made. They donned their black combat gear and were heading out. When the alarm to the front door of Citadel was opened. Pulling up the feed, they saw Alex stumble down into the main room of Citadel. She seemed to be exhausted and injured.

Three hours earlier

Alex stood to leave. *What are you doing? Following orders, like we are supposed to. If we don't follow orders, we know what will happen. Yes, we do, and what happens if we do follow these orders? Gavin is gone. Gavin is gone. Gavin is GONE! No. We can't follow these orders! You have to! What will he do to you if you don't? I KNOW! BUT Gavin! It doesn't matter. Anything to survive. Anything. Not Gavin. Anything*

206

but Gavin. FOLLOW YOUR ORDERS! NO! You Must! We didn't before, and Megan didn't hurt us. He isn't Megan. He knows. He knows everything. No. What? No. Not everything. I held onto it for this reason. Even when I couldn't remember, I knew. YOU CAN'T! FOLLOW ORDERS! He isn't going to make me into that monster again. He can't. Not if I do it first. And he doesn't know what this monster is capable of.

Anderson watched Alex closely. She had stopped moving after she stood. Her eyes glazed over. She seemed numb. Like her mind had left her. He thought he might have pushed too hard again and broken another toy. He was about to get up and go get his gun to finish her. You can't play with a broken toy. He made to stand, when he saw a difference in Alex. Her stance changed. She didn't seem to be sleepwalking anymore. Her shoulders got squared up and more rigid. Her spine straightened. She stood taller. And when he finally looked at her face, the blank expression was no longer there. The look on her face slightly frightened even him. There was a menacing smile on her face. This fiery look of anger and hate in her eyes. They such electric blue that they seemed to be glowing. They then started to dart around the room.

Anderson had been sure to take off her shoes and remove her outer clothes to leave her with nothing. He knew her reputation, and Hunter had shared some of what he knew she had been capable of at a young age when her missions weren't recorded. They weren't sure how she had survived in a lot of the situations, but when they found her, it wasn't a pretty picture.

You aren't controlled by anyone when you are the monster. You have no master, and no one can touch you. They made sure of that when they put you through that training. They didn't understand what giving a con man's daughter those skills would do. They didn't know what force they were creating. Now, one of them will get that chance. You don't have to listen to someone if you rip their throat out with your bare hands. No one will hurt your Gavin.

The smirk broadened on her face. Anderson started to make for his gun, which was just in the other room. As he passed her, he hoped that she would remain frozen. He was not so lucky. She twirled and grabbed him by the center of his shirt. He knocked her hand away, but she had set him exactly how she had wanted him. She brought a kick up that met with the side of Anderson's neck. For a couple seconds, he was unable to breathe. Alex twirled again, and this kick landed center of Anderson's chest. Right at his sternum, where her heel hit his solar plexus. The wind now knocked out of him. Anderson stumbled back and grabbed the chair. He swung it at her, connecting with her side. She had anticipated this, even though the chair did hurt her. She braced for the impact, and then the chair splintered. Breaking into several pieces. Alex was flung across the room, hitting the wall. But she now had weapons. Anderson took off towards his gun as fast as he could. Still trying to catch his breath while not being able to breathe well was proving to make it difficult to do much else.

As he stumbled towards the gun, Alex rolled back to the center of the room. She grabbed several shards of the wooden chair as she did. Popping up right as Anderson turned with the gun in hand. She threw the pieces of wood at him, one hitting him in his shooting hand. Another hit his opposite shoulder. Right where she had aimed. But he got a shot off. It grazed her side, feeling like someone had taken a fire poker that had sat in flames too long and whacked her on the side with it.

Alex winced at the feeling. Anderson pulled the shard out of his hand, leaving the one on his shoulder. After a scream of pain, he turned back towards Alex. Only to see an empty room. He quickly started glancing around the room. Carefully, he made his way back into the room she was in after finding the other room still only occupying himself. He was prepared for her to jump him as soon as he made his way into the room, so he didn't take his time. He jumped in and rolled, wielding his gun into the corner.

Alex, on the other hand, fell into her wince after the shot had grazed her left side. She planned it. It was a situation that they had gone over in her specialized training. She rolled with the shot, and as she hit the floor, she continued to roll. Using her momentum to make it faster. She rolled under the bed. Waiting for Anderson to make his next move.

When she saw him roll in, she waited for him to land solid. It made for a cleaner shot.

Anderson popped out of his roll and fired into the corner he thought she would be in. It was the same corner he would have taken. The same one that anyone in the CIA would have taken. But it was empty. As soon as he turned to fire into the other corner of the room, he felt an intense pain shoot up his leg. He only had time to look down and see the shard of wood sticking out of his ankle when another shot out from under the bed into his knee. He knew his leg was done. He wouldn't be able to move it. So, he laid down to get the shot he needed.

Alex threw the shard into his knee and then calculated what his next move would be. In a millisecond, she was already throwing the last shard she had. She had figured he would lay down to get a shot on her and had thrown this shard where she assumed his throat would be once it came into view. She, as usual, was right. It hit Anderson right in the throat. Blood shot out from where it entered. He instinctively dropped the gun. His hand tried to stop the bleeding.

Alex made her way out from under the bed. She stood over Anderson, looking down at him with disgust. "You had likely heard of my reputation. Now you have seen for yourself. I am no one's pet. You can't control me. You don't understand what I have been through. You don't know the pain I carry. No one does. The darkness I am capable of, it's beyond what the CIA taught me," Alex said, taking a cleansing breath. "I should thank you. You helped me more than you know. You threatened Gavin. And I won't stand for that. I have my orders, and you don't get to be the one to set them. Enjoy dying."

Alex walked away, leaving Anderson there to bleed out onto the floor, after going through his pockets for some money. She would call an NSA cleaning crew as soon as she was back. She walked out of the building and breathed deeply. It felt like the first free breath she had taken. Ever. She felt lighter. She knew her darkness was a monster. She hoped that Gavin would understand. She couldn't blame him if he was incapable of loving that monster. But it definitely had its advantages.

And it hadn't come out in a long time. The only thing that brought it out now was the threat to Gavin himself.

She knew her darkness had changed. Just as she had. Gavin had had an impact on her that she would never have expected. He made her embrace all of herself. Even if she felt it was unlovable. She felt whole for the first time since she left with her dad as a 7-year-old girl. Hopefully, Gavin could accept her darkness like he had the rest of her. She would understand if he couldn't, but he had already given her so much that she couldn't blame him. She would continue to grow. And hope that one day she was worthy of his love.

Alex made her way to a busier road and hailed a taxi. She knew she needed medical, so she gave the address to the Sub Express in Atlanta. Once there, she went into Citadel, hoping that someone would be watching. The blood loss and pain were starting to get to her. She made it into the conference area and collapsed.

Gavin saw her collapse and immediately called Megan and Chad. He rushed to Citadel with Charles, beating Megan and Chad there by only a few minutes. He and Charles started getting supplies ready when they got there. Megan and Chad got to work taking care of her cuts and gunshot wounds. As she was in and out of consciousness, she kept saying, "Anderson is bad."

Gavin, who never left her side, just reassured her that they already knew and that they would get people on it. Charles called Richmond and updated her on the situation. Once Alex was able to be mobile, they were going to go back to the place she was taken and clean up. They all knew if Alex was in this kind of shape, then Anderson wouldn't be looking good either. And who knows how many other bodies were left.

Anderson was struggling. The fear that this may very well be it was impacting him hard. He had given so much, but now this was it. As he felt himself fade out with what he thought was his last time, he saw a shadow stand over him. "Pathetic," they mumbled. "Grab him. The Collective still has use of him. And call Pendulum. It is time."

210

Chapter 14

:/The Heart

Gavin sat in his lab at home. He watched Alex on the monitors like he had been since she made it back. She had been cleared after a quick health evaluation by Megan and Chad. But Richmond had commanded Alex to be confined to a cell until they could figure out what kind of a threat she posed. Alex agreed to it willingly. She hadn't known everything that had happened to her and figuring out her programming had just started. She didn't fully trust herself again yet.

Gavin watched as she paced back and forth. Occasionally, she would sit, close her eyes, meditate, or get up and exercise. It was driving Gavin crazy not being able to be with her. At one point, he thought he could move on with his life if she left, but now he knew it would likely be worse than Jill. Even if he could keep going and maintain what looked like a better life, he would truly be hollow. Nothing would really matter anymore.

He called Richmond again for what was the 7th time that morning. Straight to voicemail. Again. "Hey, it's Gavin again. I know you said to leave Alex alone, but…. It's Alex, General. We know she isn't going to do anything to hurt me. He is loyal to the government. We can trust her." He hung up, realizing the voicemail would likely get deleted and ignored. The General knew all these things. She was doing this for a reason, but that reason was not explained to Gavin. And, honestly, Gavin wouldn't have cared. Looking at the monitor again, he grabbed his keys and headed for the car.

***

Alex was sitting on the bed in her cell. She was getting restless, but knew that this was just precautionary. Once Richmond felt it was okay, she would be freed and reinstated. She hadn't slept great and had a feeling the entire time that someone was watching her. Yes, there were cameras, but they were closed circuit to Citadel only. She had gone over the specs herself, and no one else stayed in Citadel. She had insisted on that. And weirdly, she didn't get the same eerie feelings that she normally does when she feels someone is watching. It almost felt comforting.

She crossed her legs in front of her, sitting criss-cross applesauce. She closed her eyes and thought back through everything that had happened. From her session with Megan and all the progress she had made. How she had come to terms with what had happened to her, as much as a person could in a single afternoon. Then, only to be taken by someone who knew everything about what had happened to her and hoped to use it against her.

Anderson had done a great job of setting everything up. He had recreated the room she had been programmed into the fibers in the boards. He had approached her with the same confident and smooth tone at first. Building to a more aggressive tone. He had inevitably led to him commanding her to prove her loyalty. Unfortunately for him, he also talked too much. Did the overconfident villain monologue. *His ego seemed to be his biggest downfall. He had underestimated her. He had underestimated Gavin. He had underestimated her love for…*

The screen outside the cell came alive, and on the screen popped General Richmond. Alex stood at attention. "You can relax, Agent Johnson. Actually, this is a far more informal visit. Alex, how are you feeling?"

212

"Much better than I was. Thank you, General," Alex said as she didn't relax out of attention still. Her agent training clearly made it impossible for her to relax in the presence of a commanding officer.

"Alex, I want you to be open with me. Right now, I need to know what you can handle and what you can't. It will not affect your position on this team. All it will do is allow me to better support what this team needs from my position. So, have a seat, and please be honest with me. I would imagine we don't have a lot of time," Richmond stated. The last part sounds slightly annoyed while also amused. It confused Alex.

"I'm sorry, General? What do you mean?" Alex asked as she took a seat on the bench in her cell.

"That is irrelevant. So, please tell me how you are feeling, what all happened, and what you feel you are ready for and capable of," Richmond said kindly.

Alex looked at her hard. Something felt off, but she couldn't put her finger on it. *If I am not open about it, I could still be taken off this team, regardless of my new position. If I am honest and tell her all that happened, she could see it as potential to use against me, or a weakness the enemy could exploit. But if I am not honest, and it is actually a weakness, then that could put Gavin in danger.* Alex took a breath. She knew that she had to be honest. The risks of not were far too much for her to play games with.

"General, Anderson used the mind control techniques that the late Director Hunter had installed into some of his top agents. I am not sure how many. I just became aware of mine recently. I am sure that you heard from Gavin and Megan about it all, so I will be direct and brief with it. He took me to a building where he recreated the room that I was programmed in. It appeared to be an attempt to reinstall the programming that I received. Like he was worried that I was breaking it. Gavin has my file, I believe, so he could likely tell you more of what is in it. Anderson told me that my Red Test was to take out another of this 'training' that was breaking her conditioning. His late wife. He also commanded me to come back and kill Gavin and steal all the information we had on the NOVA system at this time in Citadel.

"When he commanded me to kill Gavin, my body started to move on its own, but then something changed. It was like something in my mind fought back. Like it didn't care what I would be put through; it wasn't going to allow me to hurt Gavin. And I was able to fight it. Then, when it broke, I did the only thing I was able to do. I fought back. I may have killed Agent Anderson. And if not, he was not going anywhere. He should be at that place still. I know I broke several major blood vessels and left him there to bleed out. You know my wounds, and I made my way back here," Alex finished.

General Richmond sat there, thinking over what she was just told and comparing it to what Megan and Gavin had told her about the situation. "Agent Johnson, first and foremost, I want to address your future and put you at ease. It does nothing to benefit me to remove you from this post. You are still far and away the best agent that any agency has. In addition to that, you already have knowledge of the NOVA system and Analyst Woodford in ways many others would never understand. So, you are in this position for as long as you would like, and very possibly longer. We want our best with the most important information and assets that the government has. While he isn't the labeled asset anymore, make no mistake, Gavin Woodford is an asset to this government. The NOVA system or not.

"Secondly, I believe that what happened with Anderson, and what seemed to have happened with Dr. Woodford, is that you were able to defy direct orders even while under the influence of the brainwashing. That tells me that you can be trusted more than any agent to follow your assignment of protection. I have told Dr. Woodford to continue to work with you and help you make progress, as well as for you to meet with an agency psychologist to help you through the trauma that led to your being brainwashed.

"And lastly, when you are feeling up to it, I believe you had started training Analyst Woodford in hand-to-hand combat? I would like you to continue that as soon as possible. He will need to be able to be more than a guy in a van here soon, if what I feel is coming is going to happen." the General finished with a thoughtful and ominous tone.

Alex was shocked. She hadn't expected to be almost literally handed everything she could ask for on a platter. Yes, meeting with the agency Psychologist wasn't ideal, but it was still better than remaining where she was at currently. "Yes, General, I think I can agree with all of those things being the best way to move forward. I should be able to continue Gavin's training this evening if that is acceptable?" Alex said, trying hard to suppress the joy she felt at spending time with him again, especially after something so traumatic.

General Richmond hid a smirk behind the glass of scotch she was sipping. Or pretending to sip. "That may be a little quick, don't you think Agent Johnson? Maybe wait a week or so? You can spend your time recovering here and at the hospital with Dr. Woodford?" Richmond teased Alex, knowing full well that she would not want to wait, but wanted to see if she was able to suppress the feelings still.

"NO! I mean, no, General. There isn't any need to wait longer. I can still continue my recovery while instructing Gavin. That will be light duty," she said all in one breath.

"Ouch, Alex, fighting me is that easy for you, huh?" Gavin said as he stood next to the monitor outside her cell. General Richmond did not seem surprised at all to see him there. "And here I thought I put up a decent fight last time," Gavin said, trying too hard to sound dejected.

"I will leave you both to it. Gavin, I expect a report on my desk tomorrow, and you know protocol," Richmond said curtly, but without the usual sting, she had. And the screen went black.

"Yes, ma'am. No, it's ok. I know you're busy. You have a great day, too." Gavin said to the empty screen sarcastically. Alex chuckled slightly at this, causing the stitches in her side to pull and hurt. She winced just enough for Gavin to notice. "Oh, I'm sorry, Alex! I should have gotten you out of there," Gavin said, lifting his shirt sleeve, revealing a wrist computer she swore she had seen somewhere before.

Tapping away at it for a few seconds, Gavin paused, and the doors opened for her.

"Thank you, Gavin, but you really shouldn't have done that without backup here. You don't know that I am not a threat," Alex started to chastise him.

"Yes, I do. And no, you're not. Not to me anyways," Gavin said with a big Woodford smile on his face. He came up to her and gave her a hug. You could tell he was being purposefully gentle with her.

"Gavin, I am not a porcelain doll," Alex said with a laugh.

"I know, but you're injured," Gavin said tentatively.

"I know, but I am tougher than I look," Alex said with a cheeky grin.

"Well, that's terrifying because from where I stand, you look like a complete and total grade-A badass. And that is me underselling it," Gavin said, smiling back at her again. "Alex, I have been wanting to talk to you. For a while," Gavin started with a different demeanor. His shoulders slumped slightly, and he looked very unsure of himself.

"Alex, I love you," Gavin blurted out. "Whoo, I said it. I love you. I have been wanting to say that since the first time I met you. I have loved you sometime between you spilling the drink on me, and yanking me into the car, and I don't think I will ever stop loving you." Gavin took a breath.

He loves me. I was going to tell him tonight, but HE loves ME? Alex felt herself getting excited. Her cheeks flushed, and she was focusing more and more on his lips. *HE LOVES ME! Wait. What am I going to do? Does he know my past? Can he know my past? I can trust him. Can't I? What about my dad? And my mom? And Bailey?* Alex sighed, and her eyes cast down to his hands holding hers.

"Alex, I don't expect you to say it back right now. I don't expect anything from you. If I did, then that wouldn't be love. I am telling you because I wanted you to know how I felt about you. That this isn't just

216

a phase or a crush. That I don't intend to go anywhere. And that you can rely on me. For anything. And I trust you. I don't worry about your past or you telling me your past. If and when you are ready, I will listen to you. There is no pressure here. And if you don't feel the same way, I understand. And again, I don't hold it against you. It won't change how I feel about you. I just wanted you to know," Gavin said with a soft and warm smile.

Alex stood there.

Without even hearing any of my concerns and worries, he had addressed them all. He knows me far better than I thought he did. He wasn't putting any pressure on me to make me feel the same, or even if I did, which I do, to state it so boldly like he had. He just simply wanted to let me know where he was and what he was feeling without any expectations of me. I need him. I need him to know I feel the same. Why can I never just be open with my feelings like he is? Because feelings get you killed. Yeah, or they give you something more to fight for than just your own survival.

Alex sighed again. She felt free. For the first time in as long as she could remember, she felt free. She strengthened her grip on Gavin's hands and, with a giggle, quickly led him out of Citadel. He had a confused look on his face the entire way, and as they got close to the car, she stopped, stood on her tiptoes, and kissed him deeply.

Gavin's mind froze. His body froze. His world froze. Time froze. Nothing else mattered in that moment other than her lips on his. He responded to her kiss with vigor. His hands grasped at her waist, and the other cupped the back of her head. He felt himself pour every emotion he was feeling into the kiss. How he had missed her when she was missing. How he longed for her. How he knew that he never wanted his life to be without her in it.

Then, just as quickly, the intense kiss stopped. Alex pulled back and grinned great big at him as she held up the keys to the car and got in.

Gavin was still frozen in place from the kiss, waiting for his mind to catch up. Finally, his body started responding, and he, too, got in the car. He didn't have to ask where they were going. The kiss had told him. He knew Alex, while often lacking in the words she wanted to say, had no problem communicating when she wanted to. And they sped off to her apartment. As they pulled onto the interstate, he felt her hand nudge his. They intertwined their fingers, and to both of them, it felt right.

***

Coeus stepped off the airplane in the United States for the first time in what felt like forever. He almost didn't recognize where he was. Looking at the Washington DC skyline, he knew it was time to have a chat that he had been avoiding since he had contacted Gavin. He knew they would both be busy and would likely use that as an excuse to avoid it, but this talk needed to happen. And happen fast.

He made his way toward the Pentagon, sticking to back alleys and streets that didn't seem to have cameras on them. He knew he could always just divert the cameras he needed to, but even the lowly NSA would be able to pick up that kind of change in a place like Washington, DC. However, he quickly created a pass card to get into any of the buildings he needed.

Finding the manhole cover he needed, he lifted it and dropped in. He had been this way several times, but it had been decades. He made a few turns and descended more ladders. Turning again, he made his way under the Potomac River. Then, climbing up again, he surfaced, ironically, next to the International Spy Museum. He walked over a few more streets and went to the Washington Monument. He took a shorter passage to the Lincoln Monument, avoiding the cameras. And he jumped into another manhole there. Taking several more ladders down again, he returned below the river to the Pentagon's lowest levels.

He knew Catherine would still be in a meeting with Congress, so he went through her secret passage to her office. Reaching her office, he checked their system to ensure he had arrived unannounced as planned. Then he checked her schedule to confirm that she would be there in the next five to ten minutes. And so, he poured himself two fingers of her scotch and sat on the couch that wouldn't be visible to anyone who opened the door and waited.

***

Alex flopped onto the bed next to Gavin. She didn't bother covering herself up. *What's the point? He literally just experienced it all.* She thought to herself with a laugh. *That isn't how you have felt with anyone else. You wanted them out of the bed as soon as you finished,* Alex slightly argued with herself. She pushed herself over and snuggled up to Gavin's side, with her uninjured side. That had provided some complications to start with, but they managed. She had never experienced something so deeply intimate and passionate as what she just had. She decided that she wasn't going to overthink this just yet. She was just going to enjoy the moment.

"Gavin, you did a terrible job of protecting yourself just now. What if I was going to attack you!" Alex smiled through her chastising.

"You mean you didn't attack me?" Gavin retorted with a confident smirk.

"Hey, you left yourself open. I just took advantage of it," Alex said as she poked him in the side.

"Well, then, you are welcome to take advantage of me any time," Gavin said with a smile and a sigh as he laid his head back on her pillows.

Alex rolled over and propped her head up on her hands, facing Gavin. "Gavin, I hope you know that I do have feelings for you. I am sorry I am not very good at expressing those feelings," Alex apologized, her eyes struggling to meet Gavin's.

"Alex, I think you did a fantastic job expressing how you felt about me," Gavin said with a laugh and a gesture to their state of clothing.

"Gavin, I am being serious here. I know I struggle to say the things I am feeling. Especially when it makes me feel vulnerable and exposed.

And I want you to know I am going to be working on that for you. You mean more to me than my privacy. It will just take me some time to be able to open up the way that I want to and that I feel you deserve," Alex said, with some slight tears coming to her eyes.

Gavin pulled her into a hug. "No matter what, we face it together. Ok? You aren't alone anymore. I will be there, no matter what it is that happens. Ok?" Gavin kissed the top of her head. And he could feel her relax into him. The tension left her shoulders.

"Gavin. My family. It is a mess. Always has been. I will get into more of the details one day. Still, for now, I want you to know that I would never want to do anything that would jeopardize your relationship with Megan. No matter what, we stick together and work through this. I think even Charles is team first, everything else second. I don't know what you did, but you have a knack for melting icy hearts and giving people new life,." Alex said with a slight blush on her cheeks.

Gavin felt his heart flutter. Knowing that she understands his family and friends' ties. How important those people are to his life and who he is. It means everything to him. He had never felt more content than he did in that moment. The love of his life snuggled into his side. His job seemingly going well. And not having to keep secrets from his sister. *Now, just to get Kaleb to be able to hear it all.* He sighed, contented again, and felt her fingers stroking his chest. As she leaned up and nibbled his ear. "I think you may be ready for another round of me expressing my feelings," Alex giggled. And a big smile spread across Gavin's face.

***

General Richmond was about to enter her office when she received a call from Charles.

"General, I wanted to inform you that the location was clear. Everything had been cleaned already, and there was no body," Charles said, a slight hint of worry in his tone.

"Thank you, Agent Charles. Please keep me informed," Richmond said as she walked into her office.

"Hello, Catherine," Coeus said as the door closed behind her.

The general didn't jump, even though she was slightly startled. She had been expecting this meeting for a while now and was ready to get this taken care of and out of the way. "Hello, Walter. I see you helped yourself to my Scotch and made yourself comfortable. Not to what do I owe this pleasure of the rarest of rare visits from the great Coeus?"

"I think you are fully aware of why I am here, Catherine. Don't try to play dumb with me. No one from our generation who has survived this long is dumb. Why did you include him? I thought we had all agreed to leave them out of this," Walter Woodford stated with a straight face.

"It was unavoidable, Walter. You know as well as I do that, I wouldn't do anything to put them in danger," she said with a stern look. She wondered how he could imply that she would in the first place and felt a bit hurt. Though she would never tell him that.

"Well, I am here to mediate. You know as well as I do it was never me that you would have to answer to. We gave you time to get them out of it, and now she wants to talk to you." Coeus's emphasis on the 'she' made it very clear who he was talking about. Coeus typed away on his wrist computer and then pulled out a box. He set the box on the ground between him and the General. "Are you there?"

"Yes, I'm here." And from the box came a holographic projection.

"Agent Hel," General Richmond said tentatively. This was the closest thing to fear she had felt in a very long time.

"Cut the crap, General. You know why I am addressing this. You were supposed to keep them off the radar of the CIA, the NSA, and every other alphabet-soup idiot's hot list. What happened?" Agent Hel said coldly.

"Well, a few things happened. I did all I could, but your son's roommate in college was one of Hunter's pet projects. I believe he was his favorite to take over the CIA when he left, but things didn't work out that way. And that agent sent the NOVA system files to your son in an email. Files he stole from a secure government facility," Richmond said defensively. She had done all she could. There was more at play here. She knew it. "And, if I may be so bold, he is made for this work. He is unconventional, like his father, but has a drive to complete every task like his mother. He is the perfect agent in such an obscure sense that it is easy to mistake. He refuses to change into what an agent would be. He is steadfast in his morals and will not tolerate the idea of him having to have a gun."

Agent Hel seemed to grin at that statement. "Of course, he is. You know where he comes from."

"I don't like him being in this life," Walter complained. "He is a kind heart, and we have all seen what this life does to kind-hearted people."

"That is what I am telling you. He IS for this life. It's likely more than any one of us is. He can do what needs to be done and still has a kindness about him that can turn even the hardest of hearts. He came to me, when Hunter ordered his execution, to become a Field Analyst for me. It was a smart move and one I hadn't considered. But given his abilities as a well-known hacker, it made sense that he could become a faceless analyst for us, as the hacker Vidar," Richmond replied.

Walter smiled slightly. He knew his son was the Vidar. Or at least he was reasonably sure he was. But Lucile did not know. And the Vidar had been a pain in the side of the company he was undercover for a long time.

"You are telling me that Gavin was the Vidar that I had sent multiple men out to kill, but was never able to catch?" Hel said, starting to feel sick at the thought of her ordering her son's death.

"I'm telling you that you were never successful in capturing him. None of us were. The only one who was even ever able to make contact was Coeus, isn't that right?" Richmond said.

222

"Yes, but I was never able to confirm if it was him or not. It makes me proud." Coeus smiled, even as Hel scoffed. She had never been able to give him the same icy glare that she was able to with everyone else.

"There is one other thing that, even though we don't have confirmation yet, I feel you may need to know," The General said.

***

Gavin wiped his brow as he stood back up. Alex and he had actually started his training. As he stood, Alex was bouncing on the balls of her feet. She hadn't had a fight this good in a very long time. "Can we take a small break?" Gavin said, sounding slightly defeated.

"What's wrong?" Alex said with a smirk, "Don't like the thought of a girl beating you?" she taunted as she lunged forward to take another attack. Out of the corner of her eye, she noticed that Gavin seemed to freeze for just a fraction of a second. She saw the look in his eye. He had flashed. And the next thing she knew, she was on her back. Gavin is on top of her. His hands held her wrists and his hips had her pinned to the floor. "I like that counter move," she said saucily.

Gavin blinked and started apologizing as the blush sneaked up his neck into his cheeks. "I... I'm... So... I'm sorry..." he stammered out.

Alex wasn't having any of that. She wrapped her legs around him and rolled them over. Pinning him down now, she got close to his face. "Never be sorry for pinning me down like that. I'm not," she said sexily, with her hot breath cascading across his cheek. It sent a shiver down his spine and caused his body to react. What surprised Alex was that his body reaction also sent a shiver down her spine. She felt so happy knowing this sweet and kind man cared for her.

She had mercy on him. And got up. Helping him up, she said, "It finally happened! You flashed into an attack. And it was so fast that I lost track of where your movements were," she said excitedly. She was happy that he would be able to defend himself if the need should arise.

"Yeah, it felt different. Like it accessed different parts of my brain. I will have to talk to Megan and see where we are with it. Maybe after a few times, then I will be able to control it," Gavin said, sounding excited like a kid who just got a new video game.

Alex grinned at him and at how different her life had become in such a short amount of time. All her life, it had always only been herself that she could rely on. And now, she not only had Gavin, but also Megan and Chad. And even in a weird way, Charles. She was amazed at how close they had gotten. And she wasn't going to let anything keep her from being there for the people who cared for her now. "Ready for another round?" she asked as she tackled Gavin into the bed.

"HEY YO!" Gavin yelled as he happily fell backward.

***

A man was standing over Agent Anderson. "Get him upright. It's time," he said.

"Sir, he is still unconscious," the scientist and doctors replied.

"I have my orders, or would you like to talk to Denver yourself?" he snapped at them.

"Yes, Agent Brooks. We will get him prepped," they said. And got to work moving him in front of the screens. They propped his eyes open. Putting on glasses, they all stepped back. Brooks looked into the joined room and nodded. The screens came to life, flashing images. The glasses shielded everyone but Agent Anderson. And finally, they stopped.

"Check his vitals," Brooks commanded.

"Vitals are good," the doctor said tentatively.

"Everyone out," Brooks commanded, and no one had to be told twice, as most were looking for a reason to leave.

224

With an empty room, Brooks walked up to Agent Anderson. Grabbing his hair, he pulled up on his scalp, and the clamps holding his eyes open popped off.

"AAAUUUGGGHHH!" Anderson screamed. His arms held down, he tried to shake his head, but it was held in place as well. "What? What happened? Where am I?" Anderson demanded.

"Why hello, Agent Anderson. Agent Denver sends his regards. While you heal, we took the liberty of giving you an… upgrade. You are now SIA Anderson. Special NOVA System Agent. And we added skills to the list. Once you are fully healed, we believe that you will enjoy the field test we have in mind for you," Brooks said with a laugh.

"What's that?" Anderson spat at him. He had a splitting headache and did not feel like playing games. This man clearly didn't know what he was dealing with.

"Kill anyone named Woodford and anyone who stands in your way of completing your missions. But bring them to ruin first. Destroy any hope they have. And once you have been able to achieve this, we will have a bigger target for you," Brooks said with a snide grin.

Anderson started to smile through the pain. This Brooks was right. This was his dream mission.

Chapter 15

:/Family

Coeus sat in the General's office listening to Hel and Richmond talk. Well, more accurately, argue. They had always had a tendency to get after each other's throats, especially for two best friends. Both are very domineering women, both having reputations to protect. Neither were keen on giving ground within an argument.

"I do NOT like the idea of my children being used as guinea pigs for your projects that have been distorted and weaponized from my husband's original design!" Hel snipped at Richmond.

"I know you don't, and this was never our plan. We had an agent go rogue, and it threw everything off. But I am doing everything I possibly can to ensure they are kept as safe as possible." The General tried to console her old friend. She had felt guilty for years for not doing more for the kids, but she also didn't want to expose them to a threat than they already were going to be. Then Brett had to change all of that.

"From what I heard, you treated Gavin like you had never known him," Hel said coldly. She was very upset with her friend. She had left her in charge of her children, and now to hear this after all these years.

"It was for his own safety! I couldn't tell who may be watching me at any given moment. And as such, I am going to be more careful than maybe I really need to be. But their safety had always been my primary concern," Richmond stated. She felt like she was on trial. She knew she was guilty. She felt it in her bones. But she wasn't going to say that. She couldn't give them any reason to doubt her. And couldn't give Hel any reason to give up.

Coeus felt a vibration on his wrist and knew his time had come to an end. "Well, ladies. This has been a pleasure, but I must be going. No need for me to be caught in the heart of the Pentagon while on several most wanted lists. Goodbye, my love." Coeus said to Agent Hel.

"Goodbye, Walter. I'll be in contact as soon as I have more for you. Continue on to your target." And with that, Agent Hel's hologram blinked out.

Walter sighed. He missed his wife more than he could ever express. He had spent a good portion of what should have been their happiest years together, trying hard to fix their mistakes and get her freed.

"Diane. I do look forward to our next meeting. I'll keep you up to date on anything that should be pertinent to you moving forward. And if you could do the same, that would be much appreciated. If possible, then please leave the intel in the underground. I'll send a marked location that will corrupt the file after you see it once I leave. And for God's sake, let Gavin tell his best friend. You may not like him, but he is loyal to a fault." Coeus stood and walked around to hug Richmond, and she nodded slightly.

"Goodbye, my friend," he said as he backed away. He tapped several buttons on his wrist, and the entire eastern seaboard had a blackout.

When the lights came back up, he was nowhere to be seen. And no one would be thinking about checking the footage of one of the most secure buildings in the area. Diane just shook her head. "Some things never change." And she sat at her desk to continue her work.

Coeus dropped down into the tunnels again. Heading off in a different direction than the way he came in from. Langley was connected, but it was a bit of a walk. He pulled up the map on his wrist computer and started in that direction.

***

Gavin laid on the mat. He was covered in sweat and wasn't exactly sure that he would be able to get up. He knew he had more to get done today, but Alex was really taking it out of him. Even injured.

"Come on, Gavin. We have more training left. It has only been thirty minutes," Alex teased with a slightly girlish giggle. *I have been doing that a lot more lately. Since Gavin and I... well. Since we got together,* she thought with a smile. She couldn't think of a time in her life that she had had genuinely smiled this much before now. Gavin made her happy. He made her feel safe, emotionally. And that was something entirely new to her. He understood what she had gone through better than anyone else in her life. At times, it felt like he understood it better than she did.

She did feel a slight invasion of privacy because he accessed her file without permission. But, at the same time, hadn't she done the same? She got the file from Langley, sure. But he never agreed to let her know everything she did about him before they met. So, it was fair for him to be able to do the same. Even if it still was unsettling for her.

Gavin had started to bring himself up off the ground as Alex was in her thoughts. He needed to talk to Megan. He felt the NOVA system starting to help him more on that last attempt to spar with Alex. But he also felt like his head was getting overheated again. After he had blacked out that last time, it made him cautious of it happening again.

"Ok, let's see if I can keep up in any way," Gavin said as he stood. Then, jerking into a fighting stance, he said with his mouth moving extra for effect, "My monkey style is clearing no match for your crane style," he mimicked being in a cheesy kung fu movie. Similar to the ones he made her watch with Kaleb.

Alex was wiping her forehead with a towel as she rolled her eyes and laughed. She would never admit it, but he was making her try as hard

228

as she could. Short of making attempts to actually hurt him. Like bringing out the Krav Maga. She also noticed Gavin slightly accessing the NOVA system while they were sparing. She wanted to ask him about it, but didn't want to do it where they were being monitored. She was sure the cameras didn't pick it up because she hardly had. They were subtle but definitely there. *Was the NOVA system helping him fight? Or is it doing the fighting for him? Maybe that's why he is able to keep up so well. Cheater,* she thought with another smirk.

Gavin took the real stance now. "Ok, ready," he said. His mood had changed. A determined look was in his eyes. Similar to when he was at a computer. *Why is that a turn-on?* Alex felt herself flush slightly as she made a move at him.

***

Gavin was trudging up the stairs out of Citadel. He had showered and changed into his work clothes. He was sore all over, but knew he still had to work. Making his way into the Snollygoster Inc., he felt, more than saw, Kaleb come up next to him. "Hello, my friend," he said. He tried to sound chipper because he really was happy to see his friend. He realized how much he missed him, which slightly hurt him.

"Hey Gavin! I noticed you are walking a bit bow-legged this morning. Have a wild night?" Kaleb prodded conspiratorially.

Gavin laughed at his friend. *Buddy, there had been plenty of that for the first time in a LONG time. But it wasn't why I can barely walk,* he thought. But what came out was, "A gentleman never kisses and tells."

Which made Kaleb pat him on the shoulder and give a deep sigh. "I envy you, my friend. It would appear that she can't get enough," he said, nodding toward the door with as much of a feral grin as possible.

Gavin looked over to see Alex standing at the door, looking around the store for him. He hadn't gotten any text, so he didn't think it was an emergency. She spotted him and waved as he made his way towards her. "Hey, what's up? Miss me already?" Gavin teased as he walked up to her.

She gave him a kiss that may have lingered slightly longer than just a hello kiss. "I actually just got done talking to our favorite General, and I think I have some good news for you," Alex replied with a kind smile. She took his hand and started to lead him into the store.

Gavin was so confused. She wasn't going to take him anywhere private, so the idea of this being work-related was out the window, but so was something relationship related. He wasn't sure what was going on. She was leading him straight towards Kaleb. He kept glancing at her.

"Hey, Kaleb, I was wondering if you would like to come with us to get a sub?" Alex said with a smirk at Gavin.

What is going on? Is she going crazy? He can't be trusted over there! He is a food connoisseur! He will know when a restaurant isn't a true restaurant! Gavin thought. He was nervous. "Is this such a good idea, sweetie?" he said pointedly.

"Gavin, I know I can be a third wheel at times, but it's just yogurt, man. It's not like we are all going to dinner and a movie together. Though I wouldn't be opposed to the idea. Just for future reference," Kaleb rambled, not noticing the looks that Gavin was giving Alex, who seemed set on ignoring his plight.

They made their way across the parking lot to the Sub Express. *What is she doing!? He can't come in here. The General will end all of this!* He thought as they made their way into the store. "Alex, sweetheart, can I speak to you privately while we get the yogurt ready?" Gavin asked pointedly.

"Of course," Alex replied in a chipper tone.

Kaleb sat at a table by the window and watched the people in the parking lot. Gavin looked at his friend for a moment. He was a bit sad that he hadn't been the friend that Kaleb deserved.

Turning to Alex, he started, "Okay, what is your issue? I know Kaleb isn't the smartest, but he is a lot more intelligent than you seem to treat him like he is." Gavin sounded more than a little indignant at her audacity.

Alex, for her part, was smiling back at him. "Gavin. Please calm down. You think I don't have a reason or a plan?" she said, patting his cheek. Reaching over, she hit the button to lock the doors and shut off the lights.

"Uh. Hey guys… what's happening?" Kaleb said, being drawn back into the store mentally.

"Kaleb. We need to talk. But more so, I believe it is beyond time that you see something," Alex said in a serious voice.

Gavin stood there with his mouth gaping. *Is she serious? What about Richmond? He hadn't been told that Kaleb was cleared. Charles will kill us.*

"And I believe Gavin should be the one to show you before he meets up with Megan," Alex finished. The smile on her face got a bit bigger.

"Woah! Am… am I getting a sneak peek at the newest flavors??" Kaleb asked excitedly.

"Yeah. Something like that, buddy. Why don't you follow me," Gavin said. I'm not sure if he was more excited or nervous. He had no doubts about Kaleb's loyalty. *He may be upset at being kept in the dark for so long.* Gavin thought as he led the way back to the freezer.

"Okay, Kaleb. What I'm about to show you and tell you can NOT be repeated. I mean, ever," Gavin said in a serious tone.

"Gavin. Buddy. It's me. Kaleb. You know you can trust me with your deepest and darkest secrets," Kaleb said almost dismissively.

Gavin took a deep breath once *more into the breach.* He thought as he opened the freezer. *It has to be easier to show him first than to tell him.*

Right? Gavin reasoned as he made the short steps to the back of the freezer. As he approached, the hand and retinal scanners opened to view.

"A bit much security to hide a new flavor, but I suppose I can respect their tenacity," Kaleb said as he stepped up.

With this, the door to Citadel opened. Alex followed them down. She watched with pride as her now boyfriend showed Kaleb around. *That's what he is now, right? My boyfriend? We never really made it official, I guess.* Regardless of what he was now, she was proud of him. And was glad to be able to force him to have to brag on himself a bit.

"Woah... you guys take this flavor analysis VERY seriously," Kaleb marveled as he looked around at all the computers in the main conference room.

"Kaleb. Buddy. Like I said before," Gavin started.

"Yeah. Secrecy or death. I got it," Kaleb said flippantly, still in awe of the room.

"No. Kaleb. Stop," Gavin said, and Kaleb did listen for once. Freezing and turning to look at Gavin. Gavin took a deep breath, steadying himself to continue. "Kaleb. I'm not who you think I am."

Kaleb continued to stare at him, but now he wasn't sure if he could give a more confused look if Gavin had sprouted a second head.

"Of course, you are. You're my best friend," Kaleb said. Glancing at Alex with fear in his eyes.

"No. I mean, yes. I am your best friend. But Kaleb. I... I work for the government. The NSA, to be exact." *There. I'd said it. Out loud. To Kaleb. That felt freeing. Oh crap. I said it out loud to Kaleb IN CITADEL.*

Just then, the screen in the conference room came to life behind Kaleb. "Now, Analyst Woodford, I'm not sure you are giving yourself enough

232

credit. Mr. Moore, please have a seat," General Richmond stated sternly, but still kind.

Over the next half an hour, General Richmond, Alex, and Gavin all proceeded to bring Kaleb up to date on Gavin's life to this point. "So, am I being recruited? Am I part of the team?" Kaleb asked excitedly.

***

Coeus made his way into Langley. He had several stops he meant to make before he made his way back to the airport.

He knew that it didn't matter the hour. There was going to be surveillance all over the place. Good thing this wasn't his first trip in. He got into the hall of records, kept on-site and offline. I'm in a fireproof room with a spark lighter in the corner, ready to burn everything inside if ever needed. He went through and found the files he needed. He read off the file names.

Project Tyr, Project Ara, Project Oghma, and Project Spartan. He knew that Gavin had the digital copies. Still, he also knew that those left out so many of the dirtier details of any project. Can't have something like that falling into the hands of the enemy or, worse, a journalist. He quickly rifled through a few more files and found one that caught his eye from early on in Hunter's career. The main file tag listed "Treaty of Dover." He grabbed it, knowing it would be something of a good read between flights. He made his way back out to the airport. "Time to go see my family," he thought with a sad smile. He wasn't sure when he had felt this weary before. Maybe when he was forced to leave them. Who knew coming back empty-handed would be just as terrifying and emotionally draining.

Opening the "Treaty of Dover" file, he said to himself while walking onto the plane, "Maybe one-stop." Typing on his wrist computer, he hijacked the small private plane and was on his way.

***

Kaleb sat in the seat next to Gavin as Gavin took him home. Kaleb had been asking nonstop questions about what he does. And then he got even more excited when he was told that it was classified, and he couldn't tell him. He was looking at Gavin like he was a celebrity.

"Okay, Kaleb. Do I need to remind you? I'm still the same Gavin, and you can't tell anyone about this. At all. Ever. Understand?" Gavin said with a slight sigh.

"Yes. Of course. Ninjas wouldn't be able to get this information out of me," Kaleb said as he mimicked a bad ninja stance. "Wait, is that an option? Like really?" Kaleb asked, sounding excited again.

"I really hope not, buddy," Gavin said with a slight laugh. He had to give it to his friend. He had taken all the news way better than Megan had. And his support was unwavering. *Maybe this would work out,* he thought, as he dropped Kaleb off and made his way to the hospital.

***

Walking into Megan's office, she gave him a stern look for being late. "Don't start with me, Meg," Gavin said as he flopped down into a chair across from her. "It's been a long day, and I know it's about to get longer," he said, taking out his laptop and quickly got to their research.

"It's ok, Gavin. It's not like I didn't have a million other things I could work on while I waited. Let's get started. Go ahead and hook these up to your head while I get some things ready," Megan said, handing him several sensors.

"Okay, Gavin, I think I'm getting an understanding of how this truly works with the brain and why it works on some and not others," Megan said, sounding hopeful. "I know we had gotten a basic understanding of it before when we worked. But it didn't make entire sense to me. You said that there wasn't that you were accessing the NOVA system really, but that you felt it working as you worked with Alex?" Megan asked.

234

"Yes. And I have messed around with that a bit more now. And I've noticed that I'm learning the fighting styles she is showing me quickly. And I appreciate the workouts that she has given me," Gavin said with a bit of a smile.

"I bet you do," Megan laughed at her own joke as she brought up a video on her laptop. Seeing Gavin blush from her comment made her smile broader. It was always fun to tease her baby brother. "Ok. I want you to try to see if you can use the NOVA system in the same way as you watch these videos," Megan stated.

Gavin sat down and started watching a video on how to do origami. And he focused on trying to have the NOVA system help. After he felt his head getting hot, he pushed the laptop away, and then Megan handed him a piece of paper.

"Megan, I don't think it quite works that fast. I mean, with fighting, it's taken more than just a few..." he looked down and saw a perfectly formed paper swan in his hand. His vision started to blur around the edges, and his head hurt. But he had done it. And it took fifteen minutes? Maybe?

"Gavin, this is incredible! You know what this means? It means training on just about anything for you has significantly cut the time frame." Megan exclaimed as she rushed to write down her observations.

Gavin was about to shut down his laptop when the screen fizzled, and a wave of blue O icons drifted across it. "Hello, Gavin. And I see Megan is there as well."

"Dad?" Megan said in disbelief.

***

Charles was sitting in Citadel going over the mission briefing, if you can call it that, of the buffoon, learning about everything that had been going on under his nose. He grunted in disgust at the idea of Kaleb knowing about what he really does.

As he was shuffling at the papers in front of him, the screen came on. "Charles. I am going to need your team to infiltrate a base believed to house a large faction of Pendulum. We are not sure what all else may be in there, but I do believe that we have someone on your team who could figure that out better than anyone else in the world," the General stated with a hint of pride in her voice. She knew how valuable her team was, and she was going to make sure to use them the best she could.

"Okay, General, full team for this one? Do we have extras incoming? Or are we alone?" Charles growled. He could feel his adrenaline already rising. He always loved to be outnumbered. It gave the opponent a little fairer of a chance. Almost.

"You will have just one other asset possibly on the ground. I'm not sure if he will be there, but I have a feeling he will be. There is a lot at risk for this one, Charles. We need this win if we hope to have a chance against Pendulum," Richmond stated with emphasis.

"Yes, Ma'am." Charles saluted. He was ready, and he would make sure that his team was as well. He wouldn't let them down.

***

Alex was sitting with Gavin in her apartment. Gavin had come back in a bit of a daze. "So, what was it that he said?" Alex asked.

"He is coming here," Gavin said dreamily.

Alex knew that this was big. Huge even. Not just for Gavin, but for Megan as well. She wanted to be there for them both, but honestly wasn't sure how. It's not like she ever had a stable family life to fall back on. All she knew was she would be there for Gavin. No matter what happened.

"I'm going to see my father again. And I'm not sure how I feel about it. I know Megan will likely have some words with him." Gavin winced at that thought.

"I'm sure that things will be okay, Gavin. He wants to see you. That's something. Right?" Alex said softly, trying to do anything she could to help.

Just then, their phones went off.

It was Charles. They had a mission.

***

Coeus stood outside of Hartfield-Jackson Airport. He knew he needed to be Coeus for a little longer, and then he would be able to be Walter for the first time in person with someone in a long time. It was close with Catherine, but he still wasn't sure if he could trust her. He sure hoped so. She had been a great ally in the past, but this wasn't the 1980s anymore.

He made his way towards the line of taxis. He tapped away at his wrist computer, making sure none of the cameras saw him.

He entered the taxi and gave him the address. As they took off, he quietly hoped this would be over soon. As nervous as he was, the thought of seeing his children for the first time in person in over ten years was too much to not be excited about.

***

As Team Woodford was getting ready to go on the mission, Megan walked into Citadel. "Hello, I know you're going to be busy, but I feel this is an ideal time to monitor Gavin. If I can watch while he is working, then it will help my research immensely," she reasoned. These were all true, but she was also just interested in coming on a mission for once.

Gavin looked over at Alex, hoping she would say no. But General Richmond, as always having perfect timing, chose this moment to make her appearance. "I believe that this is a great idea. You and Analyst Woodford can stay in the van. You may monitor him while he works, but you are not allowed to ask questions or distract him in any way, as that could lead to your team being injured or killed. Do you understand?" Richmond stated more sternly than usual.

"Yes, ma'am," Megan said as she felt her posture improve. The General just seemed to have that effect on her. With that, the screen went blank.

"Great. Wheels up in five. I don't expect you to slow us down," Charles grunted.

"Don't mind him. He's just huffy that we may not get to have any gunplay on this one. Since they want as many as possible kept alive for questioning," Alex tried to explain, but halfway through, realizing how crazy she sounded to a normal person.

"Oh," was all that Megan could muster. But she didn't dare say more. In case the General was still listening and would tell her she couldn't go now.

They loaded up into the van and headed off to their location. Gavin was typing away furiously on his laptop. Megan tried to watch him work, but it honestly hurt her eyes trying to keep up with how quickly he was shifting windows and pulling up new ones.

"Is he always like this?" Megan asked, wide-eyed, to Alex.

"Honestly? This is a bit slow for him. He is likely distracted." Alex almost slipped and brought up their dad. But she caught herself. She didn't feel that this was the time or place for that topic. Recentering herself.

Soon, they arrived at the business complex. It appeared to be a regular high-rise building.

"Okay. I have schematics, a body count, tech layout, and control of their cameras, and I find it interesting. Based on their layouts, it looks like it could possibly be a NOVA system room," Gavin rattled off.

"Okay, we will keep an eye out for it," Charles confirmed. He had no doubts in Gavin's abilities to control the building from anywhere. Let alone right outside.

They pull up to their spot, and Charles and Alex hop out of the van. Sliding under it, they drop down into the sewers.

Just then, Gavin picks up on a tap, filtering through his current tap on the system. He isn't sure where it is coming from.

Then, it is gone.

He picks up the trace from its signature just before it disappeared. He was running it back as fast as he could. But he felt he is just short of finding the location and person running it.

"Guys, we have company. With a high level of hacking ability," Gavin said in their coms.

"Richmond said we could possibly have another person on with us. She wasn't sure, but felt confident they would show. Maybe she felt you needed an extra hand with the computer work, Woodford," Charles needled him as they made their way to the building.

***

Coeus made a surveillance pass on the building. He saw Gavin tap on their lines already. Knowing he would have his son watching over him is a comfort he rarely could afford before now. Piggybacking on his preexisting hack, he was able to see everything that Gavin could. Walking toward the front door, he saw the guards notice him and make their way towards him.

***

Gavin saw the figure approaching the front. "Guys, I think this nut job is just going to walk in the front door like some kind of Neo or something."

"Who?" Charles grunted into the microphone.

"Neo? Matrix? Are World War 2 documentaries all you watch, Charles?" Gavin said with a slight laugh.

"No. Sometimes, I'll watch a Vietnam War documentary just to remind myself what not to do." Charles growled.

Gavin huffed out a laugh as he watched the figure get stopped by the guards.

***

Coeus smirked. He knew his son was watching. It was going to be hard not to show off a bit. What father didn't want their son to look up to them?

He approached the guards, and before a word could be spoken, he threw a jab into the throat of one and spun a kick to the temple of the other. The first stumbled back, grabbing at their throat, and the other dropped dead in one shot. Coeus launched a kick into the nose of the guard, grabbing his throat, and then as he lay writhing on the ground, he stomped his head.

***

"Woah! Ok. Neo just dropped both guards. Pretty sure they are dead," Gavin blurts out. Keeping the team up to date.

"Hey, now. Don't let him have all the fun," Charles said. Actually, sounding upset at the idea.

"It's not like I can just tell him to stop," Gavin snipped at Charles.

240

"Guys let's focus here," Alex said as she reached the access point to the building. Tossing up her grappling hook, it latched onto the ledge above, and she began her accent. Charles was right behind her.

***

Coeus made it to the front desk and connected directly with their main network. He downloaded all the information he could glean from this one connection. And unplugged within thirty seconds. Moving on, he looked for a server room.

***

"Ok, the other guy seems to be focused on their data network. Hopefully, he is on our side, and we will get to compare notes before this is done," Gavin said.

Charles just grunted in response as they were in and making their way to the floor where Gavin saw the NOVA system room on.

As they made it through the building, they took out several people. But it was methodical. They were a well-run and connected team. As they made it to that floor, Gavin lost visual of them. They expected this, so no alarms were raised.

Gavin had lost sight of the other guy and was running blind. But keeping an eye on the other cameras as much as he could. Until he saw him.

Walking into the building among a group of others, he seemed healthy.

"Guys. I just saw Agent Anderson. He is in the building," Gavin said into the mics. "Guys?"

They must have entered the NOVA system room and can't hear me, Gavin thought. *Stay in the van. Stay in the van. Stay in the.* His hands were pulling on the door before he could stop himself.

"I don't think you should go in there," Megan warned him. She knew full well that there wasn't anything she would be able to do to stop him.

"I can't leave my team," Gavin said as he took off.

***

Coeus came out of the server room. He had gotten more than he had expected. As he made his way through to the front door again, he saw several guards passing him. Apparently, Gavin's team was doing its job well.

***

Alex and Charles planted the bomb in the room and started towards the entry point, when they were suddenly under fire.

"Gavin, we need an alternative exit plan here," Charles huffed into the coms.

"Head toward the front door. We are going to walk out with the other guy. He is heading there now," Gavin said while running there himself. "And Anderson is there."

That caused a chill to go down Alex's spine. She thought he was dead. "Gavin, that's impossible. I killed him," Alex said. She felt her voice losing any warmth.

"I saw him, Alex. I saw him on the cameras. He is here. In this building," Gavin panted out.

Alex felt her darkness. She tried to fight it, but she knew.

More and more guards started coming in. They were taking fire from both sides now. Charles growled. This is how he always saw himself going out. They were one floor away and were completely trapped. The guards were alternating fire now. They didn't even allow them to pop their heads up for a clean shot.

242

Over the building intercoms, a cold and lifeless voice echoed through the building.

"Alex, Charles. I know it's you. I'm sure Gavin isn't far behind, is he? I'm going to finish what I started. Should I do it slowly? I'm sure I could separate you all. Kill you one by one. Wouldn't that be fun? Or would dying together be how you want to go? I know dying alone is perfect for Gavin. Always the social person. He deserves some peace and quiet, don't you think? I believe he is about to come through the front door. I think I'll go greet him. I'll let you know how it goes," Anderson finished with a laugh that held no mirth.

And it happened. Alex felt it. That cold feeling. She vaguely remembers feeling it before, but it felt like a dream. Or maybe a nightmare. That darkness. It was consuming her. But this felt different. This felt like she could control it, but didn't want to. Like she chose it. Even if she didn't mean to. She felt it covering her.

She squatted there behind a desk. Gunfire came down on both sides, and it felt like time slowed. She could hear the pattern of the bullets. She could hear the reloads. She looked at Charles and saw he felt out of answers.

She opened the desk drawers and started pulling out everything she could find. Paper, pens, pencils, rubber bands, paper clips. Typical office supplies. She remembers from their way up that there were light controls by each end.

The calm came over her. She pulled her gun in one hand, and her knives were in the other. She may not make it, but she felt it. Neither were they.

She put her hand up and shot. A stray bullet glancing by her hand burned more than a shot. But the shot hit its mark. The lights go out. Apart from the muzzle flashes, you can't see anything. This was her queue.

243

Charles has no clue what's going on. He had heard the rumors, but had yet to see it himself. He saw that look in her eyes before she shot. He stayed hidden. Not from the bullets. But from her.

Alex leaped over the desk, the bullets much more sporadic now. She is able to dodge them to some degree. She knows she will get hit once or twice, but it should be livable, hopefully.

It was weird for her to have something to live for now. And that made this even more paramount.

Sliding under a table. She had her eyes closed. She knew where they were. She'd memorized the layout as they walked through the first time. And the pattern of the bullets told her where they were firing from.

Fifteen at this end. Ten at the far end.

She had almost made it to the first one. She knew. The picture that Gavin had seen of her. The videos. She was about to see the outcome. She wasn't sure if he was ready for that yet. But she was getting back to him. One way or another. Even if he didn't have her, she would be there to protect him.

Reaching the first guy, she twisted her body, feeling out how he was standing in reference to the other men. Knowing the drop ceiling will provide a good assist in her movements. Making it harder for them to track.

Slithering her way up his body quickly, she dropped her gun and pulled another knife. She slits at just the right spots, cutting major arteries before finally slitting his throat.

His screams caused the shooting to stop.

The silence allowed the shock for her to make it to the next two men. Spinning on her heel, she slit their throats, instantly dispatching them. She feels their blood splatter across her face.

Their gurgling screams cause the two closest to her to turn towards her and open fire. She figured this would be what would happen, and she leaped to the drooping ceiling and lifted herself up. She launched herself in the direction of the next guy, and the two who turned ended up shooting each other.

She quickly made her way through all of them. Wielding nothing but her knives. As she finished the last guy on this end, she kicked his gun up and grabbed it as it came down. Spinning and slitting his throat as she did.

Turning and firing on the opposite group as she ran towards them. It caused them to drop out of sight.

Knowing she had them now, she leaped over Charles and his desk, and as she did, he felt a drop of blood hit his arm. He hoped it wasn't hers.

Reaching the other end, she quickly ended every guy there.

In a matter of five minutes, she had killed them all. One on twenty-five. And she had a slight burn on her hand. Where one bullet almost hit her. As the emergency lights came on, and Alex made her way back towards Charles, he couldn't help but be a slight bit afraid of her.

They made it to the main area and saw Gavin enter through the door. Megan was hot on his heels behind him. She had been yelling at him that the other guy in the building was their father.

Alex and Charles popped out behind Anderson and his men. As those men were getting ready to open fire on Gavin, Alex shot three of them and Charles the other four. Anderson had turned to see them appear and took off. Knowing he would be outmatched for this round.

Megan and Gavin entered the building. All of this had happened in under twenty minutes from entry to exit.

Alex ran up to Gavin. The look on her face was relief that they made it, but fear of rejection. Gavin didn't care. He grabbed her and held her close. He knew it was gross, and they would have to talk later. But all that mattered was that his Alex was alive.

"Glad I made it too," Charles grunted with a hint of self-deprecation in it. Which caused everyone to chuckle slightly. Megan gave him a hug despite him trying to avoid her.

They heard a door open on the far side of the lobby, and all turned. Alex and Charles drew their weapons.

Through the door walked Walter Woodford. Megan and Gavin both freeze. He started walking toward his kids. A slightly shy smile played on his lips. He could see the conflicting emotions in both of their eyes. He understood and hoped they could one day move past the last ten years.

Gavin felt a rush of emotion at seeing his father. He had always looked up to him, even before he knew he was a genius. But knowing what he was, truly made everything else dim in the light of his achievements.

Megan didn't know what to feel. She truly wanted to be happy. But all she could bring herself to feel was anger. Rage at the fact that he left. That he left her to be in charge. At such a young age. How unfair it was to her. How he had stolen her childhood.

She started to speak. "Pancakes?!"

BANG!

Chapter 16

:/The Files

Time froze. Everyone felt like they couldn't move. The multiple gunshots were still ringing in their ears. The moment of slow-motion panic set in—the scramble to see who was shot at and who was injured. Just then, Coeus stumbled. Gavin's eyes bulged, seeing a blood spot starting to form on his father's shirt.

Terror rushed through Gavin. "NOOOOOO!!" he screamed. His entire body tensed up. He was vibrating with emotion. His mind was running overactive. He saw every memory of his dad he had. The time he took him to see War Games in theaters. The time he watched a Star Wars marathon with him. Making breakfast on Saturday mornings. Teaching him the basics of computers and computer programming.

He felt the anger and abandonment of when he left. How he lost his role model. The man he looked up to his entire life to that point. More than anyone. And he was gone. The only person left in the world that was supposed to love him was Megan.

He had mixed feelings about when he came back into his life. All he had learned. How he had watched over him. Even from a distance.

It hit Gavin that his dad was shot and dying. His body started working. He was shaking, but he knew he had to get to him. Looking over at Megan, he saw the same hopelessness in her eyes.

Megan stood there. She had been ready to tear into her father. She had such anger towards him. And as she saw his blood filling his shirt, even her medical training couldn't force her into action. She felt utterly lost. She had so much to say to him, but now she knew that she'd never get that chance. The placement of the shots through his abdomen made it clear he wasn't leaving that building alive.

She heard screaming. She looked around and saw Gavin yelling, but the tone didn't match his voice. Her hands reached to her face before she realized that it was her who was screaming. Her shaking hands covered her mouth.

She saw Gavin rush forward, but she knew it was helpless. There was too much blood, far too quickly. Her father was truly gone this time, and he wouldn't be coming back.

The tears started to fall as she fell to her knees. The ground jumped up to meet her. The slight pain from the fall brought her back to what was happening before her. A sob started forming in her chest, and the sorrow of the loss she witnessed was just too much.

Alex spun on her heels, gun drawn, ready to take out any other missed shooters. She fired off three rounds at the closing glass door from which she knew the shots had come.

Gavin heard Alex fire and turned to look at where she shot. On the other side of the glass door was a smiling Topher Anderson, giving them a slight wave, and then he was gone. Gavin was too preoccupied with his dad to worry about Anderson just yet. He saw Alex and Charles take off after him.

Gavin leaned down over his dad, the blood from the wounds smearing it on his clothes and hands. Walter was gasping, trying to hang on. He mustered up the little remaining strength he had, pulling off his wrist computer and the flash drive out of the pocket in his sleeve. Handing it to Gavin, he said, "Gavin. You're special. Always remember." And his pupils dilated as the color drained his face, and his body grew limp and cold.

"No. Don't go. Dad, please don't go..." Gavin sobbed out as he pleaded with his father's body. Gripping his dad's body as the tears started to fall. "I can't lose you, not again," Gavin whispered, knowing his father was gone. Once again.

Alex and Charles grabbed Megan and Gavin, who were still in a state of shock, and headed for the door. Charles also grabbed Walter's body. Making their way back to their van, they all got in. Megan sat up front with Charles, sitting in silence for the duration of the ride. Which suited Charles just fine.

Alex sat in the back with Gavin, trying to keep him from looking more at his father's body. Which was covered on the floor of the van. She tried her best to console him.

***

Making it back to Citadel, everyone was somber.

Alex went to the shower. She knew she needed to get all the blood off her before she could tell if she had any injuries. Charles set out to put all the equipment away and clean the guns. Megan sought out Chad to seek some comfort. And Gavin sat at his Citadel workstation, unsure what else he could do.

Now that he was no longer holding his father's dying body, the image of Anderson standing on the other side of that door. Smiling. The gun that shot his father in his hand at his side. Gavin felt his anger surging to the surface. He felt helpless. The blood from his father was still literally on his hands and shirt. A sob squeezing around his heart.

He felt a hand on his shoulder as he was ready to lash out and swipe everything off his desk. Turning around, he only saw blue. He was quickly encompassed in a tight hug. A kiss on his cheek, and he felt

Alex wretch. Her tears mixed with his own as she held him. *I don't have much else I can give you, Gavin. But I will give you everything I am able to,* Alex thought to herself. Feeling the pain of seeing Gavin hurting so badly. It was new and different for her. Trying to express such emotions that she normally fought so hard to bury deep inside her.

Without saying a word, she released her hold on him. Grabbing his hands, she pulled him to follow her to the showers.

Gavin got up and followed her numbly. He had never seen her cry, not in person. It wasn't a sight he wished to see again. But knowing he wasn't alone in this pain, that someone loved him enough to feel this kind of pain with him, that didn't have to. He would follow her wherever she led.

***

Gavin woke up to the morning light seeping through the curtains into his room. The usually happy feeling didn't hold the same warmth now. *He really is gone.* Gavin bemoaned. He felt a stirring next to him, and that did bring some warmth to his icy mental state. He felt an arm lazily snake around his stomach and a soft body pressed up against him.

Alex had opted to stay with Gavin at his place that night. She was determined to not let him feel he was alone in this. Even if she didn't have the words to say. She felt him wake up but wasn't ready to let go of him. She knew they had a lot to figure out and likely a lot to talk about today. But she found herself treasuring more and more these peaceful moments with her Gavin.

Gavin kissed the top of her head. Her breathing had changed. She was awake. But she wasn't moving to get up, so he wasn't about to either. For all he cared, they could lay together in this bed for eternity and let the world pass them by.

After some time, Alex lifted her head and looked at him. His brown eyes were lost in her blue eyes. "Good morning," she quietly whispered. It was almost as if she thought that speaking too loudly would scare away the peace between them.

"Good morning," Gavin croaked out. He winced at his voice cracking. But then, he smiled at the beautiful smile he had gotten at his blunder. He cleared his throat a couple times. "Good morning," he said again, in a much clearer tone.

"I have reports I have to file this morning," Alex almost whined, sounding very similar to a child. Gavin couldn't help but smile at her antics.

"I do hope I'm not interrupting anything," a slightly amused General Richmond stated, making her virtual presence known in the bedroom. She had gotten Charles's report from the mission the night before. She knew what they had gone through and didn't blame her team for seeking comfort. But sadly, there was still work to be done.

The diminutive General continued, "Please don't get up. I can see you both fine. I don't mean to intrude, but I did figure you would want to know that we received a transmission from Topher Anderson this morning very early. It is directed at you both. You don't have to view it now."

"No. I want to hear what he said," Gavin stated as he shot up in bed. There was a look of determination in his eye that Richmond had seen before. But not from him. Nor his father. And that gave her a shiver.

"Ok. I will warn you. He is seeking an emotional response, given how he has seen you in the past. I would implore you to not give him the satisfaction," Richmond said before the screen cut out and the video was pulled up.

Anderson's smirking face filled the screen. His eyes looked dead. Gray. Even the whites of them didn't look healthy. They weren't bloodshot. They just didn't seem to have any light in them. None of them had gotten a clear look at him the night before. But his face did not look healthy. It was not like his eyes were sunken in or that he looked thin, just ashy. And his eyes looked a bit crazed.

"Hello, Gavin. Alex. And everyone else who will watch this. I know, Gavin, that your first instinct will be to trace where this feed is coming from, and I hope that you do. Just so you can begin to understand just how out of your depth you are. You are outmatched in every way. Alex can tell you that I am not someone to be trifled with." His voice sounded as dead as his eyes looked. He was looking at them like it was a live feed.

"Isn't that right, Stacy? And how is your father? I think I may pay him a visit like I did for Gavin's last night. Which prison was it again that he was in? Or have you not told your current lover boy that you told me all of this? Oops. Did he even know your name is Stacy?" A smirk played on his lips as he continued. "Kind of like how he didn't talk to you about any of his plans to join the NSA." Gavin blushed at that. And Alex started to get more than a little irritated.

"Remember, all of you, that none of you truly know who your enemy is, and we look just like all of you. And I know far more about you than you do me. And I know your pressure points. I'm coming," Anderson said ominously, right before the screen cut to black.

Gavin sat there. Alex could feel the anger radiating off him. *I am not helpless. Not anymore.* Gavin's brow furrowed. "General, do I have your permission to investigate this?" Gavin asked with a strained voice. Gavin was trying hard to remain stoic and professional, but it wasn't working.

"Yes, Analyst Michael, you have my blessing to pursue this. I will get the paperwork taken care of immediately," the General stated, seeming like she was about to end the call, but paused. "And Gavin," she continued with a fire in her eyes that they hadn't seen before. "Bring this bastard to his knees." And with that, she cut the feed.

Gavin flung off the covers and hurriedly got dressed. Alex was not far behind him. She knew there wasn't much she could help with, but she still wasn't about to leave Gavin's side while he worked through this. She came into his lab with breakfast in hand, seeing him already busy typing away at a computer.

***

Several hours later, Alex was working on her paperwork. "UGH!" he exclaimed as he tossed his keyboard in front of him. "He was right. There is no way to trace him. There is nothing I can do to find him. To get a step ahead," he said with a huff, his head dropping into his hands. He did feel out of his league. He hated most of all that Anderson was right.

Just then, there was a knock at the door. Alex got up to check it, giving Gavin a quick peck on the cheek. Opening the door, she saw Megan there. She didn't look much better than Gavin did.

"Is my brother home? He has to see something," Megan said in a bit of a hurry as she slightly edged past Alex. "Yeah, he is in his lab," Alex said, now to the back of Megan's head as she followed her into the lab again.

"Gavin, you have to see this," Megan said, urgency clear in her voice.

"Not now, Meg. I am busy trying to find Anderson," Gavin said dismissively.

Megan grabbed the keyboard out of Gavin's lap, "No, you need to watch this." Gavin went to grab the keyboard, starting to protest in anger at his sister. "Gavin, it's from dad," Megan said. Gavin stopped. He didn't know what to think. "It is some kind of video will," Megan said. "I started it but stopped when I saw what it was and came over here. He must have never gotten your new address," she finished quietly. Gavin simply nodded and put the flash drive into his computer.

The video popped up with the Coeus symbol to start with, and it eventually decoded into their father's face. "Hello Gavin, Megan. If you have received this, then that means I am no longer with you. I mean. I have passed on. I hope you can find it in your hearts to forgive me for my shortcomings as a father. But I only ever wanted to keep you kids safe. Gavin, I will have given you my wrist computer and several flash drives. What is on those is vital to what is to come. I can't tell you everything, but you are not alone. Not in the way that you both have felt you are for so long. You have had people watching out for you longer than you could have known. Megan, you will be receiving my laptop, which has all my NOVA system data on it. Everything in all the research that I have done is yours. Use it to either get that thing out of your brother's head or use it to help him learn to control it. I hope that these things will help you better understand why I had to leave. Why your mother had to leave. And why she is still gone. Yes, kids, your mother is still out there. And I have been working on bringing her home for a decade now. I hope you will be able to continue my work. And please know that your Godmother is watching over you." As he said that, the camera panned the room and settled on the empty desk of one General Richmond. The nameplate was very clear.

All three stood there. Not sure what to think or do. The siblings hadn't even known of General Richmond until Gavin got that email, what felt like so long ago. Now to know that she had known them for much longer. It felt both comforting and like a betrayal. They couldn't take the time to think about that much more, as the revelation of their mother still being alive changed things. They knew that they would have to focus more energy on finding her. But even beyond that, they had the more pressing matter of figuring out what was on that laptop and the flash drives their dad had left for them.

After a quick recap of what they would do, Gavin grabbed the flash drives and wrist computer and got to work. He got acquainted with his father's design quickly and was soon flipping through all the files he could find. Most of which he had seen the majority of before. Files on the projects Spartan, Tyr, Ara, and Oghma, but one caught his eye that was different. File name "Treaty of Dover" Gavin admittedly didn't know much about it. He vaguely remembered hearing something about it in history class but didn't know much else. He opened the file and started to read with no dates given, but clearly, different entries were done at different times.

Treaty of Dover

Charter:

The United States has become weak. Less than a mirror image of itself. We, the people, seek to rejuvenate it to a new glory. One that henceforth has been unseen by this world. We are the elite of all areas. The members, for security's sake, will not be named. Nor will other members know the entirety of the membership. We start small. The best of the best. And we will build. Until we are many.

Director Hunter has instituted the beginnings of our army. We have several ready-to-follow orders given without question and without feeling. The other directors are too weak to be brought into the fold. The CIA is just the tip of the sword in this fight. But our members are growing.

The first missions have been carried out. One promising subject, young though she may be, was able to take out an entire terrorist enclave. All with only a knife. She did not remember it and was found naked but for tattered clothes and blood. She will be the first General of this new army.

There has been our first setback. One of the subjects rebelled. It was the first time this had happened. The lead subject was brought in to clean up the mess. This will not be overlooked.

Project Oghma has become more of a headache than it is worth. The programming has shown to be useful, and the need to have the intel downloaded directly into the agent in charge of the subject isn't dire just yet. We will continue to work on it, but with several lead scientists gone, it may be a lost cause.

Several handlers have shown an inability to continuously control their subjects. This will not be tolerated. The tech division is working to recreate their NOVA system. They are calling it Pendulum. We look forward to status updates.

The NSA NOVA system seems to have been downloaded into a civilian. We are still unsure how this happened, but one of our agents in charge seems to have gone rogue. This will not stand. Though the download has been confirmed and complete. The subject doesn't show any signs of revolt as the others had.

The project seems to work, though the NSA has too much input in the missions. Richmond must be dealt with. The civilian has seemed to be having adverse effects on the lead subject. We will need this dealt with as well. The Woodford name cannot continue to plague our enterprises.

Pendulum is close; they will finish their NOVA system, and we will bring in the subject. As the lead prospect went rogue, we had to have him dealt with. Richmond remains untouched as well. The next agent in charge is en route to the current NOVA system and the lead subject to see what he can do to separate them. As well as find any code that he can tell will make the Pendulum work.

The Pendulum is operational. We were able to redesign it for several uses, not just data upload. Torture, as well as mental manipulation, are an option. Continued research is needed.

Agent in charge made quick work of finding the code needed. He has been given leeway with the lead subject, as he has shown he needed to reprogram her.

Agent in charge was found. No lead subject. Bringing him in for upload.

Upload Complete.

***

Gavin reread it several times. He couldn't believe what he was reading. *Anderson is a NOVA system,* he thought as he read it yet again. Just to make sure he hadn't missed anything. The vagueness of the document would make it mean nothing to anyone who wasn't in the know of several situations. You would almost have to be read in on all the projects to understand it.

Gavin had Alex read it and called Charles in to read it as well. Charles read it once and grunted. Hitting a few buttons on the lights' main screen, the wall opened next to it, revealing a decent armory. He took out a rifle and started cleaning it. "It calms me," he grunts at the stares he gets from Gavin and Alex. "You all don't know your history, do you?" he continued.

"Not obscure things you find on the History Channel," Gavin said sarcastically.

"They don't teach much history when they are training you to kill people," Alex said with some snark.

Charles flinched slightly at Alex's response. "Ok. Well, you first have the names of the projects. Ara is the celestial body the Ancient Greeks believed was an altar where the gods devoted their loyalty to Zeus. So, it makes sense that it was named that in the sense that it was used to brainwash people to follow orders. The Norse god Tyr was their god of war. He was stronger, faster, and more agile than humans. But his true strength was his skill. He was a strategic genius and a master fighter. His skill in battle was above all. Oghma was named after the god of knowledge. The NOVA system instantly increases your brain's ability to increase your knowledge of any kind. And the Spartans were the perfect soldiers of their day. I'd imagine by this; they would be the army referenced and would be full of everyone who had gone through their projects and programming."

Gavin and Alex stared at him more. They weren't sure how he knew all of this off the top of his head. "And what about the Treaty of Dover?" Gavin asked.

Charles growled, seemingly exasperated by having to explain again. "Isn't there anything in that thing in your head?" He teased with a grunt. "The Treaty of Dover was an alliance between England and France lords during the time of the third Anglo-Dutch War. On the surface, it is a typical alliance. Still, when you read about it, they had a secret alliance before the public one. They had promised to aid each other militarily, if any of them faced an uprising from their people. It was, and is to this day, one of the most famous cabals in history. A secret society of the elite that did everything they could to make sure they would maintain power. Of that, we will have to tread carefully. I'm going to go update Richmond," Charles finished.

Gavin turned to Alex, "There isn't anyone outside of our team that we can trust, is there?" he said, sounding slightly desperate.

"Gavin, breath. We don't know any of this yet. We don't know how far this reaches or anything like that. Let's not overreact just yet. For now, we prep and train. We can't take them down without knowing what we are against," Alex said placatingly as she rubbed his arms. He seemed to calm slightly at this. "Besides, you could use more training in hand-to-hand combat before you go seeking out Anderson," she said, remembering that Anderson had almost taken her. She had been toying with him slightly, but she did have to try. Something she wasn't used to having to do one on one.

"You're right. I just can't stand the idea that my father's killer is out there, and there isn't a thing I can do about it," Gavin said dejectedly.

"Numbnuts, weren't you listening? Just like your girlfriend said, there is something you can do. You can train. Focus on getting better, so when you get the chance, you don't try to kill him with your girlish screams," Charles grumbled. He didn't like this emotional talk, but Gavin was like a brother. And he respected him. He was going to make sure that the kid was ready.

"You're right. I need to focus. I will be over to your apartment in a bit. I want to get some searches set up to track them down. All of them. I will look for keywords in all documents and files. In our networks, as well as on the dark web," Gavin said, grabbing his keyboard and already typing away before he had finished talking.

Charles grunted. He knew the kid was tougher than he would ever let on. And he knew that if Gavin wanted something found, it was getting found. After putting the rifle away, he left his apartment, and Alex followed him out.

"Charles, do you think we did this to him?" Alex asked softly.

"If anything, he was born into this. Don't take blame where there is none to be given. That kid is far more dangerous than people realize. Then he realizes. And he is about to find that out, I think. Our job now is to protect him from himself," Charles said to his partner as he opened his door. "If you tell him I said anything, I will shoot you," Charles added with a smirk. Alex smiled at her partner, hoping he was right. She left to get ready for a sparring session with Gavin.

***

Gavin finished setting up his searches and grabbed his stuff to get ready to leave. He opened the door to find Megan standing there with her face in a laptop and hand raised to knock. "Um, Meg? How long have you been standing like that?" Gavin asked with a slight chuckle.

"Huh? Oh, I'm sorry," she said as she pushed past him into his apartment. "You need to see this. I think I cracked it. I think I know how to make this work," she said excitedly.

"Make what work, Meg? The NOVA system is already working," Gavin said, slightly annoyed since he was already going to be late for sparring with Alex.

"No, it's not. I mean. Not fully. It overheats, which causes distress to the brain, which could lead to brain damage if allowed to go unchecked. You have the benefit of an overly electrical brain already. But this boosts it and can create issues. But I think I have a way to counter that. Even when you are learning using the NOVA system." Megan explained excitedly. "It's all here in Dad's notes!"

"That's great!" Gavin replied. "But can we finish talking about it later? I'm about to go spar with Alex," he said, edging towards the door. "That's perfect! I'll come with you, and then we can test it out and see

259

if it works. If it does, you could potentially get complete control over this thing with minimal to no repercussions."

"Ok. Come on, then. Let's get over there," Gavin said, slightly annoyed but ready to go. Megan rushed after him.

***

Alex let the siblings into her apartment. She hadn't expected Megan to come along. She did expect Gavin to actually spar this time, though. She was worried he might be unable to defend himself against Anderson. She was no slouch in hand-to-hand combat.

"What's going on guys?" Alex asked with a pointed look at Megan.

"Sorry to intrude," Megan started, "But I have a theory that I'm wanting to test out with how Gavin's brain works with the NOVA system and learning." Turning to Gavin, she pulled a few receptor nodes out of her bag. "We will just attach these to your head while you spar for at least a couple rounds, just to see how your mind is processing, to get a baseline. Then we can start some of the tests," she said.

Getting into stances, Gavin put the nodes on. He wasn't sure what this would help at this point, so he focused on the task at hand. "Okay, Gavin. In this first round, I want you to not use the NOVA system. Just your abilities. I want to see what you have retained," Alex said with a smile.

They went through, and Gavin did better than expected, but Alex still dispatched him with little effort. He still looked clumsy and awkward.

"Ok. Now use the NOVA system, and let's see how you improve." They get in the stance and start. Megan watches as Gavin's brain lights up. Neurons flying around. Megan watched as they fought. The different areas light up. She marked it all down. This lasted longer, but ended when Gavin's brain seemed to be wearing down. Once the lights started to dim on her monitors of his brain, Alex easily overtook him.

Gavin had to sit down after that. His mind was whirling, and he felt dizzy. "My head is feeling hot."

"Get him a cold washcloth. Then we will work on something once he recovers," Megan said.

Once he was able to sit up on his own, Megan pulled out some cards for him to read through. He skimmed through them and looked up. "Megan, this is genius! It might just work," Gavin said. Flipping back through the cards.

"What? What's going on?" Alex asked, hating to feel out of the loop.

"She wants me to try to think through it like a computer program. Break it down into segments to be processed. Slowly, at first. Instead of trying to do the entire thing at once like I have been doing," Gavin said as he started to think through the process. Alex can see his mind working through his eyes.

"That makes sense. As far as both the NOVA system and how Gavin's mind naturally works," Alex said.

"Exactly!" Megan said excitedly. "And since that is how he has processed information his entire life, it would be natural for him to do it with this. It could also explain why he has always struggled with athletics. Even though he was coordinated and has always had a decent build without trying. So, if his mind just hadn't been able to process the information correctly, then it would have created an issue to start with."

"Ok. When you feel ready, let's try again," Alex said as she took another swig of her water.

Gavin stood up. His eyes closed but moved under his eyelids. Finally, the spring opened, and he got a slight smirk. "Ready," he said, taking a stance.

Alex launched herself at him at the same pace she had before. She was surprised to see him start to move fluidly, blocking her moves with

261

relative ease. Megan watched the monitor, and his mind seemed to stay at its usual temperature and rate when he flashed. And was gradually diminishing.

Suddenly, Alex changed tactics. She changes stances and styles. Attacking the weaknesses of the one he had been using. To her surprise, Gavin followed almost seamlessly. He shifted his stance and then continued to surprise her when he shifted again and moved into a style to exploit the weaknesses of the style she was using.

They seemed to be dancing at this point, from how it looked to Megan. She watched them move, almost as one. She had never seen Gavin move like that. So fluid. So precise. He knew exactly what he was doing.

They were quickly approaching the time frame for when Gavin had overheated on the previous trial, and he wasn't showing any signs of slowing down. Every time Alex made a move, he countered perfectly. Not long after the time had passed, Gavin spun and kicked Alex's legs out from under her. He caught her and set her gently on the ground before pinning her.

Alex seemed out of breath, but Gavin seemed to barely be tired. Gavin leaned in and kissed Alex with a confidence she hadn't seen from him before.

Megan coughed to make sure they remembered she was there, and Gavin shot up. As he jumped, he stumbled a bit and caught himself on the table. *There's my nerd. Good to know he's still there,* Alex thought as she watched him with a smile.

A few days later, after more practice training on both hand-to-hand and weapons, there was a ping on Gavin's search. He had found a lead and reported it to Richmond. He turned to Charles and Alex in Citadel. With a somber face, he said, "Let's go hunting."

Chapter 17

:/The Antithesis

The team packed up and headed out to the 5th location they had found in two months. They flew through the facility and met very little opposition. But they did find a server that Gavin was able to get on and take some information.

They did take down and capture several lower-level Collective operatives. Still, most of them had a cyanide tablet in their mouth, killing them once they bit into it.

They had struggled to find this one lead, and now they felt they had nothing. This was a dead end, as far as they could tell. With a huff, they made to leave.

Anderson watched them exit the facility. "I thought you said that he was incompetent," a distorted voice on the other end of the phone call said accusingly.

"He is. He just gets lucky from time to time," Anderson responded defensively.

"His luck had better be running out quickly. Or there will be consequences," the voice said as the call ended.

Anderson continued to watch the recording. They were getting closer than he expected, and that was unacceptable.

***

Gavin flopped down onto his bed. He hasn't felt this defeated in a while. He was running out of ideas on where to go from here. He was just starting his downward spiral of self-deprecation when there was a knock at the door.

Dragging himself out of bed, he made his way to the door. As he opened the door, he was immediately pushed out of the way by an already-talking Kaleb. "Why do I not have a key already, man? I get you to have this super-secret life of Spy-atude, but it's ME, man! And this entire not spending time with me for months on end crap? That's coming to an end. I'm not asking to be a part of the team, unless you are looking? No. Ok, yeah. I'm not even asking for a spot. Just need my Gavin time. Now, I have some grape sodas, some pizza, some Sizzling Shrimp, and both the new Call of Duty AND the entire Star Wars saga. All 6 movies. On Blu-ray. Oh, yeah. Oh, and the new Star Trek movie, if we feel a bit nasty."

Gavin just stood there and smiled. He had missed his best friend more than he had realized. The toll of the life he was leading really was more than he could handle at times. It was always nice to have a reminder that, to some people, he wasn't a spy, or a big-name hacker. He was just Gavin. And that's all they expected of him.

"Yeah, buddy, I'll have to get you that key soon. And I think I'm feeling pizza and Star Wars tonight. Not in a gaming mood," Gavin said with a slight shrug.

"Say no more, my man! One Star Wars Marathon coming right up!" Kaleb says as he starts to set out the food on the coffee table.

The movies start, and the friends talk like old times. Gavin tells him about his dad dying and that it happened on a mission, so he couldn't tell him more. Kaleb came and sat next to him and gave him a hug.

They proceeded to sit and reminisce about what his dad was like when they were kids while the movie played in the background.

"You remember after we watched War Games, and your dad taught us how to Demon Dial?" Kaleb said with a laugh. "That was one of the craziest things I ever did. But that seemed to jump-start your craving for hacking. It was crazy." Kaleb shook his head with a smile at his friend. "He always had some secret to share with us. And usually, there was more to it. Some hidden..."

Gavin's mind trailed off. He started thinking, *Dad always left more than what was first seen. He always gave extra that you had to work for.*

"Gavin, you, ok?" Kaleb said, shaking his shoulder. He had a concerned look on his face.

"Kaleb, you may be a genius!" Gavin proclaimed as he shot up out of his seat and took off towards his lab.

"Well, obviously... wait. Why? What did I say?" Kaleb followed Gavin, and walking into his lab, he stopped. He knew Gavin worked for the government now, but he had never considered what that might mean exactly. Gavin's lab made his office at Snollygoster Inc. look like a trash pile. "Woah..." he murmured as he slowly looked around. Seeing multiple computers, he knew which was for gaming. He'd known his friend far too long not to.

"You reminded me that my father was notorious for leaving hidden clues and messages our entire life. Little things that not everyone would know, or pick up. And that made me think of our current mission status and how my father may have left more for me than I saw originally," Gavin stated excitedly as he typed away on his laptop.

"Oh. Yeah. Of course! Happy to help," Kaleb said, still awe-struck by the lab. He gradually walked back to where Gavin was working, and as he did, he looked over Gavin's shoulder.

Gavin knew Kaleb probably shouldn't be seeing what he was doing, but he didn't want to waste time. Typing away, he finally found it. Pulling up the file, he found it was password encrypted. *Great.* He flopped his hands down onto the desk, feeling a bit frustrated.

"You said your dad sent this to you. Right?" Kaleb asked.

"Yeah. He did," Gavin said dejectedly. He knew that if his dad had encrypted it, he wasn't getting it open without the password. No one was.

"Well. Just me thinking, but wouldn't it make sense that it would be something he knew you would know, then? Like. Not overcomplicate it, but make it something you and him would have a connection on?" Kaleb said again, trailing off at the end as he clearly wasn't sure of himself.

"That... actually makes sense," Gavin said, again surprised that Kaleb was being this helpful.

"I have my moments. Just don't let my boss know. He will expect more from me!" Kaleb said as he let out a shudder.

"Don't worry, buddy. Your secret is safe with me," Gavin said with a laugh. He started typing in things he could think of. After a few attempts, he ran his hands through his hair and sat back. His eyes landed on the War Games poster. And it clicked. He typed in

:/HE FIGHTS FOR THE USERS/:

Suddenly, the Coeus symbol came on screen. And after a brief loading screen, a video of his father appeared.

"Hello, Gavin. I knew you would find this, and hopefully sooner than later. These files will contain information that will be dire to what you and your team are doing. But be warned. There is no way to undo opening some of them. The owners will be notified, and they will be coming after you. There isn't anything I can do to stop it. Especially now.

266

I want you to know, I have contacted your sister for the last few weeks. Even though she does not know it was me. I was monitoring her progress with the NOVA system and your own. I'm very impressed with how far you have been able to take it. I am very proud. I have a patch for you that I believe will help you greatly in what you're trying to accomplish. Hit enter and ESC on the main screen with the files, and it will activate.

Please know, I never meant any of this for you and your sister. I wanted a better life for you. One away from the spy world. But it has found you and her anyway. And since that has happened, you will get access to the rest of my files as well. Our old house has them, and you will find instructions among these files as to how to find them.

Remember, you are special in a way no one else could be. I am sending this before I breach a building that could be very heavily guarded, and I hope you won't see this. But if you do, know I always have and always will love both you and Megan with all my heart."

And the video cuts out, and a folder with multiple files pops up.

"What does he mean by a patch?" Kaleb asked, startling Gavin, who had honestly forgotten his friend was still there.

"He is talking about the NOVA system. The program that I downloaded into my head. The reason I am working for the government in the first place," Gavin answered. He still wasn't sure if he was going to put the patch in or not. *Probably should talk to Alex about it first. And maybe Richmond.* Gavin thought as he started to look at the files.

"Kaleb, I know we said that this was a guys' night, but is it okay if I call Alex?" Gavin said hesitantly. He knew he hadn't gotten much time with his bearded friend lately.

"Dude, it's no problem. This is kind of a bigger deal," Kaleb said, still sounding a bit stunned by the amount of information he had to accept at this point.

Gavin had a brief conversation with Alex and then called General Richmond. Both cautioned downloading the patch without Megan looking at it first. He agreed. So, instead, he worked on the files. He figured out which ones were going to be the dangerous ones to open. And he figured out the basics of why.

***

A few days later, he called for a team meeting. He had explained everything to Megan, and she was on board with the patch as long as she could be there to monitor. And Gavin had everything ready to tell the team what he had found. He forwarded everything to his private server at Citadel.

They all met in the conference room, with Gavin hooked up and being monitored in the side room. The patch was designed to help him process physical information and help his mind control his movements and breathing. It was specifically designed to match Gavin's current brain wave activity, something Gavin and Megan had been working on with the original design.

"Gavin, are you ready?" Megan asked, glancing at the monitor displaying his brain activity.

"Yeah, I think so. It's not like this is ever comfortable," Gavin replied with a slightly nervous laugh.

"We will be right here this time," Alex said comfortingly. Which made Gavin smile.

"Ok. Here we go," Megan said as she hit the buttons, and the screen in front of Gavin came to life.

Accessing the NOVA system went on for a while, and once it was done, Gavin slumped in his chair, and the screens went dark again.

"His vitals all remained normal. That's weird. He didn't even have his brain heat up this time, but the monitor showed his entire brain was lit up like the 4th of July. It doesn't make sense with how he was in the past," Megan said, clearly very confused. "This will be something I will have to monitor."

Alex had already left and rushed into Gavin's room to check on him. She heard Megan say that his vitals showed he was perfectly okay, but he had passed out. And Alex didn't like that. She rushed up to him and unstrapped him from the chair. "Gavin. I'm here. Are you ok? Talk to me, Gavin."

"I need to get my presentation ready," Gavin mumbled, still half out of it. His eyes were still closed.

"You just sit here for a moment and recover," Alex said as she climbed into his lap.

"You are sitting in my lap. It is going to recover something, but it won't lead to me resting any," Gavin said with an edge to his voice. Causing a giggle to erupt from her chest.

"Ahem. I hope I am not interrupting anything. But we are waiting for Gavin to tell us why he has requested us to be here. If he has a moment free?" a somewhat irritated-sounding General appeared on the screen in front of them.

Quickly jumping off Gavin, Alex said, "Yes, General." And marched out of the room, leaving Gavin staring at the General. He couldn't help but grin a bit. This caused Richmond to shake her head and close the video feed before she smiled herself and betrayed her stern persona.

Gavin walked into the main conference room and pulled out his laptop. He started pulling up files but was careful to not open any of them.

"Ok. I have a lot to get into. I'll need input and permission to continue with this research. Once we do this, there is no going back. I want to make sure that everyone knows what it will mean for us. For all of us. This isn't something to be taken lightly. It's an all-or-nothing decision, too." Gavin paused to breathe and let everyone take in what he said.

"What are you getting at Woodford?" Charles growled, not liking the little dance around the information that Gavin seemed to be doing.

"Okay, buckle up, kids. We are going on a bit of an adventure," Gavin started as he started pulling up pictures, files, and slides. Filling the entire screen several times as Charles groaned slightly. "So, this started the other night when Kaleb was over, and we were talking. He brought up the fact that my father always likes to hide extras in all his work. Really, in everything. He would make little games and riddles to solve, to keep me interested and give my brain a workout before I was able to get the extra information. And he did similarly with the video he sent me and Megan." Gavin rushed out, trying to get through it all, but realizing he was talking way too fast.

"Yes, you weren't the only one he liked to do that for," Richmond injected, "It just drove most of the rest of us nuts," she finished, causing everyone in the room to slightly chuckle in recollection of the man.

"So, the extra files and different information that he left for me this time is what you see in front of us," Gavin continued. "These files are the building blocks of a mixed domestic terrorist group Slash Cabal." Gavin cycled through the documents slowly. They could read parts of them before he moved on to the next, but none of it was making sense.

"Talk, nerd for brains," Charles growled, getting frustrated at the pace Gavin seemed to be dragging this out. He respected the kid, but didn't like the feeling of being left out.

"Okay, Charles, settle down. If you read through these documents, you will find names, dates, financial records, etc. All relate back to several groups. Some of which we already know to be members of the Collective," Gavin stated, briefly pausing to let the information sink in before continuing. "It would appear that Hunter, while he was despicable, had come across this group and was treading carefully in his research. This is quite smart since, as you can see, many Fortune 500 companies are listed among the members and several prominent senators in their parties. This group is well embedded into our government, defense, and tech companies. You could almost claim they are running the country or would be with few moves. However, a majority of the major players seem to be privately owned companies or financial groups that no one has heard of, but fund many campaigns and hold many government contracts." Gavin paused for a drink.

"So, you're saying that this could be something that could cripple the US, if we were to actually take it out?" Alex asked with clear hesitation and unease in her voice. *What had I committed my life to serving? Were my actions ever about saving people? Protecting people? Serving the government? Or was I always a privately owned slave masquerading as a weapon?* Alex lamented internally.

"I am not sure. I know it will affect our country as a whole in some way, but I am not sure how deep the rabbit hole goes. Like Andersonhad taunted, I didn't understand what I was getting into. But I think I am getting a grip on it. I also believe that I have found a listing of properties that they own. We would have to work off the record for most, if not all, of this, as they would have people in place to be able to track us. I am sure that, especially after our interactions with Anderson, we are now on their radar like never before," Gavin warned slightly.

"I know that I am secure here, and I just need to know, are they after the NOVA system or Alex? What is it that made them come after our team?" Richmond asked curtly. She was clearly uneased at this revelation.

"Simply put? Everything. They seem to want control of everything. They seem content to rule from the shadows. Pulling strings and cutting strings as needed to get what they want. Achieve their goals, and then back into their private lives. Never allowing themselves to be in any kind of danger. But putting so many others in far more danger than they would choose on their own. They seemed to have learned the value of the shadows. Not wanting to be the face of anything. Recognizable, but never known. All the power, with very little of the responsibility," Gavin finished as he continued to cycle through the files.

"They sound like real pieces of work," Charles said with a scowl plastered on his face. These were the exact people he never liked, and yet, like Alex, he couldn't even tell if he had been serving them unwittingly or not for years. Given up more of his life than he would ever like to admit to, and for what? The security of some rich people's investments?

"It is good to know who you're fighting, and now we know," Richmond said, trying to sound positive. Even though she was struggling to find the silver lining.

"I did find one thing that would benefit us greatly," Gavin said with a slight smirk.

"What is it, Gavin?" Alex asked, even though she had a slight clip to her tone.

"I am pretty sure I found where Anderson is. And the specs for the compound," he stated, pulling up the location and information. Earning grunt number eleven from Charles, excitement with the hope of gunplay.

***

Landing in Colorado, they made their way silently through the forest to the compound that Anderson was said to be in the documents. Approaching the wall, they paused to discuss their strategy. Gavin had his laptop out and was in their system. He was ready to shut down the entire plant, as soon as they were ready. He just waited for word from Charles on when. Alex sat, rechecking her ammo and knives to make sure she had all she needed.

Anderson watched on the surveillance monitors as the group approached. He had hoped they would be so bold as to find him. They had set off the silent sensors in the forest that had been set up to make sure they could keep an eye on anyone who was after the one true perfect NOVA system. And now he would finally get the opportunity to take out the weaker form. Show once and for all, who the real NOVA system was. Brett had been weak. Sending it to Gavin when he was set to be able to take it for himself. Too scared to take that chance. That risk. But now it worked out for Anderson. He was now the perfect NOVA system. The perfect Agent. The perfect killer. And no one would be able to stop him. Not even Alex Johnson. He had a plan. Now, he was able to make it happen.

Gavin got the nod and looped surveillance for them to make a silent entry. They didn't want the entire compound to know that they were there. Charles and Alex took out the single guard on a post with ease and made their way toward the main building.

"I know I shouldn't say this, but has this seemed easy to anyone else? Like, too easy?" Gavin asked hesitantly. Looking around and saw very few people.

"Yeah, I don't like it. Keep an eye out. I'm smelling a trap," Charles replied. Always the marine first, he was vigilant. Not wanting his team to be at risk.

Alex stayed quiet. She didn't like this. It reminded her of too many missions that went south. And usually, those were the ones that she had blank spots on. Times she didn't remember, but then would wake up later covered in blood. Even though she had minor injuries. The times that she didn't want to know. The times that she feared what would happen if Gavin saw her like that. When Gavin didn't see Alex anymore. All that was left was the killer. She took a deep breath and cleared her mind. She had to focus. Everything else would be handled once they were no longer in danger. *Well, it's an immediate danger anyway.*

Gavin hooked up his wrist computer to the door's security panel, getting through it with ease. Before he opened the door, he accessed the NOVA system on his martial arts skill set. That did nothing to help his fear. As soon as the trio was through the door, it shut, and he heard it lock. *Not good.* He thought as he looked back at the door. Suddenly, the alarm sounded. *A trap. Of course.* Gavin took off towards the security room so that he would be able to set up and find everything he needed. Alex and Charles took off after him. But the training he had been doing with Alex and the increased influence of the NOVA system had been helping him. He was faster than them, his long legs eating up the floor faster and faster. And as he made yet another turn, they lost him. The dual doors shut behind him, and Alex crashed into them. They were locked. She kicked the door in frustration. Blocked off from the man she loved.

Charles got on the coms. "Hey Woodford, forget something? We are shut off from you. We will try to find another way through, but for now, you're on your own."

Alex put her hand up, stopping Charles. She heard boots approaching. "Charles, we have to get out of this corridor. We are truly trapped here. No cover at all." As she finished, the first of the troops came around the corner. There was nothing they could do. "Gavin, finish this," she said in her coms before setting her gun down and raising her hands in sync with Charles.

Gavin froze momentarily at hearing that they had been captured. But he knew his best bet at getting to them would be getting set up in the security room. Where he would be able to get control of the complex. He hurried around the last few corners, approaching the room with hesitancy. After confirming that there was no trap on the door, he unlocked and opened it. Walking into the darkened room, he hears, "Hello, Gavin."

Anderson was standing in front of the monitors. "You really think you are that good of a hacker? You could just walk into one of the most secure places on earth without any resistance? When are you going to learn your limits? Or that anything you can do, I can do better?" Anderson said with a smirk.

He hit a button on the keyboard in his left hand, and on the main screen, it changed to show Alex and Charles surrounded by the military. "If you hurt them," Gavin started.

"You will what? Kill me? Please. Gavin. We both know that that just isn't in your nature. You aren't a killer. You apologize for running into chairs. To kill another person is just not in you. Now, I, on the other hand. Did you enjoy the performance I put on last time?" Anderson said with a smirk. "Your father looked so helpless as he lay there. The look on his face was amazing when he finally realized he had been shot. But nothing will ever compare to the look on your face when it dawned on you what was happening. It is something that I will cherish for the rest of my life. It's almost as much as when I finally rebreak Agent Johnson and get her back to what she was made to be. A perfect, order-obeying robot. She was trained to not have weaknesses like emotions. The perfect woman. And this time, she will answer to me. You see, there is no way out for you. There is nowhere you can go. There is nothing you can do. And, as far as the government is concerned, you aren't here. So, there is no backup coming. You have nothing. And there will be no record of this anywhere," Anderson ranted on, praising himself.

"So, this isn't a military base? Those aren't US soldiers?" Gavin asked.

"You really are just so slow sometimes, Gavin. Do you need everything spelled out for you? How did you even get into GIT? It is no wonder why they kicked you out. No, those aren't military. They are in the Collective. They are provided by our generous benefactors. These men happen to be provided by Orlov Industries," Anderson scoffed at him.

Making sure that his com was active subtly, Gavin replied, "So, these guys are Russian?" Keeping the com active so Anderson could be heard.

Anderson replied, "Yes, Gavin, and $2 + 2 = 4$."

Gavin heard Charles give a disgusted grunt, and Alex softly laughed at what she heard. *They didn't have to hold back. They weren't hurting good American soldiers who were just following orders. That made this entire operation easier. And easier to report after the fact.* Gavin tapped a couple keys on his wrist computer, and the lights turned off on the entire compound. The screens went black. And he lunged at Anderson.

Alex and Charles waited for it. When the lights darkened, Charles knocked the gun away from his back and launched his head at the enemy. Breaking their nose and knocking them to the floor, unconscious. Spinning as he kneeled, he kicked out and broke the next guy's knee. He grabbed the first guy's gun that he dropped as he spun and fired several rounds at where he remembered the other guys being. The flash revealed them to no longer be there. He pauses and hears only breathing. "Alex?" He asked.

"Yeah, Charles. We are clear." She replied calmly.

"Good. Let's go find Gavin," Charles said as he got up and started making his way down the hallway. He was thankful to have Alex as his partner.

Anderson saw Gavin lunge at him and moved out of the way. He activated the NOVA system and accessed the file on martial arts skills. Smirking, he expected this to be easy. He knew that his NOVA system had been upgraded, far from what Gavin had originally downloaded.

Gavin recognized Anderson's face as he accessed the NOVA system. He had left his coms on, so he let Alex and Charles know, "Anderson, do you have the NOVA system?" Gavin asked.

Anderson didn't reply to him, this time. He just smirked and came at him with a right jab at his jaw. Gavin dodged the jab and then moved to block the left knee that followed. Anderson started out with a barrage of attacks, hoping to end the fight quickly. He landed several, but as the fight continued and he was unable to get Gavin down, Gavin seemed to be getting quicker.

Gavin felt the NOVA system kick in, the patch he had downloaded calming his mind. His emotions were still there but in a dampened state. He felt calm, even as there was slight pain from the blows that Anderson had been able to land already.

Limbs were flying everywhere. Gavin was blocking more and more of Anderson's attacks. Left jab, right hook, left kick, left knee. It was all slowing down. He felt the NOVA system reading it, and it felt natural. Not like before, when he felt rushed. Not like with Alex, where he felt something was controlling his body. This felt like muscle memory. It was like he was reacting, not a program running in his mind. He watched Anderson as arms and legs were being thrown.

276

Just then, there was a ramming sound on the door. Gavin looked up to see Alex and Charles looking through the security glass. It distracted him enough for Anderson to get a kick in. It landed square in Gavin's chest. Sending him flying back and slamming into a table. The wind knocked out of him, and he staggered. He didn't realize how tired he was.

Looking up, he saw Anderson breathing heavily but had a confident smirk on his face as he came at him. The look in his eye was of murder. He was ready to kill Gavin and end this. Gavin started glancing around the room. His mind ran as fast as it ever had. He knew that he had to do something. That kick had been more than he expected.

Anderson ran the last few steps toward Gavin to gain momentum and leaped at Gavin with his knee out in front. He was looking for a death blow.

Gavin grabbed the mouse and keyboard off the desk on top of him and lay down on the floor. The knee barely misses his head. Gavin rolls out from under the desk as he wrapped the mouse cable around Anderson's ankle and pulled. Causing Anderson to fall into the splits. As Anderson fell, Gavin sent a spinning kick towards Anderson's head. Anderson blocked it, but the force caused his head to fall back and hit the desk, slightly dazing him. Gavin followed that with the keyboard, cracking Anderson right at the base of his skull with the edge of the keyboard and causing Anderson's head to hit the desk again. As he fell backward, Gavin brung another kick up, and this one connected with Anderson's forehead.

Anderson fell to the floor, knocked out.

Gavin rushed over to the panel and opened the door. Getting a rushed embrace from Alex and a pat on the shoulder by Charles. "You did good, kid. Now, let's get out of here with him before anyone else comes," Charles said, holding up some handcuffs.

The team got Anderson handed over to Richmond's trusted transfer team and filed the paperwork to list him under private John Smith for designation to a black site. Not even they would know where he was being sent. They all got together for a family dinner. Justice had been carried out.

***

Alex knocked on Gavin's door. They hadn't gotten much of a chance to be able to talk since Anderson had taken her the first time. And most of the time they had spent together hadn't been spent talking. *It was communication, just of a different kind,* Alex thought with a slight grin to herself.

Gavin opened the door and let her in. Giving her a kiss, he asked, "Hey Alex, is everything okay?" He could read a slightly pensive look on her beautiful face.

"Gavin. I feel I owe you. I owe you a story. My story. The truth as far as I can remember. You see. None of those files you have, will tell you the entire truth. Because from the start, none of them had it. You see, part of why I chose this cover name for my CIA contracts is because my real name is actually Alex. Alexandria Lisa Kowalski."

***

Anderson sat in his cell. The trauma to his brain while running the NOVA system had done its damage. He struggled to focus on anything. Anything except his hatred. That ran too deep to be subverted to anything else. Hatred for the CIA, hatred for the people who were supposed to be looking after him. And most of all, hatred for Gavin and Alex. He hated them most of all. He knew lunchtime was getting close. The only interaction with other people that he ever got now.

A figure made its way to the seemingly abandoned building. Scanning their badge and walking into the door. They walked right past the guards, who look at them and then went back to what they were doing. They walked right to Anderson's cell and opened the door.

"About time you got here. I've been waiting," Anderson said. He looked into the dead eyes. He looked at their ashen skin. The life

278

seemingly drained from them. The figure raised their arm, and Anderson was left with the sight of a lifeless walking corpse and the flash of a barrel being the last things he saw.

Three shots. One in his head and two in his chest. They said, "We are done here," and the figure turned and walked out of the black site, leaving the cell door open.

Chapter 18

:/Repercussions

Gavin sat there. Stunned. He didn't know what to say. He had never expected Alex to open up like this. It wasn't really in her nature.

"Alex, I..." Gavin started, only to be interrupted by Alex. "No. Gavin, just listen for now. I need to get through this before I lose my nerve." Alex took a deep breath.

This is it. You can show him what he means to you, what this relationship means to you. He knows that you don't open up. That everything about you is a lie. But not this. This is real. And he deserves to know the real you, Alex thought to herself. She looked up to see Gavin nod, his face stern with determination to listen.

"My name isn't Stacy. Or any of the other names in that file that you saw. My father was a con man and a fairly decent one. He taught me all about the business when I decided to leave with him, when he left my mom. My early memories are of them fighting all the time. My dad seemed like he was the fun and cool parent, in the way that a naive kid can never understand how being responsible is needed. He would have me help with the cons. I'd fake injuries or sell cookies that were never intended to be delivered. And for a time, I loved it. It made my dad proud how I could swindle someone we called a fool. But it also meant that we were moving all the time. Which made it very difficult to make friends.

"I didn't have any, in fact. My dad was the only person I hung out with. And eventually, it became mandatory that he was the only one who I was allowed to hang out with. Of course, I started to want friends at my age around this time. And that's when Hunter found us. I'm unsure how or what he saw in me to make me someone of interest to him.

"And this is where the files you have, and my memories differ. If the parts that I thought were just nightmares are true, and I was actually sent on those missions and had those things done to me at such a young age, then it is far, far worse. And you could double my mission log. And likely quadruple my assassination count. I only remember them as bad dreams. Since it was all supposed to get erased when they said the trigger phrase. But mine, I think, have all been stored in a different part of my mind.

"But I'm getting ahead of myself. Let me go back," Alex said as she refocused.

"Take your time, Babe," Gavin said supportively.

***

The Westgate sat in his lab waiting. He never liked working with the people he had to, but he didn't have a choice. The research he has always hoped to do was borderline legal in the best of situations. They always kept him waiting. He knew why. It was a power move. They always had to prove he was on their time, not the other way around. But their money was always welcome. So, he sat.

Reading through his research, seeing what else he could tweak to help his project progress. He had some of the notes from Coeus. Scrap pieces here or there. And one full file from Perseus. It's not like he was handed the keys to the kingdom.

How was he supposed to make sense of all of this? He couldn't recreate the NOVA system with shards of a past. He would almost be better suited just starting from scratch. But he has to figure this out. He could lose much more than just a contract.

The door opened, and in walked two men. Not saying a word, the taller one set a briefcase down on the table as the other sat. Looking around the room, the one sitting nodded.

"Yes, I shall begin then. I know you are both very busy. You see, I am having an issue with recreating the project with such little of the original information," the Westgate stated. "Without more information, I feel it may be a dead end, and my time would be better used on other projects," he finished hesitantly.

There was silence from the other two men, which made him uneasy. He waited nervously as the one sitting down pulled out a wallet and took out a card. The Westgate could see a badge in the wallet. He could barely make out that the man was CIA. At least, that was one of his employers.

The man stood, took out a cell phone, and walked out of the room, dialing a number. As the door closed, the other man cleared his throat. It felt as if he had intended to say something and then thought the better of it. He looked towards the door, expecting it to open.

The Westgate was getting very nervous. He wasn't sure what more he could say. He knew what needed to happen; without more to work with, this was a dead end completely. A waste of money and time. He didn't understand the obsession with it, to begin with. After his work with the other projects, he had been in charge of. Those that had started him down this path away from the CIA and other official government agencies.

Just then, the door opened. The shorter man walked back into the room and sat down. He had a scruffy-looking beard and looked quite disheveled compared to the other taller and more clean-cut man. Both looked in their fifties, not that the Westgate could talk, being in his seventies himself.

282

The shorter man spoke first, with a slight smirk that would make most anyone's insides cringe, "Orlov said he wants this done. Now, let's talk."

***

Alex smiled at Gavin, who was giving her his goofy, nose-scrunching grin back. *I can't believe how good this feels. Knowing he isn't judging me. Won't back down, but isn't pushing either. Just accepts what I am willing to give. So, this is what love is.*

Alex sighed softly as she continued, "Okay, where was I? Yeah, Hunter showed up. At first, he was kind. He offered me a way out. My father had been caught, and my freedom was on the line, too. My mom had been long gone. I didn't even remember where she was, at this point. I hadn't heard from her in years. So, I was alone. My father was taken into custody for the crimes I had helped him commit. My mom was nowhere to be known. As far as I knew, there were no ties back to who I really was.

"I was a 14-year-old girl in a world without anyone or anything to fall back on. Except the skills my father had taught me, and then I honed myself, as well. I had gone to the small cash dump we always had whenever we settled into a new town and was getting ready to bolt, when he came up behind me.

"If I'd known then what I know now about what he was going to put me through, I wouldn't have missed. I threw a knife at him as a warning. Hitting the tree next to him. He thought it was a miss. His arrogance thought I was helpless, and in many ways, he was right.

"He kept me in regular high school for quite a while. Pulling me for, at times, full weeks to send me to train or on missions. I only remember a lot of my teens as a dream. But not for the normal reason people have that.

"I vaguely remembered what they did to me. And it was too much. But who could I tell? He was the assistant director of the CIA at the time, and I was a nobody. Literally, everything about me was erased, and he put in a file to make something official about myself. And that's where the name Samantha came from. I'd learned from my father, never trust someone who has power over you. And assistant director Richard Hunter definitely had power over me.

"Like I'd said, he started off being kind. Bought me books to read, clothing, provided housing, and food. Everything I needed. I rarely went wanting. But I realized too late that that was by design. I was trapped. I owed him too much in my mind to walk away. And then he got me to that point when he started pushing.

"The training got worse, harder, longer. At first, I'd miss school for a day. Then, a few days. Then, a week. Finally, after the first month-long mission, he arranged for my diploma to be issued. I actually left school at 15, even though my transcripts say otherwise. I was in classes with seniors to get through.

"After that, it got far worse. I started trying to push back. I didn't feel I owed him anymore. And that's when he brought my father back into it. He started threatening me that if I didn't follow through, then he was going to have my father killed in a prison riot. And then, have every memory of him ever existing wiped.

"My father was far from a good man, but he was still my dad. I hated every minute of it, but I went through with whatever Hunter told me to. Eventually, I started to have every bad thing feel like it had been a nightmare. I thought it was a coping mechanism, but as you know, it was them.

"Looking back, I remember a man that would come. He would do things to me. Forced me to listen to things while he gave commands. I assume that was the brainwashing. But it's so faint and vague it would never have made a difference now. I couldn't pick him out in a crowd."

"Can you explain to me exactly what you're wanting it to do? Then maybe I can start working on something similar," the Westgate asked, hoping to be able to salvage some kind of hope for keeping this project going.

"Orlov said that the council needs this to do everything. For starters, it is meant to be an intel transfer to agents. But they have heard you can add skills to its abilities. The very little the CIA has on this project anymore that isn't still classified to a point even I can't touch, indicates it has been done and successful in a few attempts. But most of the recent ones have been complete failures. Where the people were left in a vegetable state or just died. We need you to figure out why and how to fix it," the taller agent stated.

The one who had been seeming in charge hadn't spoken since returning from his phone call and saying to talk. He sat there typing and would occasionally look up at him. It just made him even more uncomfortable.

"Can I know your names? I need to keep a record for the counsel on who has been involved. If you don't want it, you need clearance from them." The Westgate was getting annoyed. Just because they had a badge and gun didn't mean they could bully him in his lab.

"Of course," the shorter one said, sounding in charge again. "I am Agent Denver, and that is Agent Brooks. We work directly for The Counsel. You will be answering to us for the foreseeable future. If you need confirmation, you are welcome to call," Agent Denver stated.

***

Hel closed her email. It was confirmed. Her heart ached. She knew something like this was likely to happen to one of them, but she never actually thought it would be him. Not for years now. Her love was gone. Dead.

He had kept the kids safe and out of the way. Right up until some hot shot agent, who supposedly just happened to get roomed with her Gavin in college, sent him an email containing the very thing they had sworn to end.

285

According to Walter, the NOVA system had melded with Gavin's mind like it was meant to. And with the help of his sister, they managed to make it far more effective than they had ever dreamed.

She saw his success sheet. She couldn't bring herself to call it a mission log. She hated to think what the NSA had put him through. Even with Catherine in place to help. She hoped it wouldn't be too hard. She had spent so much time away from them that she had almost forgotten what it was like to be a mom.

She kicked herself. She didn't have time to wallow. Not right now. Not with everything that had happened. She still had to be on edge. She still had to be Hel. But Lucile looked at the picture of her son. She worried he had started looking for her, and even more worried he could find her. She wasn't sure how to explain what she had had to do to get to this point.

"Hel, my dear, my love," the heavy British accent echoed through the hall to her office, making it sound far smoother than it had ever felt. Orlov stepped through her office door, "Would you mind having a nightcap with me?" He said as he came into the room holding two glasses and a bottle of scotch. "A slight celebration, if you will," he finished.

She felt the bottom of her stomach drop out. She knew where this was heading and wasn't sure if she could hide the pain this time. But she plastered the perfected fake smile on and played slightly dumb. "What are we celebrating, Ivan?" she asked.

"You act like you don't know," he said in a teasing tone. "Coeus is gone! The man who had been a complete thorn in my side has been finally taken out. If this isn't something to toast, then I'm not sure what is! With this, the business will increase 10-fold at least!" Ivan finished with a smile and offered Hel a glass.

Numb. The agent had taken over completely again. She couldn't feel anything. She smiled and took the glass. Clinking and then taking a mouthful of the scotch. Letting the peat and pepper taste burn as it went down her throat. At least it reminded her she could feel. "To growth," she forced herself to say. The crying would have to wait for later.

***

"So that's it. From there, you have more of my story than I do. What I do remember wasn't all that good. I had some fun times with different people. But it always had some kind of catch. Something attached to the attention I was given. Something was expected of me beyond just talking and laughing together. That is, until I met you," Alex said with a shy smile.

Gavin was beaming. He had stayed somber for most of her story, but he couldn't help but smile at the fact that he had given her hope for more to life than this. "When I met you, something changed within me. I couldn't understand someone being so good, kind, and selfless, especially without some ulterior motive, specifically towards me. It upset me so much when you kept it from me that you were joining the NSA. It hurt on a lot of levels. You, to that point, had been the epitome of selflessness and goodness to me. But, whenever this happened in the past, there was much more on the table than you asked. Everyone in the past who had gone to make a deal, would have tried to bargain for me to be a part of said deal. And that has never been who I am as an agent, as you know.

"Then, the fact that you didn't feel you could trust me with it. That you couldn't come to me and inform me that not only had you joined the NSA, but that you were the notorious hacker that everyone I know in this business has, at some point, tried to capture. Those both hurt. More than I ever would have told you. I couldn't understand what I had done that caused you to think you couldn't trust me. Could you explain?" Alex asked.

Gavin looked at his hands for a bit. A quiet hurt spread across his face. "The bugs in my room. And how I know the protocol for everything should go. I wouldn't be surprised to hear that you had had conversations with Hunter about when and how to get rid of me. How to dispose of the asset. Am I right?" Gavin asked softly.

Alex was stunned. She hadn't even considered what it would mean that he would know what was expected of her. She would have had to think about and plan how to dispose of him. What to tell his sister. Then, how to explain her disappearing. This was all new to her. She was not used to a protection mission being so long or involved. No one was. This wasn't covered in training. And she had had plenty of training. "Gavin," she said softly, "I am sorry."

"Alex, it isn't really your fault. That is partly why I was so confused as to what to do. I didn't know who I could trust. Or that you would be able to control what happened to me either. At one point, I had accepted that I was a walking dead man if I couldn't change my situation," Gavin explained. He leaned in and kissed her to reinforce the fact that he didn't blame her. "I love you, Alex Kowalski," Gavin said softly, causing Alex to shiver.

It wasn't that she didn't trust him anymore. It was that that name was now foreign to her. It was someone that she no longer felt she had a right to be. Someone innocent and naive. Things that she left behind long ago.

"Gavin, can you keep calling me Alex Johnson. I know that is my cover name for this mission, but can I be honest? I feel like my life truly started when I bumped into you at that club," Alex said as tears started to form. Overcome with emotion, she kissed him again. Harder than he had her. She couldn't believe how much she cared for this man. Pushing him back onto the bed. The rest of the conversation could wait.

***

Hel finished her drink and stood. She needed to be alone. She craved to be alone. Even if that was what she feared more than anything. Alone. Nothing makes you feel more alone than when you know you have people who would love you, care about you, and be there for you selflessly, and you can't be with them.

She felt her entire life had been out on hold for well over a decade, approaching two, at this point. And the only one she could blame was herself. She, in essence, had chosen this. "Ivan, I believe it is time for

288

me to go to bed. Thank you for this lovely scotch," she said as she stood to leave.

"Oh, must you go?" Ivan Orlov said with a faux pout. "One of these nights, I will get you to stay, my love. I just know it," he said with a sly wink. His demeanor showed a charm that did not meet his eyes.

Hel knew the truth. She knew more than he did. And she knew that there was no way he would ever get her into his bed. "Goodnight, Ivan," she said as she walked out. As she did, she touched the door frame on her way out. Placing a small receiver for a parabolic microphone there.

Getting back to her room, she made sure the door was locked. She swept the room for bugs of any kind. Finding 2, one she knew wasn't Ivan's, the other being their standard for bugging every room for safety. She knew she was in the clear for another night. Opening her laptop, she took off her necklace and collapsed it down. Inserting it into the USB port and holding down the power button for 30 seconds and then a minute. The one necklace lit up.

The Coeus symbol was displayed on the laptop, and she typed in her password. Up popped the face of Walter Woodford.

"My beautiful wife, Lucile. I want you to know that there hasn't been a day that I didn't think about you. About our family. About what we lost. I will forever regret not double-checking my work on that initial software.

"As I have no doubt you will know by now, this will be my last transmission to your device. I am gone. And with me, us ever having our full family back together. I know it was what we had always fought for. But we both knew we would likely lose it all one day.

"Thankfully, not all is lost. You know about our son now, and Megan is doing well. I hope soon you will be able to get away and see them. Though I understand why that isn't a good idea now, more than I ever did. In the next few days, you will be receiving files that I stumbled across, that I know now were never meant for any of our eyes. Be sure to read through every file. Commit it to memory. You will need to know it all moving forward, if what I think is going to happen does.

"Gavin will need you. Megan will need you. So please, when you can, come out of the shadows, out of the darkness. There is work to do in the light. I love you, my dear Lucile. With all my heart," Walter said. As his picture on the screen cut out, you could see tears falling from his eyes. His wedding ring shone in the camera.

Lucile kicked herself for the millionth time. She couldn't wear hers. Not while on assignment. And it still killed her inside, even after all these years. She felt naked without it.

Quickly remembering what was happening, she typed a few commands into the laptop, and a recording software came up. She played back the recording she had missed on time and a half speed. She heard a name she hadn't heard in quite a while. So, she flipped over to the video log. To make sure she got everything she needed.

On the screen, she watched it play out:

Ivan watched her leave the room. As soon as she was out of sight, the smile fell from his face. The real Ivan was on full display. He called some guards to clear the cups as he looked around the room. He was always very paranoid but never thought she would betray him. Ever. If only he knew the depths of her betrayal.

Ivan walked to a monitor, brought up the keyboard, and started working. She brought up the logs from his computer that got copied over to hers. She watched as he sent several threatening emails. A couple of world leaders. None of that surprised her. She watched him bring up payroll. Going through his books, there was nothing she didn't already know. As she was in charge of them. He was double-checking her work.

He then pulled out his phone. She flipped over to the clone of his phone she had on an app to record everything. She knew he was untouchable. Where they were, and what he had on many world leaders, kept him safe. Even more concerning was the texts he would send twice a day.

She had traced the number, but it was always a dead end. Some burner or another. Always with what seemed like an order. But nothing ever came or went. She was never told about it. It bothered her.

Hel thought back on her earlier days in the CIA. Before everything in her life went to crap. Before her world crashed. She had always trusted her gut. It had rarely ever been wrong. About Walter was the biggest one that she could remember. That brought a sad smile to her face. She had underestimated him. Just like everyone always did. And he made her pay, by making her fall in love with him.

Shaking her head, she got back to it. Bringing up the recording of the phone call. She jotted down the number. Then, any names or references to names. She never listened to it the first time on a recording. It was data gathering. She would listen to it again. And again, if needed. And those would be for listening very closely.

She rewound it and played it back again. Ivan got a call from a number she knew. She'd still have to review the logged numbers again. The recording said:

Ivan: "What?"

Agent: "He has nothing really. You sure this guy is worth the trouble?"

Ivan: "Are you questioning me? This is who we need. He will be able to create exactly what I am wanting."

Agent: "No, sir. It just seems like this scientist is a fraud. He doesn't even seem confident that he can make it when we get him everything he said he needed."

Ivan: "You underestimate him. He is the fifth brightest man I have ever known. And he knows, if he doesn't, then I'll kill him myself."

Agent: "So what is it that you are wanting, Sir?"

Ivan: "I'm wanting the NOVA system rebuilt and for my own use, but with some modifications, Agent Denver. The weakness of the United

291

States Government is its rules. Their laws. They wanted the basics of what this technology was capable of. But my plan is much broader.

"There are many more applications for it. Atreus has a vision, and he has told me what to do. I will have the specifications sent to the Westgate of what all is expected in the different designs he has planned."

Agent Denver: "Does the Collective know of his plans?"

Ivan: "It doesn't matter if they do or don't. They will fall in line, just like they always have. No one disappoints Atreus. Now, finish up there. I have another mission for you and your dog on a leash."

Agent Denver: "We will be done here in the next few hours. What is the next mission?"

Ivan: "Very well. We have the location of the current NOVA system now. Atreus has told me you will be flying to Atlanta, Georgia, to retrieve him. Then bring him to the Westgate. He will have everything he needs then to continue his work."

Agent Denver: "Very well. I will message you when we leave."

The call ended, and Hel stood there. She knew what she needed to do, but she wasn't sure how to get it done in time. She had to get to Gavin. To her family. To protect them from those thugs. She knew who Ivan was talking about. Denver and Brooks were notorious for their ruthlessness and brutality. She couldn't believe they were being sent in for such a delicate task.

She got a go bag ready. She could easily say she was off on assignment. Ivan rarely questioned her anymore. She was his right hand by design. And now was the time to take advantage of that. But not without giving a heads-up to her old friend.

Lucile grabbed her bag and left a note for Ivan saying there were issues that she was looking into in their operations in Mexico, which wasn't entirely a lie. It was something he knew she had been frustrated with for a while. But it offered her an excuse to be in that part of the world.

Sneaking out her window, she preferred to come and go without anyone knowing. No matter what.

She made her way to the private airport. Getting into her plane, she got to altitude. Sure, she was safe and alone now. She swept the cabin. It was clear as she had known since the first sweep on the ground. But she was always careful. Pulling the phone out that she had under several dials that were actually broken on the dash, she activated it.

The load screen came up with the Coeus symbol. Linking it to their satellite, she activated the call.

General Richmond was just starting her workday when the call came in on her phone that she always kept hidden. The phone Coeus had given her decades before. The phone hadn't rung since her friend went on her last mission.

Picking it up and letting it connect, she heard a voice that was known to be calm in all situations, and sounded slightly panicked.

"Catherine. He knows where the NOVA system is. He knows, and he is sending Brooks and Denver. Get everyone ready, and I hope you have a plan." The call ended.

General Richmond quickly dialed Charles.

"It's time. They are coming. A war is coming. And I'm not sure if we are ready. There can be no mistakes." She hung up the phone and slumped her shoulders. She knew this day would come. She just had hoped it would take longer.

293

Chapter 19

:/Missing

It was very early morning, around 4am. Alex rolled over in bed and saw he was gone. She figured he was in his lab, but had to confirm. Climbing out of bed, she grabbed her gun, just in case. *I know I'm safe here. This feels like home. Maybe we should do something about that,* Alex thought with a smirk. She had never even imagined living with someone before, but now that they were officially together, she hated her apartment. She still liked her alone time at times, but Gavin had his gaming time during that. Smiling to herself, she thought they should talk about her moving in. She turned the corner and leaned against the doorframe, watching him.

Gavin sat at his computer. Fingers flying across the keyboard with a memorized ease. He went through file after file from what his dad had sent him. The Collective still had operatives and bases all over. They had people in every branch of the government on their side. And from the top down, there were 4-star generals, and there were janitors. But rarely did you see names. Mostly titles.

Trying to make sense of all of it was going to take time. And time was not on their side. He saw her reflection on the screen. He felt her presence more than anything. It comforted him. But it helped him focus and motivated him, while reminding him of what he was fighting for.

"I'm trying to learn all I can about the Collective, while also trying to find my mother," Gavin said without taking his eyes off the screen.

"I understand," Alex replied as she came up behind him. She wrapped her arms around his shoulders and chest and rested her head beside his. She kissed his neck by his ear, feeling him shiver. "How's everything going?" she said softly into his ear.

"Well, that doesn't help me focus," Gavin said with a slight laugh. "But honestly, it's scary," he continued somberly.

"How so?" Alex asked, standing up a bit straighter. Paying better attention.

"Well, they are far more widespread than we knew or expected. I have next to no names beyond what we already had. They are well organized and even more well-funded. Like beyond government spending funded. And what's worse. They are ghosts. They are everywhere and nowhere. If the files are correct, they have been responsible for a large majority of the world's biggest devastations, as well as developments," Gavin breathed. He was trying his hardest to not sound like he was describing a Batman villain, but he felt more and more like that was just what they were.

"The issue is, until recently, if I'm reading these correctly, they were a benevolent group. Always trying to do what's right. And I'm using the term 'recently' very loosely," Gavin said. "I'm not sure what changed, but it seems like in the late 80s until the early to mid 90s, they started being more controlling and manipulative. Gaining power for power's sake. Rather than using it to help others.

"See, the documentation shows that it was a group created originally after World War II to help prevent anything like the Holocaust from happening again. They were there to do good and to help the world be a better place. I don't have direct links to them, but it's heavily implied. They helped with civil rights revolutions. And end of famines. And the vaccine for Polio. They did good stuff. But that just kind of stopped happening during the late 80s to mid-90s. And I don't know why," Gavin finished sadly.

"I'm sure we will figure it out. Now, you said something about looking for your mom?" Alex asked with slight hesitation. She knew that Woodford's mom was always a bit of a sensitive subject.

"Oh yeah! So, my dad left a file indicating that he had been trying to get mom out of some long-term mission that went wrong. That was why my family was ripped apart. He didn't give a lot of specifics, but I think I got it narrowed down to an operation in Russia. I'm just not sure if I should keep this to myself or if I should bring it up to Richmond. Because I don't really want to be ordered to stand down. If I don't say anything, my leeway allows me the room to act like I didn't know I shouldn't. You know?" Gavin speculated. His eyes pleading with her to understand.

"I agree. I don't know that Richmond needs to know about this little project. However, should you talk to your sister about it? She might be able to help." Alex asked.

"I don't want to get her hopes up about it, just to have mom be dead. Or worse, that she just doesn't want us anymore. Megan already dealt with that enough. I can't do it to her again. She had to fight so hard for us to not be separated, to make sure our family was intact, as much as it could be. Eventually, we learned to fight for each other.

"Maybe you're right. She and I always had each other's backs. It wouldn't be right for me to keep this from her now. She deserves to know and have the opportunity to make that decision for herself," Gavin relented. "And, Alex, I know you tread lightly on the topic of family. I'm not sure if it's because of mine or your own, but I want you to know I trust you. And that goes to talking about my family, as well. You don't have to worry about upsetting me too much with it. I know if you say anything, it's because you care about me and want the best for me," Gavin said with a smile.

Alex breathed a sigh of relief that she didn't know she was holding. "Thank you, Gavin. And on the topic of family, there is something else about me you need to know," Alex said with slight hesitation.

Gavin took her hands. "What's that?" He asked gently.

"Operation Ruins," Alex said.

Gavin's eyes fluttered. Images of a chamomile bloom came to mind. Gavin accessed the NOVA system in the mission logs. "Alex, what happened on that mission? It says it failed. And who is Agent Denver?" he asked.

"Good. It was in there. I was worried it had been entirely off the books. Agent Denver was my handler. He was known for getting the job done, no matter what. And the mission wasn't a failure. Not like I had reported anyways," Alex paused to breathe. *This is the last I have, Gavin. Please understand. I love you. This is me giving everything.*

"So, the package in the mission briefing is misleading, to say the least. It was a Russian diplomat and prominent businessman's daughter. His one child. See, after everything with Brett happened, the CIA felt they couldn't trust me. So, they gave me a handler. Denver. He was ruthless. Manipulative and mean. But effective. He sent me in to get the daughter. But didn't tell me what I was getting into.

"It turned out that she was going to inherit a large amount of money, and Denver wanted it. He believed that he could use her to get their fortune. He wanted me to just drop her off to him and leave. But I couldn't. I couldn't do it to that little girl. So, I left her with the last person in the world I trusted at the time. My mom," Alex explained.

Gavin was shocked. He thought she hadn't seen her mom since leaving with her dad.

"I hope you're not upset with me," Alex said quietly. "I didn't want to tell you, but I'd looked her up as soon as I got the clearance. I wanted to know what happened to her. She never remarried. Never had another kid. It was like her life was on pause. And, well, when I saw that little girl's face, I knew I couldn't hand her over to Denver. I'd done some terrible things before. But I couldn't do that.

"So, I reported the mission as a failure, my first one. Got my slap on the wrist from Hunter. And then got the girl to my mother. I had to call in a few favors, but I got her somewhere safe. I felt it gave my mom the daughter that she deserved. A restart on life. Not exactly the same, but still," Alex finished solemnly.

"Alex, I know and understand that you will have things that come up that are secret. And that has to stay that way. While I want to know everything about you, I don't want you to feel like it's required that you tell me everything. And given what has happened to you, I'm sure that there are things that will come up that you just don't remember," Gavin said placatingly. "I love you. Now, let's see about talking to my sister about some of this. Now that the sun is up and everything," Gavin finished with a laugh.

As they got up and headed towards the door, Alex laughed in agreement with him. She leaned in and gave him a kiss as he reached for the door. She was glad that things between them had settled, and they were finding comfort in being with each other. She felt stronger when she was with him. Not because he was weak, but because she could be, and he wouldn't judge her. She had never experienced a comfort like that before. Gavin pulled the door open, and Alex whipped out her gun.

Standing in the doorway was an older woman. Gavin froze, and Alex had her gun drawn. The woman was smiling, but Alex felt a tension that she never had before from Gavin. It made her very uneasy.

"Mom!?" Gavin breathed out.

***

Denver walked into the building. He was starting to hate this place. It was taking too much of his time. He left Brooks there to make sure that production never slowed down. He needed the NOVA system, or whatever it was called. He wanted to get on with his mission. This was

298

meant to be his last. Once he completed it, he was promised enough money that he would be able to retire with it and never have to worry about anyone commanding him to do anything ever again.

Holding the finishing plans that Ivan had for the Westgate, he made his way into the room where the man was working. "Here are the plans. Now, how long do you think it will take?" Denver demanded with a sneer.

The Westgate looked at him dumbfounded, "I have told you before. It doesn't matter what designs you give me. Without the specifications and the base coding for this that Coeus built, we are never going to get this built. It is impossible." He nervously shuffled through the files he had been given.

Brooks rolled his eyes and huffed. He always hated working with these eggheads. They overthink everything and make it all more complicated than it needs to be. He still didn't see what the big hubbub about this NOVA system was. It felt like a waste of time to him. He didn't need some computer in his head to help him know what to shoot and where. He was perfectly skilled to be able to do that on his own.

"So, what if we brought you a living, breathing, working NOVA system? Would you be able to use them to create what our boss wants?" Denver huffed out impatiently. He was tired of jumping through hoops and being an errand boy. He would much rather be able to have something he could do to be able to end this. He knew his partner had no interest in the NOVA system, but Denver had seen footage of it in action. He knew some of what it could offer. And if he could intimidate this Westgate into making a second one for him, one he could use for his own gain, to leverage others to make sure he got exactly what he wanted, and then left alone, he intended to do just that.

"Are you getting close to finishing?" Denver asked as he walked up behind the Westgate.

"You know I hate it when you guys sneak up behind me. Yes, I am finishing the little bit I can do before you bring me the subject," he mumbled while continuing to work. The Westgate was frustrated to have everyone seemingly watching over his shoulder, but that has seemed to start to come with the territory.

Denver had a text come through.

HE IS READY. LOCATION AND BRIEFING ON THE PLANE. MOVE. NOW.

"Okay, we will be back with the subject. If you aren't ready for him by then, we will terminate your contract with us," Denver said with a sinister smirk and a flash in his eye.

***

"Hello, Gavin. I have missed you," Lucile said as she came in for a hug. At first, Gavin let it happen as he didn't really know how to react. As he went to pull back, she had already. "Look, we don't have a lot of time. So, I think the best way to avoid a lot of this awkward gun pointing would be if I make a call. Can I use your direct line to General Richmond?" Lucile asked, giving a side eye to Alex.

Gavin was still stunned. His mother came back from the dead and instantly knew about his spy life. *Of course, she knows about the spy life. It makes sense that she disappeared, if she was also a part of this life. I AM excited she is back, but WHAT IN THE WORLD IS GOING ON?!* Gavin couldn't help but feel like his life was some kind of sick joke. It was like a game to someone who thought it would be fun to mess with him. *Well, I am getting tired of playing this game.*

"Gavin, Gavin!" Alex finally yelled, trying to get him to come out of his internal processing. "I know this is a lot, but I am not sure that right now is the best time to try to process it all. We can talk it through when we are alone. Ok?" She looked at him with concerned and pleading eyes.

"What? I'm sorry. Yeah. We can. Yeah, that would be good," Gavin stumbled through, trying to bring himself out of his fog. He knew that whatever had brought his mom back to them out of the cold couldn't be good news.

"Hello, Catherine," Lucile said with a bit of an edge to her kind tone.

General Richmond sat a little taller and looked with a slightly cold stare back from the screen. "Hello, Lucile. You said it was time. Fill us in. Tell us all you can." A look of determination settled on her face.

"As of three nights ago, Ivan Orlov, head and creator of Orlov Industries, had set out to retrieve what he had learned to be the only living and functioning NOVA system," Lucile started, turning to Gavin. "You. They know you are out here now. They know what you are capable of. And they are coming. They want you. To study, turn, use, or kill, I am not sure. But no option is a good one. He learned about your father's death, and it brought him out of the slight hiding place he had been cornered into. Despite his vast empire of evil, your father and I had been dealing massive blows to his organization. Him from the outside with the intel I provided from the inside. We were signed onto this mission when you were five, and the entire thing went south when you were around nine.

"We created this monster. Ivan. At one point, he was a good and kind man. William Churchill. He worked with your father on the very first creation of what is now the NOVA system. But something went wrong in the upload. Despite your father's extensive research, the algorithm was off. The original program was set to override the person's brain. To make deep cover operations easier. You don't have to study the persona you take on, because you literally become that person.

"Like I said, everything was going well until the first check-in. We met with William, and it failed when we tried to use the suppression device on him. And he tried to kill the team that met with him. Succeeding with two agents.

"That was when I got called in. I was to infiltrate his organization, which was originally meant as a cover for him to take down the current hierarchy of Russian arms dealers. And he succeeded but then just took their business. Until the only one left was him. And when I was able to get into his facility, I quickly realized that it was a one-way trip. Until we found a way to get it suppressed, your father's friend was stuck. And that meant that I was stuck. I had to stay there until we figured it out, or the threat was no longer one that we could just ignore.

"The red confirmation never came. And it wasn't until I got the letter from your father on his demise, that I learned just how deep it had gotten. Your father uncovered that it wasn't his fault that it had failed. The program had been altered by someone with clearance to access it after it had been completed. And there was only one man with that kind of access. At the time, he was the Assistant Director of the CIA," Lucile explained in a cold voice.

"Hunter," Alex said. The sheer ice coming from her voice was so chilling that even Lucile and General Richmond had a slight shiver go down their spines. They knew just who was talking there. Even in the isolation she had been in, Lucile had heard of her replacement, Hunter's Kill Switch Ker. She knew more about the things she had done than just about anyone. Given she had been sent in to clean up a few of the slaughters that Alex had bestowed on people that Hunter had felt was a threat to his power.

"Yes, and we still don't exactly know why. Walter couldn't make sense of what had made him do that to him and his friend. But that betrayal was enough to make Walter go into a place that he never should have breached alone. He went into Langley. And then into a Collective headquarters. The one where he died. I heard you were all there, though you didn't know why he was. He never said it, but I think he believes there is a link between the Collective and what was going on with everything that Hunter did," Lucile finished with a slight sigh. Even with her training and years away in deep cover, it was still hard to discuss the death of her beloved husband without getting emotional.

"What Lucile is saying," Richmond stepped in to finish the briefing, "is that we have a large, well-funded, ruthless, and cunning group of mercenaries on their way right now to grab you, Gavin. We need to get you off the grid and into a safe house. ASAP." A very stern look came across her face.

"I am not sure that there is time. I know Ivan, and he will not just give us any time to prep. His men are already on their way, if not to the States by now. They will be here in a matter of hours," Lucile said with urgency.

Just then, the alarm for Citadel went off. "It sounds like they are here," Gavin said solemnly as he hit a few keys, and up on the screen came an entire tactical team breaching the entrance to the base.

Charles came walking in as he loaded a gun, "It's time to go," he growled. He was already in full tactical gear. "Who's this?" He said, indicating with his gun who he was talking about.

"This is Agent Hel, aka Lucile Woodford," General Richmond stated.

"Good lord, what is wrong with this family?" Charles grunted as he turned around and walked back out the door to get the car ready. Gavin couldn't help but smile a little at his friend's antics, regardless of the situation. *He really has become a friend.* He thought with a slight sorrow at what was coming. He trusted his team. He just always got nervous before something like this. "Let's get moving!" Lucile barked, as Richmond ended the stream.

Alex could tell Gavin was a slight bit off as they got dressed for the coming battle, and that worried her. "Hey Gavin, everything is going to be ok. I promise." She reached out a hand, taking his in hers and giving it a squeeze.

"Thank you, Alex. I am more worried about my mom suddenly being back right before what will likely be a firefight. We all know what happened the last time that happened with one of my parents," he said, finishing as his voice trailed off with emotion.

"You can't think about that, right now. We will worry about what is in front of us and nothing more. Ok? We will get through this. All of us. Things will be ok." Alex tried her best to be comforting. It was something she had never been called before coming here, but something about Gavin had brought it out of her. He was so kind and caring. It made her want to be that for him. *What would I be without this man?* She thought with a slight admiration of the man Gavin was.

***

As the team pulled up to Citadel, they saw three vans. Getting out, Charles places charges on the undercarriage of each. Moving around the building, he went to the back to come in the rear. As Alex and Lucile both moved to go through the front. Gavin got on his setup in the van, quarterbacking from there. He was capable in the field, but they all felt better if he wasn't in direct gunfire.

Charles went in first through the service door. He cleared the back kitchen as Alex and Lucile took the front. Making their way through, they confirmed the top was clear. Getting into Citadel, they made their way down the stairs as quietly as possible.

As they reached the bottom of the stairs, Lucile was the last one down. Her back leg short-stepped and triggered a laser set flashbang grenade. Causing the three of them to drop and roll to the side as gunfire started to rain down on them.

Watching from the van, Gavin tried to call out the location on the mics, but they couldn't hear him. He locked down Citadel, causing the team to be trapped, and provided a bulletproof barrier between them and the mercenary team.

Thankfully, it worked, and it allowed the team to recover. They had been trained with flashbangs, so the recovery was quick. Once they gave the go-ahead, Gavin killed the lights and pulled the lockdown. The shield came up, and the mercenaries put on their night vision. "Going white," Gavin called in the mics. And he typed in a command, causing the lights to overload to 1000 lumens each, then back to normal levels. The team covered their eyes, and as soon as the lights returned to normal, they came out and took out the team.

A car pulled up on the monitor, and Gavin informed the team as he watched it. Megan got out and started toward Citadel. Getting up quickly, he went to ensure that Megan didn't get in. "Team, Megan is

304

here. I am heading her off." Taking off his headset and closing out the computer, he jumps out the back.

"HEY, Megan!" he starts to yell to get her attention. But she isn't there.

A cloth covers his mouth and nose as he got pulled back around the van. "You shouldn't always trust your electronics, Mr. NOVA system." Agent Denver said as he pulled Gavin around to a car, as he was quickly going limp. Pulling him into the car and closing the door, "Get out of here, NOW!" Denver commanded Brooks. The car took off.

***

"Gavin?" Alex tried to get ahold of him on the coms. "Gavin!" Alex asked, starting to get worried. Lucile was already on her way up the stairs. Turning to Charles, who nodded for her to follow, she took off after Lucile. *Please be ok. Please be talking to Megan. Please, please, PLEASE. I can't lose you!* She hurried out the door, she didn't see any car. Megan wasn't there. Running around to the back of the van, she joined Lucile, who was already standing there staring into the back of an empty van.

"No," Alex whispered. She felt herself shutting down. It hurt too much to think about. Her mind was reeling. *He is gone.* She started looking around for clues, tracks, anything. Lucile joined her. They were getting more and more frantic as they went through the van and looked around the area.

Charles walked out to them, freaking out. "He's gone, isn't he?" he said, softer than Alex had ever heard him. All she could do was nod. "I'll call Richmond. We will find him," he grunted, back to his normal tone. Turning and walking away to make the call.

"Richmond, secure."

"Charles, secure. He is gone, General. Gavin is gone," Charles growled into the phone. Struggling to hold back his own emotions, which surprised both him and the General.

"We will find him, Charles. You make sure to keep track of Johnson. She will not be stable for a while. We both know just how compromised she is with him. Heck how compromised we all have become. I will be in touch," Richmond said, sounding uncharacteristically kind.

Alex stood and left. She couldn't be there anymore. She had to get to the one place she had ever felt at home. Gavin's apartment. But as she walked in, it became glaringly clear it wasn't the place. It was the person. Gavin was her home.

She collapsed on the bed with one of Gavin's shirts. *What has he turned me into? I was NEVER the type to want a boyfriend's shirt. I didn't care how they smelled. I didn't care if they were gone or busy. Maybe that is it. I just didn't care. Before him, I wasn't a person. I was a weapon. A soldier. Nothing but a spy. Without him, I am nobody. No one will know that I am gone without him. My mother, but she has had to accept that long ago. I have everyone in my life who cares about me because of Gavin. And I won't give up. Even if it costs me everything. I need him.*

Alex lay on his bed, smelling one of his hoodies, as the tears started to fall. She felt pain she didn't know existed. Her heart yearned for him, and to not even know where he was or if he was still alive. She couldn't think like that. He was alive. She needed him to be alive.

***

Denver dragged his body into the lab. Laying him on the floor. "There, what you needed. The living NOVA system," he said with a slightly tired irritation.

The Westgate was ecstatic. He could complete his work if given enough time. He motioned for two men to pick Gavin up and put him in the chair. "Do you have the information I need for him?" he asked Denver. He was thinly veiling his disgust for the man. It was difficult when he had spent enough time with him to learn just how truly disgusting he

306

was. The man had no morals. No ethics. But none of that mattered in this work. He had a job to do. So, he turned to Gavin and grinned. "Finally. Now let's see what you have inside this brain of yours."

***

Lucile stopped by to see Megan and let her know the bad news. As she knocked on the door, she feared the worst. It opened to a smiling Megan, but the smile was quickly replaced. The hurt in her eyes was palpable. She could see her entire body change. She hated that all she was bringing her was more hurt.

"Hi, Megan," she said sadly. She really did not want to do this.

"Mom?!" Megan replied, stepping back from the door. Not sure what to do, say, or think. After watching her father be shot in front of her, right after she had gotten a chance to reconnect, left her with severely mixed emotions about how to handle this situation. She was worried that if she was upset, even if she had a right to be, it would inevitably cause the death of her mother.

"I'm sorry. I don't have good news. I came back to protect Gavin," Lucile started to say.

Only to be cut off by a sassy retort from Megan, "he has protection, mother. He has had me since you left, and his wonderful girlfriend Alex since they started dating. He is doing just fine. And so am I," she said struggling to keep her composure.

"Megan. He is gone. I couldn't save him. He was taken by men who work for the same man I have been in a deep cover trying to bring down. They wanted Gavin. They wanted the NOVA system," Lucile said softly.

"No. NO! You're wrong. Alex would have told me. Is she at Gavin's? Alex?!" Megan spilled out, walking across the street to Gavin's place, knocking on the door and then barging in. She made her way back to Gavin's room. She didn't care what they were doing. She needed to know he was safe. Bursting through the door, she saw Alex. Alone. Crying on the bed. And she couldn't help the sob that wretched her entire body as it escaped her lungs.

Gavin was gone.

Chapter 20

:/Captured

Gavin woke up. He was lying down, strapped to a chair. He felt the nodes attached to his head. His body felt like mush. He couldn't move, even if he wasn't strapped down. He tried his leg, but it was like jelly. He could barely open his eyes, but when he did, all he could see was the medical light right over him. He heard faint talking and several machines running. He tried to speak, but couldn't.

What is going on with me? Ok, don't freak out. What would Alex do? Or Charles? How would they handle this? They likely had training to not have whatever sedative is in my system any effect on them, like it does me. So, THAT doesn't help. Okay, my brain still works, right? Obviously, I am thinking. So, what can I think through while I am in a position that is less than ideal physically? There are machines running. I can hear the fans on them. Must be putting off some real heat, if they can be heard. That is either significant computing power or it is mechanical. Not sure how that helps me, but it is information. Also, it means we have power. That rules out some places. Unless they have generators. Not really helping. Ok. Think. Focus, Gavin. He thought as he frantically tried to make sense of anything that was going on.

"Hello, Gavin. I know you can hear me. I am Professor William Orcival Westgate, but many simply call me The Westgate. It's a bit more ominous for my taste, but it works. And I am sure you have a million questions going through your beautiful mind. Of course, you won't be able to ask any of them, but I will do what I can to give you some peace. I am attempting to take the NOVA system out of your mind and recreate it. I am not sure if it will be permanently gone from you, but I do know that while you are here, you will not be able to access it the same way as you have in the past.

"You may be wondering why it is that I am being so open about this? Well, to be honest, the easiest way to allow my research to continue and recreate the work of the great Coeus is to have my subject be somewhat compliant. However, the people I work for do not care about that. So, you WILL give me what I need, even if it kills you. Do not worry too much, as it is. You have already been more than helpful to me. Far more than you could ever know," The Westgate said with a sinister grin. Gavin did not like this man. He was beyond just the typical mad scientist. He was insane!

I can't help them more. I can't let them get ahold of another NOVA system. Not that it should matter. This, as far as we know, will only work in my mind. Anyone else it kills. That was the flaw in it all along. Outside of what my father was capable of creating. Who knows what they would do with it, Gavin thought.

The Westgate picked up a tablet and walked out of the room. He walked down the hall and into the adjacent room, where Denver and Brooks were watching. "Well? What do you have for us? Ivan is not going to want to wait much longer," Denver said with clear annoyance and malice in his tone. He was done waiting around to make his move.

"I don't have the entire program. But what I do have, I have been able to adjust and make it to where it won't kill the person who uses it. I am not sure what it will do, but I know at the moment it won't be pleasant," The Westgate replied with a similar level of annoyance. He was tired of being bullied by the jock types. It had happened his entire life, and he thought for a brief moment that when he was an adult, it would change, but it stayed the same. Just fewer of those people treated him that way.

310

"Give me what you have, and we will find a use for it, as well as test it," Denver snapped as he rubbed the bridge of his nose. He was ready to move on. This scientist was his ticket out, and his biggest obstacle to getting that ticket. He needed him, regardless of how badly he wanted to kill him.

"Call Ivan and tell him to give me three more days, and I should be able to have a fully working NOVA system that should be able to be copied and given to anyone and everyone willing to pay the highest price for it," The Westgate stated in a conspiratorial way.

***

Alex lay in Gavin's bed again. The pure sorrow she felt coursing through her entire body was more than she could take. *Where is he? Why haven't we found him? It has been several days and NOTHING! That is just unacceptable! We don't even know who has him, other than it MIGHT be someone from Ivan Orlov's organization. And that is coming from someone who just disappeared from Gavin's life and then reappears right before he is taken. I don't like that coincidence. I need to talk to Richmond about what is going on. If we have any updates, see what we can figure out,* Alex thought to herself as she half-heartedly dragged herself out of bed.

She went and showered and got dressed. She needed to look professional, even if she wasn't feeling it. After she had finished, she made her way to Citadel. As she came down the stairs, she overheard several people talking.

"I understand, General, but isn't there ANYTHING you can do? We need to find my brother!" Megan said, clearly feeling about as good as Alex was. *It is selfish of me to act like this only affects me. Even more of a reason that we need him back,* she remorsed. Even if she was glad to know that she wouldn't be the only one wanting to fight to find Gavin.

"I know and hear what you are saying, Dr. Woodford, but I can't just break international laws and overturn years of diplomacy for one man.

No matter how important that man is. We wouldn't even do this for the President," the General tried to explain while also understanding that she was likely falling on deaf ears.

"General, if we have any idea where he is, then we NEED to make a move to get him! Don't you DARE act like the government hasn't done extremely similar things in the past. As long as they are off the books, then no one will care," Megan argued back, and if the General was honest, it would be hard to refute her claims.

Alex stayed in the shadows, listening. All she needed was a vague location.

"This work is usually the type of thing I give to Gavin. And then, if the target is important enough, I send my best teams after them. You all. But the analysts we have left can't pinpoint exactly where, and without a specific location, we can't just send you all in blind to retrieve him."

Come on, give me a location. Give me a country, a continent, anything. Give me SOMETHING! Alex pleaded in her mind. She would hunt him down.

"General, please. If we know he is in North Korea, then we HAVE to act! Please. This is my brother," Megan begged shame over her brother's safety had left the moment she was told.

Charles heard a faint rustle overhead, but then the HVAC unit kicked on. He turned back to the screen. He agreed with Megan, but he couldn't say that. Not in front of the General.

"I am sorry. There is nothing that we can do," General Richmond said sternly as Megan left the room bawling.

Once she was out of the Citadel, the General addressed Charles. "You were not instructed to get whatever team you can trust. You were not instructed to find a way out of the country undetected. You weren't instructed to go AWOL for a few days. You weren't instructed to do what you do best. And you sure as hell weren't instructed to do

312

whatever it takes to bring my godson home. Understand, Colonel Charles?" Richmond asked very pointedly.

Charles growled in appreciation. "I understand, General. I will be sure to not report back when I am back stateside. Though I do have to inform you, General, I don't think I will be the first one out," Charles stated to his commanding officer.

"I know. Please try to not let anyone start a world war," Richmond said, and the screen went black.

***

Alex made it back to her apartment. She was going to grab her go bag and be on her way out of the country. She walked into Gavin's room to see Kaleb standing on a chair, trying to get something. "What are you doing?" she asked heatedly. *I don't have time for this.*

"Oh, me? Nothing! I wasn't doing anything. I promise," Kaleb started trying to back away, almost falling off the chair.

"Kaleb, talk," Alex commanded.

"Gavin asked me to take care of the ring he bought if anything were to happen to him," Kaleb said, trying to cower away from Alex.

"Ring?" Alex said, aghast. She knew what that meant, but she had to hear it. She had to be sure.

"Yeah, he- he is going to kill me when he gets back, but he was going to propose to you," Kaleb said, half excitedly and half dejected.

Propose? To me? Gavin was going to... She went around Kaleb without a word and grabbed her go bag and munitions bag. Going to the couch in the living room, she hit the button under the middle cushion, and the couch rose up. Her arsenal was there. She quickly grabbed her three knife sets, several pistols, a shotgun, and an M1. Holding extra clips and her strap, she clutched a spare Gavin-made cell phone. She knew it was extra, but she loved it; it was useful and reminded her of him.

Kaleb watched her load up, "You're going after him, aren't you?" he said, standing in the doorway. "I know how this will end, but I also know that he wouldn't want you risking your life to save his. He loves you too much for that," Kaleb cringed, knowing what was coming. Before he knew what was happening, he was on the floor hogtied. Somehow, it hadn't really hurt. He was shocked.

"With all due respect, Kaleb, don't ever try to stop me from getting to my Gavin again," Alex said as she walked out the door. Leaving it open so that someone would find Kaleb.

***

Lucile was dying inside. She knew that she should be looking for her son. She knew that she couldn't lose him. But if she hadn't returned to Orlov, then who knew what would have happened to Gavin. She walked back into her room and was greeted by Ivan sitting at her desk in her room.

"Welcome back, my lovely Hel," he said in a chipper tone that sent chills down her spine. She knew he wasn't happy she had left. She had thankfully had the presence of mind to address the Mexican cartel issue before she came back. So, at least then, it would look like she had done what she went to do.

"I am tired, Ivan. Can this talk happen in the morning?" she asked, trying to get him out of her room. Maybe if she could get into their system, she could find where Gavin was and then get the location to Catherine.

"I understand, Hel. You have had a lot on your plate and a long trip. I know you don't care for sleeping on planes. And I know you have a lot to do. But I do have to ask you. What reason did you stop in Atlanta?" Ivan asked as he flipped her monitor around to show her entering Citadel with Alex and Charles.

"The NOVA system is my son," Hel said matter of factly.

"Oh, how I wish that you hadn't told me that," Ivan said, and he pulled a gun on her. She knew she had a gun in the back of her pants, but she wasn't sure if she could draw before he shot.

"Now, I am going to have to do something about that. You see, as we speak, he is being stripped down by a scientist of mine. A friend, really. Even though he works for me. He has always been very intrigued by the concept of the NOVA system. And he knows that I am after it. He is less than three days away from completing his work, after which the current holder will be dispatched of. Denver is in charge of how that will happen. But now for you. What to do with you?" Ivan stated with a cold tone.

He attempted to sound tired and hurt. But it was an act. Lucile knew that. She had done the same thing for years to him. He motioned with his hands, and six armed men came in. "I know what you are capable of, Hel. I am not taking any chances. You are going to be put in a holding cell. I don't want any trouble. And once all of this is behind us, we will readdress your position in my organization. I can't tell you how disappointed in you I am," Ivan said, still in that fake hurt tone. He was trying hard to sound human.

Hel analyzed the men around her. They all outweighed her by over 100 lbs. She knew and had trained most of them. She was thankful for that. She knew their weaknesses. As they made their way to the holding cells, she waited for her moment to strike.

They turned the corner and had to stop to open the cell door. Once it was open, she struck. Jumping and kicking the two next to her in the knees, snapping their legs in half sideways. Landing on her knees, she quickly jumped back to her feet. The two in front of her had started to turn around. So that gave her a moment. She launched herself back, causing the two behind her to stumble. As the two in front of her realized what was happening, she kicked them both. Forcing them to stumble back, as well.

She kicked the door activator, closing them in the cell. She spun and punched both the guys to her sides, knocking them out as their heads hit the door frames. Grabbing one of their guns, she spun back around. Slamming the butt of the gun into the guys behind her. As they were stunned, she finished them. Knocking them out with the rifle. "Always use a handgun in close quarters. Idiots," she mumbled as she grabbed one of their radios and made her way out of the building.

She had to call in a few favors, but she was heading to Washington, DC. And she didn't have a lot of time.

***

Charles returned to the apartments and saw Kaleb lying on Gavin's living room floor.

Going up, he cut him free. "How long have you been here like that, numbnuts?" he barked.

"Not long. Two, maybe three hours. Alex is gone. I think she went after Gavin," he said, sounding incredibly worried. Though Charles wasn't sure if the worry was for Alex or the rest of the world.

"I know. I am going after her," Charles said matter of factly as he left the apartment to get his gear. Kaleb made to follow him, only to have the door slammed in his face. He checked the phone that Gavin had given him. It dinged that Alex had just left the airport and was airborne by the rate of travel. He had to hurry.

***

Alex sat on the deck of a cargo ship. She had HALO dropped onto. She avoided the crew as a stowaway and watched her progress on a Gavin phone she had grabbed. Waiting for her moment, as the ship passed within ten miles of the coast of North Korea. Once she saw it, she dove off. Flipping in the air, she landed feet first into the water. Once surfaced, she confirmed her gear was attached and began her swim to shore. The night air was making even the cold Pacific water feel warm, stinging her face. She went to shore and hid from sight in a sewer drain.

She mapped out where she could get some information and places to look for people. She made her way to the airport. Slipping into a storage room, she waited for a maintenance guy to come by. Grabbing him and snapping his neck, she took his clothes and adjusted them to hide her figure. She entered the airport to find someone who may have more information.

Alex had pulled several men into closets or bathrooms. Few had information. None made it out unharmed. She had been there a full hour and knew her time was getting short. She had gotten the names Brooks, Denver, and The Westgate. She still had no location, though.

As she saw a man in a suit, talking in English on the phone, she followed him. Once he hung up the phone, he started to dial again. She pounced. Grabbing him and pulling him into a stairwell. Slamming him against the wall, she yanked his head by his hair.

"Do you know the names Brooks, Denver, or The Westgate?" she demanded. "Answer, or I will start with your fingers," she said, as she bent the index finger on his right hand back. He had held the phone with his right, so she assumed it was the dominant hand.

"Brooks. I know Brooks. He gets a drink at the same pub I do. We play poker together. I can tell you where it is. Please don't kill me," he said as he started sobbing.

Alex twisted more, "Tell me," she said.

***

Charles was able to call in a favor and get a HALO drop right onto the airport roof. He followed Alex's dot around and watched where she went. Dropping his gear in a dumpster to the side of the building, he could retrieve it later. He made his way inside. As he passed a security checkpoint, he grabbed a radio and listened. They were screaming in Korean about a giant brunette woman who was hurting men left and right. How they spoke about her sounded like the boogey man. Charles

317

had to chuckle at that. "If only they knew the half of it," he mumbled under his breath. He followed the call for the most recent survivor.

***

Alex made her way to the bar that the man had told her. She kept to dark alleys and avoided traffic lights as much as possible. She got to the bar and waited. It didn't take long before an SUV pulled up, and a tall white man got out. The doorman greeted him as "Mr. Brooks." She had her man. Now, all she had to do was wait for him to leave, and she could follow. *I am coming, Gavin. Just hold on. Please!*

***

Gavin lay in the chair, still sedated. He was tempted to give in and willingly help the Westgate, but knew he couldn't. He wasn't sure what the plan was still, and it had only been a day. He had endured high school. If the guy thought this was torture, then he was kind of missing the point. He could lay here and sleep as much as he wanted. Sure, they weren't really feeding him, but that wasn't so bad.

The Westgate returned to the room several times and looked at different instruments. Marking down what he saw and then leaving again. Rarely would he say anything to Gavin.

***

Charles watched Alex sitting outside of the bar. He knew she was waiting for a target, and she had likely spotted them. So, he sat. He wasn't going to interrupt her investigation. He knew she would get the job done. So, he followed and waited for when she would need backup. He watched as an SUV pulled up, and she made her move.

Alex watched Brooks' SUV get pulled back around, and as he was talking to the doorman, she made her way around the SUV and into the back seat. As he drove off, she sat in the back, waiting. She would periodically look out the window to see where they were. Checking her phone discreetly was difficult. But as they pulled into what appeared to be a tall bank building, she knew she was there. *I am coming, Gavin.*

Charles saw her get in the back of the SUV and made his way to the car in front of him. He quickly put in his skeleton key and then opened the door. Shutting off the alarm before it could start going off, he turned the car on and made to follow the SUV. He watched it from about 30 yards back, being extra cautious, as he was sure the person driving was trained to spot a tail.

The SUV pulled into a bank, and Charles drove on. He would park and find a way in on his own.

Once in the bank with Brooks, Alex followed him as far as she could. She knew she was close. He went to a door lock, retina activation, and when he opened it, the inside looked like a lab. She knew she was there. Gavin was just a little way away. Now, how to get to him without alarming them to kill him.

Charles saw that she had stopped and waited. He had made it to a delivery entrance in the back of the building and was making his way toward her. But he didn't want to blow her cover. Once he was within a floor of her, he stopped and waited himself. She was still at the same place. She hadn't moved. So, either she was with Gavin already, or waiting for her opening.

Alex took out her Gavin phone and started going through the settings, trying to remember how he had shown her to activate the door algorithm matcher. She knew that once she did, all hell would break loose. She confirmed that she was ready. She had two sets of knives on her, one more in her backpack. two pistols, and five clips each. Plus, there are more clips in her pack. She was ready.

Finding the setting, she set it next to the scanner and waited. Red. Red. Red. Green. The door opened. And she was instantly greeted by two armed guards. Drawing her knives, she stabbed them both through the neck, severing their spines. Causing them both instant paralysis, followed by death. She was lucky that they hadn't been able to scream. She made her way down the hallway and looked in each room.

She found the one with Gavin in it and let out a sob. She ran to him, unhooking the nodes from his head and pulling the sedative out of his arm. She was bawling. He was severely out of it. Dehydrated and couldn't move. His eyes were closed, but she felt a pulse. "Gavin, come back to me. I'm here, Gavin. I love you. I want to marry you. I won't give up. I need you, Gavin. Without you, I am nothing. I have nothing. I have no dreams outside of you. Please, Gavin, come back to me," she pleaded through agonizing tears.

He slowly opened his eyes, and she let out a gasp. Hugging him, she heard the door open. The Westgate walked in. "I see you have a visitor. That is not permitted, Mr. Woodford. He pulled a gun but instantly fell to the floor. Charles standing over him. "You ready to leave yet?" he growled with a slight smirk.

Charles came over and grabbed Gavin, tossing him over his shoulder. And headed out into the hallway.

Stepping out behind Alex, he saw her standing there in front of Brooks. "Go! Get Gavin out of here. I will be right behind you! GO!" she said without turning around.

Charles took off, running toward the way he came in. As he turned the corner, he got stopped by a group of men. He quickly took out two with four quick shots. Then, he threw Gavin's limp body into the rest. Running up, he grabbed Gavin, shooting the remaining men. He returned to his exit right after hearing gunfire back down the hallway.

Alex stood there. *Only two? This shouldn't be too bad.* As she said, five men came out of a door behind her. And four more out of a door behind Brooks. "I've heard you have a reputation for falling for the guys you are around. Don't go falling in love with me now, girly," he said with a disgusting smirk. Nodding behind her, the guys all drew their guns.

Before they could shoot, she knelt and launched four knives. All four hit their targets, the two men closest to her, in the shoulder their guns were resting on. Causing them all to drop their weapons. She spun and planted her hand on the ground, bringing her right foot up and kicking the head of the guy closest to her, causing him to fly sideways into the guy next to him, both crashing into the wall and falling to the floor.

She pulled out four more knives and launched one at Brooks and three at the heads of the guys behind her. Brooks caught the one towards him, but the other three got embedded directly into the foreheads of their targets. Three bodies fell to the floor.

Grabbing the guy to her left, she rolled him on top of herself right as Brooks and the other two opened fire. Shooting the man in the back. One bullet grazes Alex's shoulder. She reached down and pulled out her gun.

As the three men left came near her, she fired, killing the other two. But Brooks saw her movements and dived behind them.

Out of the bullets in those magazines, she threw the guns at Brooks. Pushing the guy off her, she stood and ran at the rogue agent.

He has ejected his clip and reloaded right as she got to him. She continuously moved, pushing his gun out of the way with every stroke of her hand. With each shot close enough to her ear, she heard the air off of it. Counting them down. Nine. Block, slide, and push his wrist. Ten. Slide, roll his wrist, kick his foot. Eleven. Block, parry, counter strike. Twelve. This was it. She reached in and grabbed his throat. With her other hand, she grabbed his wrist with the gun. When he went for her hand on his throat, she released, holding the gun and twisting it free from his grip. The gun now in her hand, she kicked him in the chest, causing him to stagger back. Not wasting a moment, she fired the last round directly into his head. Right as her world was lit on fire and turned black.

Standing over her was Denver with a taser. "What do we have here? I'm sure that you will get me quite a handsome reward," he said as he pulled her body into the room he came out of where the Westgate was hiding.

"I found our test subject. Grab your precious little tablet, and let's go," he injected a syringe into Alex before picking her up and carrying her out the door.

***

Alex woke up strapped to a chair. She vaguely remembered a sharp sting in the back of her neck right after shooting Brooks. Her eyes slowly focused. Across from her was a shorter, unimpressive man. Looked aged and tired. His hair was unkept, and you could tell he hadn't shaved in a few days. His suit was wrinkled, his tie loose, and the top button was undone. *Denver, why am I not surprised?* she thought.

"Hello, Agent Johnson. You are going to be our Guinea pig for our new little toy. You see, we need to know what it does before we can send it to our employer. So, as I am not one for wasting time. Let's get started," Denver stated. Like the person he was talking to wasn't strapped down to a chair.

Denver set a tablet in front of her and nodded over her shoulder, it came to life. Coding and images flash on the screen. She felt her eyes start to burn, and then the burn quickly worked its way back into the center of her brain. Her entire head was on fire. She heard screaming and crying but didn't know where it was coming from. And then suddenly, it stopped.

She opened her eyes, and an unimpressive little man sat before her. He had always given her the creeps.

"So, Agent Johnson. How do you feel?" Denver said.

"What's going on here, Denver? How did I get here?" Alex said, angry and slightly in pain.

"Interesting," she heard from over her shoulder. The Westgate was taking notes. "It appears to be taking memories," he said, walking over to a computer.

322

Denver stood and walked off. He took out his phone and dialed a number.

When he came back, he sat back down and said, "The boss said to continue until I say. He told me when to stop," he pulled out a file.

The tablet was turned back on, and the pain was back. Burning in the center of her brain. Radiating out in pluses. It seemed to never stop. Finally, she succumbed to the pain and passed out.

Alex woke up in her apartment. She was starting a new assignment today after just dealing with everything she had with Brett. She was ready to begin cleaning up the mess that had been made. She heard her phone ring.

"Johnson secure."

"Agent Johnson. We will always have Miami," the voice on the other end said.

She felt her mind go numb. Her body followed. She relaxed, and all emotion fell from her face. "What are my orders?"

Chapter 21

:/Agony

Gavin was back in Citadel, furiously typing away at a keyboard. It had been almost five days since they had gotten him out of the facility. Essentially trading him for Alex. He had not agreed to it, but couldn't say at the time. He was only semi-conscious. The sedatives they had given him still took more than a day to leave his system.

When he got back, they wanted to do full checkups and check the NOVA system, of course. After putting him through several tests, they determined that he was fine, other than needing some rest. And the NOVA system was unphased.

But of course, they have to check it to make sure. Can't have the precious reason I am useful to them be injured. I guess that isn't fair. They came for me. Alex came for me against what they were told to do. Even Charles went against orders. I just need to get Alex back. She calms me.

As he started to trace where her Gavin's phone was, *I have GOT to get a better name for that,* lost signal for the 5th time, and the door to Citadel opened. He din't bother to look as he assumed it was likely Charles or Megan coming to check on him again.

"Gavin," Alex says, sounding weak.

324

Gavin spun around as fast as he could. "Alex!" He almost screamed as he jumped up to take her in his arms. Easing her down into a chair, he started to fawn over her. Checking her in every way that his sister always had to him when he was hurt. "What happened? How did you get out? Did you know the guys? Can you tell who they were workin' for?" Gavin asked rapidly. The questions didn't seem to end.

"I. Too. Tired," Alex murmured. She couldn't understand why they needed this guy dead, but she had her orders: Find out what he knows and has. and then kill him. She couldn't answer all of these. And definitely not this fast. She needed time to think through all her answers to all these questions at once. Her brain felt a little foggy. She wasn't thinking as quickly as she had normally been able to.

"This is all going too fast, I understand. I am sorry," Gavin said as he hugged her again. "I am just glad you are back. Though I am sure that this feels familiar, huh?" Gavin said with a slight chuckle.

"What do you mean?" Alex said, sounding stronger but slightly annoyed.

"The time you were taken before. Anderson? Ringing any bells?" Gavin asked. Holding her at arm's length and inspecting her face. There was a concern in his eyes that she wasn't used to. It was too much to bear, and she had to look away. *This isn't normal. This isn't a normal assignment. What is going on here? He looks at me like he actually cares. What have I gotten myself into?*

"I think I just need some rest. It has been a lot to handle," Alex said, sounding tired again. She felt it this time. Trying to think through everything was draining her. It surprised her how hard it was to focus. To concentrate on what he was talking about. It just made her mad. Everything about being here hurt her head. "I think I am going to go back to my apartment for a rest," she said as she started for the door.

"You don't want to come over to mine and get some rest? You had told me before that you always slept better when you were in my bed,"

Gavin said, sounding slightly hurt, but his face showed he was trying to understand.

I know. I just don't think I am ready to run into anyone else just yet," Alex said, trying to placate him enough that she could get away.

. I understand. I will be here when you are ready. I am just happy you're back." Gavin hugged her again. He felt her pulling back. *I know she has gone through a lot, but this isn't right. Something is off. She is cold to me. Like when we first met,* he thought to himself.

Alex excused herself and made her way to her car. Sitting down, she rested her head against the steering wheel. She started thinking back on what she knew. She got the call from the Director and then woke up in her bed in her apartment. *Since when did I start calling this random studio apartment 'mine'?* she thought, as she put her car into gear and headed back to the apartment. *This is even my car. Why is my personal car here for an assassination mission? What is going on? Focus, Johnson.*

She remembered waking up in her bed. Her phone rang. And when she answered, Director Hunter told her the mission details. It wasn't how he had normally done things, but given the sensitivity of this mission, it was understandable.

He had explained that she was found not remembering her last year and a half. He filled her in on her deep cover mission. She had infiltrated Gavin and his family. They were NSA moles, in deep cover themselves, working for the Collective. She didn't know what the Collective was, but something sounded twisted about it. It seemed familiar. And not in a good way.

Everything about this place felt familiar, but she had never been on a mission to Atlanta. Her missions had almost all been strictly international. The CIA normally didn't work domestically. And when they did, it was kept very under wraps. Usually, they use black sites and never use their normal names, even if they were their permanent cover names.

326

This all felt sloppy and thrown together for a deep cover assignment that had taken more than a year. It also felt like it had been planned for a long time, as well. She wished this was the only time that something like that had happened. It was always some mix of flying by the seat of their pants and expecting every detail to be plotted. She tried to put it out of her head now that she was back in her bed. She needed rest. Her headache was back.

***

Gavin made it home and went to his lab. Calling the General, he explained what had happened and how it felt weird.

"Analyst Woodford, I am sure that she was just tired. However, I have made note of your concerns. If it continues, I will be sure that she is able to get the help she needs. I assure you; Alex will be back to normal soon," General Richmond attempted to calm him, knowing that it wouldn't do much. "Try not to let it affect you too much. You need to focus on finding the Collective and getting as many of them taken out as possible."

"I will do my best. I promise. It is just hard, General," Gavin said as she ended the call.

General Richmond immediately called Charles as she ended the call with Gavin.

"General," Charles answered the call.

"Hello, General Charles, keep an eye on Agent Johnson. Woodford said that he felt she was acting off," Richmond said.

Johnson is back? I haven't seen her, Ma'am, but I will keep my eye on her when I do," he said, tempering back his surprise at the fact that she was back. It didn't sit well with him that she didn't check-in. He turned on the security for Citadel and couldn't see her there either. He pulled out his phone to call Gavin when there was a knock at the door.

He checked and saw it was Gavin. Grunting, he opened the door. "Here to talk lady feelings?" he grunted.

"Something like that," Gavin replied. "I know you know she is back, but it's not the same, Charles. Something happened. She was pulling away from me and wasn't acting like she did when she got back from Anderson. She's acting cold. Like she is mad at me or something," Gavin sighed, feeling defeated.

"I'm sure she just needs time to process everything. You know?" Charles said in a rare moment of trying to be kind and caring. He knew Gavin needed to talk it through, or he would go off the deep end.

"Thanks, Charles. I'll try to go home and sleep and not let it bother me," Gavin said as he got up and headed towards the door. Maybe he would call his sister for some female insight. He grabbed his phone out of his pocket and dialed. The worst that cou;ld happen was she talked him down.

***

Alex laid in her apartment and couldn't help but think about what she felt when she was with him. *It doesn't make sense. Why would I feel at home with my mark? Why do I have these dreams about being happy with him? I know I haven't done seduction missions in the past, but I don't think that this is how it goes.*

As she laid in her bed and still couldn't get it out of her head. *Why would he treat me like that? Why would he hold me like I was so precious to him? What made him dangerous? Especially dangerous enough to kill him. Director Hunter was very adamant that he was supposed to die. But why? You're not supposed to question your orders, Johnson. You're supposed to just do what you're told. Did Hunter mention a handler? Why, at this point, would I have a handler? What is going on?*

Her head started hurting. It felt like it was on fire. Every question that came up made it burn more. Her eyes felt like they were huge. She couldn't understand what was happening to her. She hadn't had any

328

nightmares that she could remember, which wasn't normal either. She had good dreams, amazing dreams, if she was honest, about her mark. About how he treated her. How he understood her. And cared for her.

About how he let her make the decisions at times. And how she felt for the first time in her life like she belonged somewhere. And not just with him, but with his sister too. Even his best friend had befriended her.

These are just dreams. Fantasies. Nothing more. Something her mind was creating in order to make the long-term con work. To make him love her enough to trust her. He had the NOVA system. He couldn't be trusted.

Her head started to cool. To feel better.

Why am I waiting? He lives alone. I could take him out now, and this mission would be over. The torment would be over. My head would feel whole again, and then I could figure out where to go. If I wanted to stay or move on with my life. Yeah. He's a mark. No matter what fantasies I make up in my mind. He is nothing more than a mark.

She got up and got dressed in her infiltration gear. *This ends tonight.* She thought as she loaded her gun and headed for the door.

***

"Hey Gavin, any word?" Megan answered as soon as she picked up the phone. Concern was clear in her tone. She cared for Alex just about as much as Gavin did. She'd never put the pressure on him, but she already saw her as a sister.

"Yeah, she made it back. I'm not sure how, but she showed up to Citadel and honestly didn't look like she was that roughed up. But Meg, she isn't the same. I don't know what happened, but she's distant. It isn't like when she came back from when Anderson took her. She didn't even want me to hold her. I don't know what to do, Meg. What should I do?" Gavin said, the tears starting to fall. He couldn't help it. The woman he loved felt gone, even if he knew exactly where she was.

"Gavin, I'm sorry. I'm sure she is trying to organize her thoughts right now. You know that she is the type that needs space to process everything. She loves you. Remember that. No matter what happens, as long as she loves you and you love her, then you can work through whatever it is.

"Not to be dark, but we don't know what they did to her. We won't even get into all the options. I know she is tough, but everyone has their breaking point. And she might have reached hers and is trying to figure out how to tell you," Megan said carefully. She didn't want to upset him, but she wasn't sure how she could talk about this delicately.

"I know. You're right, Meg. I'm just worried about her and want to help as much as possible. She's been there for me. I just want to be there for her. You know? Let her know I care," he said dejectedly. He was so desperate to not lose her, but it felt like she was slipping away.

He knew it was one interaction, but the last time anything like this happened, she came back even more eager to be in his arms. She processed with him. She lay in his bed, in his room, and they worked through everything together.

That was how it had been since they had been open with how they felt about each other. Every moment apart wasn't sought out. It was agonizing, and they struggled through it. Until they could be together again.

But this felt entirely different. She wasn't even this cold towards him when they first met. She had had moments when she was angry with him or when she felt she had to be that way. It felt like she was looking for a way out, away from him.

"I'm going to try to sleep, Meg. Thank you for talking. See you tomorrow?" he asked. He had no interest in going to work again tomorrow, not with this hanging over his head.

"Of course, Gavin. Just let me know when, and I can be there for you in whatever way you need. Love you," Megan said.

"Love you too, sis," Gavin said, trying hard to cover how sad he felt. But she could hear it, and it broke her heart. She hung up the phone and went to Chad and cried.

Gavin hung up the phone and went and showered. Then, he worked on some daily work before he called a night. He went to bed and tossed and turned for quite a while before he started to feel tired enough that sleep would come.

***

Alex pulled up outside of Gavin's house. And sat there for a while. She hadn't struggled with a red mission for this long in a long time. And whenever she thought about going back to bed, her head would start to burn. But when she decided to pull the trigger, it would begin to clear up.

It didn't make sense. *None of this makes sense. This is torture. Why would I feel love from someone that's my mark? I'm not that immature. I don't fall in love. Spies don't fall in love,* she refocused her mind.

Her phone rang. "Johnson secure."

Director Hunter smiled into the phone. "Hunter secure. Sitrep."

"I'm outside the mark's residence. I will finish the mission and report back. I have to complete this," Alex said. Her tone portrays her pain more than she intended.

"We will always have Miami," Hunter said. He wasn't going to lose her again. He hoped and relied on her training and brainwashing. He knew if he kept pushing it, it would force her to complete the assignment and return it to him. Then, he could figure it out from there.

Alex's mind went numb. "What are my orders?" she said without any emotion.

331

"Kill Gavin Woodford," Hunter said, then hung up the phone.

He smiled to himself. One down. Now, make another call and see where the rest are at. He picked up and scrolled through his contacts to the next item on his list to complete. He was in the end game now.

Alex felt her head cool. She was calm. She pulled out her gun, put on the silencer, and pulled her mask down over her face. She checked her body armor to make sure her form was unnoticeable. She was ready. It's just another tally on her red record. One more to join the thousands already there.

She stepped out into the night. As the cool breeze hit her face, she had a slight flashback to falling through the night as tears streamed off her face, not because of the sting of the wind but because her heart was breaking.

Why was my heart breaking for someone that's my mark? Her head started to burn. Shaking her head, she turned towards the building she knew to be Gavin's home. She looked up. Without even thinking, she knew which one was his bedroom. She started across the street and looked behind her. Seeing Megan's home, her mind flashed back to a warm morning when she snuck into the place to look for the NOVA system.

That seems right. I'd be looking through everything I could to make sure it wasn't hidden.

She got to the door and pulled out her phone to look up the code. But out dropped a key. She instinctively knew that it was for Gavin's place. Her mind flashed back to the day Gavin gave it to her. How happy she felt. How loved and cared about she felt. And her head felt the fire inside this building again.

Trying to ignore it, she put the key into the lock. She turned the knob and snuck through the door, entering the living room. Her mind flashed back to him sitting there with her. They were watching some movie. Had spaceships and laser swords. It didn't matter. She felt his arm around her. How warm and comfortable she felt. Feeling herself fall asleep on his shoulder.

"Aahhh," she grunted quietly. Her head started to hurt too much. *It will all end once I pull the trigger. Once he is gone, those fantasies will die. It will cleanse my mind. I will be back to the spy I'm built to be.* She started to sneak down the hall to their room. *HIS room! His!* she reprimanded herself.

 She passed by the bathroom, and her mind flashed back to them standing in front of the mirror, brushing their teeth together. Him teasing her about her boring flavor of toothpaste. Her response was that he didn't seem to mind the boring taste when she kissed him.

The fire inside her head was building to an inferno. She had to continue. It was all she had. *I can't fail. I must complete the mission. It's the only way for this to end. It's the only way for the agony to stop. For my mind to be free. It's all I am. A spy. He can't take that from me.*

She finally reached his room. Walking in, it smelled like him. It felt like a massive smack in the face. Her mind was awash with memories of laying in the bed talking about life. Intimate moments between them. Holding his face to hers as they laughed together. Sharing a kiss as they both lay in bed reading. Him with his comic books and her with her mission reports. How he gave her a hard time that she couldn't get away from work to enjoy life. Then both lay there. From opposite sides. Their heads next to each other. As they listened to music. Him telling her who it was and the song title. Working with her patiently to find what songs she liked.

Her head was killing her. If she didn't know that putting a bullet in his head would end it, she'd put one in her own. She had sweat dripping off her chin. Her mask was getting soaked. It was making it harder to breathe.

JUST. FINISH. THE. MISSION.

She moved toward the bed. Raising the gun to the head of the man lying there. Her hand was shaking. She was breathing heavily. Like she had just run a marathon. Her entire body felt like she was weighed down by sandbags. Aching everywhere.

"Are you going to do it?" Gavin asked quietly. His voice was thick with emotion. It was clear he was crying. But not out of fear. Out of sorrow. "Might as well. Without you, there isn't anything left I want," he said, turning toward her. Even in the dark, her eyes met his, and she felt it.

"AAAAAHHHHHHHH!!!" Alex screamed as she dropped the gun. Her entire body was shaking. She screamed and screamed. She hurt all over. It felt like red hot metal was being shoved into her body. Like she was getting slowly covered in molten lava.

She kept screaming and shaking. She hadn't even noticed that Gavin had gotten on the floor with her. He was holding her and hushing her. Soothing her. Rocking with her. And that's when the sobs started.

She had never cried like this in her life. It felt like her soul was retching with every breath she took. He took off her mask and kissed her forehead.

Slowly, he stripped them both. Carrying her to the bed, laying her down, and then lying down next to her. She couldn't stop sobbing. He pulled her close to him and rocked slowly in bed. Slowly, she eventually lost the battle with sleep. And as she lay there, she started to cuddle back. He just held her as she slept.

Chapter 22

:/Healing

Alex woke up in Gavin's bed. She shifted and felt that she was naked. Slowly, the previous night came flooding back to her. The pain, the emotions. She was set to kill him. Her brain felt like it had been put through a meat processor. All her memories were jumbled. Things all felt like a dream. Awful and amazing things, both. She couldn't place anything with any certainty. She felt lost in her own head.

The only thing she felt she knew for sure was that she was glad she couldn't pull the trigger. Even if nothing made sense with it, and it made her head hurt slightly, she knew she made the right decision. She loved this man. She trusted him. Her Gavin. She felt him shift his weight slightly, and when she looked into his eyes, she saw a spark from her dreams.

"Good morning," Gavin said softly, hesitation in his voice. He was understandably nervous. She had been standing over him with a pistol drawn to his head, after all.

"Good morning. Gavin, I am so sorry about," That was all she got out before Gavin waved her off. He was having none of it.

"Alex, you may not think this, but I know you. Last night was not you. It was someone else entirely. You would never intentionally try to hurt me. Well, unless we are sparing. You can get a bit aggressive then," he said with a slight laugh, easing the tension a little. "But I knew that last night wasn't what you would want. And once you came out of whatever they did to you, you would never forgive yourself," he finished.

"That is just it, Gavin. I don't know what they did to me. I don't know why I was thinking I had to kill you. All I know is that it made sense in my mind that that was the only way for the pain to stop. And the more I fought it, the more pain my entire body was in. Starting from my head and coursing through my body. It was the most agonizing pain I have ever experienced," Alex explained, a tear escaping from her eye. She blinked it away the best she could. Still not entirely okay with how much she had already cried in front of him.

"I am so sorry, Alex. I can't imagine. My heart was breaking when you were gone, but it broke when you came back, and you weren't you. I knew something was off. Do you remember anything about what they did?" Gavin asked hesitantly.

"That's just it. I don't know what they did to me. I can't remember," she said softly. Embarrassed at how little help she was. *Great spy, you are, Johnson. Can't even remember what happened when you were tortured? What a joke. Any other person in the world would never be able to forget it. Especially just days after it supposedly happened. But other than the headaches, nothing feels sore or broken. There is just nothing.*

Gavin was concerned again. This was not like his Alex. She didn't forget things. Ever. Even when he wished she would. ESPECIALLY when he wished she would. It wasn't adding up. "Can you remember who all was there? Who all took you?" Gavin asked, hoping to probe something out of her mush of memory.

Alex sat there. Her mind reeling. She tried and tried to remember who it was. She vaguely remembered someone sitting in front of her. But the harder she tried to focus on them, the more distant the memory got.

336

Huffing in frustration, she got out of bed. "Look, I don't remember anything! Okay?" she snapped at Gavin.

"Okay, I am sorry. I will stop pushing," Gavin said. She hated that she made him feel like this.

"Gavin, I'm sorry. When I try to push to remember, the pain comes back. It feels like a fire is starting in the center of my brain. I will try to just tell you all that I do remember, okay?" she said, trying to help him feel better about everything. She wasn't mad at him. He was just trying to help. She was mad at the pain and frustrated at the fact that she couldn't seem to remember anything useful.

"That would be great. I will try not to push more than that. And maybe there is something there that can help," Gavin offered. He wanted to figure this out. Alex may be getting back to how she was, at least in the sense that she was kind to him, but she was still not herself.

"Okay, well, I remember getting on the plane to come here. I remember reading your file and thinking that this job was going to be quick and easy. Get you to tell me where the NOVA system that Brett sent to you was and then be back in DC by sundown. I then remember the form of a man sitting in front of me. Then I don't really remember what happened, but then I know I woke up in my bed the next day. I had your file on my bedside table, and as I reread through the file, I felt like I knew more about you than I did.

"Then, Hunter called me and explained that I had been in deep cover with you for over a year and a half. He didn't know what you had done to me, but that you had wiped my mind and dropped my body. They found me and brought me back to my room, which was acting like my safe house for the time being. I asked what my mission was, and he informed me that I was to assassinate you.

"I came to see you at Citadel and then had to leave because my head started hurting. I got back to my place and got ready for bed, and I couldn't sleep. Everything felt off. Wrong. It felt like I was betraying you, and in feeling that way, I was betraying my country. Like

337

everything I was doing was wrong. My head was on fire. It felt like it was getting split open. And when I couldn't take it anymore, I knew the only way to end it was to finish my mission. I got ready and got in the car and came here. I had a brief moment of calm when Director Hunter called me and confirmed the mission parameters, but other than that, I was in pain the entire day," she finished, feeling some of the pain coming back in remembering all of it.

"Alex, I don't know who called you, but Hunter is dead. He has been dead for about a year now," Gavin said softly.

Alex stared at him like he had grown a second head. *I know he isn't lying to me. He has none of the tells, and I know his tells. I am not sure how I know, but I do. So, if he isn't lying, then he truly believes that Hunter is actually dead. So, what then? I need to talk to someone else in charge. Who else is in charge, though? Hunter is the Director of the CIA. Who is over him? He doesn't even need confirmation from the President to approve a mission.* Alex couldn't make sense of it.

"Alex, I am being honest. I know it likely sounds crazy to you, but let's get dressed, and we can figure this out. It's hard enough for me to think when you do have clothes on," Gavin said with a slight grin. His comment broke the unease that had been building.

Alex smiled back. She knew she was attractive. Enough guys had hit on her to make sure that they knew. But why was it so much better knowing it was Gavin she was making feel this way? Another thing her brain was having trouble processing, but she was okay with this one. It felt good, even if she didn't understand it.

***

After they got dressed, they made their way to Citadel. Walking in, they saw Charles's stuff on the table, but he wasn't in the room. "He must be in the firing range," Alex said without thinking as she put her stuff down.

Gavin didn't want to make it into more than it was, so he didn't comment. But the fact that she so flippantly knew where Charles was, without even thinking, told him that all the memories were still there. They just had to figure out a way for them to come out. Right now, he was just going to be thankful that her feelings for him hadn't gone away. Tempered slightly, but not gone. He started a call to Richmond. She needed to be kept up to date and at least informed of what Alex had told him.

She popped up on the screen, her usual scowl in place. "Hello, team. Well, most of it. Where is Charles?" she asked, not liking that Alex was alone with Gavin.

"I'm here, Ma'am," Charles said as he walked in carrying his pistol. He didn't make it obvious, but he wanted to make sure that Alex knew he was armed. She definitely took notice.

"Good, now, first, it is good to have you back, Alex. I understand it may take some readjusting after what wouldn't be considered a holiday. Still, nevertheless, we are glad you are here and okay," Richmond said, showing an unusual amount of sympathy.

"Thank you, General. It is good to be back. I have several things that I need to tell you. If I may," Alex said matter of factly. She felt some pain starting to build, but it was bearable.

The older woman nodded for her to continue. "Thank you. So, as you know, I returned yesterday evening. What you don't know is that last night, I was convinced that I needed to kill Gavin. Obviously, I couldn't, but the fact is still there. I believe it may be best if I am taken off his protective detail," she said, agent mask on.

Gavin looked at her, stunned. *This wasn't what we had discussed, Alex! What is going on? Why would you say that?* "General, if I may. I believe I have a few things that we talked about this morning that may shed some light on the situation," Gavin interjected quickly. Trying to act before any rash decisions were made.

"I think that that would be wise, Analyst Michael," Richmond said, her tone portraying a shock that did not make it to her face.

"So, yes, what Agent Johnson said was true. She did have a gun drawn to my head last night. However, she was unable to pull the trigger. We all know what she was put through for what can hardly be called training. I can imagine this won't be the last time something like this happens. She endured an unreasonable amount of trauma at a very young age. I think if we give her some more time, she can continue her role on this squad without any issues.

"Also, she did say a few things when I probed her slightly about what had happened and what she remembers. See, she doesn't truly remember the last year and a half. The last thing she truly remembers before yesterday is getting this assignment and the figure of a man sitting in front of her. That is it. She doesn't remember anything about the missions we went on or any people we interacted with since. Other than her feelings for me. Some of those are still there." He looked at Alex, who nodded for him to continue. Appreciating the fact that he was taking the lead on this and allowing her mind to rest slightly. She knew she could trust him.

"The other thing is that she is convinced that former Director Hunter called her and authorized the mission to kill me," Gavin said.

"Well, that makes sense. He did seem to push for your execution before he passed. It wouldn't surprise me that she is remembering a phone call with him," Richmond stated.

"No, Ma'am. She doesn't remember some call from over a year ago. She got the call yesterday. And again, before coming into my home," Gavin explained.

Richmond stopped. She slid to the side, and into the screen came Lucile. "What exactly did he say?" Lucile asked coldly. She had an edge to her that made everyone uneasy, including Richmond.

"I can't remember exactly. I remember getting the missions, and I remember him calling. But I don't remember everything that was said," Alex explained, feeling more than a little defensive towards the other agent. Though she wasn't entirely sure why.

340

"You said you got that call right before entering my place?" Gavin asked, to which he received a nod of confirmation. He quickly shuffled over to a computer and started typing away. It wasn't more than a few seconds later that up on the monitors popped several angles of Alex sitting in her car with a mask over her face. As it played, you saw her check her gun to make sure it was loaded several times. Looking out the window several times. She was fidgeting and nervous. It was clear. And then she received a call. Putting the phone up to her ear, she visibly went calm. The fidgeting stopped. She hung up and opened the car door.

Gavin went back and replayed it. Then, cut it to her getting the call. Then, zoomed in on her, and you could see the change in her eyes. She went placid. Her eyes glazed. She was no longer thinking.

"I will see what I can do to get audio," Gavin said as he started typing away again. Alex was amazed at the proficiency that he handled himself with the computer. *Must be the NOVA system,* she thought, trying to explain it, even though she knew that wasn't it. This was all Gavin.

"There," Gavin said and hit play again. It was too much static to hear at first. But a few minutes later, he had scrubbed the audio and was replaying it.

"Johnson secure."

"Hunter secure. Sitrep."

"I'm outside the mark's residence. I will finish the mission and report back. I have to complete this."

"We will always have Miami."

"What are my orders?"

"Kill Gavin Woodford."

The clip ended, and the room was silent. Everyone was thankful that she had been unable to complete the task. Lucile was the first to speak. "That did sound like him. And I know those commands. You were part of Project Ara, weren't you, Agent Johnson?" she asked, her tone sounding accusatory.

"It wasn't by choice, mom. She likely doesn't remember. I was the one who told her, after I found it in Hunter's personal files. She doesn't know everything about that yet. But yes, she was. And Tyr, and Spartan," Gavin snapped at her. He wasn't going to let her talk down to Alex like that.

Alex put her hand on his arm. "I don't know who you are, and I have never heard of those projects, but if Gavin says I was a part of them, then I was likely a part of them. Now, can someone please explain to me what they mean?" she asked, trying hard to sound calm.

Charles said, "I got this. Ara was a brainwashing program designed to make operatives conform to whatever the person who said the command wanted. Tyr was a strength and conditioning program taken way too far. It involved mental training with strategy and techniques, as well as body augmentation to make you bigger and stronger. Spartan was designed to fine-tune you into the perfect soldier. It meant you were the ideal candidate for the NOVA system. But we have since found out why that just isn't the case. NOVA wasn't designed to just go into anyone. It was designed for a specific type of brain, for Gavin's type. So, the project was canceled, and you didn't get the NOVA system. You just got sent into suicide missions and were expected to come out alive. All around the age of fifteen. Did I leave anything out, Gavin?" he finished.

"No, I think you about covered it all, big guy," Gavin responded. To which Charles grunted in reply.

Alex sat there, shocked. She wasn't sure how to process it. Her head was already hurting. She needed a break. But she didn't want to settle for half answers. These people knew more about her than she did herself. *Well, one thing is for sure. Gavin was never my target. If it wasn't Hunter on the phone, then whoever it was needs to die,* she thought.

"I think Agent Johnson needs to see the team doctors and get evaluated before she is ready to be in the field again. Agent Johnson, do you currently feel any inclination to attack anyone on this team?" Richmond asked in a clipped tone. She wanted to dig into this all as soon as possible.

"No, Ma'am. I… I don't know what happened, and I know even less of why I feel the way I do, but I love him," she said, not entirely sure why she felt the need to say it out loud. But she knew it was the right thing when she received a big smile from Gavin and a grunt of disgust that was thinly veiling a smile from Charles.

Even Richmond and Lucile seemed to be pleased with what she had said. The call ended, and she was sent to Megan to check her head. She needed to know she was okay before she would allow herself to be alone with Gavin again.

***

Hunter looked through the news again. He looked online. He couldn't seem to find anything about it. He contacted some of his sources who were still working for the CIA. He had to get confirmation, and Agent Johnson never checked in. She missed her time. She never failed her missions until recently. She had been the perfect warrior for years, and then 3 failed missions in a row, including this one. This was the second chance she had to kill the remaining Woodford, and as far as he could tell, she had failed.

He called another number. "Denver, I am going to need you to go in. She failed. Yes, I know you told me she would. This is it. You finish this, and you're out with a nice severance to go with it. I'll make sure of it. Not get the job done this time!" Hunter yelled as he hung up the phone. He was getting impatient. He had waited too long and plotted too heavily for this to fall apart now. If he had to, he would go and put bullets in the remaining Woodfords himself.

***

Orlov was livid. He knew that Hel was formidable, but he wasn't entirely ready for her to take out six of his guards and escape. "How long had she been like this? How long had I trusted her and for her to just turn on me? This will never happen again. I can promise you that," he said while he looked in the mirror.

He called in his financial advisors and lawyers and got to work cutting ties. He was going to make sure his empire would live on without her. He could find another right hand. But there was more than just Hel to cut out. He had to stand alone entirely if he wanted to withstand the storm that he saw coming. Once Hel knew the truth of what happened, even he feared what may come. And that wasn't including the rest of the team that had dealt him such significant damage in recent months.

He picked up the phone to make the hardest call he would ever make, but it was time.

***

Denver landed in Atlanta and checked into his hotel. He didn't intend to stay long, just long enough to get the job done. He got out his rifle and handguns. He would be ready.

***

Alex sat down in Megan's office and was ready to be examined. She didn't know what to expect but hoped that the interaction would at least be peaceful. She wasn't sure what Megan had been told, but when Gavin's sister entered the room, it was clear that she had been brought up to speed. She was quiet and slightly cold in a professional way towards her. And she couldn't even begin to blame her.

Megan sat down at her desk and looked at Alex. She wasn't sure how to approach any of this. She knew that Alex needed a true psychologist and psychiatrist, but Richmond had sent her to her. So, everything started with a scan of the brain. She needed Alex to be under stress in order for the scan to be effective, so she laid it on thick. In her heart, she knew that Alex would never hurt her brother. She had forgiven her the moment that she was told.

"Let's head to get you a CAT scan first. I will ask you questions while the test is run. Please try your best to stay still, or it could cloud up the images," Megan explained as she stood and grabbed some files and a notebook.

Alex stood to follow her. *I hope she will forgive me. I can't expect her to. I wouldn't forgive someone trying to take that wonderful man away from the world. But I was ready to do it less than twenty-four hours ago. I need to know what is going on with my mind so that we can make sense of all of this. And when we do, I just hope that they will still love me. I can't imagine my life without them. What? Where was all this coming from? I am a spy. The TOP spy. I am a ghost to ghosts. Why am I suddenly a mushy, sappy schoolgirl? Gavin didn't do all of this to me, did he? There must be more.*

Megan escorted her into the room and had her get ready. Then she laid down in the machine, and Megan left for the observation room. Starting it up, she started asking her questions.

"Do you remember what happened last week?" Megan asked.

Alex lay there and tried her hardest to remember last week. It was all blurry. Nothing fit together. Her mind was a jumble. "I… I can't," she said, sounding strained.

Megan watched the monitor and took notes. There was a lot of unusual activity in the hippocampus, which made sense. But it looked like it was almost short-circuiting. Every time she would try to remember something, there would be a flash, and then that activity would stop. And the flashes kept getting brighter. "Okay, rest for now. I will ask another question," Megan said into the microphone.

Alex tried to relax her mind. The pain subsided slightly.

"Do you love Gavin Woodford?" Megan asked. Thankful that Richmond had put it on the list of questions to ask so that she wouldn't have to break the rules and ask her for herself. She listened as Alex started to stumble through an answer. She had clearly been caught off guard, but Megan was more watching the monitor. The hypothalamus looked like it was trying to light up the room. She smiled. This woman did love her brother.

Megan was not looking forward to the next part. She was thankful that Alex had been strapped down for this. "We will always have Miami," Megan said into the microphone, instantly hating herself. She watched as the activity in the brain slowed almost to a stop.

"What are my orders?" Alex asked in a completely monotone voice.

Megan hated that voice. She stayed silent. She needed to know if Alex was fighting it. If she could be manipulated more. Further.

Alex lay there. Her mind was calm. *Wait. This doesn't make sense. I am strapped down. Why am I calm? What was the question? What is happening?* Megan watched the monitor as Alex's mind started to come back.

She repeated, "We will always have Miami."

Alex's mind slowed, but not as much. It showed that she was fighting. It took her longer to respond. "What are my orders?"

Megan did it one more time. "We will always have Miami." This time, the brain didn't slow down but a little. She was fighting harder. She felt it.

Alex lay there. *Those words. I have heard them. What do they mean? I know them. No! FOLLOW ORDERS, AGENT! Pain. Everywhere. PAIN IS WHAT A FAILURE LIKE YOU DESERVES. Pain. No. There is more than pain. I deserve more than pain. FOLLOW YOUR ORDERS, AGENT!* "What are my orders?" She repeated.

346

Megan knew that this was it. This was where she needed the push. "Kill Gavin Woodford," she commanded, hating every word.

Alex started thrashing slightly. But it wasn't like she was fighting against the restraints. She was fighting against herself. *YOU HAVE YOUR ORDERS, AGENT. NO! I can't do that! THEN YOU ARE A FAILURE! No! I am more! YOU DESERVE PAIN. WHAT GOOD IS AN AGENT THAT CAN'T FOLLOW ORDERS? I am loved. Gavin. Gavin doesn't care if I fail. He loves me anyway. Megan doesn't care if I fail. She will be there for me, even more. No. I won't listen. I won't.* "I WON'T! SHUT UP!" she yelled over and over. Her body hurt.

Megan tried the command again. But Alex never calmed. She just kept fighting. Megan had tears dripping from her chin, but she couldn't stop. She kept saying the command. And watched in both pride and terror as Alex fought within herself. "Come on, Alex. You are stronger than the trauma they put you through. Push through it. I know you can," she whispered to herself. She didn't realize that the microphone was still on.

Alex heard her. *She wants me to fight. She believes in me. See! She thinks I deserve more! FOLLOW YOUR ORDERS, YOU FAILURE! NO! I deserve this. I deserve love. I deserve this family that has accepted me. Even as broken as I am. And I will do anything I can to protect them. From anyone. Including my past.*

And the pain stopped.

***

Gavin was working through some basic analytics for the NSA in Citadel when the alarm went off. He knew what that meant. He had set up facial recognition to run through every camera in the city when he had started looking for Alex. He went to a monitor and brought up his software. As the profile came up on the screen, he called Richmond.

"Richmond with Hel secure," she answered.

"Analyst Michael secure. Ma'am, Agent Denver has landed in Atlanta. He was Alex's old handler, and I saw him at the facility I was kept by The Westgate. He needs to be brought in," Gavin said quickly.

"I agree, and he is very dangerous. Get your team organized and a plan sorted out. Hopefully, everything with Agent Johnson is going according to plan. We will need her," Richmond stated and then ended the call.

Chapter 23

:/Minion

Denver had been watching Gavin for several days. Learning his schedule, when and where he was most vulnerable. He needed to make this clean, or he would never leave the city to collect his reward. At best, he would be killed. At worst, they would let someone like him have him. And that thought sent a shudder down his spine.

He thought he may have the perfect time and opportunity to take out his target. So, he set up his rifle in the building across from the entrance of Snollygoster Inc. before sunrise and waited. He knew he had to be there early to avoid being seen by the crowds in the shopping area. He watched and waited.

He saw Gavin's car pulling into the parking lot. He got his rifle ready and zoomed in on Gavin. Following him to his parking spot. He watched as Gavin shut off his car, got his gear together, opened the door, and got out. This was it.

Denver steadied his breathing, and on his exhale, as Gavin got out of the car, he squeezed the trigger. CLICK. What? CLICK CLICK CLICK. He knew he put rounds in. Looking back through the scope, he saw Gavin looking at him and holding up a firing pin. And then his world went black.

THREE DAYS EARLIER

Gavin had been watching Denver through the traffic light cameras and security cameras ever since the alarms went off that he had entered the city. Richmond had told him to keep an eye on every move that Denver made. Which had been pretty easy since Denver was mostly following him. Either at a computer or on his wrist computer, he was able to watch almost anywhere Denver went.

He had a pretty good idea of what Denver was doing but still wanted to run it past Alex and Charles first. He didn't quite trust his own instincts as a spy yet.

Alex had spent the next day after what happened with Megan checked into the hospital. Megan wanted to monitor her, just in case there were lasting effects. Checking her vitals and having regular CAT scans just to make sure that everything was okay. They even checked the trigger command a few more times. And while there was a twinge there, it was nothing like what had been there before.

Alex was beyond thankful to Megan. She felt lighter than she had for as long as she could remember. It felt like she had taken this weighted blanket off her head. She was free to think and feel more fully and happily. She didn't mind the extra day there making sure everything was okay, other than she desperately wanted to get to Gavin. She wanted him to be able to see how far she'd come.

Even without those memories, my body craves him. It is confusing, but a lot less confusing now that my head is clear. I need him to explain everything that was done to me again. I hate having to ask things that I already am supposed to know, but it's better than staying in the dark, I suppose. Alex thought as she got her things together to leave the hospital.

As she got her last bag packed, Megan walked into the room. Without saying a word, she walked over and gave Alex a hug. Alex was caught off guard but enjoyed one of Megan's bone-crushing hugs anyway.

350

"Alex, I am so sorry for what I had to do. I hated seeing you like that. I'm glad you are ok. Please forgive me?" Megan said with tears in her eyes.

"There is nothing to have to forgive, Megan. You were doing what had to be done, and I am thankful you did. I can't explain to you how much better I feel. It is incredible! And you are the reason for that. Yes, what I had to go through was not fun, but it was worth it. And I would go through it 100 times to get this type of freedom from my past. I don't even know everything I went through anymore. I need to talk to Gavin about that again. But what I do remember isn't fun. It's a lot of loneliness, pain, and death. But when I am with you, Gavin, and even Charles, sometimes it has made me feel like I finally have somewhere I belong," Alex said. She couldn't help some tears welling up in the corner of her eye.

Since when did I become the type to get emotional this easy? I'm not sure I like it, but maybe it is just because of the change that has happened.

Megan smiled and said, "I am so glad to hear you say that. I know more than just my brother was freaking out at the fact that you didn't follow them and were missing. You are a part of our family now. Whether you like it or not." Her smile then dropped. She said, "Now for the doctor stuff. There has been some scarring and damage to your brain. Nothing extensive that will cause massive issues later, but you could be prone to some emotional outbursts. And with your skillset, that could potentially be dangerous for other people. Also, the scarring looks interesting. It isn't like any I have seen before. It seemed to congregate around the hippocampus. When I got a good, clear picture of it, it looked like scorch marks. Do you have epilepsy that you know of?" Megan asked, sounding both concerned and very professional.

"No, I wouldn't be allowed to have the job I have if I did," she said, looking at Megan like she should know that.

"Right, of course. Sorry. It just looks like scarring, similar to someone who experiences a lot of seizures. If I didn't know any better, I would

351

say that someone tried to upload at least part of a NOVA system into you," Megan said, almost to herself.

Alex suddenly had a vision of her old handler sitting in front of her with some type of screen facing her. She couldn't see what the screen was playing. Then, the vision was gone. "Megan, would they be able to install a NOVA system off a tablet or something like that?" she asked.

"That would be more of a Gavin question, but I don't see why not. What makes you ask that?" Megan asked, with a concerned look on her face.

"I just had something come to mind. Maybe it is a memory? I am not sure. I just saw my old handler sitting in front of me with a screen playing something. I don't remember what it was playing, though. I think I will go talk to Gavin and see what he has to say and maybe see if we can go over my past. Again," Alex finished with a slightly irritated tone.

"Hey, don't get discouraged. It is good to ask things. Get the truth from people you know you can trust to be honest with you," Megan said, giving her one more hug before they parted ways.

***

Back at Citadel, Gavin was busy tracking Denver. At the same time, he also tried to figure out what was happening with the Hunter situation. *Could it just be someone using some voice-altering software, trying to play it off as they are Hunter to manipulate Alex. But they knew the trigger phrase. Could Denver have known? I wish I could ask Alex, but she likely wouldn't even know who all was told,* Gavin thought.

He looked at his phone and saw he had missed a few texts. One being from Alex. She wanted to know where he was. As he went to reply, the doors to Citadel opened. He looked up and saw the woman he was thinking about descending the stairs. "Hey, I was just replying to you. Sorry, I got caught up in some work," he said, worried slightly about which Alex he was getting.

"It is okay, Gavin. I just feel we need to talk," she said as she got closer to him and saw his face was quite askew with worry. "No!" she said, slightly laughing. "Nothing bad. Well, nothing bad between us. I just need you to tell me about things that you have already. I am sorry, you will have to discuss it again, but I need to know about what happened to me. What caused me to be brainwashed. My history with the company," she trailed off as she finished.

"Oh, that won't be any problem. I know it won't be easy to talk about again and watch, but it will be easy to do," Gavin said.

"Ok, but first, why are you tracking my old handler?" Alex asked, looking at Gavin's screen that he was working on.

"He landed here last night and tripped my alarm system. And he was at the facility that held me before you went missing. I think he may have grabbed you and is looking for us again," Gavin explained.

Alex stared at the screen. *That makes sense. That must have been a memory I had at the hospital. I will tell Gavin after we get through my past. Again. I am sure he is right. There aren't really many things that are sheer coincidence in this world.* "Let's take a look at what you have on my past first, and then we can get into that," Alex said.

"Sounds good to me," Gavin said, hitting a few keystrokes and pulling Alex's file. He started with her family and what he had found out. Then, he went into her illegal recruitment. Then, into what Hunter labeled her training, but it was far from that. It was an indoctrination. He felt sick all over again watching those videos. Especially seeing her face when she watched it. It was heartbreaking seeing her world fall apart as to what she thought it was.

When she watched the video of her returning covered in blood, a tear started to fall down her cheek. "I thought those were all nightmares," Alex whispered, meant to be for herself. She couldn't afford a breakdown. Not right now. Not with Denver in town. If what she remembered was real, then this wasn't the time to deal with all the emotions that came with that chaos. "Ok, now on to Denver. Thank you

353

for letting me know, Gavin." She leaned down and gave him a kiss. She wanted to make sure he knew that it wasn't him or his fault.

Gavin was thankful to seem to have her back. It had been a rough few days, but getting her back was worth it. He started to pull up all the files he had on Denver. "Now, I do feel I owe it to you to tell you again before we dive into all of this. I am The Vidar."

Alex was shocked for a few seconds and then just laughed. "Of course, you are." *Is there anything that this man isn't capable of?* she thought as she looked at him with amazement.

"Okay, now that is out of the way, let's focus on Denver. I know he landed in Atlanta one day ago. He had checked into his hotel and driven around to several areas of town, but mostly over here. He knows Citadel is here since it is where he grabbed me, but I believe he doesn't know how to get in. I have also noticed him setting up on the roof of Kaleb's store, across from Snollygoster Inc. He is likely setting up an assassination on either me or Charles. Likely both," Gavin finished. He flew through the entire thing, with slides and videos illustrating what he was saying.

Alex sat there, both mad at Denver for what was taking place, and impressed with Gavin for his ability to put together a mission briefing as he did so quickly. "Okay, so we have all the actionable intel. Now to set up the plan. I do feel I need to tell you, Gavin, I think it was Denver who took me. And I believe he forced me to watch something that affected my mind. It was on what I think was a tablet, and I don't think it was only once," she said, trying not to let her emotions show. "Do you think it could have been some kind of NOVA system?" she asked.

Gavin sat for a moment trying to cool off, and also thinking it through. *It makes sense. They were trying to pull the NOVA system out of my head, but they were unable to do so fully. I know. They said it enough. The Westgate said over and over that the copy they had was incomplete. So, does that mean that the version that they do have is able to erase memories?* "Do you feel like what he played you has anything to do with you forgetting everything?" Gavin asked.

"That is kind of what I am asking you. Is it possible that is what caused me to forget? I mean, I always had issues remembering things correctly with the programming from Project Ara. However, every time it was used, I still remembered it. It just was like it had been a terrible nightmare. And this was similar. I remember our time together like it was a dream. A dream I never wanted to wake up from. Does that make sense?" Alex asked, almost sounding shy.

"Yes, it makes sense. But I gotta tell you, Alex, it wasn't always sunny days," Gavin said with a slight laugh. He was just glad that they were here now. He wouldn't have thought it would be possible just a few short days ago.

"I know that, Gavin, even if I can't remember it. No relationship is without its qualms. But we got through it. Together," she said, grabbing his hand. "Now, let's figure out what we are going to do about Denver," she said.

After they had a semblance of a plan in place, they called the team together and had a briefing with all of them, including Richmond and Hel. Once everyone agreed on what needed to happen, they waited for Denver to make his first move.

***

Gavin continued to watch Denver for another day. They waited for him to leave his room, and Charles and Alex went in as hotel staff to bug the room with specially designed bugs that Gavin made himself. They were untraceable as far as a normal sweep would find. 3D printed, so they didn't contain metal, other than a small amount of wire and soldering. He also set them with a small charge so that if they were to fall into someone else's possession, then all he had to do was send a command, and the bug would vaporize. No back-engineering them.

With those bugs set, Alex went and found Denver's rifle. She reported to Gavin that it appeared he intended to snipe whoever his target was. According to their plan, she took the firing pin out of it and put it in her pocket. Then, they made their way out of the room.

Gavin then spent the evening listening remotely from his home lab. Late that night, Denver had an incoming call. It didn't take long for The Vidar to get the call recorded.

"I am growing impatient, Denver. Get it done, or our contract will be terminated." It sounded like Hunter, but he was much more frantic than he usually sounded.

"You can't afford to cancel my contract at this point, Hunter. However, it is your lucky day. The idiot has a routine that he follows almost every day. I will take the shot tomorrow morning when he is getting out of his car and be in the air before they even find the body," Denver replied. *Well, that answers if he is still alive or if it was a voice changer,* Gavin thought.

"Get it done. I have bigger plans in store, and I need him out of the way to accomplish them," Hunter said and then hung up.

Denver had a few choice words for him and then went to bed. Apparently, he was eager to get the job completed.

***

The next morning, Alex waited for Denver to arrive, out of sight from the ladder to the store's roof. Charles waited inside of Snollygoster Inc. with a rifle of his own. The company had been closed for the day per a call from the government requesting a tax review. And Gavin put on his vest. Charles, an expert sniper himself, assured Gavin that from the range that it would be fired, if anything went wrong, Denver would go for the body. And so, they got ready. As soon as Gavin got confirmation, he was heading towards the shopping center, he notified the team and headed for his car. When he got there, he clicked on the coms to notify the team he had arrived and then proceeded to get out of the car.

Alex heard the clicks and got up on the roof as fast as she could. She got up behind Denver when she heard him huffing at the gun. CLICK CLICK CLICK. She smiled and watched him look through the scope again. Alex laughed and then tranqed him. "Denver is sleeping. Good work, team," Alex said over the coms. Only to be greeted by the sound of Gavin letting out a massive breath he had clearly been holding. She laughed slightly to herself.

Alex and Charles got Denver into the interrogation room in Citadel. They were prepping their equipment to process him when he woke. Looking around, he saw who was in the room with him, and he couldn't help but start to laugh. "Oh, how we have come full circle. I have to tell you; you guys are wasting your time right now," Denver said, still sounding slightly groggy.

Charles smiled and said, "I love it when they play tough. It makes it more fun to crack them." Ending with a pleased growl.

"No, you understand. I am more the type to survive rather than always win. I'm more than willing to talk. But I want specific assurances," Denver said with a smile.

Charles started getting mad. He was really looking forward to processing this smug punk. But he also knew you get betting intel from someone who talks willingly. He would have to settle for allowing the justice system to do what it was made to do. "Fine. I will get the General," Charles growled. Alex never turned around.

Pulling in a monitor with a direct call to Richmond, they started the negotiations. "Agent Denver, I feel you must know you are not in much of a position to barter." She was tempted to let Charles rough him up a bit just for the smug smirk he had on his face right now.

"Oh, I know, General. But I also know I have information that I can give you to help end this in a much more civil way," Denver said, feeling he had the upper hand.

"What could you possibly tell me that I wouldn't be able to get from my analysts?" Richmond snapped, wanting this conversation to end.

"If you take death off the table, I will tell you where you can find Hunter," Denver said.

Everyone froze. *So, he was willing to play. He wasn't bluffing. He was willing to give it all up. What else did he know? He wouldn't turn that fast on him without some more information,* Alex thought. "How can we know that it is reliable?" she asked. She wasn't ready to just give him this out yet.

"Like your boss said, I am not in much of a place to negotiate. Plus, if I lie, I am dead. And I rather like living," Denver said in a light-hearted tone.

"If you are willing to turn that fast without a second thought, then you have more than just a location to give," Alex said with a snarl. She really hated this man.

"I never said I didn't have more. But that is what I am willing to give for the agreed-upon deal," Denver said, trying to look relaxed as much as he could while cuffed to a table.

After discussing it some, they all agreed. Take this deal, and they could always interrogate him for more. "So, where is he?" Alex asked. Her patience running very thin.

"His base he created from the money he siphoned off from the CIA's budget over the years is in the northern Canadian wilderness in Nunavut," he said.

***

Hunter had been listening to Denver through an implant he had put in him years ago while Denver was recovering from a gunshot wound. He never had trusted him. He knew too much and was too much of a coward to take on what the job really meant. When Denver hadn't reported success on the mission, he activated his implant. Having heard that the rat had given them actual vital information, he was left with no choice. He entered the command.

***

358

"Now, for more, you are going to have to…" Denver was saying. Then, out of nowhere, one eye turned in its socket. A small amount of blood started to trickle out of his ear. And he collapsed. He was dead.

They called in Chad to confirm. "Yeah, he had something in his head that exploded. It was small but obviously did what it was supposed to do," Chad said, while clearly trying not to get sick. This was a bit much, even for a heart surgeon.

"Well, team. Good work. It sounds like we have to make plans for a trip to the north," Richmond said. "Analyst Woodford, please start scanning for any anomalies. We will send a scouting party up, and then the team will start that way as soon as we have confirmation." And the video call ended.

"Glad to see that some things never change," Gavin said with a slight laugh.

Chapter 24

:/Hunter

With Denver dead, Gavin got to work figuring out where exactly this base was. *Can we call it a lair? Does it feel like an evil lair?* he thought as he typed away, syncing with several satellites simultaneously. He was finally able to find something with thermal imaging. After confirming with the Canadian government, if it wasn't Hunter, then it wasn't welcome.

So, Team Woodford packed up, picked up Lucile, and headed to northern Canada. "Not going to lie, I kind of expected him to be in Russia." Gavin joked as they approached the base via helicopter. Charles grunted a slight laugh in agreement, while Alex and Lucile were in agent mode. They were focused and didn't flinch. Gavin looked at them and was more than a bit awe-struck by the similarities.

Shaking his head, he refocused. He kneeled to get out things from his backpack on one knee. "Okay, team, I have a few new toys for everyone. Agents Johnson and Hel, I have these." He pulled out a box that looked like a ring box. To her surprise, Agent Johnson felt her stomach fill with butterflies. *This is NOT the time for that, Johnson. Get yourself together. As far as you are concerned, you JUST met the guy. He isn't going to propose to you.* Lucile notices Alex fidgeting, and she remembered what it was like for her with Walter. She stifled a giddy smile and got back into agent mode.

Gavin, oblivious to what was going on with each of the women, continued, "These are image repeaters. Just open and place wherever you need a distraction from." Gavin demonstrated this by opening the device and throwing it to the other side of the plane. Turning to follow the device with their eyes, the two women see another Gavin kneeling behind them. "Great, I can't handle two of you. Close it up," Charles grunted.

"Don't worry, big guy, I didn't leave you out," Gavin says, pulling out several things from his backpack. "This scope acts as a spotter for you. The AI calculates wind, humidity, angle, distance, and curve of the earth between you and your target. I wasn't sure how far out you would need to be, so I looked up all the aspects a pro spotter considers in calculating the trajectory of a shot," he explained.

Charles grunted in appreciation as he held up the scope and inspected it. "You connect it to your coms and don't worry. It isn't my voice," Gavin said to which Charles grunted a thank you. "It's Megan's, so don't mess up," he finished, causing everyone to give a slight laugh.

He then pulled out another small box. "This is an EMP. This is our exit strategy. Charles, you are in charge of it. It will kill everything in the base since everything is run on electricity. So, it will likely kill everyone in there, which I hate to say, but unless they get out before the doors shut, they will die. And team, we have to be ready for anything. I tried to map out as much of the base as we could see with thermal imaging, but it wasn't clear. Coms should work. I made sure they were strong enough to be picked up underground. But if they don't, be ready to go dark. And be careful. This mission isn't worth dying on," Gavin said, looking directly into Alex's eyes.

Please hear me. I know there is an aspect of justified vengeance on this one, but please don't. Don't sacrifice yourself, Gavin pleaded in his mind with her. He just needed her to come home with them. And there was still an aspect of being worried that the deprogramming didn't work. "I will obviously be getting into their system as fast as possible. I will shut down and open up whatever doors I can. There are sure to be some that aren't digital and will need to be manually opened. I know you're all more than capable. I just want to have my team's back in any way I can. And I will also try to use any security they have to track down Hunter," Gavin finished. He was nervous about this one—more than he had been for any mission to this point.

***

As the helicopter landed, Charles and he grabbed the bags as the helicopter landed, and Lucile and Alex grabbed their backpacks.

Gavin was the last one out, and they set up his area before the rest of the team started their parts of the mission. Gavin used an auger to bore down and find their incoming lines from the power plant. He ran his line right next to theirs, directly into their system, and then set up his solar panels to run his equipment.

While it booted up, the others got into position. Alex and Lucile made their way just outside the view of the guards while Charles got posted up on a hill that overlooked the entire valley where the base was settled. When you looked with the naked eye, the base looked like a slightly large cabin. However, imaging showed a large underground labyrinth of tunnels.

"Okay, team, I am in. Let me scout it, and then we will breach. I will notify when ready." He sent a ping through the system. His specific ping was set to map where it went as it traveled through the system. This gave him a layout of where each access point, camera, and device that was connected to the system was. Then he opened every device that had a camera on it. He filtered out any that weren't active or that were blocked. When he brought up the cameras, he activated a program that scanned the image and pieced them all together with the map the ping set up, showing all it could. And it was then filling in the missing parts with a simple line drawing.

"I have a map. It looks like we are looking at about thirty-five guards spread out over around a mile and a half of tunnels. One of which is Hunter. I am still running my facial recognition to find him, but that looks like what we are seeing on the inside of the base," Gavin called out over the coms.

362

He received a grunt from Charles, and Alex and Lucile both acknowledged they received it with a double tap on their coms. They were too close for verbal confirmation.

Good work, Gavin, Alex thought as she watched her guard put out a cigarette and turn. She waited for Lucile to confirm they were breaching. As soon as she heard the whistle, she threw her knife. It sunk into the base of the skull of the guard.

Coming out of her hiding, she climbed onto the base deck quietly, seeing Lucile doing the same. They walked to the front door. "You guys are invisible. I have overlapped and surveillance to your face and body signatures; their systems are set not to see you," Gavin said. Alex knelt, picked up a radio one of the guards had, and clipped it to her hip. They entered the base and started looking for the entrance.

As they found it in a closet in the primary bedroom, they double tapped on the coms. "Okay, from what I can tell, the entrance is ready to breach. I believe we are a go," Gavin said.

"Confirmed," Charles called. Alex put her Gavin phone to the door, and it scanned the algorithm used to lock and answer it. As the door opened, Charles said, "Hold, I have movement. A lot of movement. There is another thirty plus coming out of the grass here," Charles called.

Lucile said, "I will stay and hold the exit, you infiltrate." And with that, Alex entered the base.

As Alex stepped in, a shot rang out. Charles started taking out what he could. Immediately after the first shot, one of Gavin's disabled screens on his surveillance came to life.

"Hello, Gavin," said Hunter. "I see you have finally made it. I left a welcome party for you all, but their anti-thermal blankets seemed to keep them hidden long enough. Is Charles being a watchdog and staying put? I would imagine that Hel and Johnson are breaching. And Hel stayed behind? Thank you for giving me my warrior back. I have missed her services. Don't you worry. I will take good care of her," Hunter said with a smirk and condescension.

Gavin hadn't thought of that. Alex had gone into the lair of the beast that created the monster in her to begin with. He checked where Alex was, and she had gotten pinned down by a group in one of the hallways.

"Ok, coms live everyone, they know we are there. They knew we were coming. Hunter contacted me. Is there any way for Alex to switch out with Hel?" Gavin asked.

"Not possible or practical. A group blocks me in, and Hel holds the entrance with Charles's help. I will move toward the mark," Alex said bluntly, gunfire in the background. "Gavin, on my mark, kill the lights."

"Copy," Gavin said he knew what was coming and knew that there would be an aftermath of this. He just hoped they all made it out alive. As he waited, he started probing the system. He wanted to see if there were any other exits. If his mom could join Alex, then their chances of survival were much greater.

Charles continued to take out as many as he could from his hilltop. He was sniping them with relative ease. He would have to tell the kid thank you for the scope. It made it all easier, for sure.

Lucile was posting up at the entrance and rolling between windows to fire out each one with her M1 rifle.

Alex was sitting. Waiting. *I hate doing this, but this darkness has been what has kept me alive to this point. Gavin said he has seen it before, but I am not sure if she truly knows what I am talking about. He will have to watch firsthand. Can he handle that? Can I? Am I willing to risk that? I don't have a choice. It's either accept the darkness and take the risk or don't risk it and not see him again. He would be left with a memory of who I used to be. Is that enough?*

Gavin watched Alex for a moment. He wished he could help her. "See what you have done to her? What have you done to my perfect weapon? She can't do what she needs to do to survive because you put a conscience in her. Now, she second-guesses her decisions. Don't worry. If I can call my men not to kill her, I will rebuild her. She will be without a soul this time. I won't leave anything to chance. I can finally make the perfect army with what we found in the NOVA system. All starting with Alex Johnson," Hunter antagonized Gavin.

That's it. She needs to know it's okay. She needs to know I love all of her, not just the kind and sweet side that I get. She needs to know that nothing between us will change just because she did what she needs to. "Alex, listen. It is just you and me on the coms right now. I muted us to the other two. So, just listen to me. I love you. All of you. Not just the parts that I get to enjoy. I know you have darkness, and I love your darkness, too. I saw the footage of you in a similar situation in a Collective base. You were incredible. You make even death beautiful. It is okay to let your darkness out when you are in the right environment. No matter what, I love you, and we work through it. Just come back to me," Gavin said.

He loves me. He loves all of me. He has seen. He doesn't care. No, he DOES care, even when I am fully me. My dorky side, my happiness, my sadness, and my darkness. He loves all of it, Alex thought as the gunshots faded into the background. She thought about the abuse, the manipulation, the hate that had been forced into her. She thought about being able to get some justice for it all. She thought about all the lives Hunter had affected and how many he had forced her to end.

Gavin watched as slowly the darkness filled her eyes. They were no longer the vibrant blue that he had known. They were gray. She was no longer Alex. She was Agent Johnson. That was all that was there now. He almost felt bad for the guys in the hallway with her. Gavin smirked slightly at that. He heard the double tap of the coms and killed the power to the hallway. The power to the lights also was to the cameras, and so he lost visual of Alex.

"Yes, the power can sometimes be fickle in this place." Hunter taunted. "Do you really think that she will make it out alive? And even if she does, do you think she will be able to live with herself? I did this all for her own good. She didn't remember the terrible things she had to do in the name of freedom, and I got to keep our country safe," Hunter said, playing the savior card as he had for most of his career.

"Gavin, they are through the door. I am not sure I can handle many more." He heard his mom say. "I am falling back into the base." Then her com went silent.

"Aw, it appears that my men have started to break through your meager options for retreat. I do hope you had a better plan than a full-frontal assault," Hunter said.

"I am getting overrun here. Falling back," Charles said as men started cresting the hilltop he had posted on.

"And now your overwatch is gone. Now, what, Mr. Woodford?" Hunter said as if they were simply playing a game of chess.

Gavin stared at his screens. *How could all of this have gone so wrong so fast? We went in too confident. Dad had always warned about overconfidence, and the one time I get overconfident, I could lose everything. Wait, that is it. I just need time to find another route. And someone of his stature must have a significant ego,* Gavin smirked.

"And here I thought it was The Westgate and The Collective that had done all the work. You were just middle management. A simple pawn in their grand game," Gavin said.

"A pawn? The Collective answers to me!" Hunter said, giving away his anger.

Gotcha, Gavin thought. "See, that isn't what I had heard. I heard that you were just another one of their playthings. To be used and disregarded as easily as I am. Maybe even more so now that you aren't in the CIA, and I have the NOVA system." Gavin hit record. He wanted to ensure he had every bit of the next conversation on record.

"Listen here. I am far more important than you could ever imagine. I put myself in a position of being indispensable to The Collective. They all have been answering to me for decades. I was the one who fixed the original NOVA system to keep your pathetic bonehead of a father from ruining its potential. He was going to use it as a simple learning tool, and that's it. I built half of The Collective to the power they have reached because of the corrected NOVA system. I altered the coding so that I could rewrite people's personalities, and they would never be the same. They would own who they are and only answer to me. They would follow my command.

"Your father was too small-minded. He had the power to rule the world in his hands, and all he wanted to use it for was to learn more. What an idiot! I created Orlov and half the others to get my command in place within The Collective. And then I would have the group of the richest business owners in the world at my fingertips—unlimited funding, untouchable. I was immune to all laws. All other measures of success paled compared to what I was achieving."

***

Once the lights went out, Alex listened. She heard the gunshots stop and could hear the breathing of the others in the hallway. *Two men, three feet to the left—four more behind them. Given the rate of fire, all have automatic rifles. When will they ever learn that handguns and knives are so much more effective in close quarters?* She thought with her eyes closed. It was too dark to matter anyway.

She got out her knife and flashlight. *Fifteen men. Six in striking distance. Nine more I will be exposed to.* She threw her knife into the throat of the back man and grabbed another. As he fired his rifle haphazardly around, she flashed the flashlight full power into the eyes of the closest guy on her left, blinding him temporarily, causing him to react and pull his hands to his eyes. She launched herself at the guy to her right as bullets hit the floor where she had just been.

Sinking the knife into the head of the guy she launched herself at, she turned and slit the throat of the guy she had blinded. And then threw the knife into the chest of the next guy. She threw two more into the two guys that were left that were close—and continued to roll.

She grabbed her knives from the dead as she went past them—nine *more*.

"I thought The Collective only accepted their own nominations?" Gavin guessed. He had absolutely no idea, but Hunter didn't know that.

"They did for a long time, but that is irrelevant now. It is only who I choose that gets in. I used my NOVA system to put six out of the ten in place. I control the majority," Hunter bragged.

"But then why Alex? Why the projects?" Gavin asked, trying hard to sound hurt. He needed him to keep talking just a bit longer as he watched the progress bar on his screen.

"Every empire needs an army. And for the perfect empire, you need the perfect army. People will always come for the crown. If you know anything about history, then you know this is true. And people are weak. Their minds are weak. And I was becoming a god. I couldn't have the weak trying to protect a god.

"She was, and still will be, my perfect weapon. She has more kills on her resume than the next ten agents, except maybe Hel. Hel was my first. She was the prototype. Her programming was simple. I thought at the time that all I needed was to make them dependent on the mission. But I learned. You have to suppress emotions. You must make them completely compliant. You must break them down to nothing, before being rebuilt to perfection. And, of course, you need others to help control a weapon like that.

"For Hel, I had Ivan, and for Alex, I had Brett. But then he had to get all high and mighty on me. Apparently, he felt bad for you. Something about what he did to you in college. And that was why he couldn't just frame you for the NOVA system. He had to send it to you. I rather enjoyed putting a bullet in him. Three actually.

368

"Then, Anderson. He was perfect. He was everything I had hoped for. But he enjoyed the manipulation a little more than he should. If he had backed off, I would still have two operatives. He made the one so disenfranchised, she stopped responding to the commands. Such a waste. She would be useful right now. But Alex had to be used to put her down, when she wouldn't respond.

"Belief in love is the worst human trait. It is fake. It does nothing but make you weak. It ruins everything that could be useful. These tools fell apart, and for what? Love? Some feelings? I gave them the right to rule the world with me, and they threw it away. One fell for their handler, and the other because she fell for her asset.

"I knew I never should have given the NOVA mission to Alex. But it was too late when I realized how deep she was in. She had already started not responding to commands. And Brett had bungled it up, trying to win her back from you. He fell in love with her. Then Anderson just had to push too hard. Again. Too hard, too fast. She would have fallen for him if he had taken his time like commanded. And then she could be manipulated. But no, I had to kill him too." Hunter was truly ranting at this point. Gavin just let him. He spotted a potential exit in his office, but until Alex or his mom got there, he knew it was too dangerous to tell them.

"Gavin, I am holed up in the base. I am able to hold them off here until Alex completes her task. Any ETA?" Hel asked.

Alex threw two of the knives as she rolled past a body. She was hitting two more that were farther off. And then whipped out her gun. She fired, killing the remaining seven men. "Gavin, I am on my way. I know you can't talk. Find a way to guide me," Alex said.

***

Gavin started thinking. Hunter was still ranting and hadn't even noticed that he had been quiet for a while. *Apparently, I struck a nerve of insecurity with him,* Gavin thought with a slight smile. He saw the shadows starting to move on one of the cams. *That's it!* He killed the light into the next hallway.

"Stay in the dark. Hunter is watching. I understand," Alex was heard over the mics.

"AN ETA Johnson?" Charles yelled over the coms. You could hear heavy gunfire in the background.

Gavin sent him a message. "Make your way into the base."

"Rodger, that Woodford," Charles said as he started to make his way there.

Gavin hacked into their fail-safe.

"Without me, you know where your little girlfriend would be? Like in prison or face down in a gutter. She was nothing before I came around. I bet she didn't tell you that, though, did she? Her father was nothing but a pathetic con man. And she was following in his footsteps. I made her have worth. I gave her a purpose. She wasn't even attractive when I got her.

"I formed this world today. I will continue to form the world of tomorrow. And I do it all from the shadows. It is better to have power than fame. Fame gets you killed in this business.

"Well, as you likely know by now, I have no intention of any of you leaving this valley," Hunter said, proud of himself. Several tanks and about 100 more troops came into view of the cabin. Gavin typed away on his wrist computer, as he raced across the valley floor. Charles off to his right, running backward as he fired at the men behind him. Gavin reached the Cabin and burst through the door, thankful no men were still in there. But he heard gunshots coming from the base. Charles got inside and ran to the entrance of the base. Gavin followed and shut the door after him.

"Are you there, Gavin, or did my men finally put an end to this?" Hunter asked with a clear smirk in his tone.

"Sorry to break it to you, but I am still here. However…" Gavin said, as he typed a few more commands into his wrist computer, and then hit enter. As he did, the entire base started to shake slightly. "I don't believe that you can rely on your backup any time soon," Gavin said.

General Richmond set down her phone. She hated that Gavin had to make a call like that, but she wouldn't let her team fall like that. He told her they may need a fail-safe, and he was right. The reaper drone returned home.

"What did you do?!" Hunter yelled into the line he had with Gavin.

"Ended it," Hunter heard behind him. Turning, all he could see was the bluest eyes he had ever known, right before everything goes black.

Chapter 25

:/Peace

Gavin sat on his couch with Alex. They had some show on, but neither of them was paying attention. They were just enjoying each other's company as they filled out their mission reports.

Gavin had followed Charles through the hallways. Charles was taking care of business as they came up behind the men who had his mom pinned down. Between the two agents, they caught the men in a crossfire and quickly ended the skirmish. It then continued its way towards Alex. Gavin had found a small escape hatch in Hunter's office that led to a ventilation tube. With the power still on, it would have been impossible to escape from, as the fans that pushed the air down to his office wouldn't have allowed anyone through. Let alone the air that was being pushed down onto them.

However, as soon as they reached the office and got their gear ready for the climb, Charles hit his EMP, and the fans and everything else in the base were killed. They all dropped through the hatch, and it closed and sealed. They then made their way up the 100ft climb out the top of the ventilation shaft. Richmond had a helicopter waiting for them to return to the closest airport. From there, they just made their way back to Atlanta.

Gavin looked up from his tablet that he was filling out his report on and admired the woman who had brought peace to his family. He had his mom back in his life because of her. He had a purpose after college because of her. He had a future because of her.

"What?" Alex asked, feeling slightly self-conscious at how intently Gavin was staring at her.

"Nothing. I am just thankful I have you," he said as he got up. She shook her head at him. There were times when she didn't understand his antics.

He went to his room and retrieved the ring Kaleb had brought back to him. He returned to the couch they were working on and took her hand. "Alex," Gavin started as he took a knee, "I know that everything has been insane since we have gotten together, and I don't know a single person I would rather go through it with than you. You are my future. I want to spend every moment possible trying to make sure you are as happy as you can be. You make me a better man. I want to wake up to you every morning and go to sleep with you next to me every night. I know life has its challenges. But whatever the next challenge is, we will face it together. I love you. Alex Johnson, will you marry me?" he asked, looking up at her.

He wants to marry me? He thinks I am worth making his wife? He would know. He knows more about me than anyone else in the world. And he thinks I am worth giving his life to. I can't believe this! It is more than I could have ever dreamed of. Wait, I haven't answered him, she thought, as she saw his face getting more and more nervous.

"YES!" she shouted, her heart feeling fuller than she could ever remember. "I love you, Gavin."

Ivan Orlov stood in the meeting room, The Westgate sitting beside him. "I know it is irregular for me to call this meeting, but as many of you know, Richard Hunter is dead. The human NOVA system took him out. I have confirmation from his beacon. I know he had some dirt on several of us, and I am sure we are all thankful that he is not a factor anymore. However, he did have some solid points." He paused to look around the room.

"I believe that what he was trying to achieve is the future of our world. With the advance of technology and travel, it is only a matter of time before someone is able to achieve global dominance. And why shouldn't it be us?" he said bluntly, which created a lot of energy in the room.

"I know that as a group, it is much more difficult to rule, but what if we were to add a few more, and then we elite could vote our leader into power among us? That way, the power isn't left to the simple-minded fools we know are just too easy to manipulate." Looking around the table, he sees many in agreement. "Let's start the voting," Ivan said with a smirk.

Thank you for reading The NOVA System: Nerds, Spies and Games of the Mind. I would love to hear your feedback, so please leave a review on Amazon for me!

Jon Scott Lee

Printed in the USA
CPSIA information can be obtained
at www.ICGtesting.com
CBHW010804020724
10943CB00008B/251